**ANA CHAUDHRY**

# The Mafia And His Lost Queen

*Copyright © 2022 by Ana Chaudhry*

*All rights reserved. No part of this publication may be reproduced, stored or transmitted in any form or by any means, electronic, mechanical, photocopying, recording, scanning, or otherwise without written permission from the publisher. It is illegal to copy this book, post it to a website, or distribute it by any other means without permission.*

*This novel is entirely a work of fiction. The names, characters and incidents portrayed in it are the work of the author's imagination. Any resemblance to actual persons, living or dead, events or localities is entirely coincidental.*

*Ana Chaudhry asserts the moral right to be identified as the author of this work.*

*Designations used by companies to distinguish their products are often claimed as trademarks. All brand names and product names used in this book and on its cover are trade names, service marks, trademarks and registered trademarks of their respective owners. The publishers and the book are not associated with any product or vendor mentioned in this book. None of the companies referenced within the book have endorsed the book.*

*First edition*

*This book was professionally typeset on Reedsy. Find out more at reedsy.com*

*This book is dedicated to all the silent souls that are suffering from depression. People who no longer believe in love or happiness? This book is for you, much much much more power to all of the champions and warriors here. You are loved, you are appreciated and you are valued. You are very very important. Love you loads, Kings and Queens!* ❤️💕❤️💕❤️💕❤️

Sometimes giving someone a second chance is like giving them an extra bullet for their gun, because they missed you the first time.

-Unknown

# Contents

| | | |
|---|---|---|
| *Foreword* | | iii |
| *Acknowledgement* | | v |
| *Author's Note* | | vii |
| 1 | Chapter 1 | 1 |
| 2 | Chapter 2 | 16 |
| 3 | Chapter 3 | 32 |
| 4 | Chapter 4 | 41 |
| 5 | Chapter 5 | 54 |
| 6 | Chapter 6 | 71 |
| 7 | Chapter 7 | 82 |
| 8 | Chapter 8 | 102 |
| 9 | Chapter 9 | 119 |
| 10 | Chapter 10 | 139 |
| 11 | Chapter 11 | 167 |
| 12 | Chapter 12 | 174 |
| 13 | Chapter 13 | 180 |
| 14 | Chapter 14 | 193 |
| 15 | Chapter 15 | 204 |
| 16 | Chapter 16 | 213 |
| 17 | Chapter 17 | 223 |
| 18 | Chapter 18 | 234 |
| 19 | Chapter 19 | 239 |
| 20 | Chapter 20 | 248 |
| 21 | Chapter 21 | 264 |

| | | |
|---|---|---|
| 22 | Chapter 22 | 278 |
| 23 | Chapter 23 | 293 |
| 24 | Chapter 24 | 305 |
| 25 | Chapter 25 | 318 |
| 26 | Chapter 26 | 329 |
| 27 | Chapter 27 | 336 |
| 28 | Chapter 28 | 348 |
| 29 | Chapter 29 | 361 |
| 30 | Chapter 30 | 375 |
| 31 | Chapter 31 | 398 |
| *END OF BOOK I* | | 416 |
| *About the Author* | | 417 |
| *Also by Ana Chaudhry* | | 419 |

# Foreword

*The writing style was truly captivating. The plot had so many twists and turns it was hard to put the book down. It really changed my perspectives about love and life in general. Not to mention the love scenes which were pleasantly surprising; so were the fights against the antagonist. Would definitely recommend it to those who like action and romance with a bit of heartache.*
  ~Nargis C.

*TMAHLQ holds a very special place in my heart as it spoke volumes. The author has done a great job covering delicate topics and has written her thoughts very clearly to a point that I am forced to say, it's commendable! The plot has had me on my toes throughout the journey. Definitely recommended as this book plays with your emotions very brutally. One minute, it can make u cry and the next, you will be laughing your heart out. The characters are beautiful and the story line is just so amazing....!*
  ~Mnz

*The Story of a powerful, ruthless Mafia King and His Lost Queen. I love how the starting kicks off by telling us that how Sophia was living her life with her abusive father and her cute little sister, Everleigh. On the other hand, the struggle Ashton went through because of how his father believed his childhood should be, is the start of his training for being the next leader of the Italian Mafia. After meeting Sophia, Ashton unlike other mafia stories that I have read, is totally protective and careful towards her. I love how the scenes take place with details, the sweet beautiful memories, the description of the places, the characters, the whole story is just amazing. When I was reading it, I was feeling their pain, happiness, excitement and every other emotion. I lived it and Loved it.*

~Ira

# Acknowledgement

The foremost praise and the most Mighty one goes to God, without whom I definitely wouldn't be here at all. It is His blessings, His mercy and His love that I reached to a platform that I can directly publish my book with love from almost every end of the world.

Thank you to each and every one of you who supported me through this journey. Thanks a bunch to all those amazing readers who stayed by my side, who helped me point out the initial mistakes that I made because let's face it and let's be honest, I am a human and can make mistakes. :) So, much much appreciation to all those people who supported me through thick and thin.

Then a huge thank you to my parents, for believing in me, letting me continue with this dream of mine and supporting me through every phase and part of it. And also, all those useless friends of mine, who do mean the whole world to me regardless of the fact that they annoy me a lot. Love you loads.

Thank you all.
~A.ZChaudhry

# Author's Note

Hello everyone and hope you all are doing well. A little background on how this book started and what led to Ashton and Sophia becoming characters has one answer. **Depression**. This one word alone and I am ninety-nine percent sure that many people are familiar with it, many many souls are going through this and suffering all alone. Fighting depression is never easy and trust me, I understand this a bit too well.

This book came into being when I was fighting depression, was in a terrible phase of life, had too many anger issues and I wanted to somehow channel my anger without lashing out at family because that only makes things worse, and that's how this book came into being, Ashton being my moral support character lol. This book is very very close to my heart as it's my first ever one and contains a journey which has been very close to me.

You will find every sort of feeling in this book. Love, pain, hurt, betrayal, misery, happiness, joy and so much more. Keep adding synonyms and you'll be getting it all right.

People have cried nightssss in a row after reading a few scenes and let me remind you, that it is a heavy book. It is a very heavy book that will play with your emotions and it will fuck you up pretty bad but in a way that you'll like it. Sounds weird, but a book can do wonders to you.

Hoping that you guys will love TMAHLQ and enjoy this journey as much as I did. Looking forward to having your feedback. You can email me at anach731@gmail.com or follow me on my Instagram at anachaudhry123. You can also catch some videos made for TMAHLQ on it's own YouTube channel under my own name, "Ana Chaudhry."

Looking forward to keeping you entertained with this book. Thank you so much once again.

And just a last message, I wouldn't allow anyone to copy my work. It's my work, my sweat, and my blood. If anyone sees someone copying my work, please let me know ASAP. It would mean a lot. But until then? I hope u guys will love Ashton and Sophia. Peace!

Signing off,
   A.Z Chaudhry

One

# Chapter 1

## SOPHIA

It was annoying.

I swear.

The morning alarm with my mother's screams for me to wake up were seriously annoying the hell out of me. Who does that? Who starts screaming at a person right just when they wake up? Especially from a great nap I may add.

Last night was pretty exhausting as the memories and the tiredness resurfaced in my mind. I had to give three shifts just to earn extra money to make sure that no one starves during dinner or goes to sleep hungry. Mum was already getting dressed to leave for her date and munchkin was ready to go to school. My little sister is the only one I find adorable due to which I started calling her munchkin. She is beautiful, amazing, a sweetheart and to be fairly honest, the only beautiful blessing in my life, worth living for and worth working hard for. So, cutting it short, I had to do three shifts and was so tired last night that I just passed out. Today was another hectic day and I just had to get on with it.

Getting ready, I looked in the fridge to see that only Munchkin could have breakfast and hence I made it for her. As soon as the little devil giggled and ate all of her chocolate sandwich with a glass of milk, we waved a goodbye to mother and I picked Munchkin up to drop her to school. It was so freaking hot that I could feel America burning when holding her hand in mine, we started walking.

The scorching blazing heat was burning up my skin, beads of sweat were forming on my forehead, neck and on the tip of my nose. My clothes started clinging to me as to how hot the weather was. I looked down to see munchkin already sweating profusely but we couldn't help it. We had no car, no bicycle, basically no form of any transportation, and the cab was costly and the only earning hand was me, so I couldn't afford too much expenses after basically running a whole home. Jogging for about fifteen minutes, we finally reached the school when kissing her cheek and hugging her tightly to me, I waved her a goodbye and went to the cafe to start my day.

## Chapter 1

# ASHTON

"WHAT THE FUCK?" I slammed my hands hard on the desk not believing anything I was hearing. How can it be possible? I had placed all of my fucking trust in him making him not one of the most trusted, but still somewhat of a trustworthy man I had, but I had never anticipated that he would betray me.

"Throw him in the basement. I'll personally attend to that fucker".

"But boss-" I threw Massimo, my right-hand man, a questioning glare and it was enough to shut him up as he quickly backed out to carry out my orders.

Five million dollars' worth of drugs. FIVE MILLION! And he handed it over to the Russians, our biggest enemy. The fucker thought that I wouldn't notice it but he forgot who he was playing with. I was known for being the most ruthless and cold hardhearted person alive on this damn earth and I guess it was time to give him another reminding as to on whose path of his loyalties, they lost their brains. Straightening my black button-down shirt to camouflage the blood stains, I wore my sleek black coat, readjusted the cuff-links and turned around to grab the gloves that I would use to torture him. I hardened my chin bone to add ruthlessness to my facial features and made my way out but not before grabbing a bottle of alcohol which I'll generously pour on his open, bleeding wounds to remind him of his mistake, to remind him who he betrayed and to remind him who was the real boss.

At last, there was a reason energies left the depth of bones upon hearing my name.

There was a reason burning embers stung like a bitch upon the mere sight of me.

And at last, there was a reason, I lived up to my name, Ashton Romanno.

*

I trudged down the stairs in pure anger and hatred for him. I was trained to grow into the heartless monster that I am today. I loved to spill blood and watch people scream in agony as the life slowly left their bloodshot eyes. Especially those who defy my orders. Two things I never allowed under my rule was dishonesty and disloyalty and the fucker just did the exact same thing.

The basement was chillingly cold and dark, just the way I liked it. Reaching his cell, I nodded to the guard who opened the door for me and I stepped in. There he was. All tied up, bloodied and beaten badly. His head hung low, his shirt was ripped to pieces and I could see several blood stains on his bare, bloodied chest. My footsteps didn't wake him up which further boiled my anger. Nodding towards Rafael, one of my guards, I instructed him through my nod to wake him up. One slap was all that was needed and he woke up with a stir.

## Chapter 1

Shakily, he raised his head and his black orb eyes met mine and I smirked to see the light vanish from within them just to be replaced with nothing but fear and complete horrors and I liked it. I liked it when people feared me. That's just how I ruled. You take my name and people used to cower in fear. I fed on fear and drank from the goblets of vile horrors. That's just how I am.

I took a few calculated steps towards him to slowly instill the fear within him when reaching near, I bent till my face was merely inches away from his and uttered the only deadly word in a mere whisper which I knew would send rapid waves of chill down his fucking spine, "Why?". That was all I had to say before he started crying. Another pathetic thing to see which further spiked rage within me. I was an impatient man and did not have time for all of this movie bullshit.

I slapped him right across the face and said, "I am asking you one last time Trevor, why? You fail to give me an answer, you know the consequences." and with a sneer I added "Alas, you were one of my most trusted men so you know what happens when you disobey me."

He remained quiet. I gave him another minute to speak up but when his head hung low and he didn't, I've had had enough. With a low growl of disapproval and annoyance I asked for my knife. The signature knife which I always use just to slash across a person's throat once in a swift, clean motion and they will be lying dead at my feet. As slowly as I could, I started to tear his skin apart. First the arms, then the stomach and finally the cheeks. Layer by layer.

As slowly as possible, I peeled off each film of his skin for him to undergo the agony of the thin threads peeling away, so that he could feel each sting of throbbing pain in the depth of his bones.

His screams resonated through the room but they were music to my ears. It eased me, calmed my satanic murderous of a heart down when I enjoyed this particular playlist. I spared a glance his direction and chuckled. Dare to disobey me and go against my orders! I bent low and looked at him again, "I'm giving you one more minute to speak up, you filthy dog. You fail to do so………..surely you know I can do worse." He started whimpering but I couldn't care less. He defied me.

The fucker was too loyal to the Russians that he didn't speak up. Rolling my eyes and heaving a tired sigh, I opened the bottle of alcohol and took a swig, letting it burn in my throat before I started pouring it on his wounds when the sound of his screams and the sizzling of his skin were assorted yet enjoyable.

I kept the torturous act for full three minutes, emptying two full bottles when I decided to give him a break. Anyone passing by would have had nightmares if they were to see his state right now with more than half of his skin gone and the rest, all bloodied and bruised up but at the moment, I needed answers.

"Trevor never have I ever given someone this much time as much as I'm giving to you and I myself am astonished as to how I gave it. You have two minutes exactly till you tell me

## Chapter 1

why the bloody fuck you betrayed me or I wouldn't stop at any lengths to torture you." I shrugged my shoulders, "I may even end you today, so fucking speak up." Obviously I'll end him today but I had to use the word 'may' to make him think that *maybe* he had a chance of survival but obviously there wasn't. He shivered but remained silent. Such a scum!

When I couldn't take it any longer, I rolled up my sleeves, and asked for the pliers when opening his mouth, I roughly started to cut all of his teeth unequally and in a rush making him scream in agony. I deliberately yanked away his molars and premolars knowing how fucking bad it would hurt. I took one of the knives which were on the table and viciously made as many slashes and cuts as I could on his body so that his bloodied flesh could be seen.

Blood oozed out in spurts, his arms and legs shook from the pain but I wasn't the one to stop. Raising the knife, I struck it down harshly in his open muscle when he screamed as much as his lungs could allow for the air to be screamed out. His shouts and cries calmed and encouraged me when I kept torturing the fucker. Subsequently, I felt a hand on my shoulder which instantly brought me back to my senses just to see that Trevor was unrecognizable.

There was a pool of crimson red blood surrounding my feet, he was screaming too loudly to a point where I started having a headache. My black shirt was soaked in his worthless blood. My hands were bloodied and there were beads of sweat on my face. I was breathing heavily when I decided to give him a break. If I wanted, I could kill this fucker right away. A bullet through his head was all that it would do but I was genuinely curious as to why he did what he did.

Taking a step back and cleaning my hands with a handkerchief I bellowed in anger, "Trevor, as much as you are wasting my time here it's better that you speak up or I'll make you pay for wasting my this time as well." I was actually amazed to see him breathing but quiet. He didn't give in. As much as I wanted to kill him, I wanted to know. Suddenly an idea came to me and I knew the exact thing which would make him speak up.

Turning to Rafael with a smirk on my face I said, "Bring his daughter, Elizabeth here. The one with the lung disease-" and with a pause I added, "To ME' emphasizing the ME. That ought to shake Trevor when he suddenly brought his head up and whimpered a weak no. Obviously, I would do nothing to his girl. The child had no fault and shouldn't be punished for something the father did and obviously I would never hurt a child or make her see any of this but Trevor didn't need to know that.

"What did you say again?" I growled in a deep voice.

"Please no, boss. Not my daughter."

"Who the fuck are you calling boss may I ask?"

"Boss I am sorry. I am so sorry. I was forced. I had nothing in my hands."

## Chapter 1

To say that I was mad would be an understatement. I was furious. Furious beyond anything. Taking a deep, calming breath and in a dangerously cold voice I spoke, "Trevor, you have bloody five minutes to explain to me why the fuck you did what you did or you know………you'll hate the consequences. Hurry the fuck up as I don't have all day and night to babysit a fucker like you. SPEAK UP!" I roared in anger and I was glad to see him recoil in fear.

"He-he, he threatened me boss. HE-he said-"

"Stutter one more time and you'll see why they call me the don of death. And for your fucking information, you already gave me the idea that you were threatened because being forced means nothing in a mafia until it comes with a poison of threatening. Just fucking look at you, did you speak up when I forced you? No. Did you decide to speak up when I threatened you? Fucking yes. So don't go in circles and repeat bullshit to me with synonyms attached to it, I need the whole fucking story."

I crossed my arms and looked at him. He took in a deep breath and started, "He threatened me boss. He promised to kill my child if I failed to provide him the drugs. I already have lost one child; he couldn't make it into this world and I couldn't lose Elizabeth. Especially when she was fighting her lung disease. He promised he'd hurt her and I had to protect her boss. I had to protect her."

There was a different sort of penurious begging in his eyes, a realization that he once had of having an incoming feeling of losing a battle that was never meant to ever start in the first place if he hadn't opened the gates. Hopelessness clouded his eyes, spread through his body and engulfed his whole heart, enough for him to destroy his own position which could easily be saved if he didn't make such a stupid mistake.

He was an open book for me to read, as clear as glass because failures could be easily recognizable as the scent of gloom always hung over their heads, taunting them, mocking them, laughing at them with every step they took, with every breath they breathed.

It?

It fucking kills people. Rips them off of their own life. Trevor was in a pathetic state, crying, sweating and with blood still dripping onto the floor, spreading in uneven concentric circles.

I thought I couldn't get any angrier but guess I was wrong. Taking my suit jacket off and carelessly discarding it on the floor beside me, I stepped in front of him, bent low just to be at eye-level with him and when finally, after fifteen seconds he managed to bring his petrified face up? I fucking slapped him right across the face, the sound echoing around the basement, making a big, bright red burn on his cheek. I was angry. Beyond angry. And a filthily dangerous one. My anger was always a dangerous one but it wasn't my fault, my fucking past was.

Putting both of my hands on the side arms of the chair I spat

## Chapter 1

out at him with all of my rage, "Are you really that stupid or slow-witted, you piece of a sorry pig? You work under me, under my mafia with the emblem of it burned in your fucking arm, you work under THE Ashton Romanno. The one people fear a lot. The one people hope to never cross paths with. No one wishes to disobey me or upset me. You have been working under me for thirteen goddamn fucking years you bloody asshole and you are still such a piece of worm shit that you cannot see through things?

I gave your medical fee for your child, didn't I? I arranged a private hospital for the girl, didn't I? I made sure that proper doctors were attending to her, didn't I? I made sure she was being handled with care, I made sure the equipment's being used were sterilized. DIDN'T I???" I ended up shouting in anger and he just nodded his head which was hanging low which further infuriated me. I hate it when somebody's not looking at me when I'm talking to them. Slapping him again, I seethed out, "Look one more time downwards and I'll personally make sure you keep looking down for the rest of your goddamn life."

He faced me again when I growled, "Now use your words Trevor, didn't I do all of these things for your daughter?"

"Yes boss."

"Then why the bloody fuck did you think that the Russians can give your daughter more safety? You were under my wing constantly, your loyalty lay with me, so how were you so damn sure that they will keep their word? How were you so sure that they wouldn't end up betraying YOU once their work was done? How were you so sure that they would keep a TRAITOR HIMSELF IN THEIR VERY OWN MAFIA?" I shouted.

The fucker was silent. I could see the million wheels turning in his head, all of them finally pointing towards the fact that I had a point. Taking in a breath, I spoke again, "They literally know you work for me and they know that you BETRAYED ME, then if you betrayed a person like me, obviously you will also betray them if some other party threatens you and this is your weak point which will make you unsuitable to be in any mafia and they would throw you out. They will never take you in as you have this weakness which is the main thing that can destroy a mafia in seconds so obviously, they would never take you in or do any bullshit, this is so obvious.

You could have come to me Trevor and you could have explained the situation to me. If I can heavily guard so many of my bases, clubs and hotels, is guarding and protecting your daughter that difficult for me? Is it too hard for me especially since I have been doing that for God knows how long? Answer me."

"No boss."

"Then why the fuck did you run to the Russians like a stupid dog?"

"I panicked and got scared boss. She is my only one. I couldn't lose her. I'm sorry boss. I'm so so sorry."

## Chapter 1

I just looked at him and saw the pathetic man inside him. He was weak, unstable and a major major disadvantage for me. No matter how much I wanted to end his life, I also didn't want to because his daughter was in a critical condition and needed both of her parents and if she knew that she isn't going to meet one of them ever and that he is gone, knowing how much she was attached to her father………it would crush her. It would kill her but sadly that wasn't my problem anymore. If her father himself didn't think about her, then who am I? If her father himself weakened the gates of my mafia, then I absolutely couldn't do anything in this matter to save *his* kingdom when he ruined *mine*.

Yes, the girl needed him but it is very obvious that a strong mafia cannot have a weak soldier in his army. A person who could easily shake up and spill everything out? Gurgle it all out and raise his hands in surrender? I just couldn't keep him. He had been working under me for too long so being strong should be a very easy task for him but if even after thirteen years, he was THIS weak? Then, he had to leave the mafia and the only way out of it was death. As simple as that.

I slowly bent down and placed my hands on the sides of his chair when I looked at him, "You are pathetic and as useless as any low-level mafia even wouldn't want to keep. As much as your daughter does wish to see her father again, I sure as hell cannot put my entire empire on stake and get it ruined by a scumbag like you. I told you the day that you joined that I wouldn't go lenient and that I hell wouldn't tolerate dishonesty and that lesson wasn't supposed to be forgotten till you breath your fucking last and thirteen years definitely doesn't do the trick. What I can promise you is that your daughter will remain safe and I will pay for her medical attention but I hell wouldn't let you leave this cell alive. It's not in my book of rules which you were clearly familiar with."

"But boss, my daughter-"

"Is not my problem. You should have thought of this before you took the step that you did as you knew the rules when you joined. No forgiveness over breaking any point in the million that I gave." I then pointed my finger at him, "You betray, you pay. And you Trevor? You, so fucking will."

I stood up when he started begging me a lot to leave him be and to let him see his daughter but for fuck's sake. I didn't need such weak people that could easily come under threats and give it all away. Weak people have no place in strong organizations.

And hence, raising the gun at him, I cocked it back, smirked at him and whispered, "I'll make the price of betrayal that you pay be easy for you. Quick, sweet to me and so horrifyingly painful for you for a few seconds." and with a bang I shot one bullet straight through his fucking head as his head was whipped back with the force until he lay dead with his eyes staring at the ceiling, with no life left in them.

I unloaded the gun and placed it back in the waistband of my jeans, turned around and was about to leave when I addressed

## Chapter 1

Massimo, "Get my suit clean whenever." He whispered a yes boss when as soon as I exited the cellar with Trevor's dead body inside, I saw the other man in the other one sitting on the floor, locked up with hollow, sunken eyes. He had stolen my money to celebrate his daughter's birthday. He had been receiving his punishment for six months when I decided to let him go.

Massimo followed me when I spoke, "Today I'm leaving you Matteo as the punishment is over for now. Remember this is your last chance. You fuck this up again, I'll fuck you up worse than karma can sort your shit out. You need something? Ask me. Something is troubling you? Tell me. You are supposed to inform me as to whatever the fuck is happening around here and whatever threats you too can sometimes get. You dare to go behind my back again or deceive me or double cross me?" I waited for the shudders to go through his whole body when I completed *my* threat, "I'll make sure that you are buried sixteen feet into the ground while you are still breathing. Next time, I wouldn't give a flying fuck as to who the fuck here needs you. Either prove your loyalty or I'll put a bullet through that useless skull. Got it?"

He shivered at I don't know, maybe the coldness of the cell or from my voice or the atmosphere that I created but he responded a yes boss.

Turning away, giving a curt nod to the guard I took one last arctic glance at him to show how much I meant what I said and then I went up to take a shower and clean of all the blood.

**Two**

# Chapter 2

## SOPHIA

It was a super exhausting and a super tiring day that I just couldn't wait to go home and throw myself under the warm and cozy bed covers. There were so many annoying customers today, irritating the hell out of me. Mothers couldn't handle their crying babies; kids were dropping ice cream and shakes on the floor and I had to clean up all of the mess and to be honest it was very exasperating and draining but I had to do the work because of the money.

We couldn't afford to starve to death and I especially wouldn't let munchkin go to sleep hungry. I couldn't bear to hear the growls of her hungry stomach at night as it would simply just kill me, rob me off my entire night thinking of her starved

## Chapter 2

state printed on the circuit board of my mind. Mum used to come home just to sleep and dad was barely ever home God knows doing what, so it was all on me now.

I was walking home and was in the driveway when I heard a crash from inside my house when I internally cringed because this only meant one thing that dad was home. He was always abusive since childhood and it grew till a point that I got used to his beatings, his foul language and his anger. Sometimes I just wished that I could disappear because it was too hard, too powerful to drain my mental health and scatter it to pieces. I had to cover up my scars and wounds during work as I found them humiliating.

Dad was a heavy gambler. He used to gamble and lose most of the times, just to come home drunk when he'll start to beat me to get the money which he can use to pay off his debts and to again use them to just wager and have fun. It was frustratingly annoying but I couldn't do anything because if I used to run to protect myself, he used to beat munchkin up and she was a baby and didn't deserve any of this at all especially at such a young age, so I had to take the beatings on her behalf.

Mum used to be out with her constantly changing boyfriends and I got her share of beatings as well. I was living a panic-stricken life in my own home and I couldn't do anything about it. How many times had I prayed that someone could lend me a hand, grab it and just pull me out of this situation but this only happened in books and movies. Real life was a nasty piece of shitty ass ride which never ended and kept getting more and more scarier and riskier than ever.

Heaving a tired sigh, I walked up the driveway, unlocked the door and entered the house just to hear my shoe crushing a piece of fallen glass on the floor. I carefully pocketed the key and looked up when my eyes widened in horror. The whole living room was a mess. Glass was displayed everywhere, half broken vases were on the floor, broken flowers were spewed everywhere. I could see food leftovers creating a huge mess on the ground when I felt pure rage because I knew that I had to clean this up as well after such a heavy shift at work. This was literally so vexatious.

The thing that caught my attention and sucked all air from the room making goosebumps appear on my skin and making my blood go cold was the thought of munchkin. Where was she? Was she hurt? Did dad beat her? Was she okay? Was my baby in danger?

Throwing my bag roughly and carelessly onto the floor, I just ran over the broken glass as quickly as I could fearing that she had gotten a beating when taking a turn, I saw blood stains on the floor confirming the thought that my baby sister had gotten a beating.

I rushed to find her and sure dad was hitting her again and again with his belt and munchkin was lying limp on the ground. She wasn't even moving a single muscle and all air was sucked from the room. The blood in my veins ran cold and I swear my heart stopped beating for a second. My nerves themselves were in shock that they had to pause

## Chapter 2

before sending further signals and when they did?

Without giving it a further thought, I lunged forward and pushed him off of her just to see her skin pale and yellow. Upon touching her, she was as cold as ice. Very. Very. Cold. I quickly placed my fingers under her neck to check her pulse when I was internally relieved to find a faint throb. At least it was there.

I was about to pick her up to take her to the hospital when I felt a sharp sting on my back which instantly turned into a painful pain. My dad had just hit me and I had nothing but munchkin in my mind. Anger coursed through my body like lava because hitting me was one thing but Everleigh? I wouldn't tolerate that.

My boss was a bitchy boss and didn't allow kids to sit there at the cafe as I worked and hence, I always left munchkin home with TV, snacks and sandwiches with her to keep her busy. I did have a mini camera installed and I always kept an eye on her throughout my job to see if she was okay or not. Today was such a hectic day and maybe the reason that I missed seeing my dad enter the house. But I really wish that I could have seen him.

I grabbed the nearest vase and turning around, I swung my hand hitting him with full force in an attempt to knock him out. He staggered back a bit and fell to the floor but tried to get up in a weak attempt when I wasn't having it. I had to take munchkin to a doctor and he definitely wasn't helping the situation. I grabbed the nearest baseball bat and again swung it with full ferocity, making a direct blow to his head when he laid flaccid and limp on the ground. I kept looking at him for six to seven seconds to make sure we were out of simple threat. He wasn't moving and I dreaded that I had maybe killed him but that was the least of my concerns at the moment.

Grabbing munchkin in my arms and wrapping a shawl around her, I rushed towards the entrance, grabbed my bag and ran out of the house taking her to the nearest hospital.

They took her to the emergency immediately and started treating her when I just stood outside to catch my breath. I wanted to call and inform the police but I couldn't as I knew that Dad would hit me again if he got free and I was too sore for that. One other thing I knew was that dad worked for someone who had power and if his boss made a harming beeline for us? We would be dead before even saying a 'please'. So, I just went to the bathroom to clean off munchkin's blood that was on my t-shirt and waited for the doctors to come out.

After about an eternity, the nurse came out to tell me that she was in a stable condition and that I could meet her but she needed rest so the meeting had to be precise. I tiptoed in the room just to see my baby sister lying on those colourless white sheets with monitors and needles attached to her. The silent beeping of the machines brought tears to my eyes but nonetheless I went to her slowly. "Hi munchkin." I whispered as if talking to the most delicate thing to exist in the entire universe.

## Chapter 2

Her voice croaked, "H-hii."

"How are you feeling baby?"

Her little chin wobbled, "It hurts sissy. My back and my legs hurt a lot."

I removed some hair from her forehead and kissed it, "I'm sorry munchkin I wasn't there for you. I'm so sorry I got late. You should have rushed in the room, locked it and given me a call when dad came."

"I didn't know he was there. I was sleeping because I was tired after school when I felt a sharp pain on my back and legs and he was hitting me. I wish he stops sissy."

I felt tears pool near the corner of my eyes and I wanted to smack myself for not being there for her. She was four, about to turn five but for me she was still just a baby and didn't deserve to suffer this at all. She would get nightmares and would be scarred for life and this was the last thing I wanted her to face. As though knowing the internal battle raging inside of me, she spoke holding my hand, "Don't blame yourself, it was never your fault. You did all you could do to protect me. Just look after yourself too. You should look after others till a certain point but never forget yourself."

Whose wordings was she speaking herself?

I just hugged her but made sure that I didn't crush her under the hug, "Ssshhh munchkin, the doctor said not to speak too much. Just go to sleep baby, you need rest. Also, where did you hear this from?"

She grinned, "Mrs. Brown."

I nodded and ruffled her hair when she asked, "Are you fine sissy?"

I couldn't believe her. She was asking about me while being in immense pain when I smiled and affectionately rubbed her cheek, "I'm fine munchkin. Just go to sleep."

She nodded when I got up and laid next to her, hugging her till she was snoring soundly within minutes and I silently smiled to myself. I didn't know where mum was or what was happening at home but I wasn't going to leave munchkin here alone and go there. My stomach started growling and I got up to go to the cafeteria to get some sandwiches when I sighed. When was I ever going to get a break?

## THE NEXT DAY

The doctor came in to check up on her. Humming satisfyingly, she said, "Her vitals are perfect, just her skin is bruised and it will take time to heal. Her blood pressure, sugar levels and heart beat are all normal. Just take good care of her."

I nodded in agreement while looking at her peaceful sleeping figure when the doctor looked at me suspiciously and asked, "Did someone beat her?" I almost choked on my own spit.

## Chapter 2

I wasn't used to telling people of what we were enduring so I quickly said, "Umm no. She fell from the stairs." and I averted my eyes. She gave me a scoff, "She was beaten and I am supposed to inform the police. It's in the rules."

"No don't need-" she rolled her eyes and left leaving me sweating. What if dad gets a helper who will beat us up if the news went till the police? What if his so-called boss kills us on the spot? What if he takes munchkin and tortures her in front of me and then later on kills us? I shook my head ignoring all these thoughts but I was genuinely scared. I quickly got up and went to find that doctor who was talking to a patient. Waiting for when she got free, I asked her, "When will she be discharged?"

She was a rude ass nurse when she just looked at me with a bored expression and kept chewing her gum, "Today. Once the police see her, you can take her away." I just nodded and went back to my room to see munchkin looking better than usual. Her drips were all done and the nurse just had to pull it off, when I knew how to do it, and so carefully taking off all the needle and the drips, I picked her up in my arms, wrapped a shawl around our bodies and heads and wore black glasses so that no one could recognize us and just exited the hospital as fast as I could.

I was sweating as hell and just made sure to get out of this area. I looked around to see where we could live as I sure as hell wouldn't go back home. I had already collected all my money to make sure that we could afford a motel and decided to stay there till we could easily afford some place better. I wanted to make sure that munchkin didn't go through this again ever. It was too horrible.

## ASHTON

The club was due to open any time as we had invested a large sum of money to open a new club near one of my bases in America. Massimo came and gave me all the files regarding the club when I scrutinized them and gave him a nod dismissing him and went back to my work. When I didn't hear the shuffling of his feet, I looked up narrowly to see him still standing. "I thought I conveyed it quite clearly that you could leave. Is there any problem?"

He seemed anxious and nervously shifted on his feet and started to stammer. "B-b-boss-"

How annoying I found it when people stuttered when I interrupted him, "Massimo, get your tongue fixed and then come to me. Till then, get the hell out."

"Bossparkerhasntcomeyetandheisntresponding." He said in a complete rush and I would be kidding myself if I said that I understood even a word of what he said except of Boss, because he said it all so damn quickly.

"What?"

"Boss, Parker hasn't arrived yet and he isn't responding."

## Chapter 2

"What do you mean?"

"You told him to collect the shipment of marijuana-"

"Massimo don't tell me what the fuck I asked him to do. I very well know what I told him to do. What the fuck do you mean he isn't back? He was supposed to be back by," I checked my phone to see it was already Monday the 26th, "Sunday. Where is he?"

"No idea boss but we contacted James. He said that Parker had collected the shipment on Saturday and he is neither back nor is he responding."

I closed my eyes in frustration and pinched the bridge of my nose, "Release the search party and search for him. I need his whereabouts by tomorrow morning 9am."

"Yes boss." Massimo started to leave when I stopped him, "Needless I need to remind you that 9am means 9am. Not a minute before not a minute after. Do you get that?"

He gulped in fear but gave a yes boss and left.

I swear I could kill anyone with my bare hands at the moment. First Trevor, now Parker. Who the fuck was next?

*

My head was hurting like a bitch and that's how I woke up with a start. I groaned and rolled out of bed to go get dressed as I had a flight to catch to America. I sent a text to Phoenix, my second in command to get me an aspirin for the headache. Taking a shower, I got into my black button-down shirt, black dress pants and wore my suit coat. I checked my phone to see it was already 8 55am. Quickly downing down water with three tablets of aspirin I headed to my office. I entered and collected my pack of cigarettes and my wallet when I heard a knock.

"Come in."

Massimo poked his head and entered after a second's hesitation. I glanced at my watch to see it was 9:06am. He was six minutes late. He took quick, hurried strides, put a navy-blue hard file in front of me and stood with his head hung low. He knew he was in trouble for being late as I didn't tolerate disobedience. Putting my hands in my pockets and straightening my back, I looked at him, "I guess I clearly mentioned 9:00am. I was in my office at 8:57 so what excuse do YOU have to come in six minutes late than asked?" Sometimes I myself was astounded to see how chilly my voice sounded.

He spoke something incoherent. I was honestly frustrated by telling people to just answer me there and then as I did not have day and night to witness them stutter.

Rolling my eyes in annoyance I growled, "Massimo. I swear-"

"Boss, Ella added laxatives into my morning coffee as a joke and you know, I-i- had a you know like a really-really bad- I

## Chapter 2

hope you get it." I was interrupted by his beautiful confession. He said all this with his head hung low in embarrassment. Ella was just a girl he had found on the street with torn clothes and all poor, when he took her under his attention and wanted to care for her. They became friends and then really close friends and as much as I have seen what's going on in my house, those two were definitely now a thing, and as it was brought to my attention that they now even sleep together.

I had to stifle a laugh here. Poor Massimo. How could I punish him because of this? As much as I wanted to bark a laugh at this, I had to maintain my demeanor when regaining my posture, I replied in a gruff voice, "It's okay, I'll leave you this time. Get my things ready for the flight."

He saluted a yes boss and was leaving my office when I turned away from the door, towards the window just to say with a smirk on my face, "And if that happens again, I still need you on time so you can use baby diapers. They are still available in the market." My cheeks heated with amusement but I swore I heard him choke. He whispered a nervous yes boss and was about to exit when I again stopped him, "And Massimo?"

"Yes boss?" It was barely more than a whisper.

"Don't worry, they are cheap. I can pay for them if you ever happen to need them. Don't hesitate, just ask."

His cheeks blushed a bright red colour and he awkwardly nodded his head, completely at a loss for words when he hastened out of my office before, I could say anything else. Who knew mornings could be this amusing? I chuckled deeply when I remembered to check the file for Parker.

I opened the file just to see a picture of Parker lying unconscious on the floor. He was sprawled like an eagle on the ground with broken glass near him and a baseball bat right next to his head. I furrowed in confusion to see that his shirt was torn and had little faint patches of blood on it. I was so perplexed, when I turned the page to find some explanation and read the printing just to make my anger boil.

***drunk***
   *passed out*
   *no sight of marijuana*
   *a couple of money in his back pocket*

**Upon interrogation**:
   *really drunk*
   *no "full" shipment*
   *hardly any drugs left*

I screamed in frustration and threw the nearest glass against the wall. It smashed and fell on the floor and broke into a million pieces. First those five million worth of drugs and now this. He had a death wish and I'll personally be the host of it. I called Massimo and he picked up on the first ring, "Yes boss?". He was still nervous from the previous discussion but the fun time was over. We were back to work.

"Lock him up in the cellar. No food will be given to him for

## Chapter 2

a day. After that, one meal per day. Make him urinate in the same cellar he is staying in. I'll come and have a look at him once I come back from America. Beat him up daily but make sure he doesn't die. He's mine to kill." I didn't wait for him to say anything else and just disconnected the call. Grabbing my keys, I exited my office, ordered the guard to tell a maid to clean up my office and wearing my Raybans, I exited the house and sat in my car to get to the airport to travel in my private jet.

America, here I come!

The pilot came to inform me that the flight would be twelve hours long when I just nodded in response. Twelve hours was no big deal, it was easy.

\*

It was nowhere near easy. For the first time in my life during the whole flight I was nervous. I couldn't figure out why the fuck I was so nervous but I was. I kept pulling my tie to free my neck a bit to breath properly when I genuinely couldn't understand as to what was wrong. Guess I just would have to wait and see.

The plane landed after what felt like eternity. I got out of it just to enter a matte black Lamborghini. Oh, how much I loved the colour black. I was ready to go to my house and rest for the day because I was tired. The club could be attended tomorrow.

## SOPHIA

I just carried munchkin in my arms to the nearest motels as a cab would be too costly and we had to save money wherever we could however we could. We found a motel a few minutes away from the hospital and I went in with munchkin asleep in my arms. The reception area was too hot with barely even a fan working. There was a middle-aged man probably in his early thirties who was sitting with his feet on the broken desk writing down something in his register. He had pale yellow skin, jet black hair and an earring in one of the ears. I shivered at the sight of the guy but still nervously staggered towards him to make the arrangements for the stay.

We booked a small room enough to accommodate two people. He was quite some rude guy and I made a mental note to stay out of his way as much as possible. He threw the keys onto the table and went back to working on whatever he was doing. Picking them up, I silently made my way towards our room, the sense of being tired suddenly hitting me again very badly. Turning the key in the lock I opened the door and entered it when-

I. WAS. STUPEFIED.

My mouth fell open on its own accord and the bag I was carrying dropped from my hands which I had bought over containing all our clothes. I had to ask my work partner Josephine to go to my house to collect the essentials as I couldn't leave munchkin alone. The room was breathtakingly gross. The bed was broken. The wallpapers were torn.

## Chapter 2

There were dusty cobwebs around the corners. The hinges to the bathroom door were broken. The floor was very dirty and I felt like puking but we had nowhere else to go. This was the cheapest one available.

I opened the windows with a creaking sound to let some fresh air come in just to get hit in the face by the foul smell of the garbage can outside. Gritting my teeth in annoyance, I closed the windows and placed a shawl on the bed and then placed munchkin on top of it to sleep. It was a miracle the bed didn't break down as I had expected after looking at the conditions.

Swiping all the sweat from my forehead I turned on the fan, set an alarm of 7 30am and laid down on the dismantled sofa and dozed off to sleep, amidst me wanting to puke so many times because of how gross this place was. It was a hectic day and I just needed rest, because tomorrow I would be finding a new place to sleep as this dirty, nasty ass place was not good for Everleigh's health. She was a baby for me and could get sick pretty badly but right now, I needed rest as I was genuinely exhausted.

**Three**

# Chapter 3

## SOPHIA

I woke up from the sound of some packets opening. I opened one eye just to see munchkin eating crisps, HER MORNING BREAKFAST, while watching YouTube on my mobile. Oh, how cute she looked.

I rubbed my eyes and yawned, "Good morning munchkin."

"Hmm."

Okay. The lady was busy eating her crisps so I stifled another yawn to check my phone. 8:03am. I had set the alarm but I forgot to press OK. Mentally facepalming myself I jumped as if someone had electrocuted me. I had to be at the cafe by

## Chapter 3

0800hrs. Quickly putting on a pair of denim blue trousers and a pale white shirt I quickly brushed my teeth, washed my face and put my hair in a messy bun. Snatching my phone and pocketing it, I picked munchkin up and rushed out of the room locking it when she protested with a moody whine.

I kissed her cheek and kept on running, "I have a job munchies and I am late." She made a cute ass pout and rested her cheek on my shoulder when I just smiled. I loved her. I really really loved her when at the last moment she too kissed my cheek when I giggled and hugged her closer. And the next thing I knew was that we both were laughing and running side by side to get to the cafe quickly.

My boss was on vacations today and hence I could bring my little devil along with me.

*

It was once again an extremely exhausting day and somehow, I was getting annoyed. I was getting frustratingly agitated due to some reason I couldn't quite figure out yet that it got to a point I actually snapped at a customer and had to apologize there and then. I was serving the last buyer of the day when I felt my trousers getting wet. Oh shit! I forgot. My monthly had started. I mentally face palmed myself, yet again, quickly served the customer, wrapped a scarf around my waist to cover up the stains and pulling Everleigh along, dashed for the door to go home. Now I understood why I was being agitated. I reached the motel and quickly freshened up and decided to eat something from whatever was left in the bag when my phone started to buzz. It was Josephine.

"Hey what's up?"

"HEYYYYY. Okay, I decided to cut to the chase as I don't have much of a time. Send me your location, I'm coming to pick you up."

I whined as I was pretty annoyed and tired, "Whyyyyyyyy?"

Excitement was evident in her tone, "There is a new club which has just opened and I cannot wait to go there and obviously you are going with me."

"But, Josephine, I am on my period. Besides, I don't even have anything to wear. Furthermore, no way in hell is Everleigh going to a club at this age and nowhere in my right senses will I leave her alone in this………." I didn't know how to describe this dingy place when I just somewhat grimaced with disgust and ended the thought with, "motel."

"Leave it to me. I'll fix you up something. Just send me your location."

I sighed and looked at Everleigh eating a burger, "What about munchkin?"

After about a few seconds she said, "I'll bring my maid along. She can look after her."

"Can she be trusted? Are you sure?" I was genuinely worried

## Chapter 3

as I have never let munchkin alone with anybody and she meant the world to me when-

*bleeeeeeep*

She hung up on me. How rude! I was antagonized but to be really honest, I really wanted to go. I had been running day and night doing duties, earning money, sleeping less and eating less for the past around six to seven years and I was genuinely very exhausted and so I really wanted to go for maximum an hour, have some time to myself, breathe a little and then back to normal routine, back in hell itself. I sent her my location and just waited for her to show up.

Josephine came at my doorstep twenty minutes later which was pretty quick. She entered the room and tried to cover up the disgust on her face. I felt ashamed but it was quickly gone when she ran towards me. Shoving a black dress into my hands she pushed me into the bathroom to get dressed. I wore it and looked myself in the mirror when I gasped.

It looked truly beautiful on me as it was long and very pretty, I must say but I couldn't wear it there. It was too revealing with a slit through my one of my legs exposing it fully, the neck hung low but fit pretty well. It hugged my curves quite majestically but still unsure of it, I went to Josephine whose mouth shaped an O, "Babe, you look stunning. You're totally getting laid tonight." She added with a wink.

I cringed and made a face and started to back away when Josephine got confused, "No Josephine no. First of all, this dress is too revealing, I can't. Secondly, I'm definitely not getting laid because first being I'm on my period. And even if I wasn't, I never intended on it because Everleigh is home alone and I don't have time for random flings. No way. If this is what you want to do you can leave without me but I'm sorry this isn't happening." There was a finality in my voice and she understood that.

"Jeez fine woman. Just tag along. You can have some fun and I'll drop you back home."

I raised an eyebrow with my hands folded into my chest and looked at her. Rolling her eyes, she held her arms up high and said with a sigh, "I promise."

I grinned to her and let her doll me up. After about half an hour we were ready to leave. Kissing munchkin on the head and making sure the caretaker was looking after her, I left with Josephine and just prayed that nothing went wrong. Now let's see what hell could break lose?

## ASHTON

Getting into my black trousers and a white button-down shirt I went to my wardrobe to wear a slick clean black coat. I adjusted my Rolex watch, wore my shoes and ruffled my hair to put some volume as I hated putting gel in them. Yuck! Adjusting the tie and the cufflinks I looked at myself in the mirror when I hummed in satisfaction. Yeah, I looked representable. Today I decided to pay a visit to the new club

## Chapter 3

we had opened and I was ready to leave. Taking large strides, I got into the car and nodded silently to the driver who raced out of the driveway. We arrived surprisingly early when the chauffeur opened my door and I got out.

Opening the buttons to my coat I entered the club and was met with a whoosh of cold air. The air conditioners were on and the atmosphere was cool. There were dim purple and pink lights. A rectangular bar was at the far end and a huge dance floor was in the middle. There were surprisingly many people, something I didn't expect. I went and sat at the far end of the corner when an intimidated looking bartender rushed towards me to take my order. Did I scare everyone that much?

Sipping my drink slowly, I put my right ankle on my left knee, eased myself back on the plush, soft emerald green sofa and saw the scenario unfold. I saw many people come in and out. People were smiling and laughing. They were enjoying this time as much as they could. I could see females happily dancing and laughing with supposedly their boyfriends and I couldn't help but wonder that what if I was never in the mafia?

What if I could lead a normal life? Nothing to worry about, not always stressing out. I was trained to grow into the heartless man that I am today. Neither did I know how to love, neither did I know what happiness was. What I knew, was pain, cruelty, bloodshed and power. I couldn't help but think that how much I have always wanted a normal life. How much I have wanted to be at ease and not worry about anything but those things weren't for a mafia boss. I zoned out thinking this when I focused on what I was staring at. Not a what, but a who.

I brought my glass down and just stared at her. She was gorgeous. Like a beautiful goddess. Her features were soft. She had rosy cheeks, plump red lips, fair skin and maroon red hair. She was very skinny but very very beautiful. She was wearing a black dress that perfectly covered her soft curves. One of her legs was exposed and I felt my cheeks heat up when I caught myself staring at them.

I looked up to see her laughing softly. Her laugh was so soft and so delicate that it could break glass. I put my drink aside and laid back easily just to watch her. She was with another girl who looked like a rubber duck. Ew!

The lights further dimmed down when some soft music came on. People started dancing and I couldn't help but wonder what if it was me dancing with her in the middle of the room. What if it was me holding her waist in my possessive grip and swaying to the music? What if it was me holding her finger while she spun till, I could pull her harshly towards me till she hit my chest and looked me up in the eye?

Tucking some strands of her hair behind her ear she moved back and sat at the counter. She refused to dance with anyone and I couldn't help but smile internally. Obviously, I wouldn't allow anyone to touch her. She was mine but she didn't know that yet.

## Chapter 3

As soon as this thought crossed my mind, she looked in my direction and started staring at me. The lights around me were dark and so she couldn't see me properly. And just to see her reaction, I placed the drink aside, bent forward and intertwined my hands together looking straight at her when I made sure my eyes bore into hers. She suddenly realized that I had caught her staring when her eyes dilated and she quickly looked away and coughed a small cough. She clenching her legs together definitely did not go unnoticed when she turned her back to me.

After about ten minutes the lights were switched back on, the DJ put some rock music to change the atmosphere and the club was once again in full swing. Gulping down the rest of my drink in one go, I went to put the drink on the counter and deliberately brushed my knee with her exposed leg. She sucked in a deep breath but I turned on my heel and with a smirk I left the club.

And oh, how extravagantly beautiful she smelled.

*

Getting home, I called Massimo and told him to get the camera footage of today's day at the club. He seemed surprised by the tone of my voice and I knew he wanted to ask why but he knew better than to ask me questions. He went to get the recordings and returned after a few minutes. I played the CD on my laptop when I found her.

She looked as gorgeous in pictures as in person. I paused the recordings and pointed my finger at her lone figure, "Get me her details. I'm giving you one full day. After that I need every piece of information regarding this lady or consider yourself dead. Did I make myself clear?"

Massimo clearly nervous, responded a yes boss, took her picture on his phone and left my room. I loosened my tie before taking it off and throwing it onto the nearest sofa, my thoughts always on that single woman that caught my eye when never ever had a woman ever caught my eye even once, let alone my breath. I think I might need to stay in America for a little while more.

## SOPHIA

Holy smokes he was hot.

Four

# Chapter 4

### SOPHIA

The party was in full swing. People were enjoying and dancing and I was just getting bored. Josephine never told me that her boyfriend Mark would be there so I was being totally ignored and I didn't want to tag along with the both of them as I hated being the third wheel. The party continued when I suddenly felt the temperature of the surrounding drop low.

I looked around to see what had happened but everything seemed pretty normal. Nobody was looking around with a frown on their face like I was, nobody had a crease on their forehead or some sort of confusion evident on their faces. I felt light goosebumps on my arm and a tingling sensation in the lower region of my stomach. Shrugging and ignoring the feeling, I went back to enjoying my water.

A slow romantic song came on when I just enjoyed the environment as I was definitely neither getting drunk nor was I going to dance with anyone. I just couldn't afford getting wasted. I was like a mother to munchkin now and a drunk mother can't look after her child. Many people asked me for a dance including girls which shocked me to my core but all I could do was politely decline. Some had to be told harshly as they just wouldn't stop budging me.

Watching other people dance so merrily, full of happiness and them laughing made my heart flutter and a small smile melted on my face. The moment was going flawlessly well when I felt as if I was being watched and I would be kidding myself if I said I wasn't freaked out. I was creeped the hell out as that cold feeling was there again and I once more tried to ignore it when I felt some heat on my back. Turning to look backwards my eyes met directly with the most handsome man that I had ever seen.

He was sitting a bit far away from me, was in a bit of darkness and I couldn't see his face clearly but from what I could see, was all him. Just him. His body screamed power. Sexiness dripped from every part of his skin. I did not know who he was but he seemed pretty presiding.

He had his black hair ruffled which honestly looked hot on him that I wanted to do nothing but move my hands through them, just to get a feel of it. From what I could see when the

## Chapter 4

nearest neon light to him turned on, was that he had a beige skin colour, neat high eyebrows, a sharp nose with big full lips.

He was wearing a white button-down shirt, had a black coat on and some black trousers. His shoes were spotless clean and I must say my room was never that clean as to how much his shoes were. I could see a tattoo peaking from under his left sleeve and I wondered what it could be about. I pondered if he had more tattoos and where. He was sitting on a sofa with one ankle on top of the other knee and seemed so relaxed, almost as if he owned the place.

He looked so……perfect. Composed. Smart. And above all he looked…handsome?

He changed positions and I peeked up to have a look at his face again when he was already looking at me with a smirk on his face. He had caught me checking him out and never in my life had I felt more shamefaced. My cheeks blushed with embarrassment and I swiveled around turning my back to him. Something caught in my throat and I had to cough to clear my passages and instinctively I closed my legs. How embarrassing could it get more?

The song ended and the DJ played some rock music. I was done for today and was about to get up to inform Josephine how I wanted to head home when the atmosphere shifted again. This was honestly confusing the hell out of me when Mr. Hot brushed his knee against my exposed leg.

I sucked in a deep breath as I felt all the nerve endings within me light up with fire. Electricity coursed through my body with the highest energy and I couldn't help but look at his retreating figure. He directly walked out into the night and I couldn't help but gawk at his figure. Even his walk was handsome for a man. I decided to leave a bit late, just to avoid running into him because I knew ignoring him would be difficult.

I looked into his glass and then up at the bartender when I called him, "Um excuse me, what did that man just have?"

"Spirytus."

"Can I have one too?" I wanted to taste what he just had and besides, today was the second day after opening and the owner of this club was kind enough to make everything free for the first three days.

The bartender raised one of his eyebrows, looked at me blinking his eyes and just walked away.

What was that?

"HEY!" I shouted at him when he came back in annoyance, "Kiddo, this is the strongest you can have. What's your age?"

I felt my anger boil. Kiddo? Did he just call me a kid?

"Did you ask him his age?" I retorted back in resentment.

## Chapter 4

"He's the boss young lady. We do whatever he asks. Now…
…….If you'll excuse me, I don't have much of a time."

He left me sitting there dumbstruck. Boss. So, he WAS the boss. My assumption wasn't wrong but he looked so young as to be the owner of a club. I rolled my eyes and got up to go home. Boys do confuse me a lot at times.

Josephine was SO not ready to go home so I decided to walk all the way back to my motel. The night felt juvenile and beautiful and I just rushed home hoping my little munchkin was okay.

## ASHTON

I couldn't sleep all night. I just couldn't stop thinking about her. Who was she? Why was she so damn gorgeous? What was her name? How did her voice sound like? How- I furrowed my brows on the thought that how she was the first woman who made me think that how would her lips feel like? How would her body feel like pressed against mine, my hands on her waist keeping her close to me, never letting her go. I desperately wanted to know everything about her. My thoughts wouldn't stop directing towards that one girl who caught my eye since the moment I laid eyes on her. My thoughts were interrupted from the buzzing of my phone. I had the annoying habit to keep my phone on silent. Always.

"What?" I growled in annoyance.

"Boss we have a problem at the mansion."

Viktor babbled from the other side. I had appointed Viktor to take control of whatever was going on in my absence when I responded, "Then fucking deal with it. Why do you think I left you in charge? Just to call me and tell that boss we have a problem, what do we do now? Seriously?"

He was clearly nervous when he said, "No Boss. A man is here for you and he is adamant on meeting you. Says he wouldn't leave without talking to you."

"Who is he?"

"Boss he claims to be Ferdinand Alaksor-"

I didn't hear anything then. My blood boiled in anger. My ears turned red from the sudden anger that was running ferociously through my veins. I suddenly sat up on the bed and tried to control my anger. I couldn't help but wonder how the fucker still had the audacity to come to my house and demand my presence. Like hell he would. I was more livid at the guard who let him come through the fucking gates. Guess my workers needed some reminding of who was the fucking boss and what were their duties.

"Viktor Ryan John," I growled lowly into the phone taking his full name which was my way of showing how mad I was and I think I did get my point across when I heard his shiver, "If you value your goddamn life and your wife's life which I recall is carrying your child, get this fucker out of my home

## Chapter 4

right now in less than a goddamn fucking minute. Make sure my orders have been carried out or believe me you wouldn't like the consequences. Throw this son of a bitch out even if you have to grab him by the scruff of this neck. Don't snap his neck in half though………..that blood to be spilt is mine and mine alone."

I disconnected the call and flung my phone across the room. It was exhausting. This mafia was exhausting but that's all I could do. Think that it was wearing me out and then go back to work again. It was a shitty world in my opinion but only one ray of light was all I could see now. She. The soft dove. The white swan. The light to my fucking darkness. The only blossoming flower in the dense graveyard that I was living in. A soft smile played on my lips and I exited the room to take a cold shower.

Walking out of the bathroom with the towel hanging low on my waist, I just saw one text from Viktor.
    BOSS.

This was alone to tell me that the fucker was thrown out on the roads. He was the subject I'll love to deal later with. Best blood is spilt when it runs too much and becomes too hot from the continuous flowing. I would need to snap that flow and I'll gladly do it with my bare fucking hands, tainting my soul with the blood of the person I hated the most AFTER my father.

\*

Wearing my clothes, I just picked up my phone when there was a timid knock on my bedroom door.

"Come in."

Massimo entered the room when I saw a file in his hand. Aaahhh! The information on my kitten was finally here.

"Boss we collected as much data as we could about the young lady."

I took the file from his hand, nodded my head and dismissed him. I was taught never to be nice to people. Never to say a thank you or a sorry. I was just trained like this and now I was used to this and easily comfortable in my skin. Neither was I willing to change it nor would I ever. Opening the file as it was the most gentle piece of item I could ever hold, I started reading.

**Name : Sophia Greene**
  **Age : 23**
  **Gender : Female**

I mentally scoffed at this. Why would he write gender? Idiot.

**Parents : None**

What does he mean none? Is Massimo high on something? He should've written dead if it is as what I presume.

**Siblings : A young sister**

## Chapter 4

**Work : Timmy's cafe**
**Working days : Monday to Saturday**
**Work Timings : 0800-2300**

Wait what? She bloody worked 15 hours?

**Pay: 250 dollars per month**

WHATTTT? THAT'S SO LESS FOR SOMEONE WORKING SO MUCH.

**Place of residence: A motel**

Excuse me what? A motel? Is Massimo kidding me? But then why would he? Why would she live in a motel? Why would the queen of beauty live in a motel? I was genuinely confused. Or maybe because she had no parents to support her. But then, what about the parents? Massimo better should have done all the research.

There was a picture of her at the end of the page and I just stared lovingly at her. Who was she? How was she so breathtakingly gorgeous? Why hadn't I met her before?

I kept gazing at her picture, her perfectly shaped nose, her big blu- wait. I was dead silent for a minute. She had blue eyes. I couldn't believe it. It stole all breath from me. The only woman I have ever adored up till now was my mother and she was the only one I knew who had blue eyes. I had my father's eyes, fucking grey. But she?

She had the same eye colour as of my mother. Glancing down her face she had the most beautiful lips anyone has ever had. Her tiny ears were so cute and she was so adorable. She was just like a fucking queen. I don't know how much time I spent looking at her but I just kept staring. I couldn't seem to peel my eyes off of her as she was the epitome of all beauty. Fucking gorgeous.

I forgot that it was her file I was looking at and somehow, I was hungry for more information on her. I wanted more. I hadn't even met her, yet her thought and her image clung to me like a drug. We hadn't even talked, yet she already had me wrapped around her delicate fingers which I bet were soft and calming to touch. We hadn't even exchanged names, yet I wanted her to be mine already. What was happening to me all of a sudden, I didn't know, but I liked it.

I liked the feeling, it was new, refreshing and something that I loved. I just had never felt like this before. It was for the first time and I wouldn't let it go that simply. I wouldn't let her go that easily. I was a stubborn man and I hunted down what I wanted and I didn't sleep in peace till I had it. I was not used to losing. I just won and won and won. And I'll definitely come out victorious in Sophia's case.

Sophia.

The name rolled smoothly over my tongue. It felt pure, fresh, just like sweet honey. Her name felt like strawberries. So soft, so gentle, so alluring. A gentle smile tugged on my face and this was probably the first since I had lost everything.

## Chapter 4

What was this girl doing to me?

Smiling like a maniac I turned the page only to find it empty. What? WHAT? OH MY WHAT? What sort of information was this? Whenever I had asked data on anybody, Massimo always produced the best reports, containing all the details. What happened this time? Furiously dialing his number, I called him when he picked up on the fourth ring, "Yes boss?"

"Are you having explosive diarrhoea or what?" My voice was laced with anger.

He gulped in fear, "No boss, why?"

Obviously, the fucker was lying. I can tell when someone lies.

"Did the laxatives kick in so bad?"

"Boss, what did I do wrong?" He was clearly frightened. As he should be.

"What kind of a report is this?"

"We gave you everything we could find."

"Find information about her parents, her background, where is she from. Check her movements. Is my mother supposed to do all this?"

"Yes boss, sorry. I'll do that tomorrow first thing as soon as the sun rises."

"You better." I shut down my phone in annoyance.

Honestly, the number of times I was getting angry someone could easily say I might be on a period.

## MASSIMO

The laxatives were so bad. Ella will definitely pay for this. The bit**.

## SOPHIA

I couldn't sleep. Who was he? I kept thinking about him. My heart has never tugged for someone so strongly before but then again, who was he? I tiredly glanced at my phone to see it was two in the morning. Thank God it was a Sunday so I didn't have to wake up early. I could easily think about Mr. Hot all night long.

How could someone look so flawless? So elegant? so......
..hot. I grinned like a lunatic and started imagining scenarios if I was with him which had somewhat become a habit for me. Imagining myself in fake ass scenarios and then crying over why I couldn't get a prince charming EXACTLY like I imagined. I kept thinking about the hot ass boss from the

*Chapter 4*

club, his sexy features, hot smirk, handsome walk, beautiful aura when suddenly, I was wide awake. What if he has a girlfriend? What if he is engaged to someone already? What if he is married? WHAT IF HE'S A GRANDFATHER? Wait what? He didn't look that old so I discarded the last thought. Mentally shaking my head, I went back to sleep. I had to stay away from this man.

Or could I?

# Chapter 5

## ASHTON

It was a clear Wednesday morning and I decided to pay a visit to the cafe to have a look at her again. She was like a drug for I needed it again and again and I just couldn't stop. Not that I wanted to anyways.

Walking up the grey marble steps I entered the cafe and I have to say, it was beautiful. The atmosphere was cool, not too hot, not too cold. Just. Perfect. The walls were painted a light blue colour. There were round steel grey tables for the seating of the customers. There was an exquisite aroma of freshly baked cookies and the smell of waffles was wafting around the cafe.

## Chapter 5

Purple flowers were hanging from the roof giving rise to the beauty of the cafe. There were clear glass walls between the lounge and the counter. The only thing I hated were the tiles. Ugh. Disgusting. I could see a few customers at the moment, I guess because it was 1000 hours in the morning. People were usually at work at this time of the day and so was I, but not today.

I kept my black glasses on and my fake mustache and beard on to make sure that she didn't recognize me instantly. I started walking towards the counter when I felt as if a cushion had hit me in the leg.

Looking down, my eyes adjusted to see a young boy on the floor holding his head in his hands. His mother came rushing to me and started apologizing frantically, "Oh I'm so sorry. Johnny just keeps running blindly. JOHNNY! How many times have I told you, you are going to hurt yourself and the people you hit? Now say sorry to the sir. You hit him." The child just kept on crying to a point it was annoying me. Rolling my eyes, I started to walk away when the mother grabbed my arm. A bit harshly may I add. "I'm so sorry. He bumped into you accidentally. I'm so sorry."

I looked at her hand on my arm, then at her, then back at the hand holding my arm and when she didn't get the catch, I yanked it away angrily and growled, "It's okay and who do you think you are to grab my arm without my permission? Do it next time and I'll cut your arms in half."

I failed to understand why at times I got so angry that easily?

Small things made me so irate and sometimes I couldn't help but lash out. The woman gasped and backed away quickly. Giving her a pointed look, I swiveled around and started walking towards the counter when I stopped dead in my tracks.

There she was.

She was there. My dove was there. My angel was there and she looked as beautiful as ever. She looked stunningly gorgeous even in her simple work attire but for the first time in my life, I felt empty. I have always felt empty but this feeling of emptiness was different. She was looking at me with disgust on her face. Pure loath was openly displayed and she was doing no effort in hiding it. That expression alone killed me.

Taking a deep breath, I chose to ignore it and sauntered over to her. As soon as I reached and opened my mouth, she started to walk away which made me furious. How dare she walked away when I was about to speak to her? No one back at the house or office dared to just to walk away but again, she didn't know me yet. Enraged I grabbed her elbow, gritting my teeth there and then because I just did what that woman did, but ignoring it, I kept my hold onto her when she turned around. Looking at my hand she arched an eyebrow upwards and spoke in the most deadliest tone I have ever heard anyone speak with me before, "Leave. My. Arm."

"No." I replied as calmly as I could. I decided to play along. It wouldn't kill to have some fun.

## Chapter 5

She grinded her teeth in anger, "I said. Bloody. Leave. My. Arm. Exactly what you said to that woman behind. Leave it or…. or-"

"Or what?", I interrupted her.

She seemed at a loss for words. Quirking up as if she got an idea she stammered, "I-I'll call the police."

I chuckled. Oh kitten. Even the police never dared to cross their paths with me but I wasn't ready to start that subject now.

She looked at me and seemed horrified, "Why are you laughing?"

I stifled a laugh and said calmly retracting my hand away, "Look kitten, just take my goddamn order and I'll leave you. Believe me it's that simple. You wouldn't take my order I'll make sure YOU take my order. So, either do your work like a nice girl or you'll see the hard way. So, your choice."

She had her brows furrowed in anger when she spun around, took calculated steps and came to take my order. Hmm. Good girl.

"What the fuck do you want?"

"Tsk tsk kitten. Language."

"Stop calling me kitten. I'm no kitten to you." She retorted back in anger and I'll be lying if I said that it didn't turn me on. She, angry, turned me on even more.

I decided to ignore her yet again, "What's your special?"

Rolling her eyes she said, "Iced mocha Grande."

I was feeling mixed emotions at the moment. Firstly, I was mad at her for rolling her eyes at me as I hated it when someone did that but I decided to let it go for now. Secondly, I loved the way she pronounced the name. The way she rolled her tongue to produce the r in Grande almost made her seem Italian.

I decided to control myself, "Yeah okay I'll have that." and with a smirk I added, the most dirtiest thought entering my brain, "With extra cream." She looked at me from under her eyelashes and furiously typed in. I handed her the payment giving her a huge amount of tip when her eyes widened. "So now you think I'm a stray dog?"

WHAT IS THE MATTER WITH GIRLS? WHY DO THEY TAKE EVERYTHING SO NEGATIVELY. I was genuinely exhausted when I sighed, "Just keep it."

She interrupted me in anger, "No no why? Why are you giving me such a huge amount of tip. You think that I can't earn? You think that I can't take care of myself? What is it?"

Heaving a sigh, I took off my glasses, the fake beard and the fake mustache and looked at her, "I. Said. Keep it." And she?

## Chapter 5

She was rooted to the spot. Her curvaceous body froze in place and her hands stopped midway when she looked at me. Her mesmerizingly beautiful eyes widened and that's when I noticed how pretty they were. Electric blue. I loved it so goddamn much.

She just kept looking at me, her whole being frozen as she drank in my image. Even I was left breathless due to her charming beauty and the power she radiated off just by standing in front of me. We both held each other's intense gaze, hers with wide eyes but mine filled with amusement when I raised my eyebrows in an amused expression, turned around and walked away to sit at the very end. I smirked to see her still standing there when she shook her head and went back disappearing behind the counter.

The drink was pretty good I must say, it had good taste after all. I got up, gave her one last heated look and walked outside. She was still standing there fumbling with her hands and I daresay………..she did look cute.

## SOPHIA

I heard a child crying when I rushed out of the kitchen. A young child maybe I guess five or six years old was on the ground with his head in his hands and was crying loudly. The mother started consoling him and muttered an apology to a young man who was standing there. My guess was that the child had bumped into him and that's why the mother was apologizing. What was more horrid was how that man snapped at her, "It's okay and who do you think you are to grab my arm without my permission? Do it next time and I'll cut your arms in half."

I. Was. Horrified. Who does that? How can a person be so rude? I felt bad for the mother who whimpered and backed away. Poor woman. The asshole started coming towards me when I just felt disgusted by him and decided to not even talk to him as he had just lost respect in my eyes for how he treated that woman there who was just trying her level best to control her son.

Turning on my heels I started to walk away when I felt a deadly strong grip on my arm and for some reason, I felt electric sparks run through the septum of my heart. What confused me more was that he didn't even look THAT good with a horrible beard and moustache on, then why did I feel something towards him was beyond my understanding.

Turning around, I saw him holding my elbow when I felt so furious. The blood gushing in my arteries boiled at the sight of him when I gritted my teeth and asked him to leave my arm just as he had RUDELY said to that woman behind him. What further angered me was the audacity of this bastard when he calmly said no. He literally said no with a stupid face and kept on annoying me when I decided to save the upcoming headache and just get rid of him because he sure wasn't letting it go and looked like a stubborn bastard.

Taking his order, he paid the bill and gave me an insanely large sum of money as tip which offended me a lot. No one

## Chapter 5

in their normal mind suddenly gives large tips and for as long as I had worked here, I had never seen him here before too, so a new customer to be giving this much to a person he doesn't even know? Felt very weird.

I had always worked on my own and made a living on my own that I wasn't used to people giving me large sums of money, then why in the name of his ugly ass beard was he tipping so huge on his first visit? Did he think that I was a long-lost puppy? Or was he so into me that he was trying to buy me by paying me? Why so damn much on the first sight? He really was so full of himself.

I again started arguing with him to take the money back when suddenly my knees felt weak. All breath was knocked out from me, my heart was slamming against my ribcage and my inner fairy girls were squealing at me and begging me to just let them observe him when he took off his glasses, fake moustache and beard. I was frozen to the spot, all energy suddenly exiting my body and no neurons coping at all. He was the same guy I saw at the club. Mr. Hot.

Up close he looked even more gorgeous than I could ever imagine. He had steel raging grey eyes and a beautiful calm expression. His face had the most handsome cut I had ever seen. I totally forgot the incident with the lady and then me when I just started gawking at him like an idiot. How can someone be so devilishly sexy but so cold and rude, I failed to understand.

I kept standing there stupidly staring at him even when he

had already gotten back to his seat, my brain not telling me to put my right foot in front of the left one and to basically move away. I kept looking at him when the next thing that he did was, smirk at me. And that ought to bring me back to my senses when shaking my head, I went to kitchen to make his drink. The ingredients fell from my hands a couple of times due to how nervous I was seeing him again.

I couldn't go back there so I sent Josephine instead to hand him his drink. Standing at the counter while taking more orders I kept stealing glances his way and had to say, even his way of drinking was very hot and decent for a man. After about half an hour he got up, looked at me for a few hot seconds, letting me feel heat creep up my body and headed out into the open air.

I was sweating so profusely as only one thought kept running in my head……………*what was that?*

## AFTER A FEW DAYS

## ASHTON

I was leaving for Italy after three days and I was hell not going there without my kitten and that's when I called Massimo in my room.

"Yes boss?"

## Chapter 5

"Come in."

He entered and stood by the coffee table. I eased back on the sofa, took in a deep breath, placed my right ankle on top of my left knee, my phone on the table and looked at him, "You will follow Sophia, the woman I told you about. Follow her to her motel and right before she goes in………" I told him the whole plan. He just kept nodding his head in response when I asked after telling him everything, "Got it? Any problem?"

"Just one question Boss. What if she refuses? There is a high probability that she will refuse."

I knew it. I knew this damn well and I know she will refuse. I mean…………who fucking wouldn't? Anyone in their normal senses would. Smiling a little smile, I opened the cap of the bottle of alcohol, poured some in the crystal-clear glass and took a sip letting it burn in my throat, letting it remind me of my past falls or gruesome loss of energies when I fell weak to the worldly burdens, letting it ignite the pain within the scars I carried on my body, the blood that was tainted not only on my skin but also in my soul, when I used this same drink to drown down the pain. I took another sip when I smacked my lips, and stared into air when I calmly responded, "We forcefully abduct her."

## SOPHIA

Today was one of the greatest days of my life. My boss gave us an off early as he had a date to go too and he was very happy about that. Seeing him being less rude when he was happy made me wish that he could stay like this for the rest of his life only because we could get an off early, no other specific reason.

It was 1800 hours when I started walking back to the motel. Today was Munchkin's birthday as well, the major major major reason I was even more happier and the reason that I was also carrying six small cupcakes she loved from the cafe. I couldn't wait to take her out to celebrate her finally turning five. My little devil.

I had to leave her at the motel today as she was hell not in the mood to go to the cafe and was being very stubborn. I was already running late when warning her that this was the last time I would be leaving her, I left for my job, but not before giving her my phone as I kept calling her every half an hour from the cafe to check up on her.

Humming to myself, I turned to the road where my motel was when I saw around five armed muscular men standing with their legs a bit apart, arms crossed and were wearing heavy armour. I was confused but still I decided to mind my own business and started to walk away when one of them stopped me, "Ma'am we have to talk."

He had a gruff voice, a very rigid face showing anger at

## Chapter 5

I really don't know what. He had a stiff body structure and it genuinely felt like as if his uniform was suffocating him. My thoughts immediately went to munchkin wishing she was fine when I looked back at the guard. He still had that arrogant feature on his face which was now kind of intimidating and made me get more alarmed. I was befuddled but still responded a questioning yes.

"You need to come with us along with your sister."

A million questions bombarded into my mind. How did he know about munchkin? Who were they? Why were they so armed? Why me all of a sudden? Where will they take us? What if they kill me? What about munchkin?

Trying to keep my tone as calm as ever I asked, "Where?"

"I'm sorry ma'am we cannot tell you that but you need to come along with us. This is our boss's orders."

"Who is your boss?"

"I said ma'am we cannot disclose this information."

I was scared shitless but I decided to put on a show of bravery, "Well then tell your goddamn bitch of a boss to shove his request up his ass. I'm not coming and you better not force me. Be decent men and for once think something like this happening with your mothers, sisters or daughters at home. Disgusting."

I quickly started walking away from them and tried not to break into a run to not give them an opportunity to place a hand over a weak point of mine. I turned around and to my surprise they were getting in the car and moving away. Huh. That was easy. But obviously it wasn't that easy as it looked. Such low-level people did not give up easily.

Still shook from what had happened I decided to move out from this motel and shift into another one as fast as possible. I packed up our things, picked my sleeping, cute little munchies up and walked out to change the place we were living at. When will I ever get a break?

## ASHTON

Massimo called me and I was eager to know what had happened though I already knew.

"Boss, we are launching plan two tomorrow at dawn. We need your permission." Hmm. So the kitten had refused just as I had assumed and expected, like obviously. In a deep voice I nodded, "Granted."

Sorry kitten but that is the only way. Sorry to scare the shit out of you but I have to do this. I will obviously make it up to her later but for right now, I needed her. I got up and went to the bathroom to take a shower. She was coming tomorrow.

## Chapter 5

# SOPHIA

I heard some noise when I sleepily opened my eyes. The new motel was a bit better than before but expensive. I discarded the thought thinking that maybe it was a cat in the lane somewhere and was about to doze off again when I felt the knob of the door rattle and turn. My heart froze and sweat started accumulating on my forehead as my eyes widened.

I quickly jumped up in fright but still as carefully as possible as to not wake Everleigh up. My hands were shivering due to the fright that who the hell was outside and what was about to happen. Since I had never been in a situation like this before, I picked munchkin up, carried her in my arms, hugged her close to me and hid under the bed. I was petrified and I didn't know what to do when I covered my mouth to muffle any sounds coming when I felt people coming into the room.

"Check every area. She must be here."

Thank God I had kept my mouth muffled as I sucked in a harsh breath. That voice! I knew that voice. It was the same which belonged to that armed man in the street. I bloody well knew, that such low-level people never stopped their bad habits but the question was that how did he find me?

The sheets of the bed rose when I felt a rough hand pull me out. I kept a tight grip on munchkin, with me being close to tears as I was not afraid for myself, but for my mini Everleigh as I feared what will these people do with her. She was a baby to me and did not deserve any harsh treatment.

Rough hands held me, keeping me at my place when I whimpered and started begging them to let us go. I started crying and fighting with all the energy I had as I was scared, I was panicking and I feared they will hurt munchkin. I feared that they will beat her and as harsh as the reality sounds, may sell her into brothels and my mind exploded at that option.

No.

I couldn't let that happen to her. I kicked out my legs and started hitting them wherever I could when I did hear one groan. Other than that? My efforts were feeble as they were way too strong. They had bodies like of army tanks, very very powerful and muscular. After about a couple of minutes I felt a cloth around my nose and I succumbed to darkness after a few seconds of inhaling it. The last thought on my mind was munchkin when I muttered her name and fell limp in someone's arms.

## MASSIMO

I couldn't understand why the boss wanted this lizard in the house? She was such a troublesome woman. Kicking her legs without seeing shit and what annoyed me most and made me call her a lizard was the fact that she hit me in the groin and that shit hurt bad. Her hit did send sparks of pain skyrocketing to my sensitive part when I accidentally

## Chapter 5

groaned out. I was mad at boss for making me do this work and when I couldn't take it any longer? I sprayed strong chloroform on a cloth to make the process quick and put it harshly against her nose when after a couple of seconds, she lay limp in my arms.

Thank God.

I couldn't control the urge and looked sideways to make sure that boss didn't ask anyone to record the scene when I pinched her in the arm furiously. That was for the knee to my groin you bitch. Huffing annoyingly, I threw her in Javiar's arms, another one of Boss's trusted guards and decided to move out but not before grabbing her little sister in my arms.

She was fast asleep when I stopped in my tracks, tilted my head and looked at her. Pink outfit, check, some random barbie on her shirt, check, strawberries on her trousers, check, some cute looking bands on her tiny wrist, okay check, two mini ponytails and a cute pout with no care in the world as to what had just happened while she was maybe dreaming about unicorns, mermaids and her evil sister in the costume of the giant squid. Check.

I squinted my eyes and kept looking at her when okay, she was an absolutely adorable young child with chubby cheeks, an innocent face making her look even more cuter and just by looking at her, it gave me a vibe that she was naughty. Very hell naughty. This thought had just crossed my mind when I vowed there and then.

I vowed that I, Massimo Labrant will protect this young sister of her at any cost. I'll make sure that no harm reaches her and she doesn't shed a single tear. I'll make sure that she is happy and well stuffed with cupcakes, pizza, pasta or whatever she likes. Shaking my head, I chuckled and walked out to get the girl and her lizard of a sister to boss, but not before grabbing those cupcakes which Sophia had brought for her little sister. She could eat them when she wakes up but my sugar patience went low after a few seconds in the car when again looking sideways to check that no one was seeing me? I opened the box and had one when my eyes rolled up in my head.

Wow.

Simply and massively, a wow. They were so gooey, so soft with molten chocolate coming out of it when I again looked at the little girl who was still sleeping. Thinking that she would forgive me as she looked better than Sophia, I popped another cupcake when I accidentally giggled. These were amazing man.

We hit the road and I couldn't wait to go home and just go to sleep as it was a very long day.

**Six**

# Chapter 6

## SOPHIA

I woke up with a soft moan and a grand ass smile on my face. This motel was so much better than the last one as the mattress was so comfy, practically swallowing me in like clouds and since I hadn't slept that well in so long, this was just pure, blissful heaven. I was really enjoying the feel of the softness of the bed, of the cool air around me, of the calmness that was already living in my body that I didn't feel like waking up at all. Turning sideways to check up on munchkin, I opened my eyes and was confused for a second.

I never rented this room. I never ever rented this room at all and I sat on the bed with a jolt of realization that I didn't recognize this place even for once.

The room I had rented for a couple of days was not this lavish, elegant and beautiful. The room had a large queen-sized double bed on which at one end I had been lying down and at the far end Munchkin was sleeping on her stomach, her cute, round, small butt high up in the air when I smiled softly. I swear she was so adorable.

There were cushions around munchkin to prevent her from falling off the enormous bed which befuddled me even more as I never remember doing it last night. The walls had a light beige skin colour. There was a beautiful ceramic fireplace directly in front of the bed and glass mirrors of different sizes, shapes and designs were surrounded on top of that. A little to the right was a beautiful golden and skin coloured sofa which looked so comfortable that I immediately felt like plopping on top of it already.

To the extreme right was where I yet again was left speechless. There was a breathtaking view of the balcony behind enormous sliding glass doors. Pearl white light was pouring in from the long clear glass windows and light skin coloured curtains were covering the ends. To the left there was a small circular table and a beautiful vase was on top with the prettiest flowers anyone had ever seen.

A glance at the floor showed me that it was all carpeted. There were two small tables at the end of each side of the bed. It had a beautiful golden lining around the corners with pale skin colour filling it in between. There were three draws which I opened up to find nothing in them at all and a beautiful coffee mug on the top as decoration.

## Chapter 6

The room was just so breathtakingly gorgeous, I could spend my life staring at this and never grow tired. And the bed. Oh, the bed. It was the most comfortable one I had ever laid on. It felt like sleeping in clouds for how soft it was.

I was looking in the air, zoned out, when the memories of yesterday hit me with the force of a truck. I remember those people storming into my motel room and kidnapping me and munchkin. I jumped out of bed in fear. Where was I? Who had captured us? What was happening? I was frightened beyond imagination.

I rushed to pick munchkin up in my arms to flee as fast as I could but I felt the sudden urge to use the bathroom, so abandoning her, I rushed to the bathroom when I entered it and it stole all of my breath away. It. Was. Beautiful.

Everything was so flawless. The main theme of the washroom was gold. There was a huge jacuzzi in the middle with golden plating around the rim of the bathtub. To the far end was a shower, an alluring sink was attached to it and it was practically shining. There was a huge mirror above the sink. An enormous walk-in-closet was situated on the extreme right.

I just stood there gaping at the interior. Never in my life, had I even dreamt of living in such a fabulous place. It was simply such a beauty. I turned to open the walk-in-closet and gasped.

It was full of clothes.

Some big in size while others small. I knew the small ones were for munchkin and the big ones were for me. Or so I guessed. With one hand on the door handle of the closet I lightly grazed my hands across the clothes to feel the fabric and nearly fell on my knees. It was so soft and so tempting but I backed away. I couldn't wear them. I didn't know who they belonged to and my aim was to run away when finally, the whole scenario came back into my mind.

Mentally facepalming myself that I was kidnapped and that I had to rush out, I quickly used the toilet and washed my face. There was a new toothbrush there and I opened it up as revenge for kidnapping me not caring as to who it belonged to. Yes, small revenge for a crime as big as kidnapping but what else could I do right now?

Freshening up and running my hands through my hair in an attempt to settle it down, I rushed out, picked Munchkin up in my arms and slowly opened the door of the room.

I silently looked sideways around three times to see and confirm that the corridor was clear and was about to tip toe my way out, when munchkin started stirring in her sleep. I froze there and then, my feet being rooted to the spot. My heart started beating fast, there were beads of sweat on my forehead and nose but I tried to calm myself down. She went back to sleeping lightly when I started to run silently.

I didn't know where I was, I didn't know who were the people who had abducted me, and I had no idea what they will do with us. Looking at the state of their rooms I knew they were

## Chapter 6

filthy rich and so they must have high security hence it would be tough to run away but still keeping my fingers crossed and without thinking much, I dashed to wherever the path was taking me as I had no idea where the front door was, my only fear being that they might use and hurt my munchkin which I couldn't afford.

It wasn't a house I was kidnapped in, it was a fucking mansion. The most beautiful I had ever seen in my life. Everything in here screamed money. I wish I could afford a mansion like this someday but even I knew that was impossible. Running as fast as I could, I kept turning around corridors in an attempt to find my way out but it was hell to impossible. It felt like eternity that I was running when I got tired and stopped to catch my breath.

I placed munchkin on my knee and breathed in through my mouth harshly to catch my breath and calm my racing heart down when it just sped up more when I heard a deep voice. That voice was enough to awaken butterflies in my stomach, for my inner fangirls to squeal and blush, worsening my situation at that point. I started to feel a tingling sensation deep down which was later followed by an ache in my pelvis as I just tried to control myself.

"Done?"

I slowly turned around to see the hottest man I had ever seen. He was wearing a white button-down shirt with black trousers and a black coat. He was standing with his arms folded and was looking at me with a smirk on his face. I could see black tattoos peeking from under the sleeves of his coat and he stood with such a handsome stature especially with his feet mere inches apart.

I just stood there looking at him, admiring the view when suddenly it clicked me. He kidnapped me. He was the one behind this. What a bastard! I grew angry all of a sudden when I picked Everleigh up and swiveled around in anger to face Mr. Hot, "How dare you? Who gives you the authority to kidnap us and make us live here? Let me go."

He looked down at his spotless clean shoes, WHY WERE HIS SHOES ALWAYS SO CLEAN, when he smiled a big smile and I had to say I felt a bit giddy. He looked so.......gorgeous? Really Sophia? Shaking my head to set aside my feelings for him, I again set a hard glare when he said, "Kitten, I do what I want and no one can stop me."

What rubbish? How arrogant! I pinched my eyes close tight in anger, when taking in a deep breath I said, "Listen, let's get straight to the point. What do you want from me? I don't even know you so I have no idea what use I am to you so tell me what you need and let me go." He smirked at me and took a step closer when I took a step back and thankfully, he stopped. Very much thankfully. With a very calm voice he said, "You are going to Italy with me."

What? Whattt? WHATTTT? Was he crazy? Was he out of his mind?

"Are you actually stupid?"

## Chapter 6

He smirked at me again, "Believe me kitten, I win every time. So, it's better for you to come along with me like a good girl that you are or once again needless I need to remind you, that I have my ways and I wouldn't hesitate to make you come forcefully."

I was fuming in anger. Who WAS he at the end? What did he do? What did he think of himself? What did he want from me? WHAT WAS HIS PROBLEM? Blinking back unshed tears from my eyes as I was tired from this life and nervous for what lay ahead, I calmly replied, "Look, I don't know who you are, my work is here, I live here and I cannot just get up and walk away with a STRANGER I may add, to a different country for crying out loud. I just can't. What is the problem with you? Tell me what you need and please just let me go."

My voice cracked in the end and subconsciously a tear left my eye when I hastily removed it. He took large strides towards me and I started backing away when I hit the wall. He came exceptionally close to me and had me trapped around, interfering in my personal space.

Putting both of his hands on either side of my face he leaned in close when our faces were mere inches apart. I could feel his intense gaze boring into my skull and his minty breath which somehow it calmed me down a bit. He gazed deep into my eyes, blue to grey, when he said in a low voice, "All of your questions will be answered shortly. Till then, you WILL come to Italy with me, you WILL behave like a nice girl and I WOULDN'T tolerate any disobedience. I know this is new for you but believe me it's for your own good."

How the hell was it supposed to be good for me? I barely even knew him. Keeping my tears at bay, I just whispered a "please" to him knowing he was the stronger one amongst us in every sense and I couldn't fight with him especially while I had a five year old with me. I was begging for him to let me go when he removed the wet trail of the tear with the pad of his thumb and suddenly my body was on fire.

His unexpected touch sent electric pulses raging through all of my body making me sense a feeling that I had never sensed before. He looked into my eyes as if debating something when he came close and placed a feathery, soft, gentle kiss on my forehead, which relaxed the rapid beat of my heart when he backed away, "I promise everything will be fine kitten. I promise."

With that he turned around and started to walk away, leaving me there all alone, so confused and so scared. He was about to turn around the corridor, when he stopped in his tracks, looked a bit over his shoulder back at me and said the one thing I was dreading the most, making me one of the most unhappiest woman on the face of this damn earth, "And don't think about running away. You can't. So, save everyone the trouble."

## ASHTON

I heard someone running and it confused me. Who would run in my house? *Run?* I started to walk in the way of the noise when I heard some sneakers screech. Everything

## Chapter 6

suddenly made sense. The kitten was running. I secretly began observing her when she kept running with no use. She could never get out. I gave her time to exhaust herself which she surprisingly did after about half an hour of constantly running with her little sister in her arms and that too in circles.

Maybe she didn't get the fact that she kept running back in the same corridor after every six minutes, but it was amusing to watch. At one point, I was scared her body might fall from the constant exercise and that too, with a little girl in her arms. And what confused me more was that how the fuck did she sleep through all of this?

When Massimo came in last night with the girls, I nodded in Sophia's direction as I had expected her to be here in an unconscious state but my eyes widened when I saw Everleigh in the same way. I would have shaved off Massimo's head if he had made Everleigh smell the chloroform too but gladly, he told me that she was already sleeping.

When she came to a stop and started breathing hard, I had had all of the fun and was tired of following her around uselessly. Walking out I faced her with only one question in my mind, "Done?"

She seemed to be rooted to the spot the way her body immediately froze and became rigid. I could see from her back how she was taking in deep, rapid breaths and it made me smirk for whatever reason. She took her time when she slowly turned around and looked at me. I could read my queen like an open book. She liked me. She found me attractive. It was written all over her face and I could easily read her. She took her time admiring me and I gladly gave it to her when her expression suddenly changed and she became furious.

She begged me to let her leave but I couldn't. I just couldn't no matter how much I tried. I was attracted to her so bad. She kept on saying to let her go and all I did was refuse her when suddenly my heart broke into a million pieces. It shattered when her voice cracked and a tear left her eye. I hated to see her cry, I just completely loathed it. It killed me. I never wanted her to feel sad or cry ever but I had to do this.

Walking towards her, I trapped her against the wall, letting my heat envelop her and letting hers envelop me when I whispered, "All of your questions will be answered kitten. Until then you WILL come to Italy with me, you WILL behave like a nice girl and I WOULDN'T tolerate any disobedience. I know this is new for you but believe me it's for your good." and mine. But she didn't need to know that. It would freak her out.

Heavily whispering a dense and a miserable please again, she looked at me when it again broke my heart to see her that way. I wanted to hit myself, I wanted to punish myself because I knew she was here, upset, and in a troubled state right in front of me, all because of me and there was nothing, absolutely nothing, that I could do about it right now. Wiping her tears away with the pad of my thumb I whispered, "I promise everything will be fine kitten. I promise." And I

## Chapter 6

meant that. I sure as hell meant that.

Unable to look at her in this condition, I turned on my heels and started to walk away when right before disappearing I gave her the warning to not even try to run away again. She just couldn't.

# Chapter 7

## SOPHIA

I sat grumpily on the bed. I wish my parents were in a better condition and could come to rescue us but even I knew that it could never happen. Munchkin stirred and woke up when she looked sideways towards me and smiled a toothy grin. Her hair were disheveled, her clothes wrinkled, one look at her face and you could tell easily that she had the best sleep of her life. I smiled widely and opened my arms for her to come but what shocked me and made me laugh more was that she just ignored me, smiled again and went to lie down. Hmm. She loved the bed then.

Shaking my head amusingly, I started to stare in the open air feeling sad again when suddenly she jumped towards

## Chapter 7

me, wrapped her arms around me and nuzzled her face in my neck making me laugh. I swear I just loved her so much, which made me wonder how would I feel when I will become a mother one day. I knew that I would give my child so much love and immense amount of adoration because one look at Ev and I just knew.

Cuddling munchkin close to me and moving my fingers through her hair, I tried to put her in a comfortable position when she asked, "Sissy, where are we?"

I didn't know what to say to her when I thought of the best I could come up with immediately, "Baby, we are in another house at the moment but we will move out soon. Now listen to me munchkin." I got serious all of a sudden when I looked at her as she looked at me, "Don't talk to anyone here, don't listen to anyone here and stay close to me at all times. Got it?" She looked at me with confusion clouding her eyes when she just shook her head yes but still whispered, "Why?".

"Because they are bad men Munchkin."

She giggled in my arms, "I love bad men. Especially the ones with guns." Then she made her hands into a small gun and started pretending as if she was shooting when she closed one eye, imagined killing someone and went in her thin voice, "Tashoo tashoo tashoo."

My eyes widened in horror. How old was she? A……….a five year old and that's when it struck me as I patted her hair down, "Um happy birthday munchkin, but no no. Listen to me. These are really bad men. They carry big guns with which they kill people." I tried to emphasize the point when she giggled more, "I love them even more now. I can make a film and ask them to act in it. Then we will play it in cinemas."

I. Was. Baffled. I put my hand across her forehead to check whether she had a temperature but no, she was fine. More than fine when I shook my head and sighed, "Go to sleep baby, you are tired." As soon as I said this there was a knock on my door when I allowed whoever it was to enter, "Yes?"

A young maid entered the room, "Morning miss, I am Elizabeth. Boss told me to inform you to please get dressed. I'll bring you your breakfast up here." She awaited no response and left the room when I annoyingly mimicked boss, the feeling of being severely agitated dominating over every cell my body owned. Huffing a tired sigh, I picked Everleigh up as I knew there was no point in arguing with Mr.Ho-, no Mr. Arrogant. Yes, it was Mr. Arrogant now. Rude ass.

I started walking towards the bathroom when Munchkin asked, "Who's Boss?" which further annoyed the hell out of me when I accidentally snapped at her, which reminded me that I was on my period and needed sanitary pads as well, "No one."

She saw the sudden sourness in my mood and became quiet. I went inside the bathroom, locked it and went towards the walk-in closet. I decided to get munchkin ready first when I gave her a bath especially after all those hospital incidents

## Chapter 7

and living in dingy, gross motels especially in the intense heat making us smell worse than accumulated sweat.

After her shower and drying her hair, I made her wear a white cotton frock which had a beautiful pink coloured belt around the middle. It ended below her knees and she looked cute in it not going to lie. I combed her hair and put it in two ponytails as she loved and made her wear white sparkly shoes.

She ran to have a look at herself in the mirror and oh the dramatic queen that she was. Her eyes widened, she placed both of her hands on her cheeks, giggled and twirled around three times when she looked at me, still with the both of her hands on her cheeks, "I. Love. It. And. I. Will. Never. Take. It. Off."

I laughed and washed her face, brushed her teeth with another brush and made her sit on the bed outside and told her to wait for me. I went back and opened the drawers in hope that pads were there when I was glad to actually find some. Taking them out, I decided to take a shower first when I thoroughly enjoyed it. The warm water was enough to calm my tense muscles down, the expensive shampoo smelled so beautiful that I actually felt nice and giddy after a while. Stepping out of the jacuzzi, I grabbed a blow dryer from the cabinet and dried my hair. Wrapping a towel around myself, I went to look for a dress to wear. I wanted to wear something simple yet beautiful.

Looking through the dresses, one seemed to catch my

attention as it was a grey coloured, beautiful looking crop top and would look well with blue jeans. I decided to wear them and found some black sneakers in the 'shoes' area which surprisingly, had my exact shoe size right there apart from munchkin's.

I found it quite appropriate to wear, because I also had the feeling that we would be meeting him soon, so quickly adjusting my clothes, I looked at my reflection and was astounded to see how I looked so much better since the day I came here. I looked so……..young, composed and……..and pretty. Opening the drawers beneath the sink, my spit caught in my throat.

There was so much of expensive cosmetic there. I didn't want to do a heavy makeup so I just put on a bit of foundation to cover up especially the dark circles and scars, applied matte pink lipstick since that was one of my favourite colours. I applied minimal amount of silverish glitter to my cheekbones just because I wanted to and it made me look more fresher and prettier. I tied my hair up in a ponytail leaving a few loose strands hanging out and looked at myself in the mirror to find myself satisfied by my look. I looked nice. It wasn't that bad after all. Walking out of the bathroom, my mouth opened on its own accord and I was stunned to see the most lavish breakfast of my life. I was staring at all of the food while Munchkin was staring at me.

"Woah." We both said in unison and giggled.

"You look beautiful sissy." I felt so happy at her remark when

## Chapter 7

I smiled and hugged her, "Thank you munchies."

The breakfast was so lavish. There was a basket of fresh fruit, a large bowl of salad, pancakes decorated with blueberry sauce and topped with raspberries. There was a dish full of sandwiches, chocolate and vanilla cupcakes topped with frosting and sprinkles. There were a dozen doughnuts and surprisingly, all my favourite. I could see waffles there decorated with chocolate syrup and lined with vanilla ice cream. Mini pizzas were abundant in number accompanied by croissants. I was shocked. I had never seen such a breakfast in my life.

I stood there gawking at the food when my stomach started growling. Putting some pancakes on a plate I handed them to Munchkin first and then helped myself to waffles. The moment I bit into it with the hot chocolate sauce, I moaned in appreciation. God they were perfect. They were simply, utterly, deliciously perfect. I felt like I was in heaven and suddenly out of nowhere I started to like Mr. Hot for kidnapping me. This wasn't bad after all.

After eating as much as I could, I felt as if I might explode at any moment when I quickly went to use the bathroom. Coming out, I saw a maid poking her head through the door, "Miss, boss said that we will be leaving in ten minutes for the flight so please be ready."

"What do you mean be ready?" It came out harsher than I expected. Come to think of it, the maid had no fault.

She gulped when she answered, "Just be ready is all that he said. You don't need to take any clothes along, that will be taken care of." She added as an afterthought. I scowled when she hurried out of the room.

Munchkin turned towards me, "Where are we going Sissy?"

I heaved a tired sigh and massaged my temple, "Munchkin, I have some work to do in Italy so we are going there for some time." To say she was excited was an understatement. She was ecstatic. She was jumping up and down and shrieking in happiness when she came rushing towards me and gave me a bone cracking hug to a point it was hard for me to breath, "Thank you thank you thank you thank youuuuu." was all that she was saying. Shaking my head in disbelief, I reapplied my lip gloss and just sat there waiting to see what fate held for us.

\*\*\*

After about exactly ten minutes, a knock came on the door and a muscular bodyguard came in to escort us out when munchkin shrieked and scurried to my side. I was already mad at Mr. Hot for kidnapping us and being cold towards me, and now this guard, when I sent him a hard glare for scaring her. He raised one eyebrow as if to say really? -my-fault, but I didn't care for reasons I don't know.

I held munchkin's hand and together we started following him. I gazed down at her to see her mouth open, staring at the roof, walls and surroundings in amazement when I

## Chapter 7

covered my mouth to stifle a laugh. Yes, the mansion was beautiful after all, who wouldn't want to live here?

We exited the front door and I had a mad plan to just run away but I knew it was of no use. The doors were heavily guarded and guards were standing all along the driveway making me wonder who even in the name of hell was he? He sure as hell didn't look like Donald Trump to be living a lavish life as of a country's president, with so much security and riches.

Getting into a sleek black Audi, I readjusted my top when the door opened and Mr. Hot slid in the car, in the backseat with Munchkin and I. I gave him a sour expression and turned my face away but not before catching him smirking at me. I saw from the peripheral side of my vision how munchkin was looking at him in awe. Not looking, staring basically with her mouth open when he extended his hand forward to greet her.

She kept on looking at him when as slowly as she could, she shook his hand. I was waiting for him to maybe pass a hurtful comment her way or to hurt her in any way and he'll see hell if he hadn't before. Everleigh swiveled fast in her seat and whispered a bit harshly into my ear, harsh enough for him to clearly hear her, "He issss hot."

And I? I felt my cheeks redden in embarrassment.

"Everleigh!" I scolded her in anger and looked up a bit to see him smirking. He took her hand in his, laid a kiss there and said, his deep, gruff voice doing something to the wires of my heart, "Thank you princess."

And Everleigh? She was resembling a tomato at that moment. She lowered her head, trying to cover her smile and the blush on her cheeks when she got on my lap and nuzzled her face in my neck hiding her face from him. I rolled my eyes but smiled a bit at my little, five year old sister as I found her very cute. The car drive was smooth and we reached the airport in no time. Walking behind Mr. Hot, he led us through a private elevator. One look at Munchkin and you knew she loved this. I wish I could give her this type of lifestyle but I couldn't ever afford it and this extremely gorgeous man standing right in front of us was spoiling her like mad.

I didn't want Munchkin to get used to this ever because it will get hard for me in the longer run but there was nothing that I could do at the moment. You know that time when you want to do something and you know you can do something about it so you do, but then there are times, the matter is totally out of your hands, you can't do anything about it and I was in this exact similar situation.

I was helpless.

I didn't want her to get accustomed to this because after leaving this life, she would find it extremely hard to adjust to the normal one and I sure as hell wouldn't be staying here for long. Given the chance, I'll escape.

We came out into an open land and saw a small plane waiting

## Chapter 7

for us there. I guess it was his private plane which somehow made me more nervous as no one else would be there if something went wrong. We were about to climb the stairs when Munchkin dropped my hand and ran to him. Tugging on his trousers she asked, "Is this yours?" Even her small voice was adorable that it automatically brought a smile to my face. Just hearing her too, calmed me down a lot.

He bent down in the most handsome and graceful manner that any hot man could and put his fingers under her chin, "Yes princess, it's mine." And suddenly, out of nowhere, I started to imagine scenarios in my head that what if he is bent down like this and talking to our child. How, I could be standing right here as his wife, the mother to our own son or daughter. Shaking my head, I went back to looking at them and had to admit, they did look adorable together.

Her mouth fell open when he asked, "You want this to be yours?" She eagerly nodded her head but I had had enough. I wasn't letting her get used to this when I went forward and held her hand, pulling her close to me, "Munchkin, this can't be yours, we cannot afford this so please get on the plane and stop it."

She whined, "Whyyyy?"

"That's enough Everleigh! Stop this nonsense. Move!" I felt bad for shouting angrily at her when she bent her head down and started walking with me. I couldn't get her get used to this life as helloooo, we were being kidnapped. I had no idea who this man was, what he did for a living, what was he taking us for, what would he do with us, was he like the men who are involved in human trafficking, would he hurt munchkin or not? There were so many questions revolving in my brain and I had no idea for what was lying ahead of us and hence I couldn't get my baby sister get used to this at all until I was sure that this man was good and that I may have some sort of future with him.

I rubbed her hand and walked up the steps and entered the plane. I could feel his presence right behind me and it was so warm that for one wild moment I wanted to just wrap my arms around him as I was sure that it would be peaceful and after leading the stressful life that I led in America. I just needed a peaceful hug by someone. I kept walking when some idiotic sense in my mind told me that this was right. That whatever was happening despite being wrong was somewhat right. What was happening to me?

The air hostess guided us to our seats. Munchkin sat on my lap while thankfully, Mr. Hot sat one alley separating us. A booming voice was heard over the microphone, "Please fasten your seat belts, we are about to take off."

Suddenly I felt a hollow feeling in my chest because firstly, I was afraid of heights and secondly, I had never been on a plane before. I felt my blood pressure going low, beads of sweat started forming on my forehead and nose and basically? I was shit petrified. Munchkin was sitting perfectly normal which I thanked God for. One less person to look after.

## Chapter 7

I started taking in heavy breaths to control my heart rate and my sanity. I opened my mouth to help with the breathing and tried to control myself. My head was mildly spinning in circles and shit started to hit the fan when the plane started moving. Suddenly, I was taking in deep breaths and sweat was dripping from my forehead. I couldn't breathe. I felt nauseatic. I felt as if my world was crumbling down, tears pooled in my eyes and I felt like dying. The moment the speed of the plane increased, I held my head as it was paining like mad and once the plane took off is when I lost it. I shoved Munchkin off of my lap, took off the seat belt and fell to the floor.

I clutched my chest and started rasping for breath while crying simultaneously. It was hard, it was too hard. The world was blackening out and I felt as if I was losing consciousness. I heard a shout and some shuffling.

Suddenly I felt as if Munchkin was being dragged away from me and I felt cold. Nothing but coldness. As if cold death was wrapping me in its' hold and there was nothing that I could do. Nothing at all. When I felt all hopeless and drained out, was when I felt pure warmth. I felt as if I was soaring in the clouds with a cushion under me, supporting me and suddenly I felt comfortable before I totally lost consciousness.

## ASHTON

I called Elizabeth and informed her to tell Sophia to get dressed and serve her breakfast in her room as I knew she wouldn't eat with me at the table owing to how mad she was and I couldn't blame her. It will be okay with time. I went into my room to take a shower, got dressed in my Armani clothes, slipped on my Rolex watch, combed my hair leaving it a bit disheveled as I liked it that way. I made my way downstairs to go have breakfast but decided against it and went to the room Sophia and her younger sister were staying in.

I put one of my ears against the door in hopes of knowing what was happening inside when I heard a clatter of dishes. Good. They were having breakfast. I was about to leave when I heard Sophia moan and wrong wrong wrong. I instantly got hard but I had to control myself as this really wasn't the time. Shaking my head and smiling that at least she liked the food, I went downstairs to have my fill.

We were leaving in ten minutes so I told the nearby maid to let Sophia know. Trudging towards my room I grabbed my pack of cigarettes, took my wallet, gave the room one last glance to check if I had missed something and headed out to leave. I reached the parking area to see my kitten and her younger sister already inside the car. I gave a curt nod to the guard and sat in the same car as in which they were sitting. Deliberately.

She looked utterly mesmerizing. She was wearing a greyish

## Chapter 7

crop top and I could easily see her sharp collarbones which damn, looked sexy as fuck. She was wearing blue jeans, black sneakers, had minimal make up done with her hair in a ponytail and a few strands hanging out which honestly gave her a decent yet a beautiful look.

I thought that maybe she would need a lot of different products for her makeup, so I bought everything a girl might need and arranged it for her in the room she would be staying in for the night. She also had pink lipstick on which actually suited her and I wanted to do nothing but just kiss the breath out of her.

She was pretty slim which made me frown as people usually sick were this slim or people who ate less but she seemed fine to me. Or maybe she was hiding it that well, I didn't know. Guess I had to find out. She gave me a furious glare which I gladly returned back with a smirk when I noticed her younger sister, Everleigh, gawking at me.

Massimo had to spy on her to see which school she goes to and so we got the name from there. She was gawking at me when I found the child amusing. Laying out my hand, I asked for her to shake it when her small, cute hand actually shook it after a few seconds, a bright red tint appearing on her cheek which made me chuckle. And right after this, she swiveled around, leaned into Sophia's ear and said a bit harshly, harsh enough for me to hear, "He issss hot."

I smirked a bit and took a peek at Sophia to see her cheeks redden in embarrassment. How adorable! She scolded her furiously in order to tell her to behave herself but I wanted to win the mini one's heart. I took Everleigh's hand in mine, leaned down to give it a kiss and said, "Thank you princess."

Her cheeks flushed and she looked red as a beetroot when she just hid her face, got into Sophia's lap and nuzzled her face in her neck as Sophia strengthened her arms around her, pulling her close.

It looked so sweet. I gazed out of the window and couldn't help but imagine how it would look like if it was my child in her arms cuddling her. How it would look like if Sophia was hugging our child? The picture looked beautiful but it had to wait. At the moment she was angry and the reason was me, sitting right next to her like the stubborn man that I was.

We reached the airport and were travelling from the private plane that I owned. Sophia started following me into the private elevator when we reached the fifth floor. Walking out, we were nearing the plane when I felt a soft tug on my pants. Looking down, I saw Everleigh when in the softest voice she asked, "Is this yours?"

I smiled a genuine smile, bent down so that I was at eye level with her when placing my fingers under her chin, I nodded, "Yes princess, it's mine." I think she really liked the word princess because whenever I addressed her with it, she always used to blush causing me to chuckle at her cuteness.

Her mouth fell open when I asked, "You want this to be yours?"

## Chapter 7

She eagerly nodded and I did not miss the sudden spark in her eyes. It seemed like the first genuine spark I had ever seen in anyone but this seemed to strike some nerve because Sophia got angry and told Everleigh how they couldn't afford it. She started whining a sad 'why' when Sophia lost it and snapped at her. I hadn't seen this side of her and I didn't know how to feel. Everleigh dropped her head low, released the grip on my pants and went back to her sister extremely despondent. Sophia walked past me, her lips in a thin line and entered the plane.

We sat separately with an alley separating us and Everleigh sat on Sophia's lap. We heard the announcement on the microphone and I put on my belt, ready for the plane to take off when I sensed that something was off.

I looked sideways a bit and saw Sophia taking in deep breaths with sweat forming heavily on her forehead while Everleigh was calm as fuck. I didn't understand what was happening at first but when the plane started moving and her condition worsened was when I understood that she was facing a severe panic attack and that she was afraid of heights.

I quickly took off my seat belt and was about to get up when the plane took off and shit went worse. She threw her little sister on the floor, took off her seat belt and fell to the ground gasping for breath and clutching her chest. I rushed towards her side, called Massimo with a shout who came running in a split second.

He grabbed Everleigh in his arms while I cradled Sophia

in mine. She was shaking terribly almost as if she was having a fit. She was extremely hot………no not as in hot hot which she was, but hot. She was having a temperature when taking large strides, I started carrying her towards the private bedroom in the plane when she fell limp. She just fell limp in my arms and her breathing evened out. I was scared shitless as to what had just happened as I had never experienced such a thing in my life, but I kept my expression calm.

I had learned it over my past to act calm when nothing was calm.

I was still contemplating as to what had happened when I made eye contact with Massimo who just gave a nod and rushed to call the first aid. That was the best thing about Massimo, one look at him and he knew exactly what I wanted.

I continued carrying her towards the room. She smelled so clean and pure, like fresh roses plucked out of the garden. I could lay next to her and inhale her scent all my life as somehow it was just extremely soothing. I gently placed her on the soft mattress, removing the loose strands of hair from her face and just gazed at her.

She looked so beautiful, so peaceful. Just like an angel. My angel. Her outfit covered her curves in the most perfect way when I just kept staring at the red head beauty laying down in front of me.

## Chapter 7

I made sure she was unconscious and looked sideways three times to see that no one was watching me when I slowly inched my hands towards her and touched her bare skin slightly. Suddenly, a shot of fire erupted in my body, my nerve endings went crazy and I felt a tingling sensation in the pit of my stomach and the central region of my heart. How can someone be so beautiful I didn't know, but she sure as hell was. She laid there, looking all peaceful when someone rushed into the room and I swiveled around, taking the gun out of my waistband, aiming at the intruder when I saw the doctor.

The idiot looked at me in horror, dropped his suitcase on the floor and raised his shaking hands in surrender. His whole face went pale when he looked at Massimo who had a funny expression on his face. Both of them were looking like Bugs Bunny I swear.

Scoffing, I put the gun back in my waistband and looked at the doctor as if saying get-up-donkey. He quickly scrambled to his feet, checked her pulse and started examining her. I always kept a doctor during flights in case something happened to my men who may need medical aid. Because the men I have, are one in a million. I train them worse than a motherfucker trains a fucker and hence I cannot afford to lose them.

After about five minutes he turned to me, "Boss, her blood pressure is very low, she is extremely weak and pale. All she needs is rest and a comforting hand. There must be something that either triggered her or in usual case scenarios, she is afraid of heights. These sudden panic attacks happen to those people who are petrified of heights. She is not in danger, she just needs care. And here are some medicines I am giving for her to feel better for the rest of the journey."

I nodded my head in agreement and gave him one last look which was my indication that he had been dismissed. Bowing his head and picking up his suitcase, he left the room until I was the only one left alone with her.

I wish I knew she was going to face this, I could have sat with her and held her hand assuring her that everything will be all right and that nothing would happen to her. I hated to see her hurt, scared or ill, even for a bit, and since the moment I had kidnapped her, I had done nothing but bring pain to her.

I was scared I might never be able to give her the love that she needs. I was afraid I would never be able to keep her happy, that one day she will say it to my face with all her heart how much she hated me and God knows I wouldn't be able to take it. Not even a bit. Inhaling deeply through my nose, I pinched the bridge of my nose and went out to have a look at how Everleigh was doing.

She, by God, was having the time of her life. She was laughing openly in Massimo's arms and Massimo was laughing along? Honestly, it was a very weird sight.

Looking up at me, her expressions changed and she came running to me, "What happened to sissy? Will she be okay? Is she fine? Is she in pain? Where is she? I want to see

## Chapter 7

her please." She started looking past me when I bent down, grabbed her face in both of my hands and gently whispered, "She is okay princess. Your sister is just tired and is resting for the time being. She was just overworked and is taking a break. Okay?"

Her expression was a bit doubtful when she pleaded with a pout and tears in her eyes as she whispered, "Please don't let anything happen to her, I can't live without her." Her chin wobbled and tears were filling her eyes WHEN WAS MASSIMO CRYING ALONG? WHAT WAS THE MATTER WITH HIM?

I heaved a gentle sigh and promised her, "Nothing would happen to your sister, princess. I promise." That ought to make her feel better when she ran back to Massimo and begged him to play with her. He took her in his arms and did as she wished. Rubbing my forehead in uncertainness I turned around and glanced once more time at the sleeping form of my angel, and took a seat waiting to see what would happen next.

\*\*\*

But what I didn't expect next was Massimo to start singing Taylor Swift. He was giving me a headache and I was in no mood to start downing down tablets and tablets of Advil. God. What did I get myself into?

# Chapter 8

## SOPHIA

I gained a bit of consciousness feeling nothing but pure numbness. I couldn't perceive anything, neither my legs nor my feet. My arms felt heavy and I was suddenly having a massive headache. I wanted to massage my head to ease out the pain but had no energy to lift up my arms. I opened my eyes to see that my surroundings were nothing but complete darkness. I had to squint to have a better look at where I was, when I could only figure out a small table a bit far from me and the door through which sharp rays of light were peaking from underneath.

I tried to sit up but cried from the immediate pain in my head and fell back on something soft just to realise later on

## Chapter 8

that it was a bed. What? A bed? On an airplane? Wow.

I tried to sit up again but it was too arduous for me. I simply didn't have the energy. My throat was exceedingly dry and I desperately needed just a jug full of water when the thought had just crossed my mind and the door creaked open a bit when I saw a head poking in.

Instantaneously, the light turned on and the figure ran towards me as I quickly shut my eyes from the intensity of the sudden brightness. I felt the bed dip as if a heavy weight was suddenly put on it when I felt big, calloused warm hands gently grab the side of my face, as gentle as fearing as if to break glass. I wasn't thinking straight when somehow, I felt like home and slowly rubbed my cheeks back and forth against the hand, feeling peace proliferate through my body. They felt so warm, so relaxing and somehow......... I felt solace, comfort and tranquility dominate myself. I was confused for a bit when it hit me. It was him.

I jerked my head away when I felt a sudden sharp pain in my head. I grabbed my head and groaned loudly when he quickly got up, ran towards the table, just to come back with some medicines in his hands. I didn't question what the medicines would do because at the moment, the pain was too intense that I wouldn't have given two shits if it had poison. At least I proudly would have been able to say that I was murdered some thousand feet into the air on a private plane with an extremely handsome man with me. Romantic!

I quickly swallowed down the medicine and went to lie down

again, closing my eyes, letting the effect slowly kick in. We were silent for at least some time when the pain started to get numb and I started to feel better. I opened my eyes and looked at him when he spoke, "How are you feeling?"

His voice felt raw and as much as I was mad at him and didn't want to answer him, I still nodded and replied, "Better."

"You should have told me you were afraid of heights."

"Well, I told you I hated being kidnapped, did you listen to me? No you didn't." I retorted back.

That ought to shut him up because he didn't respond. After a few seconds he got up and started to leave, "If you need anything the bell is on the bedside table right next to you. Ring it and your problems will be solved." He replied in such a gruff voice that I peeked a glance at him, to see his forehead stretched firmly in tight lines and his expression- oh. He was mad. He was livid. I made him too much angry, I guess. Not even sparing me another look, he opened the door and left the room closing it with a soft thud. Suddenly I felt the room go cold, the temperature dropped promptly and I just missed his warmth and his presence. Sighing, I decided to go back to sleep to lessen the pain.

# Chapter 8

# ASHTON

"Well, I told you I hated being kidnapped, did you listen? No you didn't."

Pure mock was laced in her beautiful soft voice and somehow what she said made me mad. I was angry and I couldn't help but just get up and leave as I usually preferred being alone when I'm mad or I'll hurt people and she was the last person on Earth I would want to hurt either mentally or physically. I was seething in anger when I decided not to bother replying. I just got up, told her, "If you need anything the bell is on the bedside table right next to you. Ring it and your problems will be solved." and turning on my heels I swiftly left the room and went towards my seat. Everleigh was fast asleep next to Massimo who was typing furiously on his phone. Guess everyone from the Romanno family was mad at the moment.

I sat back on my seat when changing my mind, I walked towards the next passage of the plane, away from all the others, stood near a window, lit a cigarette and tried to calm myself down. Her words kept ringing in my ear. She hated me was what I thought. She completely loathed my presence but I couldn't let her go. I liked her a bit too much.

I did make her come forcefully; I just didn't know what would happen if she decided to leave me. It would be too hard to let her go knowing the fact that it hadn't even been a whole week of me being with her but her aura, her power and her beauty was enough to make me want to keep her and slowly build my place in her heart.

And if even after that she wanted to leave me? I will. I will let her go because if she is happy that way? Then so be it. I want nothing but her to be happy even if it it's not with me, even if I'm on the verge of cracking. I just want her to be happy. As far as my angel is content, I'm content.

But till then, I would fight for her love and adoration till the last of my ability. I would use all of my power to win her over. I wouldn't lose this fight that easily. It would be a hard battle, yes, but I knew how to play my innings when my side of the match got tough. I would battle till the last of my breath. Gazing out of the window, I took another long drag of the cigarette and wished the flight to end soon. I was already too damn tired.

## SOPHIA

I woke up after what felt like eternity. I was feeling much better than before and the first thought that crossed my mind was that I had to apologize for snapping at him. At least he took care of me, kept an eye on me and asked me how I was and that's how I repay? By snapping at him? Yes, he had kidnapped me, yes, he was an asshole for doing that but somehow, I couldn't find myself ever being too rude with people.

I just couldn't do it.

## Chapter 8

And somehow knowing that I didn't like the idea of being kidnapped, I still did like his presence. I felt at peace when he was near me. I felt calm, as if no one on the face of this earth could hurt me. I felt safe, something that I had never felt in years before.

I was also fearing that he might hurt us, especially Everleigh because I made him upset since I didn't know who he was yet and what work he did but I don't know what made me brush that thought away for the time being.

Slowly standing up on my feet, I readjusted my dress and was relieved to see it was the same one I wore before leaving. At least no one tried to redress me. I steadily started walking towards the door and opened it a bit to see Everleigh and the other guard sleeping peacefully. I slowly walked up to her to check if she was okay by laying the backside of my hand against her cheek and smiled to see her perfectly well.

I looked around but didn't see him anywhere when there was a door at the other side and I decided to check it for once. Slightly opening it and not wanting to make any noise, I saw him standing with a- A CIGARETTE IN FRONT OF HIS MOUTH? HE SMOKED? I wanted to do nothing but snatch it right out of his hands but decided against it. I couldn't show him right now that I was developing more feelings for him, he didn't need to see that weak side of me yet.

He didn't notice me yet but when he did, he discarded his cigarette and quickly came towards me giving me his hand to hold on to. I grasped his hand firmly and suddenly my legs gave away. Touching him sent sparks up my body and I couldn't do anything about it. He reached just in time to put his arms under my legs, picked me up and carried me bridal style to one of the luxurious seats. I think he was still a bit mad at me because he wasn't saying anything and that was somehow disturbing me a lot, his silence when he got mad. He gently placed me on the seat, bent down and started observing my ankle to see if I had hurt it or not.

My heart swooned at his actions and I suddenly wanted to do nothing but just embrace him. No one had ever done that for me, no one had ever been this kind to me and taken this much care of me. Ever. Instantly I felt more bad at snapping at him when I whispered a mere whisper, "I want to talk to you."

I expected him to not hear me owing to how low I spoke but surprisingly he looked up at me. Our faces were mere inches apart making my mind go hazy. We gazed into each other's eyes silently, never once breaking contact. Grey to blue. Raging. We were lost into each other for a few seconds, sweat forming heavily on my forehead owing to how intense it was getting when I could see how perfect he was.

He had the perfect skin colour, properly shaped eyebrows, a big nose and full lips. You could see he had a smooth skin and I wanted to feel it. Just once, but I wanted to. He had hair that I wanted to run my hands through. He. Was. Just. Flawless. We were gazing into each other's eye's fiercely that for a second, I forgot what I wanted to say when in a soft voice he asked, "Hmm?"

## Chapter 8

That snapped me back to reality. Tugging some of the loose strands of hair behind my ear, I looked down as I suddenly felt ashamed and started stammering, "I-i am- s-so-". I felt his fingers lift up my chin when he brought his face unbearably close to mine and whispered, "Easy hun."

I swear his voice was sexy but it calmed me down. Taking a deep breath, I tried to duck my face again in embarrassment but his strong fingers didn't let me. I looked him in the eye when I apologized, "I'm sorry for snapping at you earlier. I guess I was just too disturbed. I'm sorry, I didn't mean to."

His face expression was calm and suddenly it was like as if he was thinking a million thoughts at the same time. He exhaled deeply through his nose and his face contorted as if in deep thought. He abruptly pulled me impossibly close to him that even if I took in a deep breath, our noses would touch.

He looked me in the eye and I saw nothing but love there. Pure adoration was dripping from his beautiful eyes when it further warmed my heart. Nobody had ever looked at me like that and here I was, sick on an airplane with a man looking at me as if I was his world. I believed that these things only happened in the books or movies but I guess I might have that right now. Who knows?

He spoke in a low, gruff voice, only for me to hear, "Don't you ever apologize for something you never did-" I tried to interrupt him but he held his hand up and surprisingly it shut me up. Wow! The power of his hand. "Don't interrupt me, let me finish. Okay?" I nodded my head in agreement and allowed him to continue. It was as if my mouth was sealed when he continued, "As I was saying, don't apologize for something you never did. Since the day I kidnapped you-" a pained expression crossed his face and subconsciously I held his cheek in the small of my palm and rubbed my fingers softly against them to calm him down as I couldn't see him in pain.

His expression displayed pure shock at my sudden movement but he quickly masked it and moved on, "Since the moment I kidnapped you, I have done nothing but bring you pain and believe me this was never my intention. I never wanted to cause you any harm, any pain but I guess you have been feeling that since the moment you came. I promise everything will be okay but just keep in mind that don't you dare to ever apologize to me especially. Queens don't apologize. Angels don't apologize at all."

He said all this in a mere dark whisper and I was left speechless. Words weren't forming and making their way out of my mouth. I was left gazing into his raging steel grey eyes and funnily enough he was doing the same, the only difference was that I had blue ones.

We were looking at each other when I came back to my senses. I quickly removed my hand, looked down and mumbled a small yes. He lifted my chin up with his fingers and looked me dead in the eye, "Is it clear?"

I replied a confident yes when he got up and started to leave, "Sit here and rest, I'll get you something to eat." With that he

## Chapter 8

turned around and left the compartment.

I exhaled a deep breath I never knew I was holding in. I didn't even know the name of this guy, yet I wanted to spend my whole life with him and thinking about it, he was not so bad after all. Yes, he spoke with sincerity that he didn't want to hurt me and I believed his words. I believed every bit of it and if this is where my love story begins? Then, I would go to any lengths to secure it. I would fight for us to be a perfect us. I wouldn't give up too damn easily. I would fight till my last breath and give us a chance to be together and be happy. I had barely participated in any contests during my childhood or my teenager life but this seemed to be the only one in my mind right now worth fighting for. And for the first time, I was hungry for success.

\*

I ate all the food he bought for me and honestly, I wasn't expecting such a delicious meal but nevertheless I was feeling much better than before. He held my hand tightly during the landing and I was grateful for that. I was nearly crushing his hand as I was too scared but he didn't even complain once, nor did he make any sound to indicate that I was hurting him. How he did that, was something beyond my understanding.

The plane landed thankfully and it wasn't as bad as before because he was constantly with me. I was nearly on his lap owing to how scared I was, but neither did he complain nor did I, as long as I survived the landing. Munchkin held my hand all the way till we sat in a car which came to pick us up to take us God knows where. No words were spoken during the ride and Mr. Hot was extra quiet this time which left me frowning as to why was he suddenly all so silent. Trying to ignore that, I kept looking out of the window only to realise later that my mouth was gaping open.

This part of Italy from where we were passing by, was so beautiful I didn't know. I had heard that Italy was a gorgeous place but this much gorgeous? I had absolutely no idea.

The roads were clean, no litter could be seen anywhere. The pedestrians were looking pretty with their extravagant way of dressing. The sidewalks were fully decorated with plants and flowers of all colours, it looked so mesmerizingly beautiful. The air seemed fresh clean that I was actually enjoying it. I snapped out of my thoughts when I heard the driver say, "We are here boss."

I didn't understand what he meant when I glanced confusedly towards him and then I turned my head to see where we were when I was left speechless. My eyeballs were practically jumping out of my eye sockets as we were outside of a mansion and oh. My. God. Was it prepossessing!

The enormous gates opened to reveal a huge mansion. There was a massive parking space and a huge round fountain was located entrancingly in between, with water flowing out from all sides and reaching an impossibly high point. There were different coloured lights surrounding the fountain which made it look even more attractive. There were many expensive looking cars parked at one end, all funnily

## Chapter 8

black and silver in colour. Basically, this placed screamed expensiveness.

Never in my life could I ever afford this. From the gates till the fountain, in between came a small, beautiful dissection leading to four different ways. One was to reach the gate behind us, the other was to reach the main house in front and the right and the left roads led to huge and vast gardens which themselves were nothing less than a magnificent, royal sight. Behind the enormous fountain was another driveway which looked extravagant. It was lined with high different types of trees which looked so perfect that it was hard to believe they were real. The way the leaves were formed, their shape and colour, everything about it was perfect. Simply flawless.

More small fountains were attached at the base of every single pine tree and pure water was continuously flowing out of it forming a peaceful shower of water. A beautiful shade was cast down by the high lengths of the trees and it looked simply, utterly gorgeous. The driver parked the car in front of a HUGE black, grey and white coloured mansion, which honestly looked nothing less than royal with the colour choosing, colour coding and the smallest of the shine in each area, illuminating the whole house.

A guard held our doors open for us when I cautiously walked out with Munchkin walking alongside me, her mouth half open too in utter shock when I just chuckled. It actually was pretty huge with small white pearly lights attached to it at so many sides, giving rise to another shade of colour within the already blended ones. One could see a beautiful layout of the rooftop if you glanced above but before I had time to register more of the beauty of it, someone cleared their throat.

I looked sideways to see Mr. Hot beckoning us to move inside. Nervously questioning my sanity and my situation and knowing there was nothing that I could do, I gulped, held munchkin's hand strongly and started walking. Here goes nothing.

I entered through the set of double doors and my breath caught in my throat. I couldn't believe I was inside such a charming looking place. I gazed down at Munchkin to see her eyeballs practically on the ground. Woah! We entered to see a very very large entrance, the inside being way too huge than what looked like from the outside.

It had a vast empty space in between, several rooms on the right and the left where I could see a kitchen as being the first one on the left, since the door was open. I could see a living room, a guest room which the room themselves looked like a merge of five to six rooms altogether. Looking at the sides, there were two sets of spiral steps leading to different wings of the mansion. The steps were made of marble as it seemed, they had a light, shiny grey colour and beautiful small circular lights were attached in the middle giving it an appealing look.

The railings had an intricate design on them in a shiny black colour with small, glossy white marble balls as decoration on them. There was a lovely looking small sofa in the middle and as much as it may sound weird to have a small sofa at

## Chapter 8

the entrance, believe me it looked gorgeous.

The two flights of steps connected together at the top and it was nothing but just pure beauty. Looking above at the roof you could see a lustrous looking chandelier which itself had a complicated design and gleaming white light was shining in rays from it. Looking up from below, one could see polished clean roof of the second floor which further had small spotlights attached to them making it look more than stunning. Then the third floor, then the fourth and then the fifth. This place, this place was for royals.

I was still gawking at the beauty when I saw (s)him walking up the steps. I had no idea what to do as it wasn't my home in the first place. I kept standing there looking like a complete idiot when he reached mid stair and stopped. He looked back at me with an eyebrow raised in question.

I swear I sounded so dumb when I asked him, "What?"

"Why are you standing there?" His cold, sharp voice pierced through the flesh of my heart and somehow it hurt me. He was back to being Mr. Rude and I had no idea how he did that. One second, he was so soft, loving, romantic, the man of my dreams and the very next he was the biggest asshole to exist on the face of this earth.

"What should I do then?"

He rolled his eyes and stated the obvious. Well, obvious to him, "Follow me, what else."

I released a confused 'oh' when he suddenly got mad, "You know what? Marco!" He shouted in annoyance when a heavily armed bodyguard came running in. Munchkin as usual got scared and pressed herself against me, wrapping her arms around one of my legs when I rubbed her back.

"Yes boss?"

"Show the lady her room and tell Lily to attend to her needs. Give her the room right next to mine."

With a swift move he turned around and resumed walking up the steps.

I felt my cheeks blush when he said to give me a room right next to his. I started to feel butterflies at the thought of him and I staying so close together. Marco eyes widened in shock when he looked me up and down as if examining me. He sucked in a harsh breath and I was so bewildered as to why he was looking at me that way when I just scowled in annoyance. He came a bit close to me and whispered a dreamy wow. What the fuck?

I asked a perplexed 'what'? when he cleared my confusion, "Boss never allows anyone to even stay a night on the floor of his room, let alone in the room right next to his. You are damn special then." He added with a smile. I should have felt disgusted, I should have felt scared but somehow, I felt happy. I was internally screaming in delight when all of a sudden, I remembered that I wasn't alone. I looked at him and formed my lips in a thin line. Thank God he got the message across

## Chapter 8

and beckoned me to follow him and that's exactly what I did only to see Munchkin way more excited than I was.

# ASHTON

I entered my house only to see Sophia gawking at the interior in admiration. Oh kitten, this was just the entrance. I smiled at myself and shook my head when I gave her exactly thirty seconds before I had had enough. I was a man of low tolerance and I couldn't stand there for long. I started walking up the steps when I felt that she was not behind me only to turn back and actually see that she was standing at the exact same spot.

This was seriously getting annoying. First the hectic flight, then the thought that I had to see Parker and now her acting dumb. It was honestly too much.

I raised an eyebrow in question when she asked innocently, "what?" I was getting mad but I couldn't lose it with her so I decided to ask her instead of snapping at her right away, "Why are you standing there?"

"What should I do then?"

I asked her to follow me which I guess was obvious but she still sighed a perplexed oh. And that's when ladies and gentlemen, I lost it. I called Marco and informed him to take her to her room. One look at her and I saw massive hurt in her eyes. They turned glossy but she quickly removed the unshed tears away. I wanted to run down the steps, towards her and wipe them away myself but I didn't. I guess it was due to my sudden change in behaviour that she got upset. I mentally slapped myself and sighing I just went to my room. I needed to be alone before I did something stupid again. Tired me is an asshole me.

# Chapter 9

## ASHTON

I woke up the next day feeling nothing but like a total piece of shit. I was still tired from last night and I couldn't sleep as the only thought which kept disturbing me was that I had hurt my angel. I had hurt her and I didn't even check up on her before parting ways. I felt like an asshole and there was nothing I could do about it now. Grudgingly, I made my way out of bed to take a shower and get dressed for the day. Today was the day I decided to meet the fucker and ask him about the delayed shipment. Why I kept meeting assholes and why at times I myself was an asshole was beyond my understanding.

I slipped on my coat and made my way to the office. Informing the nearest guard to call Lily, I entered my workspace. I walked towards the window behind my desk and gazed silently at the tall buildings which could be seen from this floor.

There were many people walking, mothers with children clinging on them, men dressed in work attire going for business, children dressed in absurd ways going to school, I guess. The whole population was busy, people were working just to earn bread and butter for their families, to make sure none of their children slept with the sound of their stomachs growling in the middle of the night due to the harshness of the extreme hunger.

There were so many people in the whole of Italy, in the whole of this world, there were millions and gazillions of people walking around this earth but I had to fall in love with a pretty dove who was either mad at me at the moment or severely hurt and I had no clue, absolutely no clue as to how to make it up to her.

There were so many people in this world I could form a family with, a bond with, could spend my life with, but I had fallen in love with someone who was the epitome of beauty. I had to fall for someone who was flawless, beautiful and utterly mesmerizing and I was attracted to her like an old magnet. A very strong ancient magnet that was hard to separate.

I was lost in my thoughts when I heard a knock on the door.

## Chapter 9

"Come in."

Lily poked her head through the door when I nodded my head and she entered. Her head hung low in utter respect and fear which was something I always liked about my people. Respect and fear. No one dared to cross any boundaries that I had set up as they knew the consequences to that and no one would be willing to be at the receiving end of it.

"Yes boss?"

"Lily, you are one of the most trusted maids I have here and that is the sole reason I am appointing you this job. You will receive a pay rise if you do your job the right way. This is something damn important to me and one wrong move, I'll cut your throat in half. Understood?"

She gulped in fear when she nodded her head and that made me mad. I shouted angrily at her, "Words Lily! Do you have a tongue or did someone cut it out?"

"Yes-yes boss, I'll do my job the way you want." Her tiny voice made it to my ears when I started instructing her, "I have a guest here with me, Ms. Sophia and her younger sister as you would have known by now owing to the fact that you served them last night when they came?" I asked questioningly to her.

"Yes boss, I did."

"Okay. You will be looking after the both of them for anything that they need. Make sure they both eat proper meals, don't let them go on a hunger strike which at times Ms. Sophia might. If they demand anything, get it for them and if you need my assistance for that, come directly to me. If she isn't taking care of herself at all you are supposed to come to me immediately and inform me. I would hear no excuses as to why you didn't. If you value your life, your loyalty lies with me as you are under me. Got it?"

"Yes Boss."

"And one more thing. Even if any one of them gets slightly sick you are to inform me and take them to our private hospital and no time should be wasted. Do you get it or do I need to repeat myself?"

"I got it Boss."

"Now go and prepare breakfast for them. I wouldn't have breakfast today."

She kept her head bent low and didn't move when I placed my right hand inside my pocket and my left one on the table, "Is there anything else you want to say?"

She nodded and finally looked up at me when I became more alarmed to see fear written all over her face. She was kind of shaking and was practically scared when she whispered, "Leonardo. What about-"

I deadpanned, "Killed."

# Chapter 9

Massive relief washed over her face when I looked at her with no expression over mine, "I don't tolerate disrespect for any gender under my rule, whether it be a male or a female. And harassment is a straight up 'no' tolerance here. I confirmed that yes, he had crossed many lines with you and upon further investigation, it was not only you whom he had harassed and made you feel uncomfortable, many female workers here had this issue and he has even raped one of them.

It's in the best of your interests to not start pondering into this matter and just let it be. But the fact that he crossed boundaries and forced himself into someone and took away a girl's innocence meant death. So, he is killed, you don't need to worry about him anymore. You are safe as long as you are here and as long as I am informed for whatever wrong is happening here."

She lowered her head and whispered a thank you when she hurried out of the room. I rubbed my forehead as it was paining a lot. I didn't feel like eating anything. I felt nauseatic, mainly because I had hurt my angel unintentionally. It was never intentional. That's just how I had grown up and it wasn't my fault how my upbringing had been done. Rubbing my forehead to ease the pain, I sat on my seat and began to inspect the dozens of files which were displayed in front of me.

\*\*\*

I inspected Parker's file again and decided to meet the fucker.

I desperately wanted to take out my frustration and he was the only punching bag I could find at the moment. I glanced down to see that I was indeed wearing a black shirt. Good. While torturing someone I prefer wearing a black shirt as it hides blood well than any other colour. I tightened my belt and made my way towards the basement.

As usual the underground was cold and dark but this time it stank. There was a horrible smell of like, rotten meat in the air. Rotten meat mixed with old blood. I gagged at the scent and tried to avert my conscious from it. Giving a curt nod to the guard, I entered the cellar and found Parker in a, well- a bad shape.

It smelt more horrible down here than in the passageway of the underground. I took a few calculated steps and stood in front of him with my arms folded and legs a bit spaced apart. I was livid and I was pretty sure my eyes and expression could easily tell that.

Parker was strapped to a wooden chair with chains around his body digging into his raw skin. I could see blood frozen on his skin and everywhere on the ground. He was taking deep ragged breaths as if it was difficult to inhale. Every time he took a breath, his face contorted. Sweat was dripping from his forehead like a broken waterfall, his shirt was barely covering his bloodied chest anymore as it was torn apart brutally but the only thing I was concerned for now was that he was alive, and I had yet to interrogate him.

Massimo placed a chair behind me. Lifting up my pants a

## Chapter 9

bit from my thigh area I sat on the chair and eased myself stretching one leg out and playing with the blade of my knife with my other hand. He slowly opened his eyes and looked at me. I internally cringed at the sight of him but didn't let that expression make way to my face. Defy me and this will happen to you. I was known to be a heartless monster and that's just how I liked it now.

"Where did you drop off the shipment after buying it?"

No greetings, no welcome, no how are you. Straight to the fucking matter.

He was silent. The fucker was silent. I was growing mad when he opened his mouth to speak but quickly started spitting out blood on the floor. I raised one eyebrow at the guard and demanded an explanation. If he was ill, I never knew about that and I would have given the guard a hard time for not informing me but my suspicion was buried deep when he informed me of a few broken teeth and a slashed tongue. Hmm. Okay, he was brutally dealt with, so I decided to go a bit easy on him.

"I'm asking once again, where did you drop off the shipment after buying it?"

He started shivering. The temperature wasn't that cold, rather it was hot, sweating obnoxiously hot, and I wanted to do nothing but just rush to have a shower. It was too stinky and hot in here and the more time this fucker wasted, the more I'll give him hell.

When he failed to answer me, I slowly started walking towards him when he started to whimper. He was so weak. So pathetic. I circled slowly around him giving him time to adjust to the ruthless side of me which he himself was inviting to, with welcoming hands, "You know Parker, I'm fucking mad today due to so many reasons and you? You happen to be one. Now looking at you, I guess you have had enough and you know I wouldn't stop at any lengths to torture the fucking nerves out of you if you don't answer me. So, stop being a pussy and answer my question straight away or God knows, I'll release my anger on you and you don't want that. You are just my punching bag for today and don't make it worse than it already is."

He muttered something which my ears didn't catch. I walked closer towards him and bent a bit, putting both hands on my knees and brought my ears close to his mouth, "I didn't hear you. What did you just say?"

I heard a faint whisper, "I'm s-s-sorry Boss-" and I landed a furious punch on his face.

"That is not an answer to my question Parker. Bloody answer what I asked you." He was cowering in fear and I was glad for that. I'll grasp this opportunity and feed on his fear.

"Boss I didn't do it intentionally." I rolled my eyes in annoyance. Neither was I speaking French nor was I singing a lullaby in Italian to him that he didn't understand me. For crying out loud it was basic English language.

## Chapter 9

"Parker, look at me."

He raised his head and looked at me shakingly. I looked deep into his eyes and motioned Massimo to come over.

"Massimo, does he look that stupid or is he acting like one?"

Suddenly the temperature of the room dropped low and everyone knew that now I was livid. I had had enough of the bullshit when Massimo silently retreated back into the shadows. I took my suit coat off and discarded it onto the chair. Picking up my knife, I walked towards Parker and made a harsh cut on his chest. He hissed in pain and clenched his teeth together.

It was causing him pain while it was relaxing me. That's the reason I was called a horrible monster. I wasn't capable of being loved or of giving love. I didn't know how to give that, heck Sophia was an example. Pushing her out of my mind as just her image calmed me down, I went back to concentrating at the scenario in front of me as I sure as hell didn't want to feel calm at the moment.

I looked at Parker one more time. When he refused to open his mouth, I sighed a tired sigh and asked the nearby guard to get me a bottle of the strongest vodka available in the house. That ought to shake him up because he knew what I was up to, when he suddenly lifted his head and whimpered a scared no, "No boss. No, no. Please no."

"Then fucking answer me. Where. Did. You. Drop. Off. The.

Shipment. After. Buying. It?"

"I'm sorry boss."

WHAT WAS THE MATTER WITH HIM? WHAT WAS THE FUCKING PROBLEM WITH HIM? Seeing that I was suddenly irate as burning anger swallowed my eyes like lit embers, he quickly started stammering when out of the blue he stopped. He stopped moving, he stopped hissing in pain and his head hung low when I kind of understood that he too realized that there was no way out of this. Either he tells me without getting any torture or he tells me after getting torture. And a sensible man knows which is better.

After taking an impossibly deep breath, with his head hung low he told me something which made my already boiling anger boil much much much more, "Boss, I lost the shipment and money to gambling. I wasn't in my straight mind. I'm so sorry boss."

I had no idea how to react to such a pleasant piece of information.

"How are you planning to pay back?"

"Anything you say Boss."

I wanted to test him and play some fun, "How many children do you have?"

That, as I had thought, seemed to strike a nerve. He whipped

## Chapter 9

his head up in terror, his eyes widened in fear and pure fright was openly displayed on his face for me to see. I smirked a bit, folded my arms and stood in front of him.

"No Boss please no. Not my kids. Punish me all you want boss but not my kids. Please."

"How many kids do you have Parker?" I ignored him. Obviously I wouldn't hurt his children. Why would the kids pay a price for something their shit of a father did?

"Boss plea-"

"I ASKED HOW MANY KIDS DO YOU HAVE, YOU FUCKING DOG!" I shouted in pure rage. I hated repeating myself.

He whined but still managed to answer me, "Three Boss."

"How would you feel if I end up serving you their heads as a gift with your breakfast?"

Tears streamed down his face as he begged for forgiveness, "No Boss, I'm sorry. Boss I'm so sorry, it wouldn't happen again but please don't do anything to my kids. Boss please." He was crying and in such a pathetic state. I gave him an icy glare when I cleaned the blade of my knife with a cloth, tucked it in the waistband of my jeans, wore my coat again and silently made my way to him. I bent down putting both of my hands on the armrest and moved close to him. Fuck, he stank like a stink bug.

"This is the last time I'm letting you go. Your children will be left unhurt. You upset me once again, see what the fuck I'll do to you. Got it?"

He cried a painful cry and muttered a yes boss. I gave him one last look and started to walk away to go upstairs and take a shower. Before exiting the room, I gave the guards my final order, "Beat him till he is unrecognizable, shift him to the hospital for maximum two days and then? I need him back on duty."

I deliberately didn't torture him today because I was suddenly feeling very weak, as if all the energy had left my body and I just wanted to relax under the shower and calm down till I got my energy back.

## SOPHIA

I woke up to see munchkin already heavily passed out as the flight had worn her out a lot. I stretched my arms and glanced around my room for the umpteenth time. I had already fallen in love with it. The main theme was space grey and it looked so elegant. There was a king size bed which Munchkin and I were sharing, to my left was a beautiful mini sitting area with two comfy sofas and a fairly large size of a fireplace. There was a beautiful black and white coloured painting resting on top of it with two small, gleaming white lights attached adjacent. In every corner of the room were large lamps casting a soft glow in the room.

## Chapter 9

Directly above the bed was a small chandelier, it had no complicated design as most of them in this house had. It was actually quite the opposite, having a simple pattern which well matched with the beauty of the room. Everything which was placed here was beautiful.

The grey coloured coffee table was made of some soft grey cushion material and it felt so calm to brush my hands against them. Since I had no idea why I was brought here in the first place and I had no clue as of what to do, I decided to get fresh first and then let's see what destiny awaits for me.

I took a shower and opened the wardrobe to see myself smiling like a maniac. There were so many dresses there which seemed too expensive. I started to look through the dozens of them to select any one to wear for the day. Today, for some odd reason, I felt to doll myself up. I always had those days once in a while where I wanted to get dressed up and look pretty. Looking through them, one seemed to catch my attention.

I carefully took it out of the wardrobe and began to get ready. Opening the high cabinets, I saw a hair dryer and surprisingly a flat iron. I dried my hair and started to curl them around. I left my curls down and did a bit of makeup, never forgetting to add the silver shine to my cheekbones as I always loved it.

I wore black hoop earrings to match with the dress which was a black coloured plain shirt, tucked gracefully inside black jeans which were hugging my curves beautifully well and showed a bit of my ass too, but I didn't care. There was also a beautiful belt which held my outfit in a graceful manner. I wore heels under it and looked at myself in the mirror when I twirled around carefully, making sure that I didn't trip. Yeah, I looked representable.

I exited the bathroom and saw that Munchkin was still fast asleep when I decided to walk around the house to get a know-how of it. I quietly closed the door as of not to wake her up. I started walking to wherever the corridor was taking me. This mansion was fabulous. It was super amazing and I wanted to do nothing but stay here for the rest of my life. As much as an asshole he was at times, the man did have taste.

It looked like a goddamn castle. Every decoration over here was expensive. From the multiple chandeliers hanging far apart which seemed damn costly till the floor which was so clean, it almost felt so fragile to walk on it. My hands were sweating because I was a ball of nerves. I was nervous to walk around and I felt as if I was trespassing but I didn't give a shit. He kidnapped me and left me teary eyed last night….. I wouldn't bat an eye towards him anymore. Yes. Decided.

I was walking through the corridor when I came in front of a room with its door slightly ajar. I took a peek inside and sucked in a harsh breath. It was a piano room.

The most beautiful piano room I had ever seen in my entire life. The main theme of this room was a creamy white colour. There were large windows at one end from which the entire city could be seen. Resting in front of one of the windows, was a beautiful looking, sleek black coloured piano. It was

## Chapter 9

shining as to how clean and polished it was. The atmosphere was so cool, not too hot or not too cold. There were multiple sofas there and a simple yet elegant coffee table in the middle with a large flowerpot resting on it.

Towards the extreme left was a small gorgeous shelf with different coloured lights and small bottles displayed in them. My curiosity got the better of me when I silently tiptoed my way inside to have a closer look. There were bottles of wine or champagne from different companies and they all looked costly. I started gazing wonderingly around the room when my gaze landed on the piano. I took long, painful slow steps towards it. It had been decades, decades since I had last played it.

I remember playing the piano for my grandmother when she was fighting cancer. We got to know that she had stage-4 leukemia and only had a couple of weeks left to live. Her last hours were near and we had to bid our farewell. It was too emotional for us and me especially, since I was so damn close to her. I was closer to her than I had ever been, even with my own parents.

I remember vividly, her gazing at me with eyes full of tears, face full of wrinkles, her body so thin that one feared that she might not even be able to stand properly. I remember two hours before she passed away, she requested me through long, painful breaths to play her her favourite song. We had brought her home because she wanted to die here peacefully.

I started playing the piano when the whole family stood

around her in a circle. It was so sweet yet so burningly agonizing. She closed her eyes and relaxed under the rhythm of the soft music. Her expression was displaying ache yet she was calm. Her milky white hair were almost all gone and she looked so…..peaceful. She whispered a low 'I love you' and closed her eyes to go to sleep.

I played it for a bit more when I saw how serenely she was breathing. Getting up, I walked towards her and laid my head in her lap and dozed off after a few minutes, only to wake up after some time to realise she had passed away in her sleep. A long smile was stretched across her face and her weak hand was resting on my head. Never in my life had I cried that much as much as I did that day.

Looking at the piano in front of me, her memories came flooding back in a rush. I hadn't played since she left. With shaking hands, I brought my hands over the keys.

They were hovering in the air as I was too nervous and at the same time, too overwhelmed. I wish she was here. I took in deep breaths and tried to bring my hands to touch the keys but I couldn't. I kept trying and trying but I. Just. Couldn't. That's what love does to you. And my grandmother? She was the most adorable love of my life, after Everleigh. A blessing no one can ever take place for.

Blinking back tears as I didn't want to ruin up my makeup, I started to walk out of the room when a guitar caught my eye which made me think, did he play both or what? Shrugging my shoulder, I silently closed the door and left. Never in

## Chapter 9

my life will I ever go inside that room again. Taking in a deep breath, I started walking again when I turned around a corner and my eyes widened in pure horror. What the fuck? What the actual fuck?

He was standing in front of me with his clothes full of blood, his hair disheveled. He was holding his left arm with his right hand and was walking a bit slowly than how he used to. He looked up at me when our eyes met and he stopped dead in his tracks.

My knees got wobbly just by looking at him and I started to kind of sweat. He kept looking at me when I don't know if I was imagining it or what, but pure love was dripping from his face when my face heated up. I decided to ignore that and see the fact that even with blood on him, he looked damn handsome and that was when I snapped out of my thoughts. Blood? What the hell happened?

I ran towards him and started checking his arms and hands for any sort of cuts or injuries. One touch and I felt a spark, another touch and I felt another spark but I couldn't just suddenly withdraw my hands away. That would have given me away too quickly. I looked up and met his gorgeous grey eyes. Oh, how beautiful they were. One could easily get lost in them.

"What happened?" It was barely more than a whisper.

He looked at me as if in deep thought when he smiled a breathtakingly gorgeous smile, "Nothing much. I was just going to go and take a shower. You should go and get some rest."

He was the one covered brutally in blood and was telling me to rest. He was about to leave when I grabbed his arm and the flashback of the events of the cafe made its way into my mind. What if he didn't like me touching him like this suddenly? What if he got mad? What if he jerked his arm away? Well…
…..fuck it, I wouldn't leave him. He gazed down at my hand holding a grip onto his arm and I nervously gulped but didn't let him go.

"Let me tend to it, you will feel better."

He looked at me when after a moment's silence he refused my assistance, "No. No need. I'll do it on my own." There was a sudden harshness in his voice and I felt as if there was a story behind this but I wasn't letting it go that easily, "No please, let me help you."

"I said no, what part of it don't you understand?" He raised his voice at me in anger and I? I had had enough. Withdrawing the moistness in my eyes, I replied back to him, equally in rage, raising my voice a bit, "You know what? Stop being an asshole for once! One, you kidnap me and my younger sister and make us come here forcefully. Two, we do come along without putting up much of a fight. This-" I said motioning to his mansion and waving my hands in the air madly, "is all new to me, I have never lived like this before. I left everything in my homeland and came here, I left everything behind just to stick up with your ass and that's how you treat me? You

## Chapter 9

suddenly get angry and start shouting at me? Seriously?"

I turned back, again blinking back tears as I used to get emotional a bit too quickly and started to walk away when I heard a sigh and felt his hand on my arm stopping me from moving. I knew that he was stronger than me so there was no use in struggling with him to let me go so I just stood there with my back turned towards him when he slowly pulled me back.

He turned me around when we were standing a bit too close. His chest was touching my breast and our noses were mere inches apart. He was staring intensely into my eyes to a point I could physically feel the heat radiating off. He had a deathly strong grip on my arm but I couldn't feel it anymore. I was so lost into him. He was so handsome up close, I wanted to do nothing but close the distance between us. He, close to me, made me feel safe, protected and loved. I felt as if no one can harm me, even a bit. We were staring into each other's eyes hungrily when he whispered, "Can you forget it?"

Oh, someone kill him already.

"Is this what you say to a person when you hurt them?"

"Yeah- I mean no, I mean… obviously not but can we forget this?"

I was so mad at him. Why couldn't he just say a simple sorry? What would it take just to say a sorry? Shaking my head, I turned to leave again when he sighed and stopped me from advancing. He took in a deep breath and opened his mouth to say something but closed it. He opened it again but shut it. He wanted to say something but couldn't bring himself to. What was wrong with him? He finally rolled his eyes, exhaled a deep breath and grimaced, "I'm sorry."

I could feel his breath on my lips as to how close we were and felt some tingling in my legs. He said sorry and somehow it made my heart flutter in happiness. I was feeling content when all of a sudden, I felt my body ablaze in flames with the next abrupt step he took. He brought me more closer to him, rested his forehead against mine, skin to skin, and whispered. Only for me to hear.

"I'm sorry. I didn't mean to hurt you. It's just that I have had a lot on my plate recently."

With equally the same passion I whispered back, "Why would you reject help then?"

He seemed a bit off by my question when he replied, "Just tend to my wounds, will you?"

I eagerly nodded and asked him to guide me to wherever the first aid kit was. He grabbed my hand and started walking to I don't know where and I just followed him, hypnotized by his mere existence.

# Ten

## Chapter 10

**ASHTON**

I held her hand and made my way towards the hospital wing. Her hand felt so warm in mine, so fitting and so uniquely perfect like a puzzle. She walked alongside me and I couldn't help but wonder the day she will walk around like this as Mrs. Romanno by my side. It felt so……..so perfect. The moment she saw me in blood, the colour drained from her face and she rushed towards me inspecting my wounds. If I would be honest, I hadn't expected that from her especially after what I had done but this little action of hers made my day.

Hmm. She cared about me. Interesting.

## The Mafia And His Lost Queen

She wanted to help me take care of my wounds and I immediately stiffened up. A man like me can never forget his past and I sure as hell couldn't. Neither could I do anything about it in the past to make it better, nor could I do anything now. The damage had been done. I was used to looking after myself alone and people were instructed not to be with me while I bled, lying half unconscious on the floor, inching closer to death but still not allowed to wrap my arms gladly around the angel of the death as I was pulled mercilessly back, to suffer more within the confined chains of the monstrous hell my dad made me live in.

Snapping out of my thoughts, I gave her a rigid response and declined but she was not having it. She insisted which infuriated me more and this ended up in me shouting at her in rage without meaning to and suddenly her eyes clouded with tears but she blinked them back taking in a deep breath when I knew she wanted to cry. Between pained breaths, she replied back even heatedly and it felt as if someone was slashing my heart with a sharp knife.

It hurt me so badly to see her breaking down like this, again because of me. She swiveled around and started to walk away when this time I decided that I wouldn't let her go. I didn't want her to cry so much since the moment we arrived. Releasing a tired sigh, I grabbed her arm and she stopped. She didn't fight against my hold which I had expected that she would. She just stood there facing away from me when I gently pulled her close and turned her around.

We were close, so close to a point that one could say we were

## Chapter 10

sharing the same breath. She looked up and her innocent dove eyes gazed into mine. They were so blue, royal pure electric blue and I was so mesmerized by her eye colour, so lost into them that I just wanted to stare into that abyss of a beauty forever. I wished one of our children in the future could have her eyes.

"Can you forget it?"

Her facial expression suddenly turned funny which was honestly very cute but also confusing as I couldn't understand as to why she made that face. I had a bit of an idea but that was where the problem was. I wasn't used to apologizing, I just never did that, so the word sorry just wasn't making its way out of my mouth, and I could sense that she wanted me to apologize for my rude behaviour.

"Is this what you say to a person when you hurt them?" Her question caught me off guard but I knew this was coming.

"Yeah- I mean no, I mean… obviously not but can we forget this?"

She seemed upset and turned around to walk away again when I held her arm to stop her. To establish a relationship, both had to make sacrifices. She made one by coming with me forcefully and living with me without putting up much of a fight and now was my turn. I decided to put away my ego only for her. Only for the woman I loved so dearly and was so damn close to my heart.

I brought her close and tried to apologize. I hadn't said sorry in nearly the past twenty-three years of my life. I opened my mouth and closed it again, again opened my mouth but closed it again, damn opened my mouth again but it closed shut on its own accord. I kept on trying but the damn words just weren't getting out. Swallowing a large lump in my throat, I rolled my eyes, exhaled a harsh breath and grimaced under my breath, "I'm sorry." What the fuck was she doing to me?

Suddenly, there was a different sort of gleam in her eyes. She felt happy and I? I felt content that she was happy, but on the other hand, I myself was surprised. Never have I ever apologized to anyone. I was taught this, never to say a 'thank you' or a 'how are you' or 'I'm sorry'. Nopes. Nothing at all.

During my whole time as a mafia boss, I had never apologized to anyone and I was known for that, but here I was, apologizing to a woman who didn't even know my name yet. I wondered how she will react when she gets to know who I am. I expected majorly for her to run away and I was mentally prepared for that and I definitely wouldn't let that happen.

Pushing aside my ego, my habit, I apologized to her and the sudden change of her behaviour, her sudden happiness made me content. She was happy.

And so, I decided to take it a notch up. I pulled her even closer and rested my forehead against hers and at the spot, the moment my forehead touched with hers, the pain in my

## Chapter 10

heart vanished only to be replaced by a burning sensation of pure deathly red fire ball of love and peace. I felt my muscles relax, my shoulders slouched down and I felt easy, calm and not restless or angry anymore.

Her forehead was so soft and fragile, it felt like home. I told her how much I had had on my plate at the moment and how I was sorry to take it out all on her and without wasting any time she asked me why I refused help which made me angry again. Why does she always keep sending me to the deepest, darkest pits of my life, was beyond my understanding but then again, she knew nothing. Ignoring her question, I asked her to take care of my wounds which she gladly agreed to and we started to make our way towards the hospital wing of the mansion.

\*\*\*

Basically, we were attacked today.

I was visiting one of my hotels to see how they were operating when we were attacked mid-way. It was an ambush. I never told my people when I was coming for inspection because they would have definitely done everything right upon the hearing of my arrival to avoid my anger if anything went wrong. I used to come at any time of any day and just have a look as to how things were being run.

We were on our way when there was a roadblock ahead. I raised one eyebrow as to why was this happening. There were many people standing outside with their backs resting against the hood of their cars, wearing a smirk on their faces and were loaded with guns. What? What was all of this about?

We came to a stop and some of my men got out of the car. They were snickering like the bull dogs that they were which made me more livid. One of them shouted in a hoarse voice, "Get your boss out. Tell him to come out."

Massimo spoke, "Ashton Romanno doesn't listen to pleas even. He orders and people listen, so tell, what the fuck is all of this about?"

It was a pretty serious situation going on but to assert dominance I think, they kept on laughing which was kind of a weak attempt as it didn't affect me. Crying women on their period affected me more than these men as I never understood how to deal with a crying person, especially a hormonal woman and apparently, telling the person that there are clouds in the sky doesn't help them.

The only problem I saw right away as they had a dialogue exchange act, was that we were outnumbered. Heavily. For the damn very first time. Through my ear pods, I commanded Massimo to keep stalling them when I immediately contacted Viktor at home to send backup, and that, we had no time to waste. Massimo successfully stalled them for about six minutes when they opened fire. Quickly jumping out of the car, I pulled out my gun from the waistband of my suit pants and started firing at them.

## Chapter 10

It was pure bloodshed. I could see splotches of pure red blood dripping on the road. Screams of nearby people could be heard over the roar of the guns. The sound of the guns shooting uncontrollably, were becoming deafening but we kept on going. Two of my men fell on the ground, dead, and we were more outnumbered than before.

Seeing that how they had killed one of my men, I felt my veins throb against my forehead. I was angry and livid beyond knowledge when taking cover behind my car, I slowly raised my gun, aimed straight at one of their men's head and with a bang he was lying on the ground, dead, with blood oozing out of his muscular body. That was for one of my warriors you fucking pig.

Massimo took out another one when I quickly rushed to the other side of the car. Aiming at another one of their strong looking men, I aimed for his heart but decided against it. They definitely would have been wearing a bulletproof vest. Turning my aim down at his shins, I took a deep breath and fired a total of six rounds in one go. As soon as he bent in agony, I fired a bullet straight through his head and with a heavy thud, he also lay on the ground, gone. Forever. That was for my second warrior you piece of dog shit.

The fighting continued with more blood spilling on the floor when I heard a roar and looked back to see my army arriving. I smirked and turned around to continue fighting because now was when the fun began. We were attacking them heavily when I felt a sudden deep stinging pain in my arm.

## The Mafia And His Lost Queen

I looked down and saw little traces of blood on my arm. I had been hit. The bullet marginally pierced through my elbow tearing a bit of muscle. I was wearing a bullet proof vest but that shit did hurt pretty bad. I clutched my arm at the impact of the bullet and again took cover behind my car. I was taking in deep breaths when I felt a hard tug on my arm. Someone pulled me up and on reflex I hit them with the butt of my gun only to see it was one of my men. What the fuck?

He held his head in his hands for a moment while I was in a trance. Why would one of my own men try to hurt me? Didn't they know my power up till now? I was thinking this over and over again when he grabbed me harshly once more, opened the door of my car and threw me inside. *Threw me.* Wow! What an audacity! Taking deep dragged breaths he said, "Don't come out boss. We will take care of this."

Oh. So he was on my side. I mentally scoffed and saw my arm. I was shocked to see that my entire white shirt was soaked in blood. I was losing so much of it, so quickly. I grabbed the side of my arm to stop more blood seeping out when I heard the final gunshot and everything went silent.

I looked up to see my men standing victorious. They dragged the unconscious bodies to the other car and took them home. Obviously, I had to give them my love first before shooting their fucking brains out. They needed my hugs to remember in hell. I was very affectionate with these kinds of people.

Massimo rushed into the car and his eyes widened when he looked at me. I shrugged it off with a wave of my hand, "I'm

## Chapter 10

fine. Just drive me home." He nodded his head in agreement and the engine roared to life. We reached home fairly quickly and I was walking up the steps when I saw my beautiful angel turning around the corridor and oh. my. god. She looked ravishingly gorgeous. Fuck.

***

I held the door open for her to enter the hospital ward and indicated to where the first aid kit was. Without wasting any time, she rushed to get the required equipment whereas I sat on the bed and waited for her to come back to me. After seven seconds, she stood in front of me and asked where I had hurt myself.

I had never taken my shirt off in front of my mother when things started to go downfall, let alone anyone so I was kind of hesitant a bit too right now. Even during random sexual encounters, I never took my shirt off due to some personal reasons and hence, I looked at her contemplating if I should take it off or not when I remembered how I had already made her cry a dozen times. I rolled my eyes and started to unbutton it.

From under my eyelashes, I saw her eyes widen and her cheeks turned a light shade of pink. How cute!

The guard at the door had taken my coat to send it for dry cleaning as it was full of blood, so that was one less of a hassle to look after. I was sliding the shirt down my shoulders when a sudden pain shot across my arm. I hissed in agony when

I felt her hands holding my arm in place. She had placed the first aid box next to me on the bed and cautiously slid the shirt off of me. I was aware of the sudden temperature drop in my surroundings. She looked up at me and silently asked for my permission to take off my vest. I couldn't bring myself to disagree so I just let her do what she had to do.

She slowly pulled the vest off of me and discarded the bloodied clothes on the bed. Taking my arm, she started cleaning the blood with an icy cold cloth to numb it, which actually did ease me a bit. She took some cotton in her hand and applied a bit of disinfectant on it which made me clench my muscles there and then. Oh, how this shit used to hurt me.

"It might sting a bit." She said in a low voice.

I just nodded and waited for the pain to come. She dabbed it a bit and I kept my eyes open with severe difficulty but gritted my teeth due to the sudden harshness of the pain. I clenched my hand in a fist and avoided screaming my lungs out. It hurt me like a sonovabitch. She kept on doing her work when finally, I could feel one of the veins on my arm throbbing due to the agony I was enduring.

The pain lessened a bit after a few when I took a look at her. She looked so………beautiful. I had never paid myself that much attention as to how much I was paying on her.

Her beautiful eyebrows were furrowed in concentration, she seemed lost in my arm trying to make the pain go away.

## Chapter 10

She blew on the wound a bit and applied some more of the disinfectant she was using, but I couldn't feel anything. I was so lost into her. Her pretty looking black eyelashes were simple perfection. God did take his time on her.

She started bandaging my arm when I snapped back into reality. It looked so clean and better than before. After she had attended to my injury, with her head hung low she whispered, "It's done."

Turning away, she grabbed my clothes and went to the nearest bathroom and started to rub my shirt under the flowing water to remove all of the blood. Rolling my eyes, I got off the bed and stood behind her gently taking the shirt away from her hands. Blood was running down in streams in the sink when I said, "It's okay kitten, I'll do it."

She insisted on doing it but I hell couldn't allow that. I wasn't going to make her wash my clothes for crying out loud. I swiftly replied a clear no and left no room for argument when I grabbed her hand to come along. Thankfully, she got the message and shut up. Stepping outside the hospital, I looked at her, "Did you eat anything yet?"

She shook her head a no and I was livid. Lily! Tucking a strand of her soft silky hair behind her ear, I told her to go eat breakfast and that I'll join her later after I change. She nodded her head and started to walk away when I already missed her warmth so much that I just kept looking back at her retreating figure. And my God! She looked like an angel. My angel.

## SOPHIA

The breakfast went smoothly. He did join us later as he had promised and sat next to Munchkin, so that she was squeezed between the two of us. She kept on blushing throughout the entire breakfast which was seriously annoying me. I tried to bring her attention back to the lavish breakfast displayed in front of us by pinching her arms and all that I could do to gain her undivided attention back, but she was so lost into him. Rolling my eyes, I tried to feed her and ate myself to the full.

The food was definitely delicious and mouthwatering. They had croissants, chocolate and vanilla cupcakes topped with chocolate chips, frosting, sprinkles and many other different kinds of toppings.

There was a large chicken bread in front of us, with a plate full of bread and fried eggs, some French toast, freshly cut fruits, a jug full of milk and another full of crystal-clear pure water. There was a beautiful basket of nothing but red cherry coloured strawberries which looked so inviting. There were mini pizzas there surrounded with some cold sandwiches. It was all too good.

He got up after about ten minutes, bent on his knees in front of Munchkin and took her hand in his, "I have some work to do princess, as soon as I get back, I'll take you to wherever you want to go in this house, whether it be the cinema, the swimming pool or horse riding, whatever. Okay?" She giggled in response when he placed a soft, gentle kiss on

## Chapter 10

the back of her hand and got up to leave.

But before he left, he stood behind me and without any warning, placed a lingering kiss on my forehead and whispered gruffly in my ear, "I'll be back gorgeous." And as swiftly as he came, he left. I exhaled a breath I never knew I was holding in since the start of breakfast and relaxed against the chair. I looked sideways to see Munchkin giving me a toothy grin. I gave her a scowl and went back to finishing my sandwiches.

The day was quite boring to be honest. I spent most of my time in the kitchen with Lily and Munchkin, baking some cakes and a bunch of pastries as I had no clue as of what to do and this was getting pretty boring actually. He better come home quickly and give me some form of entertainment or I'll be leaving within the blink of an eye. Even the kitchen this Mr. owned was fabulous.

It was huge with polished, shining brown coloured cabinets, a large stove and a baking area. There was a separate area for the pantry which looked beautiful and fully stocked. There was a proper exhaust system so the kitchen wasn't stuffy at all.

On the contrary, it was quite comfortable with the gentle scent of waffles wafting in the air, giving it a homely feeling. We spent around three hours baking and I spent the next an hour and half gazing at the walls of our room while Munchkin was taking her evening nap when I heard a knock on the door.

"Come in."

The door slightly opened when he poked his head through. I straightened up as if on queue and started rubbing my hands together in nervousness. This was one of my oldest habits. I used to rub my hands when nervous. He looked at the sleeping form of munchkin when he said, "I thought to give her a tour."

"I'll just wake her up."

I turned away to wake munchkin up when he interrupted, "No no, no need. Let her sleep. Let's go for a walk."

I gulped nervously. At this point my hands were practically wet from how much I was sweating when my voice came out a bit squeaky, "Who?"

He looked at me with an expression as if saying what-do-you-mean-who, "You and me, who else." I could hear the unsaid duh in his voice.

I exhaled and got up slowly when I replied in a small voice, "Okay, just let me change."

He waved his hand in the air, "No. No need. Just come along."

I tucked a curl behind my hair and started to go when I suddenly turned and ran back to munchkin. I placed cushions around her from all four ends to make sure that she didn't fall. Turning around, I started to walk towards

## Chapter 10

him when I caught him looking at me. I swallowed a large lump in my throat and closed the door softly. He gave out his hand for me to hold which I held tenderly as sparks flew across my body upon the contact of his skin with mine. We started walking down the steps and I was clearly aware of the tension surrounding the air.

"Where do you want to go?" His voice was so rough, so deep and so goddamn sexy, it made me nervous. I started thinking that where would I possibly want to go. You know the moment when you want to go somewhere but no one is there to take you and when someone is actually there to take you along, you cannot think of one? That was the exact same situation I was in. Thinking through, I suddenly remembered that he had mentioned horse riding to munchkin so that's what I wanted to do. I had never sat on a horse before and I wanted to do that.

"Horse riding." My voice came out smaller than I expected it to.

He just nodded his head and picked up his speed to a point he was walking too fast and it was difficult for me to keep up.

We exited through the double doors of the mansion and took another long walk towards the stables. During the whole time, he held my hand and if felt so warm. Surprisingly, our hands fit together perfectly. It was a cute sight and I wanted this to last forever. I was gazing at our entwined hands when I glanced towards my left one and imagined a ring lying on my finger, indicating to anyone who saw, that I was his and only his. No one else's. I smiled to myself silently when his voice cut me through my thoughts, "Which one do you want to ride on?"

I looked at the horses and then back at him, "I have never ridden on a horse before, I can't do it myself."

He looked adoringly into my eyes when he said, "You don't have to. I'll help you."

"And what if I fall?"

He snaked his arm around my waist, pulled me flush against his chest, brought his face unbearably close to mine until his lips grazed the side of my earlobe and I shivered.

My heart constricted and fire erupted in the whole of my body. I could feel fireworks exploding in my body and I couldn't think straight. My whole mind was foggy and blank. I closed my eyes at the sudden blooming feeling when he whispered in his devilishly sexy voice, him pulling me even closer to him, his hand leaving an imprint over my back as he placed his lips over my ear, "I would never let you fall kitten."

He placed a kiss on my earlobe and before fully withdrawing, nudged the side of my face with his nose. I was screaming internally like a lunatic on loose. My whole body was on fire and my heart was going crazy when I wanted to do nothing but just kiss him. This was too hot and I couldn't handle it. My cheeks heated up and there was a sudden amused

## Chapter 10

expression on his face when he looked at the side of my face. I chewed the inside of my gums and closed my eyes in embarrassment as I knew what he was seeing. My ears had turned a dark shade of red. He smirked a bit and asked me again, "So, which one do you want to ride on?"

Coming back to my senses, I looked at all the horses which were in front of me and it stole my breath away. They. Were. So. Beautiful. There were around five to six of them and they all looked so……..pretty. Their stable was clean, their bodies so beautiful, I just kept on gazing at them when one caught my attention. I didn't know whether it was a he or a she but it was standing at the far end and somehow, I assumed that it must be a she.

She was pure white in colour. White as snow, so frostily white as a rich, white Toblerone. Her white mane looked so soft and were waving elegantly due to the silent breeze of the wind. She had clear round eyes and a perfect shape. She just looked utterly beautiful and I suddenly fell in love with her. The others were all black or grey in colour and so so so fucking beautiful but she was the only one who was white. Guess she was special then.

She stood there looking all powerful when I turned back and met his steel grey eyes. I was confused for a second. Is he more beautiful or the horse? I wouldn't be shocked if they turned out to be siblings to be really honest.

I whispered, "The white one."

A sudden expression crossed his face but I guess I had imagined it because he wiped it off straightaway. I was sure I had imagined it as he looked angry. A dark, pained expression had crossed his face but he hid it pretty well. He nodded his head and walked towards the horse. I just stood there with my sweaty hands moving back and forth in extreme nervousness.

Who was he? What was he hiding? How can he be so romantically sweet one time and dark as thunder the next? Why was he like this? He was a very closed book which pissed me off. You couldn't read him that well but he could. He could read anyone in a second. I wanted to know who he was at the end of the day. Guess I'll just have to wait then.

He went to the horse and gently moved his hand across her mane. She lowered her head and just enjoyed his touch when he went a bit forward and placed his forehead against her. He looked deep in pain and I changed my mind. We could use any one of the other horses, I don't know why this was hurting him so much but it was. I was about to take a step to tell him that I had changed my mind when he suddenly straightened his posture, turned towards me and started inching close with the horse.

She trotted in a smooth way as if walking on clouds. It was graceful for an animal. They came and stood right next to me. She suddenly neighed when I shrieked and hid behind his huge, muscular, well-built body. He chuckled softly and I looked at him. That was the first time I had heard him chuckle and it was so cute. I looked at him when he said in

## Chapter 10

his usual heavy, deep voice, "She wouldn't say anything to you." So she wasssss a she. AHAAAAA!

I raised an eyebrow in uncertainty when he said, "What? Go on. Try it." He urged me to see whether she would do anything when I shakily brought my hand towards her head. I clutched the back of his coat tightly with the other hand when I nervously hovered my hand above her head.

What shocked me more was that she bent her head and sat on two legs in front of me. What the fuck? Why was she bowing? I looked a perplexed look at him when I saw him even more shocked than I was. Suddenly, his face broke into a smile but a broken one. He was smiling but it wasn't quite reaching his eyes.

"What is all of this about?" My voice felt so tiny when he glanced at me.

He opened his mouth several times to say something but at the end he just shook his head and said, "She accepted you."

I felt like the world's biggest donkey to exist when I moved in front of him and placed my hand on his forehead, just in case he had a severe temperature. The moment my hand touched his forehead, sparks of electricity coursed through my body and I felt as if I was being electrocuted. I had never thought in my entire life what a single touch could do to a person. He chuckled at my move and said, "Come on, let's ride Pegasus."

## The Mafia And His Lost Queen

I was confused, "Who?"

He rolled his eyes in annoyance, "Me. My name is Pegasus. Ride me. Will you?"

I choked on my own damn spit and my cheeks turned beetroot of a colour. He. Did not. Just. Say. That. To. Me. I was pretty sure my face had a funny expression when I slowly turned around and started to head in the complete opposite direction, "I-uh, I need to use the bathroom." I quickly swiveled around to move when I felt his hand around my stomach and he pulled me back.

Huffing he whispered, "Her name is Pegasus. My mum gave her this name."

Oh. I mentally slapped myself hard when I relaxed. He seemed annoyed but he said, "Get on her."

To avoid any other embarrassment, I put my foot on the saddle and tried to get on her but I just couldn't. She was too big. I kept on trying when she suddenly just shrugged me off, sending me falling down and hitting some soft grass. Two things surfaced in my mind at that moment. Did a horse just shrug me off? Whattt? What the hell? And two, when did the ground become so soft when I felt myself being lifted up.

I mentally became hyper aware of my surrounding. Surely, the ground couldn't lift me up so I turned my head back in an awkward position to see myself in his arms. He was looking directly into my eyes and it felt as if there was high intensity

## Chapter 10

of current passing between us, grey to blue, lightening to dark sea, but sadly the moment passed away quickly when he hefted me on my feet.

I was feeling like a kid again for some reason when I put both of my hands on my hips and went to stand in front of the horse. She gazed at me boringly which to be really honest offended me more. I put a scowl on my face and with my forefinger pointing towards her I whispered, "Bad horsy!".

Obviously I didn't mean it, but she *shrugged* me off for God's sake. I looked at Mr. Hot who was standing with an amused expression on his face and with both of his eyebrows raised. I looked back at her who had an expression as if saying bitch-please before I saw stars. She kicked me with one of her legs and I literally flew in the air before landing on the ground with a hard thud. on. my. butt. I let out a sharp pain as it did hurt me. Suddenly he was at my side and picked me up bridal style. Worry was laced in his voice, "Are you hurt? Are you okay?"

I got out of his arms as I was mad, "A beautiful horse you have there."

I was horrified to see him smirking. What an audacity! "Who told you to tell her that she was being a bad child."

"*She shruggeddddd me off!*" I tried to emphasize my point when it came out all loud and squeaky.

He started shaking his head amusingly, "Come on, she

wouldn't do it again. And stop being her mom."

I wanted to smack him across his beautiful face but decided against it. We walked past the horse when I scowled at her. He indicated me to put one foot on the saddle which I did when I felt his strong hands on my waist and he easily lifted me up, as if I was as light as air. I was shocked. He was MUCH stronger than I had thought. He placed me gently on the horse when I felt a slight stomach ache coming in due to me being nervous for this was my first time sitting on a horse and I had seen videos of people falling from horses. He then himself mounted it and sat behind me. I could feel him against me and I could feel all of his *organs* against me. Instantaneously, I was feeling hot and started sweating. What was he doing to me?

He snaked his arm around my waist and pulled me impossibly more closer to him. My back was touching his torso and I could feel the light rising of his chest. He was calm, or maybe not. He was good at hiding his emotions. Better than anyone I had ever met. Maybe he was feeling the same thing as I was, maybe he was as nervous as I was. I wish I could read him as easily as he could.

I sensed him coming closer to me when I felt his soft, warm breath on my neck. I closed my eyes in satisfaction ad it was soothing me so much. He had a tight grip against my waist holding me close when he brought his head a bit in the crook of my neck. He was slouching with his eyes focused in front, when he pulled the reins and she started moving.

## Chapter 10

I was silently freaking out and was sweating profusely when I backed more into him. He gave my waist a hard squeeze and whispered, "Just breath baby. Keep on breathing. Take long deep breaths and go easy." With an even more seductive harsh tone he then whispered, "I won't let you fall down."

Honestly, my heart was beating like a wild animal against my chest that I was frightened it might burst out at any minute. I took long deep breaths as he had instructed but the horse was a bad one. I kept trying to calm myself down when she kept on gaining speed. I wanted to smack her on her head to let her know to slow the hell down but decided against it as she was just like Mr. Hot. Moody.

She kept on gaining speed, and he kept tightening his hands around my waist to a point she raised her front legs and started to run across the field faster than I had ever seen any horse run. Without thinking any further, I just started hitting Mr. Hot behind me, "Slow her down, slow her down, slow her downnnnn dammit!"

He chuckled when she started running faster, "You'll enjoy this believe me."

I didn't care where I hit him but I kept on hitting him harshly when he toughened his voice, "Sophia-"

"No, don't Sophia me, stop her, she's going too fast."

My heart beat was immeasurable and I was scared out of my fucking wits when I started to take in deep breaths. Knowing that they too weren't being enough, I just audibly started to breath to take as much air in as I could. I was feeling nauseatic and sick when he suddenly tensed and I felt his right arm pulling back, the one with which he was controlling the horse. She came to a slow stop and I started to feel a bit better as my heart beat slowed down a bit.

He grabbed me from under my armpits and raised me into a sitting position but it was a bit hard for me. He pulled me against his chest when I rested my head against his shoulder. He shouted to the nearby guard to bring me water and held me in a sitting position again, supporting my back and started rubbing it. Instantly, I started feeling a bit better than before. In less than a minute, a bottle of water came and I drank it like a thirsty camel. He asked if I wanted more to which I respectfully declined. I was feeling better now.

He turned me a bit and looked at my face, "You okay?"

I nodded a yeah when he asked me if he should start again. Was he mad? I wasn't going on that deathly ride again, that too seeing how he had acted on my first ride. I shook my head frantically no and openly let him see the fear in my eyes, feeling pathetic. He looked at me sympathetically when he put his fingers under my chin and lifted my face up to meet his, "Kitten, I wouldn't stop." There was some sort of finality in his powerful voice which left no room for argument.

"I want you to overcome this fear. Conquer every fear which comes in your pathway so that you come out stronger than ever. The weak cannot survive." He then looked me deep in

## Chapter 10

the eyes and whispered, "And I want you to be strong."

I wiped the sweat from my face and nodded. He did make sense. I glanced down at the horse and silently after thinking for the thousandth time, rubbed my hand on her head. She relaxed when he finally tugged on the rope and she started moving. He slowly made her pick up speed letting me adjust to the changes, and he himself kept on repeating in my ear to breathe and to stay calm. I was feeling much better than before when after about half an hour, she was running freely into the fields and I was perfectly calm. I was relaxed and was surprisingly enjoying it.

She galloped like a happy mother runs in the field to go give her children food. Strong currents of winds whipped across my face and I felt as if I was in air, as if I was in heaven. I spread my arms sideways and felt free. Happy. Content. I could feel him smiling behind me and to be honest this was the best experience of my life. She ran and ran and ran when I laughed openly. It felt so good, so free, so………amazingly fresh.

We ran for about some time when he stretched the reins and she made a turn to go back to the stables. It was one of the most wonderful experiences of my life. She marched into the stables gracefully, with style and I laughed. She wasn't bad after all, just like Mr. Hot. Moody at first but then relatively good.

She came to a stop in front of her stable and I couldn't feel the cold wind blowing my hair in all directions anymore. The air was hot again when suddenly, I missed it. I missed it so much. Turning behind, I gave him a sad pout when he said, "We can come here again. Don't you want to go and have a look at your sister now? We have been riding for about an hour now I guess." He looked at his watch and then said, "Or maybe more than that."

My eyes grew wide. Munchkin! Shit. I forgot about her. I slapped myself on the forehead when I tried to get off of her but I just couldn't. Excuse me ma'am, but I want to desperately get off now. I forgot my sister. I heard a deep sigh when he lifted me from my waist easily and put me down on the ground softly before he himself got off.

I went and stood in front of Pegasus, for a fairly long time. She looked at me without saying anything when I smiled slightly. I loved her. I loved her so much and for some odd reason I felt some sort of connection with her. I kept eye contact with her when she herself didn't break the gaze. Slowly, without breaking contact, I brought my forehead against hers and rested it softly against her forehead. I brought my hand up and gently rubbed her face when she closed her eyes and relaxed. I heard a sharp intake of breath but I kept my eyes closed. This was too peaceful. I loved it. I felt calm, relaxed and peaceful.

Breaking away contact, I bent my knees a bit and stood in front of her and whispered, "Thank you."

She neighed again when she nuzzled her face in the crook of my neck and I laughed while rubbing her. Slowly, she

## Chapter 10

retreated back and started to go back to her stable. I looked at him and was confused for a moment. He was gazing at me but was somewhere else. His face was blank and pure shock was evident on it. He quickly cleared his throat, became normal again and followed her. He placed food in front of her with water, tied her again before he rubbed her affectionately and started advancing towards me. He came and took my hand in his and started to go back to the mansion, "I think you enjoyed that."

Words weren't making their way out of my mouth. No one had ever made me this happy. I was speechless. I didn't know who this man was or what he did or why he kidnapped me but one thing I knew was that I couldn't live without him anymore, even if it had been just a few days of us being together. He meant the world to me. He gave me happiness, he gave me strength, power and everything a girl could dream of.

He took my hand and went with me through my fears so that I could overcome them. He made sure that I knew that I wasn't alone. Anytime. Anywhere. This man brought me unlimited amount of happiness and I just couldn't leave him. I mean, I could but I didn't want to. I wanted to be his and him to be mine. I wanted nothing but to sleep in his arms at the end of the day.

We were walking back when the sky was a deep shade of orange red. Bright orange light was casting in the sky and he looked gorgeous as ever. I glanced at him and fell more and more in love with him. If that was even possible. He was perfect. Smoky orange light was bouncing off of his face and he looked gorgeous. He was flawless and I couldn't help but get lost in him once again. Not finding my voice at all, I gathered some courage and managed to whisper, "I loved it."

He looked at me, into my eyes and broke into the first genuine smile I had seen him give while he held onto my hand.

And that, I guess, was the start of a new chapter in my life, something I would never leave mid-way and give all of my strength to, to finish it one day with a happy ending. Let's see what happens next. Until then, I'll fight for it day. And. Night.

That, I promise.

# Chapter 11

## ASHTON

I woke up from the shrieks of the annoying alarm from my phone. It was honestly giving me a headache and I wanted to do nothing but just throw it against the wall. Disabling it, I groaned and turned on my side to rest for a couple more minutes.

The bed was as usual soft and comfy and the sweet memories of yesterday resurfaced into my mind. It was one of the best days of my life. It had been a while since I had smiled or felt happy or relieved and just a couple of hours with her seemed to do the trick. The way she was at a loss of words for how happy she was and she didn't have to say it, I could see it in her eyes. The sudden gleam, the first light that I had seen in the Romanno house since I had gained consciousness, I guess.

The way her red blonde hair whipped in the air, the sweet scent of vanilla mixed with lavender entering my nose made it nothing but more peaceful and the most shocking bit was Pegasus accepting her. I was more astonished than she was. How could it happen? What was she thinking? It was all beyond my understanding. For the first time since so many years, after my mother's death, Pegasus galloped freely into the field and oh how much I had missed this.

I remember smiling an amused smile when she tried to teach her how she was being a bad child and Pegasus being Pegasus did the exact same thing that I would have done been in that situation, kick a leg out and hit the person right in front till the person fell fifty-five feet away and felt their bum hit the ground harsh.

Pegasus was a bit proud and not going to lie, that must have hurt her pretty bad. I smiled silently and got out of bed to go get dressed for the day and confront whatever shit was waiting for me at the doorstep. Little did I know it was a massive one.

\*

Her little sister was already loving me loads. She couldn't stop doing mini talks with me, most most most of the time talking about some animated movie 'Frozen.' I knew Sophia was getting bored by it but there wasn't anything that I

## Chapter 11

could do. Dammit this was the first time a child was here in my house and I didn't know the basic thing as to how to take care of them, or how to make them happy or stop them from crying or loving them. I had never been at the receiving end of love nor had ever given it in the first place so I had absolutely no idea. Conclusively, I decided to use was a strategy. A highly stupid and a ridiculous one but nonetheless, a strategy.

I decided to do the exact opposite of what I did with my prisoners. Weird I know, but it worked.

Everleigh was chirpy, bubbly, energetic, beautiful and innocent in her own way. She did not resemble Sophia at all and I thanked God for that. Secretly, I was elated that Everleigh did not look like her because if she would have, then anyone passing by could have easily said that they were a mother and daughter as to how Sophia took care of her and it would have boiled my blood. I wanted Sophia only to be the mother of my child or children. Thank God they both looked like animals of different species.

Chuckling to myself, I got up from the table, gave Everleigh a kiss on her small, beautiful hands which somehow became a ritual now before stopping behind Sophia. She immediately stiffened up which happened every time I came near her. I knew she used to get nervous as she would start rubbing her hands harshly together and would start sweating which was a clear sign of nervousness.

I bent till my mouth was near her ear and could feel the rapid movement of her chest when I huskily whispered, "How are you feeling today?"

She was sweating. My angel was sweating and I smirked to myself. She replied with a highly squeaky fine. I was amused when I whispered again, "I'm talking about the landing you received from the horse yesterday, darling. I hope your bum is okay now." I HAD TO CONTROL MY LAUGHTER AT THIS.

Her ears turned bright red which I had also noticed yesterday and it looked even more cute on her with her fair complexion. She swiveled around in her seat and gave me a hard glare, "I'm good. Thank you."

Oh my! Guess I did touch a nerve there. I brought my face close to hers to a point I could feel the pressure of her gazing eyes in mine, the power being too strong, "That's good to hear kitten." Giving her a wink, I straightened my posture and walked out, making my way to my office.

\*\*\*

I was going through some files showing the monthly expenditure made in one of the hotels I owned in Spain, when I heard a timid knock on the door. "Come in."

Andreas, one of my men came into the room and softly shut the door behind. He made quick strides towards me and placed an envelope on my table, "Boss, this came in the mail today. It's for you."

## Chapter 11

"Who sent it?"

"It's not mentioned Boss."

Huh. Weird. I scrunched my eyebrows in confusion and nodded giving him the sign that he was respectfully dismissed. He backed out of the office when I wore my black gloves and then picked up the envelope, turning it back and forth. I had trust issues and hence, didn't rely on my men a hundred percent. Not trusting an envelope with no name on it, there could be a possibility that it's smell could get me unconscious and my whole mafia would be weak if I was out of the picture. Or, the smell can get on my hands which I can accidentally inhale and get weaker and hence, the reason being, I wore my gloves.

The envelope actually had nothing written on the outside. No address, nothing at all when I tore it open. Inside lying, was a neatly folded white piece of paper. Opening it, I read what was written on it and felt like exploding. What the fuck? Who the fuck dared to do this and mess with me? I tried to make out whose writing it was as it was manually written and not computer typed which was a rookie mistake but the problem was that I couldn't figure out that too. I couldn't remember it.

Yes, I had seen this handwriting before but where……….I had no idea. My blood was boiling in rage, I could feel my veins popping out of my forehead. Never in my life had I been this livid before. Messing with me was one thing but messing with someone I loved…………that was a whole new suicide mission. I definitely wouldn't tolerate this bullshit of a crap.

I called Massimo and asked him to assemble all the guards we had apart from the security ones in my office right. This. Instant. I would deal with the security ones separately as right now? Right now, anger was dripping out of my voice but I didn't give two flying fucks.

There was a soft knock on my door when I roared in anger, "COME IN!"

Massimo and an army of my guards rushed in and closed the door behind. I beckoned Andreas to come forward. When he was near enough the table, I threw the paper on my desk and gritted my teeth in anger, "What is this?"

He gulped in fear when he responded, "I don't know Boss."

I scrutinized everyone in the room standing and pure confusion was evident in their eyes. Who the fuck would do that? Who the bloody fuck would even think of messing with me? I looked around the room when I narrowed my eyes at Andreas, "Why the fuck are you still standing here? Go back." He scurried back and stood with everyone else who by now had their backs straightened and were on full alert.

"Listen to me carefully now, all of you. I don't like it when people fuck with me. So don't you dare try to be smart with me because believe it, if I catch you-" The temperature of

## Chapter 11

the room dropped on its own accord. My voice came out all bloody and icy and everyone was sweating. WHAT'S WITH THE SWEATING?

"I'll fuck you up. I'll fuck with your life, I'll fuck up your family's life and I'll fuck you up before you'll even be able to say 'sorry'. So, it better not be one of you. Now if it isn't one of you, then I don't know who the fuck it is but believe me I will find this fucker and feed him his goddamn liver with his melted kidney and intestines for dinner, I swear to God. Now listen to my instructions damn carefully and follow them properly with full caution. And if I catch anyone, and I mean, ANYONE going against my orders, I don't think I need to mention what I'm capable of doing. So do things wisely. You only have one thing to do, only one order to carry out and only one life to sacrifice yours for if necessary."

They all looked at me with deep concern and fear in their eyes. I put both of my hands on the desk in front of me, bent down a bit and stared into the air, "Protect. My. Angel."

# Chapter 12

## ASHTON

My voice resonated through the office and I was pretty sure everyone had heard it. The situation was deathly and I would fight till my last breath to protect my angel, to protect her from any harm and to make sure that she was safe at all costs. I had sworn in to find that bastard who had the nerve to do this and would definitely give him a long, excruciatingly agonizing death. I wanted to see the life slowly and painfully leave his eyes as this couldn't be forgiven at all.

"Protect. My. Angel. Protect her at all costs."

I raised my eyes to have a look at my men and everyone was high on alert. They saluted me and bowed their heads, ready

## Chapter 12

to sacrifice their life for my queen if necessary. I chewed the inside of my cheek as I wanted to hurt somebody, I wanted to take out my anger but I had no idea on whom. The anger was boiling up inside of me like lava, like hot molten lava and I couldn't control it. I could sense my body getting extremely hot and I knew I was about to burst.

The only thing which confused me like hell was the person who had written the letter. The name was so damn unfamiliar. Like, I had never heard of it before. I racked my brain hard to try to remember who he or she was but I couldn't get ahold of it. Saerdna. What the fuck. Who was this person? Did I know them? Had I ever seen them? I was livid and wanted to punch the living daylights out of someone when suddenly the prisoners of yesterday's roadblock came into my mind. Fine, then so be it. I'd attend to them later in the day.

"Someone must always be with Ms. Sophia and her younger sister at all times. Not once should they be left unattended. I find that she was all alone somewhere, I'll rip your fucking hearts out. Do you get me? All of you?"

Fear was high in concentration in the room, I was feeding on their terror and it relaxed the gushing hot blood in my body when they all nodded in unison.

"Her safety is your duty and your duty is your loyalty towards me and whoever the fuck is not loyal..." I did not need to complete that sentence since they already knew the outcome. I dismissed everyone but asked Massimo to stay behind. He was like a brother to me. The only one who was a bit close to me and I trusted him. I trusted him with all my fucking heart which was the reason I told him to stay back.

I threw the letter towards him and he caught it midair. His pupils dilated when he read what was written. His nostrils flared in anger when he looked up and his expression, I swore, could have scared anyone. Except for me of course. His eyeballs were a deep shade of brick red, the veins in his neck and forehead were bulging out and he was fuming in anger.

With a heavy voice he said, "Don't worry at all Boss, I would protect her. I will lay out my life for her if it means her utmost safety. Don't worry at all."

This was the thing I loved about Massimo but I didn't let the content make way to my face. I swallowed and nodded at him when he left the paper on my desk and was leaving when I stopped him.

"Massimo."

He turned around, "Yes?"

And I pleaded. I fucking pleaded and this was the first time in history that someone in the Romanno mafia family had pleaded and yet I did. I didn't care if I was letting my guard down, or if I was letting my heart feel different things. I didn't. I didn't give a bloody ass shit.

"Protect her Massimo. Protect my angel. Don't let her suffer

## Chapter 12

if I fail to keep her safe. Be her safeguard even if I die in the process. Just. Protect. Her." I gritted the last words out.

Massimo was shocked. There was a painful, pin drop silence in the room till the point that even the sounds of our deep breaths could be heard easily, without effort. Never ever had he seen me in my lowest. I was practically slouching but I hid it well. I was gazing down at the floor when I felt him coming near me and I immediately tensed up. I hated it when people came near me, especially to console, as I never got that in my childhood as far as I could remember. He laid a hand on my left shoulder and gave it a hard squeeze, "You don't need to say it brother."

My world stopped for a moment. I was shocked. Brother. He called me his brother despite knowing the ugly shit that I do. He gave me a tight-lipped smile and turned around to leave when he stopped, swiveled around and said the last thing I was expecting him to say.

"Don't give up on her."

With that, he turned around and marched out of my office leaving me standing there dumbstruck for about all evening.

## MASSIMO

I was livid. Who would dare to mess with us this way. Who was it? And boss? He fricking pleaded. I couldn't believe my eyes. Or my ears. Ashton Romanno pleading? What the doughnuts?

I had my suspicions that he had feelings for her the moment he told me to keep eyes on her and to track her as she was of no threat and we used to majorly track people who were of danger to us. That suspicion was confirmed when he ordered me to abduct her. I knew there was something going on in his heart for her, for the way he looked at her and took care of her, the sudden gleam and a tint of happiness in his eyes whenever he glanced at her but for his love for her to get this deep this quick and this powerful? I didn't know. Never had I ever seen him this way.

Yes, he had several girls as a one nightstand but he used to kick them out angrily right after the random fuck or the very next morning if they wouldn't have left the night before, but it was never anything more than that. And he never slept with those girls too.

He was soft around her and I could see the reason. She was pretty after all and her little sister was adorable. A sweet young potato. I saw Sophia as my sister, someone Boss loved and nothing more than that. And nor will I ever. After reading the letter, the way I had made a vow while abducting the sisters that I would make sure that Everleigh never shed a tear, just like that today I made a vow with myself, to protect the both of them at all costs, even if it meant my graveyard being wet the next day. I didn't care.

I always looked up to Ashton Romanno as my brother because he pulled me up and made me stand upright in the

## Chapter 12

darkest of times, when no one was with me, when I was giving up on life slowly, he was the one to hold me by the scruff of my neck, made me get up and live a life. He gave meaning to my life and made me lead it and form it till a point that now my life is empty without him.

The least I could do for his happiness was protect his queen, the only person he loved and showed care for after nearly many years that I had worked with him and that, I would graciously do. I got up from my bed, wore my armour, looked myself into the mirror and promised to bet here for her and be her protector. No scratch would even make its' way on her arm.

Looking back at my reflection, I remembered what was written in the letter and somehow it was implanted in my brain. I just couldn't forget it. I made my way out of the door to train my army. You fuck with my family means you are fucking with me. And that, I hell wouldn't tolerate.

*Protect your angel all that you can but you can't for long. Your efforts will be futile Mr. Ashton Romanno. Believe me I'll fuck her and toss her in the river and let you find your way to her body and bury her. You won't be able to find me ever because you? You are nothing but a dumb sack of an illiterate sick piece of shit. Get ready for hell to break loose and needless I need to say it but let's say it earlier, Merry Christmas!*
*Signed,*
*Saerdna.*

**Thirteen**

# Chapter 13

## SOPHIA

I woke up from the glaring sunlight rays peaking from between the gaps in the curtains. I stretched and yawned, feeling a sudden dizziness in my head and slumped back heavily in bed. Looking sideways, I saw Munchkin sleeping peacefully when I internally smiled to myself.

It had been two days since I had gone horse riding with him and it was one of the best days of my life. Everleigh was mad at me for leaving her all alone and going horse riding especially with the handsome man, so it took me nearly an hour and half to make it up to that moody butt of hers but she finally complied.

## Chapter 13

I can never forget that days' events, it was like as if it was implanted into my brain forever. He made me happy, he made me live a small moment of my life that I had been dying to live for. And he gave it to me without me even asking for it in the first place. I was happy for a single moment, nothing to worry about, nothing to fear about………nothing at all. It was calm, total peace and he gave it to me when no one could. Not even me, myself. I sighed contentedly and rolled out of bed to go get ready for the day.

I wasn't in the mood for wearing a proper elegant dress and I wanted to feel a bit comfy so I settled for a set of denim ocean blue jeans with a black shirt. I rolled my hair up in a messy bun leaving a bit of strands hanging out plastered to the side of my face and did a bit of makeup to look at least representable. Wrapping a scarf around my neck to make it look a bit better, I walked out of the bathroom when I saw Munchkin already up, rubbing her eyes to make the sleep go away. Cute baby.

I went and took her in my arms and ruffled her messy hair when she just clung to me. She had pure curly hair which she had inherited from dad and they looked so beautiful and soft on her. She wrapped her arms around my waist and nuzzled her face in my neck when I closed my eyes in utter satisfaction. I loved her so so goddamn much. Kissing the top of her head, I took her to the bathroom and dressed her up for the day.

We were about to go downstairs towards the dining room to have breakfast, when suddenly I felt nauseatic. I was feeling sick again which had been happening since the past couple of days and I couldn't quite figure out the problem yet when suddenly my eyes grew wide.

It was my monthly. Again. I have been having early monthlies for a few months which to be honest were a pain in the ass, but I was suspecting that it had happened this time again.

Slapping myself on the forehead, I rushed to go to the bathroom but midway turned around and warned Munchkin, "Munchkin I'm coming from the bathroom baby, DON'T, and I repeat, DON'T go anywhere. Wait for me." and without awaiting any response from her, I rushed into the bathroom.

*

She DID NOT wait for me which left me panicking. I had no idea where she would have gone and this mansion was so damn huge, it would take me ages to find her, not to mention, I still didn't know much about the paths of this house yet. The thing which further dreaded me was that what if she met him? I couldn't trust Munchkin on her mouth at all. She could say anything to anyone at exactly the wrong time.

Wiping away the sweat from my forehead, I rushed out of the room when I finally felt the cramps kicking in and I swore, it hurt me like a bitch. My first instinct was to check the dining room as Munchkin loved eating and that is exactly where I went. And sure enough, she was sitting next to him eating and talking at the same time. Oh. My. God. I hated,

## Chapter 13

I absolutely loathed it when someone talked while having food in their mouth. Ugh! Disgusting.

Tucking a strand of hair behind my ear, I timidly walked in with my face hanging a bit low as I was suddenly nervous. I always used to get nervous when I was around him or when he was in close proximity with me and I wanted this weakness to end pretty soon.

"Good morning." His deep voice resonated around the room, sending shivers down my whole body and I clenched my legs shut together. My heart was beating wildly in my chest and I was trying my best not to sweat. Looking up, he was staring at me intently and I could feel the heat from such a distance. I could feel his intense gaze boring into my body when I shivered and replied back in a small voice, "Good morning."

I sat alongside Munchkin and gave her a hard glare. She was eating a sandwich when she gave me a toothy grin and went back to attempting to talk while she was eating when I hit the back of her head softly, "Don't talk while you are eating. Finish it first and then talk."

She rolled her eyes at me and dramatically started to slow chew obnoxiously. My very own eyes widened. Did the little missy just role her eyes at me? How the tables had turned! I placed waffles in my plate topping it with chocolate syrup which was mostly my morning breakfast nowadays as I loved this so damn much when he interrupted me and said something when I choked on my own food. Everleigh!

"Your sister here was mentioning you liked to dance a lot in a crop top and shorts. Freely to the music." He gave a painful pause before he continued with a smirk, never once meeting my gaze as he looked in front of him with his glass of wine in his hands, very close to his lips, "And how much you absolutely love it."

What? WHAT? OH MY WHAT?

I saw the corner of his lips turn up slightly in a smile when I coughed and started to stutter, "Um what? No-no, I mean no hah." I attempted to make a weak laugh and glared at Munchkin. I laid back a bit in my chair and turned so that I was fully facing Everleigh, "Munchkin, when did this ever happen? When did I ever dance like that? I had no time baby."

She looked at me as in deep thought, swiveled her head fastly and looked at him. He had both of his eyebrows raised at her in amusement and had stopped eating. So had I. He looked expectantly at Munchkin and I swear my heart beat was going places. And she being an asshole quickly replied, "She is lying. She does that all the time when we used to live in our house. And she does look pretty. You should see her."

My. God. What. The. Fuck. What. The. Actual. Fuck.

I remember dancing occasionally in shorts and a crop top with the whole of my heart as sometimes I loved dancing away my tensions to the beat of the music. My cheeks heated in embarrassment and I was sure they had turned a deep

## Chapter 13

shade of red. He raised an eyebrow and looked at me and then back at Munchkin. He bent a bit and grabbed her tiny hands in his, "Yes I know your sister is beautiful and don't worry, I'm sure I'll get to see that someday."

He. Did not. Just. Say. That.

Suddenly, I wasn't feeling hungry anymore. I was having a bad stomach ache and the stunt which Munchkin just pulled out was enough to put me in a deep slumber for a lifetime. It was like as if my mouth was sealed. No words were making their way out.

He cleaned his hands on the napkin and put it graciously on his plate before moving to get up to go to work, I guess. He kissed Munchkin's hands and stood behind me. Then as if he changed his mind, he came to stand right next to me, bent a bit and placed his mouth right next to my ear. I could feel his hot breath on my earlobe and it tingled me when he whispered in his hot, gruff voice, "A beautiful hobby you have there. I would love to witness it sometimes."

With that he moved and kissed my forehead, straightened his suit and walked out of the room like the king he was. I exhaled a breath I never knew I was holding in. What was he doing to me was beyond my understanding.

Suddenly coming back to reality, I scowled at Munchkin and she had a wide smile on her face. I grabbed the leftover sandwiches from her, placed them back on the table, and grabbed her by the elbow dragging her to the room. She kept on complaining about her sandwiches but it was time for some grounding. Stupid girl.

## ASHTON

I smirked to myself as soon as I left the dining room. My kitten was as red as a tomato. Everleigh without hesitation told me the wonderful piece of information and I would be kidding if I say it didn't fascinate me. I imagined her dancing her heart out with her eyes closed in front of the music playing and that scene looked oddly satisfyingly beautiful to me. But then imagining her dancing in shorts had me scolding my own self as I had to control my desires for now wasn't the right time.

I just kept talking with her when Sophia entered the room. She looked beautiful even in simple denim pants and a crop top I think girls called it, with a scarf around her neck. But nevertheless, my angel looked simple, elegant yet beautiful.

The breakfast was entertaining as fuck when I decided to pay a visit to my office before making way to the training grounds to practice.

\*\*\*

I entered the training grounds to see Massimo and many of my men soaked in sweat yet were training vigorously. Massimo was shouting orders here and there. On my left, were people doing some heavy exercises and on the right

## Chapter 13

side Arthur, one of my men, was training people on how to shoot. That wing looked weak to me and hence, I stood away from their peripheral vision, witnessing it when I concluded that they all had a poor aim. An extremely poor aim sorry to say. Finally choosing between the two options, I headed towards Arthur.

"Since how long are you teaching them as to how to shoot?"

He was breathing hard and was practically dripping in sweat yet, he straightened his back and answered, "A month boss."

I was livid. It had been a month since he was teaching them and no one had a good aim. No one had learned anything.

"Are they all newbies?"

"Yes Boss."

I raised an eyebrow in anger when I told Arthur to step aside. Eyeing each one of them until their faces were white from terror, I picked up a gun lying on the table and stood right in front of the target. But my way of explaining wasn't that simple. My way, was to scare the living fuck out of my men and then train them. I had my reasons for this method and somehow it always resulted in better results. Have a look at Massimo.

I looked around at all the newbies when I saw a young boy, maybe in his early twenties who was shaking a bit but was displaying a fairly good attempt in hiding it. I could easily tell that he was the weakest of them all, so needed harsher of a training.

I beckoned him to come towards me and as expected, the life drained from his eyes. He swallowed and took small, weak steps towards me when I got angry. I was an impatient man and my men were never scared of anyone, except me and if I called them, they were bound to come quickly without a second's hesitation, without a slight delay. Those were one of the rules.

"QUICKLY!" I roared in anger when he practically ran towards me. He came a bit close when I put the barrel of my gun in front of me, touching his chest, "Maintain a distance next time. Got it?"

He swallowed again when he nervously shook his head back and forth, stepping back. Another wrong step to make me angry. Not replying to me. Swinging my gun, I hit it on his thigh in a swift motion when he yelped in pain and the sound reverberated in the area causing everyone to look our way but they knew better than to watch as they resumed their training.

"Words."

He stuttered, "Yes-yes Boss."

I wanted to hit him again with the gun but it would have been a bit too much, but then I remembered it had been a month. A month since he was here, training. So, I swung my

## Chapter 13

gun and hit his thigh again, "Stutter one more time in front of me and you'll see what the fuck I'll do. Got it?"

"Yes Boss." This time he uttered it pretty confidently without stuttering. Good.

I looked at him with a hard glare, then looked at the target right in front of me. I know this was a wild thought but beckoning the gun towards the target I said, "Go and stand in front of it."

To say he was scared would be an understatement. He looked like he might faint when he stuttered again, "Wha-what Boss?"

I closed my eyes in annoyance and took small, dangerous, calculated steps towards him when the temperature of the room suddenly dropped. Bringing my face close to his, I gritted my teeth and said, "I won't say things again buddy, so do as I say, or get the fuck out."

He gulped but turned around and stood in front of the target. He was constantly rubbing his hands and was taking in deep breaths. Clear fear was written on his face when I started, loud enough for everyone to hear as well, "First thing you should learn, is to never let your enemy see your fear. Never let them see what is in your heart. Don't let any emotion make way to your face. Wipe it off."

I knew he wouldn't be able to do it in the first lesson, so I let it go for now. He did try his level best to wipe the fear off of his face but the latter expression looked funny. I raised my gun at him. He was shivering when with the gun still aiming at him, I spoke, "Stop shivering or the bullet will pierce your shoulder, grazing your muscle."

I looked sideways to see all the newbies gazing at the scene in front of them in pure horror. I closed one eye, looked at my aim, took in a deep breath and shot three rounds. The boy pinched his eyes close but opened them a second later. He hesitantly looked left and saw three holes right in line with each other.

He glanced back at me and was horrified. I had always been brilliantly skilled at shooting. My father dear had taught me. A wide smile made its way on his face but I kept my expression normal. He looked at me expecting me to smile back and when I didn't, he slowly became serious again.

"Stand with your feet a bit apart."

He looked at me confusingly when I rolled my eyes, "So that I can shoot you close to your dick."

That seemed to suck the air out of the room. His eyes grew wide but he must've thought better now when he silently did as I had asked. I aimed my gun right below his center when I looked up at him and saw tears leaking from the corner of his eyes. Flexing my muscles, I counted till three, waited for him to keep shitting himself as all the other newbies seemed to not even be breathing by looking at the scene playing right in front, when with a bang I fired, and the bullet pierced

## Chapter 13

straight through the cardboard with a satisfying sound.

The boy exhaled a huge breath and slumped against the wall. I wanted to fire again and order him to straighten up and never slack when I decided to let him off the hook for today. I glanced at the other newbies, glaring at each one of them, "Don't make me do this to you too. In a week, I need your aims to be perfect. You all get me?"

They all responded back with a frantic yes when I eyed Arthur sending him a silent warning to pick up the game when I swung the gun towards him and he caught it midair. I looked at Massimo to see the men he was training were fairly good. He was good at his job. Always was. Giving him a slight nod, I walked out of the training area to go take a shower because one thing I knew for sure was, that the boy was now on one hell of a ride. One of the many rules for becoming a part of the Italian mafia was, that once you come? Baby there is no going back. Either you make it into my army, with powers perfect as the word perfect or you don't.

In case you failed? BANG! A bullet to the head and your body is sent back to your family for mourning because nobody is allowed to leave the training headquarters of the Italian mafia. Basic, common fucking sense, because they have seen the insides of the house. And letting any kind of information go outside would be the most harmful thing that can happen.

People can even leave behind small hidden cameras here to watch over us which I hell wasn't having. And even if people were executed here? It still didn't make a difference as my whole house was daily literally x-rayed for hidden cameras or anything which weren't under my knowledge. So, it was recommended that it's always wise to think before deciding to step through my kingdom's doors. Because once you do? There is no going back. Absolutely none.

Welcome.

To the Italian Mafia.

# Chapter 14

## SOPHIA

This was actually becoming too boring for me and I couldn't spend any more of my free time here. I was used to working day and night, giving multiple shifts just to feed my mum, Munchkin and I, and hence, it was difficult for me to sit around here idle all day. Finally mustering up the courage after the embarrassment from today's breakfast, I decided to go speak to him. Munchkin was fast asleep, so tucking some cushions around her so that she didn't fall, I straightened my clothes and walked out, just to come back in. I readjusted my clothes, did my hair in a messy fish braid and left it hanging on my shoulder when I applied some perfume and decided to go meet him.

The mansion was as usual abnormally huge and I didn't know the way to his office so I went to the dining room where I hoped to run into a maid but there wasn't any. I turned around to leave when a heavy muscular man passed by me with some papers in his hand walking up the stairs. Seizing the opportunity, I ran and called out to stop him. He turned around and I shivered. Why did all the men here scare the living hell out of me?

But oh wait, he was the man who came to kidnap me. I placed my hands on my hips and scowled, "Youuu."

He looked at me with a confused expression on his face when he also sang, "Meeee."

I pointed my finger at him, "Do you have a mother?"

"Dead."

"Sorry to hear that. Do you have a sister?"

"Close to none."

What? "What does that mean?"

"Next question."

"Do you have a daughter?"

"Not right now, but I can definitely say that I am trying for a kid."

## Chapter 14

My eyes widened at his boldness when I cleared my throat, "I just wanted to tell you that whatever you did was indeed a very low-level act. Imagine this happening with the female of your family, how would you react?"

He gave the wall next to me a bored look and then looked at me, "Why do you even exist is out of my understanding."

Was he drunk?

"You kidnapped me-"

"Missy miss, why are you roaming here like a homeless person and why did you come to me in the first place?"

And that's when I remembered and asked, "Do you know where his office is?"

He raised one of his eyebrows and looked at me, "Whose?"

I gulped, "Him."

After a minutes' silence I added," Who brought me here." and that's when it dawned on me, that I didn't even know his name and he even knew my interests.

After a second, realization dawned on his face when he said, "Oh, you mean boss?"

I nodded my head yes when he beckoned, "Follow me."

I was a ball of nerves but still went along. Suddenly, I was hyperaware of how I looked and I had a feeling I was looking a bit ugly but nothing could be done now. I couldn't turn back. After walking for about three days, because that's how far his office was, we came outside a large wooden oak door when he raised his knuckles and knocked. A deep gruff voice resonated from the other end, "Come in."

I swear it made my heart tickle and my toes curl. His voice was so deep, so gruff and so- sexy that it sent tingles down my body. The guard slowly opened the door and stepped in, beckoning for me to follow. My breath caught in my throat once I was in, for his office? His office was so damn gorgeous.

The main theme was wooden black, from the spotless shiny floor till the high, professional looking cabinets, it was a very long office. There were high plush sofas on the extreme left and an enormous library on the extreme right. Exactly in front of the huge shelves of books, was a mini coffee table with a comfortable looking sofa adjacent to it. There was a unique aroma of perfume lingering which wasn't bad to be honest.

He was sitting at the far end at his desk with his face buried in a bunch of files with his forehead creased in concentration. Or maybe tension, I couldn't figure it out. His table was huge, with many folders lying together in a mess, a silver apple laptop resting right next to him, a pack of cigarettes to his left and he had a glass full of wine, it looked like.

## Chapter 14

Right behind him was nothing but glass. Huge glass windows were displayed at the back and you could see nothing but the whole city there. It was all visible to you, right there in front of you, under your very own eyes to watch. It was a beautiful place to sit and work in peace.

He didn't look up when we entered which I had expected he would.

"Yes Massimo?" His voice did wonders to the nerve cells in my body but suddenly I was confused. How did he know who had entered? He could have called him, yes, but then anyone could have come before him. Massimo, I guess was what he was called, cleared his throat, "I got the CD you asked for."

With his head still buried deep in the file, he nodded, "Leave it here, I'll have a look at it myself. And till then, go over the auditing again till my suspicions are confirmed."

He nodded, placed it on his desk and turned to leave but not before saying, "And the young miss wanted to meet you."

That seemed to grab his attention when he looked up at me. Suddenly, I was taking in shallow breaths and could feel my body go warm. I was somehow at peace and felt relaxed. He looked deeply into my eyes and I tried to look back but I couldn't. He nodded when the guard walked out, softly shutting the door behind him.

"Have a seat."

### The Mafia And His Lost Queen

I nervously walked up to him and sat in one of the seats placed in front of his desk. My hands were sweating and I kept rubbing them back and forth till a point where it became painful and turned a light shade of red.

"Would you like to have a drink or anything?"

I respectfully declined when he sat back and relaxed, "So what brings you here today?"

Mustering up the courage and finding my voice I replied, "I want to talk to you."

He nodded, "Go ahead, I'm listening."

Taking in a deep breath I said, "I want to leave."

I don't know if I had imagined it or not but it was like as if the life had left his eyes. They just turned empty. He looked at me for a second when he asked, "Why?"

I knew this question was coming and I was mentally prepared for it. Waving both of my hands in the air, I said, "Look, I don't know why you brought me here in the first place and upon asking, you don't even tell, but I can't live here anymore. I'm used to working day and night, earning and then making a living out of it. Neither am I being able to study here, neither Everleigh-" but that's where I stopped, he may not know who Everleigh was, "Everleigh is my little sister just by the way. That's her name."

## Chapter 14

He rolled his eyes and nodded which seriously annoyed me, but I still continued, "So, neither am I working here or studying, neither is Everleigh and I can't afford that. I have to make sure she is educated so that she can stand up for herself on her own, so that she doesn't have to beg anyone for anything, so that she is pretty confident in herself. So please, it's a humble request, let me go."

I could never read this man's expressions, he masked it too well. He looked at me as if in deep thought when he bent forward and rested both of his arms on his desk. He looked me dead in the eye when he whispered, "Where are your parents?"

I sucked in a harsh breath. I wasn't expecting this question at all. I seriously wasn't and I never wanted to reply. It always brought back bad memories. Always. And it always resulted into me having panic attacks and nightmares and waking up in the middle of the night shivering like a mad person, convulsing with no one to hold me, no one to calm me down, no one to help me out of the situation. I swallowed in a large lump of saliva when I looked down and said in a hoarse voice, "They both died."

He was quick to respond, "Both?"

I looked up at him and it was like as if he was mocking me. I closed my eyes shut in anger, frustration, agony and hurt when I croaked out, "Yes." I never realized that I had tears in my eyes upon the memory of my parents who were never happy to have us, their taunts, their screams, their hurtful words. I mean…………..what kind of parent's do that? He looked at me as if reading me, when seeing the unshed tears in my eyes, he moved back and said, "I'm sorry, I didn't mean to-"

I just nodded my head back and forth as if to say it was okay. Sniffing, I repeated in a clear deadpan tone, "I want to leave."

He locked his arms together and looked at me when after a short silence he had the audacity to refuse me, "No."

I was angry, livid, boiling in anger when I quickly got up, "What's wrong with you? What is your problem? Haven't you heard not to keep anyone anywhere against their will? And don't you know kidnapping is never a good thing to do. I said let me go so please let me go!" I was looking at him angrily, feeling the need to just throttle him when he gave me a bored look, looked me in the eye as if thinking that this all was wasting his time when he again said in the same monotone voice, "Take a seat."

As if on impulse I shouted, "NO!" and that's when I heard rapid footsteps and the next thing I knew, I was up against the wall. His hand was around my neck and he was so damn close to me caging me in. We both were breathing heavily and the only difference was our genders, other than that? We both were looking angrily at each other, feeling the need to strangle one another. He tightened his hold against my neck a bit and rasped out, "A no means a no. You will live here, you are living here and you will be here for the rest of your life."

## Chapter 14

And that's when I lost my battle and let the tears flow down which I was holding in for too long since I was literally kidnapped by a person I didn't even know, who took us to a whole new place just to feed me strawberries??? What even?

He looked at the tears which leaked from the corner of my eyes when his eyes softened and he removed his hand from my neck and wiped the tears away. It was a small gesture but I liked it, it was warm and giving me a homely feeling somehow. My breathing was slowly returning to normal when I felt both of his hands travel to my waist when he held it firmly, awakening the butterflies within me. He pulled me in close when my breast was touching his chest. I could feel the intense gaze of his eyes boring into my eye sockets and could feel the warm breath on my nose which tickled me.

He touched his forehead against mine, lighting up the different nerve cells in my body which even I didn't know I had till that point and just gazed at me when somehow, I was enjoying it. I felt as if the world had stopped, as if time had forgotten to move and we both were just lost into each other, completely forgetting that we each had duties to do. He whispered, "Just stay a bit longer. You'll know why."

It was as if he was pleading me, as if he was requesting me and I couldn't deny it, I couldn't bring myself to refuse and I was falling in love with him more and more and I couldn't stop it. My heart felt so many things at once when I was with him that I was quite sure no one else can give that to me. It was as if my mouth had been sealed shut when I just swallowed. He moved back and I felt empty and hollow. I loved the feeling, the warmth that radiated off of him when he was close to me. I missed it.

He said, "I'll arrange a home tutor for you and your sister and you both can continue studying."

I was still a bit mad at him for capturing me like this when I accepted his offer for Munchkin but declined for myself. I wanted to continue in a proper medical university and wanted to graduate from there since the feeling of properly graduating and throwing our caps in the air had a different feeling which I wanted to experience. He didn't question my answer but silently nodded. I whispered a light thank you and started to back away to leave when I felt his hand on my arm halting my movement. I looked back at him when he said, "I promise you it'll be okay."

Not believing a single thing, I just pulled my arm away and walked out of his office.

## ASHTON

I hell couldn't let her out of my sight, let alone the house. I still couldn't figure out who sent the letter, who was out there threatening my angel but I couldn't let Sophia go out like this. It was just like letting a sheep enter a lion's den knowing I'll get her bloodied corpse back and that, I couldn't afford. I couldn't even think about it.

## Chapter 14

Yes, it hurt me to see those fat tears leaking out of the corner of her magnificent beautiful eyes and I swiped them away as it pained me to see them, but there was nothing that I could do. Sometimes, I wished I had never kidnapped her and had closed myself off like I had all those damn years but no, I had to let her get into my heart.

Holding my head in my hands before going off to bed, I wished that I had never brought her here like this. What kind of a person was I? Putting the only woman I love in danger? Because of me, she was the target of all my enemies because somehow, they knew that she was my weakness, that I was slowly falling for her more and more as time passed by and I couldn't help it, but the question was how?

How did they know that I had my eyes on her when neither did I take her out anywhere nor did we go anywhere together since the day she came here when suddenly my head snapped up. If we didn't go anywhere together, if no one came here to visit me, if no one outside this mansion had seen us but still someone from outside knew what was going on inside meant only one thing.

The traitor was one of my own men.

My own fucking men.

But who?

# Chapter 15

## ASHTON

### THE NEXT DAY

I kept pacing around my office as I was disturbed, a bit too disturbed. I always created problems wherever I went. No one was ever happy with my presence, especially my father but I didn't even want to think about him. The mere mention of his name angered me to a point where I wanted to do nothing but take it out on someone or something badly, resulting in blood spilling from my knuckles leaving them freshly raw. I guess my mum was the only one who had loved me but that wasn't for long either.

## Chapter 15

It was all useless, this mafia, this world, this life. It was all fucking useless and amidst this, the only light I saw was her. Sophia. My angel. The beauty between the darkened fields, the rising cold currents of air between the ferocious, uncontrollable storm, the light to my darkness and the reason for my sanity. I couldn't lose her and I never wanted to, but the thing was, that she wasn't happy. When you finally love someone, all you want is for them to be happy, for them to be safe and to never shed a single tear of pain or grief.

But what had I done?

The complete fucking opposite.

I had made her cry countless times and fuck I couldn't help it. I kept trying I swear, but I couldn't. It was like, as if happiness was never meant to be in my life. I tried to make an effort to make her feel at peace, to make her happy but I kept failing. Miserably. I had never done this before. I knew what I did to her, how I made her feel, but did she have any fucking clue as to what she did to me?

Did she have any idea that when I look at her, all I can see is her walking down the aisle in a magnificent, royal white dress in front of everyone ready to be mine? In front of thousands of witnesses and God? Did she know that when I get stressed out of my fucking mind, when I'm not in the right mood, the mere presence of her calms the rushing vicious blood in my veins.

I couldn't lose her and I never wanted to for which I promised myself, I promised that I would keep fighting till my last breath for her, till the last of the strings break, and if even after that she doesn't want me..........I'll let her go.

I'll love her but still let go of her. I'll tuck away my feelings in the deepest pits of my heart that at least for once..........
…..she was with me. Right here. So so so damn close with our foreheads touching, the heat practically enveloping us. But if she was happy without me, then so be it. I never cared about myself ever, because what did I do? Bring destruction everywhere. Never was there a happy moment in anyone's life because of me and I had grown used to it. Downing down the glass of alcohol, with my throat burning from the impact, I walked out of my office to go and strengthen the security as much as possible.

\*\*\*

I threw the glass against the wall shattering it into a million goddamn pieces. I had never been this much stressed out. Ever. Sophia's safety was my number one priority now and I had drilled it in everyone's heads. Now all I could do was hope for the best.

I took off my coat, swinging it across the room, jerked my tie loose, and made my way to the chair. Inserting another CD inside my laptop that I had asked Massimo to get for me, I resumed the footage from where I had left to see who had dropped the letter. I was fast forwarding it when there was a knock on my door and without awaiting my permission, it swung open. I heard the clicking of heels when I looked up

## Chapter 15

to see the intruder and groaned at the sight. Oh God, why the fuck?

Her heels clicked against the wooden floor creating an annoying sound that I wanted to do nothing but just break off the heel and hit her with it continuously. She was wearing a long red dress which was too revealing. In former times, although it never turned me on, I still managed to spend some time with her but today, I felt anger. I was livid.

I couldn't touch another woman when I was in love with another. I couldn't touch another woman when I was chasing the other. It wouldn't have been fair on either of them. Yes, Nina was one of the best assassins on my team and also my usual nightstand but I had never shown her or indicated that I had feelings for her, neither did I ever want to start anything with her.

I closed my eyes in frustration and pinched the bridge of my nose. Who the fuck gave her the authority to enter without my permission. Shutting the lid of my laptop, I leaned back against the chair and held the side of my head with my right hand, "Did I allow you to enter?"

She seemed taken aback but still had the audacity to seductively approach me with an ugly smile on her toad like face. She said with an even uglier tone, "Oh come on, you know I don't need permission."

"What? When did that happen?" I feigned confusion, which was another way of saying that I am pissed off so better stay the fuck away from me.

She came more closer to me while swaying her hips, "Oh babe come on-"

"I ASKED YOU, WHEN DID THAT HAPPEN?" I shouted in anger.

She grew serious and stopped all of her fake acting, "What happened to you? I know something has been worrying you that's why I came. Come on, let's get you laid." She added with a wink which further made bile come up my throat. I was hating this right now and I was fuming in anger.

"Get the fuck out." I kept my tone dangerously calm.

"Huh?"

"I said. Bloody. Get the fuck out."

She came closer to me and I was ready for anything but certainly I wasn't ready for what came next. She threw herself on me when on impulse I pushed her away. She staggered against the table when her skirt skid up a bit. I got up from my seat, took a step back to maintain some distance when I pointed towards the door, "Leave."

She started pouting, "What's wrong with you, what has gotten into you? You never refused me so this time too I wouldn't go without some fun." She displayed a wide smile and came closer to me and pulled me by my tie when I pushed

## Chapter 15

her back a bit forcefully.

"What part of leave don't you understand?"

She was about to say something when I cut her midway, "It means, drag yourself the fuck out as you are not invited. Your presence is not appreciated."

She whined, "But whyyyy? What happened? Did I do anything?"

I closed my eyes in annoyance again, "No. Now leave."

"Ashton, what is going on? Tell me."

"I SAID NOTHING! NOW LEAVE!"

She made her way towards me again when I lost it. I grabbed her by the elbow and started to drag her towards the door but I didn't see what was coming next. She pushed me forcefully from the side when I fell on the floor and she started straddling me when I wanted to do nothing but puke. I felt disgusted, impure, filthy, and that's when I put my hands on her bare thighs and tried to pry her off of me but the bitch wouldn't move. She just wouldn't budge. She had gotten more powerful since the last time I had seen her.

I felt her breath on my skin when she started to plant wet kisses along my neck and I felt revolted. Gathering all of my strength, I pushed her away, stood up and looked at her. Her face expressions immediately changed, from lust to fear. I was livid. I was burningly mad and not in my right mind anymore.

Taking a deep breath, I pulled her up harshly from the ground, curled my fingers around her neck and held her up in the air, choking her, blocking her windpipes from getting air, preventing her lungs from getting air, her body from getting enough oxygen. How dare she touched me when I had refused. What did she think of herself? What the fuck was this woman thinking? She was just a nightstand and nothing more, nothing less than that. And I had clearly always shown that. I had Sophia in my mind and I didn't like any other woman touching me now. The sounds of her choking got me out of my trance when I looked up at her.

Her face was turning purple, the veins were popping out and somehow that made me more mad that I started squeezing her neck further. She scratched her nails on my hands and tried to pry off my fingers from her neck but that just added fuel to the fire and I kept on increasing the pressure. I heard the faint sound of the door opening and a shout but I was too far gone, I wasn't in the present anymore. I didn't see who it was, hell I didn't hear the approaching running footsteps when I felt a pair of hands on my wrist, trying to pull me away and suddenly it felt, as if all the weight had been lifted off of me.

I felt at peace, calm and serene. I turned my head and saw the woman I was falling in love with day by day, hour by hour, minute by minute, second by second. She stood there in her full glory looking like a goddess when I felt a harder tug.

## Chapter 15

Sophia was tugging me when I looked at Nina whose face was harsh purple of a colour. I was seething in anger when I jerked her towards me and whispered in her ear, adding a bit more pressure squeezing her windpipe, "Next time, watch it. A no means a hell fucking no. Lay a finger on me next time without my permission and say hi to your relatives in hell from me."

And with a hard thud, I threw her on the floor.

Sophia looked petrified and shook from terror and I couldn't blame her. Rubbing my forehead, I asked in a low voice, "What is it?"

She opened her mouth and closed it shut, opened it again and closed it again unable to create a sound when in a low voice she replied, "I wanted to talk to you."

Heaving a sigh I nodded, "Go to your room, I'll come by."

She swallowed and nodded when she was about to leave but came back slowly inching towards Nina, ready to help her when I held Sophia's arm, "Leave her. She'll be thrown out." and gulping, she nodded and left the room silently.

I sighed and pinched the bridge of my nose when I shouted at the nearby guard, "Clean this fucking mess!"

What a gorgeous day!

\*\*\*

I had promised to meet Sophia but I forgot, which I realized at three in the night. She would have been sleeping at that time when I decided to meet her tomorrow morning and as the asshole I was, I forgot that too.

**Sixteen**

Chapter 16

ASHTON

I couldn't sleep all night. I couldn't comprehend that there was a chance of one of my own men being a traitor. But why? What did I do to them for them to betray me? To hurt me and the woman I was madly in love with. If someone was angry at me, then they should come deal with me, face me. Fuck with me if you have a problem, but not with the people I love, because if you do that, you sure as hell would regret it all your life. Placing my hands on top of each other while lying in bed, I gazed at the ceiling before drifting off to sleep. Who could it be? Guess we will try to find out tomorrow, but I knew it would be useless.

\*\*\*

I wore my coat, tucked my gun in my waistband and looked at myself in the mirror. Yeah, I was ready for what I was about to do next. It was petrifying but I was ready. Glancing at myself one last time, I called Massimo in my office.

"Yes boss?"

"Tell everyone to get ready, to dress up properly to show which family they belong to as we are about to leave." and after a silence I added, "But that, is a surprise."

By Massimo's expressions no one could tell he was confused, he masked it pretty well but of course I knew better. I trained him for God's sake.

He was about to leave when I stopped him, "And Massimo?"

He turned around.

"Tell everyone to get their own signature knives. They might need it." And with a smirk, I dismissed him.

*

I didn't eat breakfast as I was too nervous. I felt nauseatic. What if something went wrong? What if something bad happens? That place was so damn close to my heart, what if hell breaks loose? I wouldn't be able to control myself even for a bit. I knew I would collapse but who would hold me and I definitely wouldn't appear weak in front of my own men. I wouldn't calm down and I knew that for sure. Sophia

## Chapter 16

wouldn't be there and I sure as hell wouldn't take her there. She didn't need to know that she was facing threats, it would scare her badly and I didn't want that now. I wanted to make sure she was living with a free mind at peace. Let the trouble remain with me, I'll handle it.

Walking down the steps, I nodded at one of the guards who opened the door for me and I sat in the car. Massimo, Phoenix and Andreas accompanied me while the rest sat in the other vehicles. The driver asked me where to go to when I bent forward, brought my mouth next to his ear and whispered the location with a smirk. His eyes grew wide, sweat broke down on his forehead but he nodded silently, changed the gears and pressed down on the accelerator. Fingers crossed, nothing goes wrong in an already failed mission.

*

The whole drive was a long and a painful one. In these times, I wish Sophia was with me. I could have held her soft hands which I knew would have instantly calmed me down, hell it did yesterday when I was strangling Nina and come to think of it, what happened to her.

"Massimo, what happened to Nina after yesterday?"

"Boss, we took her to the hospital, she is recovering. Will get discharged today."

I nodded at him. I liked this thing about Massimo, he always got to the point and never beat around the bushes. I didn't have time for bullshit.

After about a few minutes, I felt the atmosphere darkening, as if all the cold air had been sucked to be replaced with a hot haunted one. I was nervous, nervous as fuck, my hands were sweating and I rubbed them along my suit pants but I couldn't show the agitation to anyone. It would give me away. We stopped when Massimo, Phoenix and Andreas turned to face me with one of their eyebrows raised. I just ignored them when I got out, "Follow me."

I didn't need to turn around to see whether they were coming or not. I knew they would.

The graveyard was dense and every time I came here, it haunted me. It sent cold violent shivers down my spine and it scared me. I sometimes used to drop on my knees whenever I came here making sure no one was watching me. It was too painful and there was nothing I could do about it. There was nothing that would stop the nightmares I got after visiting this place. My chest felt heavy, I felt like suffocating but I walked as confidently as possible.

\*

I stopped in front of my mother's grave. It was no longer wet. It was too dry. The soil was cracking, it looked so… .depressed. I turned around to see all of my men looking at me in sheer confusion when I commanded, "Surround."

## Chapter 16

In an instant, they circled around the grave. I stood at the fore front scrutinizing each one of them. Taking a deep breath, I started, "There is a reason my name symbolizes fear, there is a reason no one crosses my path and even if they do, doesn't get to see his or her family ever again, let alone the rays of sunlight and I wouldn't let that name fall apart. Ever. I spent my entire fucking life training, to be the head of this empire, to rule it and make it one of the best there ever is and the most feared one and look-" I spread my arms, "I succeeded.

No one dares to cross my paths and whoever does, you know what happens. One thing which everyone should know and not only you guys, I mean everyone, from the people who work with me till the people who don't even know me properly or that how do I look like. Don't. fuck. with. me. or. my. family. Just. Don't.

Each one of you knows the consequences and I, for once, would do the honors of killing the man or the woman who dares to hurt my family. I'll make sure to skin you alive in front of everyone as an example and without a second's glance, I'll slash your throat apart, feed your meat to the stray cats and dogs and people wouldn't even know any one of you ever even existed."

I was livid. I was suddenly beyond angry. Dare to hurt my angel, I would go at any lengths to protect her. Any.

I exhaled a harsh breath, "I wouldn't tolerate any of you stabbing a knife behind my back. I wouldn't. I just simply wouldn't. So-" This was the hardest part. The goddamn hardest part. I pointed towards my mother's grave, "I couldn't protect her. I couldn't. She left me and I couldn't save the only woman who knew me too well, the only woman who cared about me, who carried me for nine months, went through hell and back while giving birth to me and then taking care of me, and I? I couldn't protect her. I wish I could have done something but I couldn't."

I looked up at them, "But that doesn't mean that I'll make the same mistake again. I won't. The day you entered my mafia, you swore your loyalty to me and me only. So obviously, if you are doing nothing wrong behind my back, the next task should be damn easy for you. Why? Because you are fucking loyal right?" I laughed a humorless laugh and could feel them internally shaking from terror.

"You know what my mother meant to me and believe it or not, Sophia means the same. She holds immense value in my life, she is very important to me and someone I would give my life for. I would do anything to protect her." And that's when I internally sucked in a harsh breath. I just let my guard down, they now knew that I had strong feelings for her but I didn't care. I wanted my kitten to be safe, my queen to wake up safe and smiling and happy. I wouldn't tolerate her suffering in pain. Ever.

"I wouldn't tolerate anyone hurting her, anyone abusing her, using her or even keeping a romantic eye on her. No. She is mine and only mine. And I would go at any lengths to protect what is mine."

## Chapter 16

I started pacing around them, "Now you know about the letter I got, right? Anonymous I may add. Remember?" They all whispered a 'yes boss' in unison.

"Right, so you all know now. Since I don't know who that fucker is, and since all of you have pledged your loyalty to me before," I mocked, "then it would be damn near easy to do what I'll ask you all to do now."

They all looked at me dreading what would come next and honestly, same. I was dreading the exact thing. I stood behind the marble stone of my mother's grave, pointed at the ground and said in the harshest and deadliest tone possible, "Spill your blood of loyalty."

They all were staring at me as if I had grown two heads and they couldn't understand what I meant which I had expected. Growing a wide smirk and putting my hands in the pocket of my suit pants I explained, "Your loyalty should leave no holes open and you all know what my mum meant to me and now you all know what Ms. Sophia means to me and that I would go at any lengths to protect her as well as her younger sister, so, prove your loyalty to me. Cut a vein in your arm and spill your blood on my mother's grave. Think twice before you do so because once done, and if I find you guilty," the atmosphere changed, "I'll personally drop you to hell."

The air was damp with fear and terror was crawling up their skins. I looked at them sinisterly to see if anyone hesitated a bit, if anyone even flinched a bit because that would give it away but to my disappointment, this didn't happen. Something I was expecting since the start but still wanted to do this. Everyone was displaying bravery with no other expressions of guilt on their faces. Part of a problem of being in my mafia, army strong as fuck as to hard to read.

Massimo was the first one to step forward. Rolling back the sleeves of his right arm, he placed the sharp blade to his skin, looked up at me with a dead serious expression and said in a loud clear voice, "I pledge my loyalty to you, Ashton Romanno, for now and forever until death do us part, brother." And without hesitating for even a second, the blade pierced his skin, with blood immediately pooling around the cut when he held his arm on top of my mother's grave and the dark red blood spilled and I watched it hit the dry soil, the blood immediately seeping into the ground.

He looked at me, nodded and took a step back. My main men then followed suit, Phoenix and Andreas later followed by other men such as Tony, Viktor, Vasili, Marco, Matteo etc. I observed everyone closely while they made their vows and none of them flinched, none of them hesitated. They all seemed pretty confident while they spilled their blood of loyalty on my late mother's grave.

It was confirmed then. None of my men was the traitor because they knew what they had just promised, they knew what they had just signed up for and they bloody well knew the consequences. Once the last of my men were done, I turned around on my heels and made my way back to the car to head home. The night was deadly and somewhere in

## Chapter 16

the forest, a wolf howled.

But I knew. I fucking knew it was one of my own men. He could be one of these behind me and he could be not. And if he was one of these behind me? Then, he played like I played, but both with different motives, both with a deadly path. But sadly, he messed with the wrong person. And time will prove that to him.

Or her.

\*\*\*

We were on our way when a guard called me, him sounding weirdly frightened, as if worried, "Boss when are you coming home?"

I shut my eyes in anger and frustration because of the tiredness when I just responded, "In a bit." and shut off my phone.

\*

I downed down the tenth glass of alcohol but the headache just won't go away. Maybe I was overthinking. Maybe there was no traitor and I had just assumed it. Maybe I had accidentally slipped some evidence without knowing, and maybe that's how someone from outside might have guessed or known that I had feelings for Sophia. I decided to let it go. For now. I would worry about that later. Till then, I would protect her and her little sister with all of my power no matter the fuck what. The thought had just crossed my mind when the door of my office burst open and a small body came running in screaming as if the world had ended.

Everleigh?

# Chapter 17

## SOPHIA

I had never felt so drained, so exhausted, so………..tired. Both mentally and physically. I was tired of him playing the feeling game with me and I was exhausted of sitting alone all day doing absolutely nothing. Munchkin's tuition was going well, I was teaching her alongside to kill time, but that wasn't helping me much. It was too much now. I had wanted to talk to him before which he had promised that he would come, but never came.

Sighing, I changed into my comfy nightgown and decided to go to bed. I'll meet him tomorrow and clear all things out and the moment my head hit the pillow, I drifted off into darkness only to wake up wheezing and breathing heavily.

I was gasping for breath. My mind was all hazy and foggy, it was spinning in circles and I couldn't stable myself. My legs were shaking and I was trembling violently when I knew it was the panic attack from the nightmare I just got. My dad was beating Everleigh and then he started beating me brutally, smashing any glass on our heads that his hands could get hold onto. I grabbed the bed sheets in fists and tried to control my breathing but I couldn't. I just couldn't control my leg movements as I was shaking bad. A severely bad stomach ache followed which made it difficult for me to even stand properly.

I had been having these attacks since childhood, when things took a bad turn and this time too, it was horrible once again which meant only one thing. I was having a panic attack with no one to hold me close, no one to embrace me, no one to calm me down. I wanted someone to hold my hand and pull me out of this situation, for someone to just embrace me tight, kiss my forehead and to tell me that it will be all right when his face came into my mind.

Yes.

Him.

He was my protector, my guardian, my man, my……….love? I wanted him and him only. I fell off the bed in an attempt to run and find him. I held the walls and tried to walk on wobbly, shaking legs all the way to the door with my heart beating wildly against my ribcage and beads of sweat breaking down on my skin when I immediately collapsed. It was too bad,

## Chapter 17

too severe and too intense this time. It was so………so nasty. I tried my best to again get up, open the door and slowly make my way out.

The attack's intense began to lessen after a few minutes as I took in deep breaths from my mouth and rubbed my chest quickly. I clenched and unclenched my fist looking right and left in case my father appeared and beat me again. I started to slowly feel normal once again but it wasn't fully gone.

I slowly walked and walked and walked when I don't know where the energy came from but I just ran. I ran and ran wherever the corridors took me. I was crying heavily, I was panting and felt like collapsing, because suddenly the thought crossed my mind that I left Everleigh alone, and for some odd reason my mind was so hazy that I forgot the path back to my room.

I couldn't find him anywhere. I checked each and every room but he was nowhere to be found when I turned around the corridor started running madly trying to find Everleigh. What if my dad was here? What if he hit her? He nearly killed her last time, what if he actually kills her this time? My brain was not at all cooperating with me when I just kept running with no idea in mind as to where I was going, with tears running down my cheeks and sirens just banging in my ears, tearing my eardrums apart.

I turned around a corner harshly and hit a wall, but before I could fall, there was an arm around my back and someone held me firm from falling when I looked up to see a muscular man standing right in front of me. He was looking scary which added to my panicked state.

My hair was a mess, there were carpet cuts all around my knees and they were bleeding a bit. He looked at me horrified and opened his mouth, when I just blurted out, "Where is he? Where. Is. He? I need him. I need him I need him I need him."

I kept ranting this when I couldn't understand anything. I held my head in my hands and breathed heavily. This was so bad. My last hopes were crushed when he said, "Ma'am, he isn't home at the moment-" and I didn't hear the rest. I just left his arms and ran back, following the only path that made sense to me. I could hear him shouting my name but I just ran. I wasn't feeling well at all. I could feel my head melting due to the sweats. It was all too hard, too bad, all of a sudden.

I was wheezing, when I reached a room with its' door open and I saw Everleigh sleeping inside. Entering it with a strong dull pain in the depth of my chest, I closed the door and stood against the wall when I closed my eyes trying to calm myself down.

*He was not here. He. Was. Not here. That gorgeous man with the mysterious grey eyes was not here, not at home.*

He wasn't with me at the moment and suddenly the room was spinning and I felt like puking when I had had enough. Without thinking with a stable mind, I rushed to the bath-

## Chapter 17

room, opened the tap of the tub filling it with cold water, grabbed a pair of some sharp razors, and once the tub was full, with a hazy mind, I shut off the running water, closed my eyes and with a deep breath slashed the both of my wrists. I groaned in pain as it was very painful but I wasn't thinking straight. This attack was massively bad.

Spurts of blood fell on the floor and in the tub from the deep cut in my wrists and I felt a sudden dull throb in my head. I started to feel nauseatic when I staggered a bit and tripped when I fell into the tub and sank below the water.

I was losing consciousness, I could feel the water turning a deep shade of red when I heard a shout, a crash and I drifted off into darkness.

## ASHTON

Everleigh?

Everleigh barged into my office and was screaming her head off when I immediately placed the alcohol aside so that she couldn't see it. She was crying so much that it was hard to understand why. She ran towards me, and started tugging my pants. She was trying to tell me something but I couldn't understand her. I couldn't understand shit when I sat in front of her and looked up at the maid standing at the door who herself looked flabbergasted.

"What happened to her?" My voice felt gruffer than usual

and I understood, it was due to the heavy amount of alcohol I had just consumed.

Before the maid could give me any kind of response, Everleigh jerked my tie down and touched her forehead to mine. The little princess couldn't stop crying. I had no idea what had happened and where was Sophia? Usually she was always with her.

I couldn't think of anything when I hugged Everleigh but I didn't stiffen up this time. I wasn't used to hugging people, it had been a while, almost like fifteen years but I felt some sort of connection with her, some sort of comfort and happiness in hugging a child. She was very small, cute and above all, the sister of the woman I love.

I picked her up and put her on my lap hugging her and rubbing my hand up and down her back to soothe her. I patted her ruffled hair which were so soft making me wonder how would Sophia's hair feel like. I embraced her tightly and tried to calm her down in hushed whispers, "Ssshh sshh, it's okay, I'm here. I'm right here. What happened princess?" but she was too far gone at the moment. She started to hiccup harshly when I decided to ask her later. I just tried to calm her down when I looked up at the maid who shook her shoulders. She also had no clue as to what had happened.

"Get her a glass of water. Quickly."

The maid rushed out of the room and returned back quickly with a glass of cold water. I removed the hair covering her

## Chapter 17

face, when I brought the glass to her lips. Her eyes were puffy red from crying and a tear leaked out which gave me a deep pang in my chest.

It hurt me to see her like this when I removed the tear with the pad of my thumb. She downed the glass of water in less than a second which was astonishing. I asked her if she wanted more to which she refused. I rubbed her back again when I asked, "Good now?"

She nodded a silent yes when I asked her again, "What happened princess? Tell me."

Tears started to pool in her eyes again when she started to hiccup badly. Oh lord, please don't make her cry. I had no clue as how to behave when someone cried. I just didn't know what to do. Between ragged breaths, she said the last thing I was expecting to hear when my blood ran cold, "Sissy, sissy. I found sissy in bathroom, she she she….. she was covered in blood-" and that's it.

My mind went blank, I didn't hear what she said next and all I could hear was Everleigh's voice echoing in my mind. Blood, blood, blood. It was ringing in my ears as if to mock me, as if to laugh at me and hold my heart in its bare hands and squeeze it painfully. Not hearing anything else, I quickly jumped on my feet, placed Everleigh on the ground and rushed out while giving an order to the maid, "Take care of her."

I couldn't understand anything. Just the thought of my angel in blood left me feeling hollow. Taking three steps at a time, I rushed up the stairs, quickly making way to her room when I barged in. I quickly scanned the room to find her nowhere when the bathroom door was open and I ran inside just to advance further to my horror.

I. Felt. Like. Tying. Myself. Up. And. Making. Myself. Suffer. For. Everything. That. I. Had. Done. To. Her.

The air in the bathroom was humid and hot and stank of blood. There were splotches of blood on the ground, the tub was full of bloody red water and I could just make out the top of her head. She was immersed in water when I ran and pulled her out. My queen was pale, she was deathly pale and so……….so weak. I didn't know when it had happened, what had happened, how it happened and why the fuck had it happened when I brought her close to my chest and …… ….I started to cry.

Never ever in my life had I cried for anyone other than my mother, which was fifteen years ago when she left me, but today I cried. I cried for the woman I loved, for the woman I wanted to spend my entire life with. For the woman I wanted to have a family with. My heart broke into a million pieces and I was sure I might never heal again. There was hardly any chance after this suicide attempt of Sophia.

Cradling her in my arms, not caring whether my clothes was getting dirtily wet or not, I rushed out and placed her on the bed when I noticed her wrists. They were cut badly and blood was still coming out profusely meaning she had just

## Chapter 17

done it some while ago. I ran to the bathroom, opened the closet in a frantic search for any two pieces of cloth when luckily, I found them. My coat was too big and wouldn't have covered both properly the way I wanted.

Running out, I called Massimo, putting the phone on speaker and shouted to call a doctor quickly. I wrapped the cloth around her wrist to stop more blood from flowing out when I just looked at her sleeping form.

Why my gorgeous, why?

She looked bruised, pained, helpless, hopeless yet strangely calm. She was lying there not knowing what was happening, not knowing what I was going through and there I was, standing there and crying my eyes out. I cursed myself. She did this because of me. I had found a razor lying in the bathroom when I felt shame, I felt disgusted and sick of myself. She tried to kill herself because of me. I couldn't believe it. I couldn't believe that I gave someone so much pain, so much hurt that they tried to kill themselves? Was I actually that horrible?

I tried to calm my breathing down as never in my dreams even did I expect to witness this ever. I went and sat next to her and put my fingers against her neck. Instantly, I felt more sick than before. I remember doing the exact same thing with my mum some fifteen years ago and the pained memories resurfaced, hurting me more, slashing my heart more, but I tugged it away, placed those haunted images in a drawer of my cupboard and locked the compartment, hiding the cupboard in the deepest pits of my heart forever.

I bent forward and placed my mouth next to her ear, laid the side of my head against the side of her face when I painfully whispered knowing she can't hear me, "Please wake up angel, I-i-" It was hard, it was too damn hard. I couldn't and I didn't want to but there was no other way, there was no other option. I had to do it.

Taking in a deep breath I whispered, "I'll let you go my love, I'll let you leave me, please, just wake up. Don't do this, I can't handle it." Biting my lower lip and controlling my sobs I continued as I closed my eyes and touched my nose with her cheek, "I'm sorry that I hurt you Sophia, I'm sorry. Please. Just. Wake. Up".

I looked at her close eyelids and noticed how fucking beautiful she was. Her face was nothing but pure beauty, her lips, her cheeks, everything about her was so damn gorgeous. People say everyone is flawed somewhere but I disagree. My queen? My queen was flawless. She was one in a million, someone I would sacrifice anything for but that was where the problem arose. She didn't have the same feelings towards me, she didn't like being here and I wouldn't keep her against her will. I will let her go if she is happy like this.

I never believed in love before, ever. I knew it wasn't meant for me and when I did start believing, look what happened. It hurt me, it killed me, it showed me how I was meant to suffer and now I was ready. This was the last time I had fallen in love and failed. Never would I fall for it again and as the

## Chapter 17

man I was, I was used to never giving up, I was used to going till the last of my strengths and winning but I was tired now.

I was sore from all the fighting and for the first time in my fucking life, I gave up. I gave up that there was a chance for Sophia and I, for an us to be an **us**. It was all over and I wouldn't go after her now. That. Was. Decided.

Heaving a sigh, I decided that the moment she feels better, I'll arrange her a flight back to America with guards still around her for her safety and I'll forget she ever existed.

Someone knocked on the door and opened it, when I saw Doctor Bills peaking his head through. I nodded at him, heaved a sigh and got off the bed for him to inspect her. He undid the knots on her wrist and began to look after her when I felt anger course through my body. I didn't like anyone touching my queen, my angel when I mocked an internal laugh.

But was she mine though?

# Chapter 18

## ASHTON

Doctor bills bandaged her arms and cleaned up the blood while Massimo called in a maid to tidy up the bathroom. Sophia was lying still which agitated me. I wanted her to move, to give me a sign that she was awake, that she was here, with me, but she didn't even move an inch, let alone a muscle. Doctor Bills turned towards me, "Boss she has lost a lot of blood and we need to give her a transfusion. I just took a sample, now I need to rush to the lab to have a quick look to see her blood type-" when I interrupted.

"No need. Massimo, the file you made for her, can you have a look at what her blood type is?"

## Chapter 18

Massimo gulped when he said, "I never had a look at that."

Giving him one of my best glares, I looked back at the doctor, "Rush. I don't have that much of a time. And let me know the results ASAP."

He nodded and rushed out, Massimo following along. I sat next to her and removed the few strands of her hair sticking to her forehead. Drying some off the water left on her face, I half closed my left hand and moved my fingers against her cheek and felt fire erupt in my body. They were so soft and so beautiful. Fuck, anyone could fall for her, just have a look at me.

I was sitting, staring into nothingness when my phone rang.

"Boss her blood type is O negative which is quite rare. Does anybody have that?"

"I'll check and inform you. Give me a minute."

I hung up and ran out looking for Massimo who was standing at the far end. I told him how we needed samples of O negative blood when he started asking everyone through his earpiece. After a painful wait of two minutes, we had no one, no donor, no one to give blood. No one had that blood type. What the fuck?

We were running out of time and Sophia needed it. Hell, she needed it bad. Doctor Bills didn't have any sample available in his hospital. The nearby hospitals were short of blood as well when the atmosphere around me darkened.

I knew one man who had that blood type but I had vowed to never talk to him. I had vowed to not even see his bloody face again as I? I hated him, I loathed him. I could strangle him and break his neck in half if he was to ever come in front of me but it was my angel we were talking about. She was going through life and death and I would be selfish if I brought my problems and my ego in. I would do anything for her, would go to any lengths to protect her even if it meant stepping aside my ego, breaking the damn wall I had built for over seventeen years. I was ready to give it all up. I was ready to throw it all away.

I took out my phone, found his contact and with a deep breath was about to dial, when Massimo shouted, "FOUND IT!"

I breathed a sigh of relief. Massimo didn't wait for my orders and just started to run in the opposite direction when he shouted at me, "YOU STAY WITH HER, I'LL GET IT."

I nodded, realizing later that he couldn't see me nodding my head but I didn't care. I slowly made my way to her room and sat next to her.

I wouldn't let you go angel before you heal.

\*

Phoenix, one of my people who was in charge of the weapons

## Chapter 18

in the warehouse had that blood type and he rushed to the hospital to donate it. Doctor Bills ran into the room and I immediately stepped aside when he started to attach the IV tubes to Sophia.

It was injected into her arm and blood was being given to her through a cannula. Doctor Bills attached an oxygen mask so she could breathe and get enough oxygen in her body. Seeing her like this made me lifeless. I felt hollow, completely empty, devoid of emotions or any other type of feelings. Why? Why did she try to hurt herself? If she was feeling this way, she could have come to me and just hit me as much as she wanted. I was the one to put her in this situation, she was hurting because of me and she was the one who was suffering whereas I should be on that bed, dying, leaving this world, leaving everything behind. Not her.

After a fairly large amount of time her breathing became normal and the colour started returning to her face. I breathed a sigh of relief and thanked God for saving her. I made a mental note to reward Phoenix for that.

I got up, readjusted the covers and took a look at her sleeping angelic face before I bent down, placed a soft kiss on her left cheek and left the room to go look for Everleigh.

*

Peeking in through the living room, she was sitting with Lily, arms draped around each other and was watching a movie, but her face told that she wasn't concentrating much. Not finding the energy to break her warm embrace with Lily, I turned around and went to the gym to take my frustration out.

I kept hitting the punching bag to a point my hands were bleeding, my skin was burning hot, it was cut apart and blood was seeping out but somehow, I was numb. I couldn't feel the pain. I couldn't feel anything. There was sweat pooling all around my body and my hair were sticking to my face when I got up and went to my office where I started to drink.

Anything to calm me down.

Anything to silent my thoughts.

Anything to prevent me from going insane.

Literally. Anything.

# Chapter 19

## SOPHIA

I woke up with a groan to see IV drips and an oxygen mask attached to me. Confusedly, I took off the mask and felt more comfortable than before. I wasn't feeling any pain, any kind of discomfort anymore. On the contrary, I was feeling numb. My body felt heavy and I found it difficult to move.

I wanted to sit up which became hard for me when I turned on my side and sliding slowly, I tried to get up into a sitting position. After a lot of effort, I finally managed to sit up and relaxed against the bedrest.

I looked at my left, then at my right and tried to remember what had happened. I was getting blood, that I could see, and another bottle was attached which looked like glucose to me, the room was exceptionally clean, there was no sign of Everleigh, my body was numb and my head felt heavy. What the hell happened? I was racking my brain hard to think when the door slightly opened and *he* peeked his head through. I swear I instantly felt happy, light and giddy. Whenever I saw him, I felt content, peaceful and above all, safe. No one had ever made me feel like that before but he did.

I was practically itching to throw myself at him and hug him when he took a harsh intake of breath and ran towards me. He placed his hand on my forehead and cheeks, attempting to check my temperature which by the look at his expressions was normal. He became slack and slowly sat on the bed next to me and looked me in the eye.

"How are you?"

His deep, dark voice always managed to do wonders to me.

"Huh?"

"How are you?"

I was confused. Why all of a sudden was he asking me how was I?

I shrugged, "Fine, I guess. My head feels a bit heavy and my body feels numb. But other than that, I'm fine."

## Chapter 19

Furrowing my brows together, I leaned forward when I asked, "What happened?"

He looked at me as if he couldn't believe what I had asked, when he ignored my question and asked his own, "Do you need water?"

I instantly felt that my throat was dry when I nodded. He got up, went to pour me a glass and came back taking large handsome strides. He brought the glass of water close to my lips and I attempted to hold it but he swatted my hand away and helped me down it down. Okay, that was new. Him swatting away my hand was something brand new.

I gulped down the water which was very refreshing and I could feel it going down my body giving me a sense of comfort somehow. He asked me again, "How are you feeling now?"

I nodded and whispered, "Okay" when he grabbed my left hand which was resting on the bed and squeezed it. His calloused hands felt so soft, warm and comforting. I kept staring at our intertwined hands and at his thumb rubbing the back of my hand when I asked again, "What happened?"

He looked unsure when he asked, "Are you hungry?"

WHAT WAS WRONG WITH HIM? And come to think of it, I suddenly felt hungry and my stomach started growling. The corner of his lips just twitched a bit into a smile but it was gone there and then when he got up and was about to leave when I harshly grabbed his arm, "Tell me, what happened?"

He narrowed his eyes and forehead in uncertainty, "You don't remember?"

I nodded my head no.

He took a deep breath when he opened his mouth to say something but closed it and in a rush just said, "Ignore it. Just... just focus on recovering. Okay?"

Oh. My. God. I hated this and this was seriously annoying me. I scowled when I narrowed my eyes into slits and looked at him. He finally did give in when he whispered in a low voice that I had to bend forward to hear him clearly, "You tried to take your own life."

And that's when I remembered, I had tried to kill myself. The events of yesterday's attack came back into my mind with the force of a truck. The uncontrolled panic attack, me running in a frantic search to find him but failing miserably, then rushing in the bathroom, filling the tub with water, cutting my wrists with the razor, sinking in the tub and submerging myself in the water. Oh God. I sat back and drew my knees together in shame.

Everyone knew, everyone knew the coward that I was and there was nothing I could do about it. Nothing at all. The damage was done.

He hurriedly came and sat next to me and took me in a warm

## Chapter 19

hug. It was so sweet and I was swooning. I loved him so much. He rubbed my back and kept saying comforting words to me when I started to cry. I felt ashamed, disgusted and I hated my existence. He moved my arms apart and brought my face up. Worry was laced in his eyes when he came more closer and kept shushing me. He proceeded to remove the tears from the roughness of his palm and I even liked that, it felt so soft, so……..peaceful.

He kept on talking and trying his best to make me feel better when I gradually calmed down. My breathing became normal when I asked the next question I was dreading the most.

"Who found me?"

He tried to divert the question but I wasn't having it. I insisted when he finally gave in, "Your sister."

Shame clouded my eyes when I covered my face with my hands and cried my eyes out. He tried to move my hands apart but I wouldn't budge. What a shame? My little sister finding me in that state? It would haunt her for the rest of her life and I didn't want that. Witnessing a suicide, especially at a young age was never healthy.

I couldn't stop crying when I felt myself being lifted up. He placed me on his lap when I was straddling him and pulled me close when I rested my head on his shoulder and just hugged him, sobbing and letting my emotions off of my shoulders. He hugged me back tightly which was hell comforting and we just sat there in silence for a long time when my breathing became normal and my crying slowed down.

Sometimes all you need is someone to hug you, someone to embrace you showing automatically that things will be okay. And today was the first time in my entire life that I was getting that and this was the man giving that to me. Something I never expected. He let me cry all that I wanted as he kept sitting there with me, and surprisingly, I felt quite light after my episode.

I removed my arms and just sat in his lap with my face down in embarrassment, when he lifted my chin up and gazed into my eyes. I swore they were so beautiful. Raging steel grey, so beautiful that one could easily get lost in them. We were so close together, sharing the same breath when he asked me, "Shall I bring food now?"

I made a pout and nodded a yes when he smiled a bit, placed me on the bed and told me to wait. He left the room leaving me in complete shock.

He smiled.

He fucking smiled.

Oh my croissants! I was so happy. So. Goddamn. Happy.

I had hardly seen him smile since the day I came here but he did smile today, even if it was just for a bit. And it was so fucking gorgeous. I craved to see it again when I giggled in

## Chapter 19

front of no one. If living a second with this man brought me this much of happiness, I couldn't imagine what a whole life would feel like. And I was ready to strive for it.

*

I was sitting staring at the wall when the door opened and he walked in with two plates in his hands. I smiled silently to myself as he looked cute though. He came and sat next to me and handed me a plate.

I wanted to meet Everleigh but I hardly had time with him alone so I decided to let it be, I wanted to be with him. He eased a bit and sat half cross legged on the bed, rigidness still evident in his posture, screaming away his power. After a few seconds, he tried to start small talk with me, but he was horrible. Extremely horrible, which was extremely fine by me. I chuckled when I began the conversation.

We spent nearly half an hour talking, chuckling a bit and sharing veryyyyy smallll secret smiles when I felt better. I felt light, as if all the burden had been lifted off of my shoulders. I wanted to sleep with him tonight but I knew it was too fast and I didn't know for sure how he felt about me especially after my suicide attempt. I feared he would want to stay away from me now and I would understand his reasoning. Who would want a suicidal person as their wife or their girlfriend? No one.

I was lost in my thoughts when he snapped his fingers in front of my face, "Where are you lost?"

Obviously I wouldn't tell him that I was thinking about him, so I said the first thing which came to my mind, "I wanted to meet Everleigh."

He swallowed his piece of food when he nodded and got up but before I could stop him to let him finish his dinner first, he was already out. Hmm. He did walk fast. Impressive.

After about a few minutes, the door was thrown off its hinges when I saw a wide-eyed Munchkin running towards me when she threw herself into my arms. She hit my chest hard and hugged me when I just giggled and hugged her back. I ruffled her hair asking her, "How are you munchkin?"

She just whipped her head up and looked at me, "How are youuu?"

"I'm fine munchkin, much better."

Her lips pouted as if she was about to cry, "But I saw you in blood."

I felt bad for her when I embraced her to calm her down but she forcefully pushed me away and moved back. She looked at me and tried her best to glare at me, with painful tears swarming in her eyes when she whispered, pointing her small finger at me as if warning when a small teardrop left her eye, strolling gracefully down her cheek, "I don't want you to leave me ever. Don't leave me please. Promise me you won't."

## Chapter 19

I looked up blinking away the tears when I saw him standing close to us, watching all of this. I picked her up and just hugged her tightly when we both started to cry. I never loosened my grip on her when I heard a faint whisper, 'I'm sorry', but when I looked up, the door had closed softly and he had already left the room.

What? Why would he say sorry?

# Chapter 20

## ASHTON

We were on our way to the meeting I had been looking forward to since a very long time. We were one of the best and the most strongest mafias to ever exist and I wouldn't let that fall apart. At all. I had spent my entire life building this empire and holding it up. I had spilt my own blood a numerous amount of times that now I had lost count. I had laid half dead and unconscious that now, I don't even remember how many times. All partial thanks to my dearest of a father.

I couldn't forget that man. And neither did I intend to. Ever. I cannot forget two kinds of people, one: who are the reason for my happiness and two: who are the real fuckers. I cannot

## Chapter 20

forget these two people and my dad was one of them. I just cannot erase the memory of what he made me go through since I was barely even six. I just cannot magically forget what the type of fucked up shit he did with my mother and how she suffered.

No.

Never.

I cannot forget that and that was partially the reason I never wanted to call him to ask for blood for Sophia in the very first place but my angel was more important than the old man, the reason for my fucked up world, for the suffering, never ending darkness. I hated him but now was not the time to ruin my mood by his pleasant memory of the fucked up shit he had done.

I had been waiting to sign this contract all my life with the French. I always made sure that we had heavy amount of ammunition than any other mafia empires, that we always had up to date, latest weapons, skilled armed force, fearless, lifeless, emotionless thug of a warriors. I always made sure of that.

The new guns manufactured by the French were to come in the market in two days but they had contacted me first to check if I was interested because I had managed to maintain a good reputation in the mafia world. And obviously, I was interested, damn interested and ready to buy them for whatever price.

The French had always been good at making weapons, machinery and stuff like that, and I had always preferred purchasing some from them. Since I got the threatening letter about Sophia, I had been working on strengthening my security more and though we didn't need new weapons, I still decided to upgrade them. Just in case.

We were about to reach the club where I was invited to make the deal when my phone rang.

James.

James was one of my guards. I was confused that why did he call me just moments after I left home when I picked up the call, "Yes?"

"Boss, Tara wants to speak to you, says it's urgent."

I narrowed my brows in confusion, "Okay."

Tara was one of the kitchen maids and I was confused as to what did she want to talk to me about? Obviously, I hadn't given her my number, not every person had my number as it was hell confidential.

She took the phone and spoke, "Boss, we have an intruder and I don't know what to do with her."

"Her?"

"Yes Boss."

## Chapter 20

"Hmm. Lock her up in the basement, I'll attend to her."

"Yes Boss."

And with that I hung up. Wow! This was the first time I had gotten a call for a female intruder. She must be a daring one I must say. I laid my head against the seat when another thought came into my mind. An intruder! How the fuck did someone enter the house? I made sure that the security was damn tight. If someone broke in the house this early into the game………I decided to hold up a meeting later to knock some fear and sense of responsibility into my men because this meant that Sophia and Everleigh were not safe in my own house. At all.

The car stopped outside the club and the driver opened the door for me. I got out of the car when I took off my Raybans, readjusted my suit, straightened my cufflinks and entered the club.

I was met with a whoosh of cold air and a brain splitting headache. The music was blasting at full volume to a point it was annoying me. There were plenty of half-naked girls dancing around the dance floor with half-drunk males clinging to them, which was quite cringy. Yes, I liked to be a bit PDA if it ever came with Sophia but for God's sake, not like this. Anyone entering could clearly see that more than half of the population was drunk. Drunk out of their fucking minds.

Pushing through people, I tried to make my way across the

floor but it was too damn hard. There were so many people pushing and swaying here and there, I wanted to do nothing but just spread my arms and push past them.

I forcefully started to make my way through when I felt some sharp nails on my arm and someone tugged me, when I instantly slowed down in my path a bit but not to the point where I could fall as I had kept my stance rigid. Because if any enemy comes to hurt, then falling is clearly not the first thing that would help my case.

I looked back to see a young girl with heavily lidded eyes, a bright red lipstick on, a black miniskirt and a high ponytail, pulled me towards her and groped me. Like, she literally groped me. I instantly flared in anger when I pushed her hands away as I had decided not to touch any woman as I had my eyes on Sophia. Not even a single one.

I gave her a glare when she again grabbed my hands and started to pull me when I had had enough. Already the music was giving me a headache, and the last thing I wanted was, was to deal with a drunk prostitute. I wasn't interested in that thing anymore as the only woman who had caught my eyes was still at home and I'd rather do it with her than anyone else. Anyone else would be straight up sickening.

Pulling my arm harshly, I raised a finger to explain to her how I was not interested when the bitch just threw her arms around my neck and clung harshly to me when I felt her tongue lick the back of my neck. I straightaway felt revolted and wanted to puke when as swiftly as I could in a quick

## Chapter 20

motion, I took out my gun, pushed her back and laid the muzzle of my gun to her forehead, cocking it to make sure she heard that it was loaded and not on safety. Her features instantly became serious when realization dawned on her of the situation she was in.

"Back. Off."

She staggered back and stared at my raised gun when I looked at her and asked in a deadly tone, "Understood?"

She seemed at a loss for words and was swaying owing to how drunk she was, but she just nodded.

I said a low, "Good", tucked the gun in my waistband and turned around to make my way towards the VIP room. I hadn't noticed that the noise had lessened and many people were looking at me, staring and shaking in fear, while many were still drunk, dancing madly, unaware that right in their vicinity was a deadly mafia boss with a gun raised at one of their own kinds. But no. They were busy dancing like baboons. I ignored the cartoons and looked at the people who were still in their senses, displaying open fear and I loved that. I loved it when people used to cower in fear. I smirked and went upstairs.

\*

The door to the VIP room opened and I walked inside, accompanied by none other than Massimo. The French leader, Augustin stood up from his chair and extended his

## The Mafia And His Lost Queen

hand towards us. I went up and shook it when he gestured for me to take a seat on the chair placed in front of the desk when I sat and eased out, placing the ankle of my right foot over my left knee showing to them how I was low of guard when in reality, I could get up and start a fight any minute. Massimo also sat beside me but with a straightened posture.

"Bonjour Monsieur, long time no see huh."

I displayed a forced smile. "Yes yes, you are quite right. Been quite busy actually."

He sat a bit forward and joined his hands together nodding, "I know I know. I can understand. How's the mafia going brother?"

My jaw clenched at the word brother, anger surging past my body like lava as I was no brother to him and vice versa, but I didn't show it to him as I replied, "It's good. Going perfect actually." I couldn't show anyone that we were getting threats. It would be more dangerous.

"Obviously obviously, who am I asking." He chuckled.

To display a little bit of an act, I had to laugh as well and that's exactly what I did, but I chuckled. I didn't laugh because…
………I mean what a waste of time. My rule was and always had been, come, meet me, get to the point, then fuck off and bye. I had always hated these greetings and how are you and how is your family and how are your servants and is there water still coming in your bathroom? Like………..what the

## Chapter 20

fuck. Just get straight to the bloody point man.

"Would you like to eat anything?" He asked politely but I guess my patience level was running low when I respectfully refused, "No. I was actually in a hurry so I came here for the deal so let's get straight to the point."

He clearly wasn't expecting this by his face expressions and honestly, I didn't give a fuck. I wasn't here to please other people or whatever. He relaxed back in his seat and took a long breath, as if in deep thought. I felt something was wrong as I could easily sense it. His guards shuffled around nervously and looked back and forth between Augustin and I.

I narrowed my eyes and looked at Massimo asking the silent question, making sure to keep my expressions totally normal, not at all showing any kind of alarm, when his eyes gave me the answer. Good. Our guards as well were high on alert outside. Massimo deliberately didn't nod to not let it slip that we were communicating about our army outside. Hidden, in case, anything happened which surely could. Anything could happen in the mafia world.

Augustin scratched his small beard when he beckoned one of his guards to come and told him to bring the supplies. The young man hurried out while Augustin poured some alcohol and gave each one of us a glass but obviously, I didn't want to drink it owing to what staring game just took place making everything suspicious, but to keep their eyes covered with mud, I still pretended to drink some to show that I didn't suspect anything for them to carry out whatever they wanted to in front of my eyes, as I would observe.

Placing my hand inside the pocket of my suit pants, I silently pressed the emergency button once of the mini remote I carried, which was my way of showing for every guard outside to remain as active as possible as anything could happen.

Pressing the button twice meant for them to barge inside and attack. Knowing my force was strong, I focused back on the meeting and took out a pack of cigarettes, placing it on the table to show Augustin as to why I had placed my hands inside my pocket. To lower the suspicions from my side.

We were sitting, making small talk when the door opened and two heavy boxes came in and were placed on the desk. Augustin got up and readjusted his belt when he opened the boxes and took out the guns and GOD WHAT THE FUCK! They were bloody gorgeous. I loved them instantly as they were so goddamn beautiful. They were practically shining and showing off when I knew I had to buy them. I just fucking knew it.

He sat back on his seat and gave one to me to hold and one himself. He relaxed back and started talking, "This is the finest productions I have made so far, its' aim is perfect as fuck, it's neither too light to hold, neither to heavy, rather its moderate which I guess is ideal for using." He glanced at Massimo at this before looking back at me and continuing, "Have a look at its aim, it's the best you could ever get."

## Chapter 20

And sure enough, when I checked it, the aim was actually clear as glass and perfect as fuck. I looked at Augustin, cocked an eyebrow and pointed to a clear glass resting in one of his cabinets in his office, "A shot?"

He chuckled and nodded, "Sure sir. Whatever you wish."

He looked at one of his guards and instructed him to take the glass out of the glass cabinet. Loading the gun with a clip, I stood up from my seat. Everyone was dead quiet observing my next movement, when the glass was very very far from me as his office was huge. It was a difficult aim but not something that I had never done before. A newbie possibly couldn't do this at all but I hell fucking could.

I momentarily dangled my right arm by my side and clenched my fist, holding out two fingers in a way that no one could see which was a sign for Massimo to stay alert. He shifted in his seat meaning he had seen and acknowledged when I strengthened my stance, stood with my feet a few centimeters apart, brought the gun up till my elbow, in front of my face, closed an eye and focused on the object in front of me when I slowly placed my finger over the trigger, my finger never shaking even for a bit.

And anytime now?

That glass would be laying broken all over the fucking floor. I counted till two and on the count of three, pressed the trigger when a shot rang out and the next thing we heard, was the sound of glass breaking and pieces falling gracefully onto the floor, scattering around like a broken ice queen, shining like a beautiful damsel in distress but a fucking broken soul who just needed her knight in shining armour to fix her.

Bullseye.

I lowered the gun and looked at Augustin when I nodded. It was so fucking beautiful, so gorgeous. The gun was screaming royalty, expensiveness and I was so down to buy it. It's shiny black colour, smooth surface, clean barrel, more area to load the bullets. The perfect thing I could ever ask for.

He continued, "It took me nearly ten years to build this model and no one has ever built of this type, you can have a look around the market-" and this was where he was interrupted by the buzzing of my phone. I looked at the caller ID to see- Marco calling me? Why would the house guard call me? I excused myself and started talking in a low voice.

"Yes?"

"Are you kidding me Mr. Extremely Rude?" Sophia's voice entered my ears and I fought the most hardest urge not to smile in front of everyone because that could arise suspicions and give it away because I never smiled. Just the mere mention of her name was soothing, her voice was just the cherry on top. But the question was what had I done now? Excusing myself and just glancing at Massimo, I walked outside, closed the door and then talked with her.

## Chapter 20

"What?"

"What is wrong with you? Why did you do this? Can I get a good reason huhhhh?"

"Did what?"

"What did she do to you? She is, believe me, as innocent as I am here, but all I'm thinking is that what the fuck is wrong with you?"

What? WHAT? WHATTTTTTT? What did I actually do?

"Did you have breakfast darling?"

"ARE YOU FUCKING KIDDING ME?"

Somehow the word 'fuck' coming out of her mouth turned me on even more but now was not the time.

I took in a deep breath, pinched the bridge of my nose and calmed myself down, "Angel, what did I do?"

"Why did you lock Everleigh in your *prison*?" She spat mockingly.

Wait what? When did I do that?

"Angel, I never did that. Who told you?"

"Well, believe me or not but my little sister is down there

crying her eyes out and screaming and sweating and..........
where are you?" She ranted in a single breath.

"I'm in a meeting at the moment but explain to me. What happened? Why is she in the baseme-" and that's when it clicked me. Tara. She thought Everleigh was the intruder.

What the heck!

"Angel, I'll call you back."

She was saying something when I disconnected the call. Calling James and asking him to give the phone to Tara, she spoke after a few seconds, "Yes Boss?"

I was about to say something when she interrupted, "And Boss, the intruder has been locked up and don't worry at all, we are safe. She wanted to pee when I remembered what you do so I snatched her from her hair and made her pee in the cellar. She is damn scared I have to say."

She seemed so proud of herself and I was so horrified. My eyes widened in complete shock when no voice came out. I tried to speak but it was as if my tongue had died.

"Boss?"

"Tara. Explain to me how did she look?"

She seemed a bit confused while replying, "Umm, cute? Sweet and very little. She was wearing a pink frock and

## Chapter 20

was running around and OH GOD. BOSS, she was stealing."

I swear I was about to pass out and die on the spot. How did these people come out of their mother's womb was beyond my understanding.

I closed my eyes, trying so damn hard to control the tone of my voice when I asked in a strained one, "What did she steal?"

She said in a breathy rush as if I would reward her for catching a thief, "Boss, she stole cupcakes. Although it isn't much but boss, stealing is stealing."

I slapped my hand on my forehead, the voice coming out loud when I angrily whispered, "Tara, are you out of your fucking mind?"

"Why Boss?" Confusion was evident in her tone.

"Tara, she is Ms. Sophia's younger sister. Have you gone completely berserk?"

Before she could say anything I angrily interrupted, "Uh, berserk means extremely fucking mad like a donkey, which you are at the moment."

She sucked in a harsh breath and quickly ended the call before saying, "Let me fix this Boss."

I rolled my eyes in annoyance when I called Marco.

"Yes Boss?"

"Can you give Ms. Sophia the phone?"

"Yes Boss, she is standing right here."

I heard some shuffling when I heard her melodious voice, "Well?" I could picture her tapping her foot, arms crossed with a scowl on her face. Beautiful.

"Angel, princess is in your room, I'll come back and talk to you, I'm in a meeting. And sorry for whatever happened, a stupid person did a stupid mistake because their brain was high on idiotology."

She huffed an angry okay and disconnected the call. Another problem to look after to.

*

I massaged my temples and eased the tension a bit when I went inside again. We talked for about half an hour about the guns and the new weapons when I got tired and wanted to go home.

"I'll buy both of your boxes. Name the price and I'm ready to pay."

"Monsieur, they are a bit expensive as I said, these are one of the bes-"

## Chapter 20

"Price?" I had heard enough of that they were the best and all, he had to cut it short.

He suddenly became serious, "I won't charge you."

Huh? "What do you mean?"

"Let's play the barter system Mr. Romanno." He relaxed back in his chair and just looked at me intertwining his hands together.

I was confused when I asked, "What do you mean?"

"You take the guns and pay nothing, just to give me back one thing in return. I won't charge you even a single penny, that's my promise and I can guarantee you these guns won't wear out. That, I promise."

"What do you want in return?"

He leaned forward, looked me deep in the eye when only two words left his mouth stopping my entire fucking world.

"Sophia Greene."

# Chapter 21

## ASHTON

All I could hear was just a shrill bleeping noise and nothing else. And that noise too, seemed far away, where I couldn't quite figure out the source. My blood ran cold, I could feel the colour draining from my face and I was quiet. I was dead silent as I couldn't believe what I had just heard. It was as if I was frozen to the spot by some spell and I couldn't even move a limb. I felt hollow. Empty. As if the world had just ended.

And suddenly, all of that feeling converted into rage. Pure anger, loath, rage. I just saw blood everywhere. My surroundings appeared red when I could practically feel the arteries about to burst in my head. How. Dare. He? How

## Chapter 21

dare he tried to involve my queen in this and lay her on a platter for everyone to feed on, to aim on, to shoot on and to rip her apart on?

How dare that instead of fighting directly with me in a battlefield like a man should, he involved my girl into this? MY GIRL? How. Fucking. Dare. He? I was growing mad to a point I could feel my ears, face and my forehead getting hot. I wasn't in my senses anymore.

As if on impulse, I jumped out of my seat, bent over his desk and harshly gripped him by his collar jerking him forward when I swiftly took the gun out from my waistband and placed it on his forehead, my teeth gritting in anger and my mind ablazing in flames like never. I was seething in fury. This motherfucker had the audacity to involve my girl in his bullshit of a mess. I definitely wouldn't let that happen. I promised that I wouldn't let Sophia get hurt in any way and this man wouldn't be able to even touch her. I, for once, will make sure of that.

Suddenly the temperature of the room shifted. I had my gun pointed towards Augustin and Massimo was aiming at one of his men while they had their guns pointed towards us. We were outnumbered. Heavily. They were approximately around ten of them and just the two of us.

Augustin wasn't fazed by the sudden commotion. He calmly looked into my eyes when I whispered, "Tell your goddamn useless of a dogs to lower their fucking weapons or you know what I can do."

He looked into my eyes, thinking through his thought process and chewed the inside of his cheek which just fueled more anger within me. After a few seconds, as I suddenly strengthened my hold around his collar to a point where he could choke, maintaining eye contact with me, he ordered them, "Boys, lower your weapons." They obeyed him but I wasn't ready to disarm myself. Hell no.

Suddenly, I was worried about Sophia. I had no idea if she was safe at home and currently, I was in no position to call backup for myself, let alone call home to know whether my queen was okay or not.

I inhaled and kept looking at him, talking in a low voice with him that only we could hear ourselves for the time being. There was a possibility that he was recording our conversation but I didn't give a fuck and there was a possibility that he was bluffing to confirm that I had Sophia, or that maybe I finally had a girl in my life which they could use as my weak point obviously, but the fact that he took her full name was what confirmed that he knew.

I spoke, "How the fuck do you know about her?"

I was freaking from the inside that how did he know but I kept my hand firm on his collar and my gun steady on his forehead, something that I had mastered at the age of seven. To remain calm when nothing was calm.

He looked me deep in the eyes for a few seconds and just began to chuckle. I didn't pinch my eyes close in frustration

## Chapter 21

as I wanted to, but keeping the aperture same, I let the lens of my eyes contract in anger when I clenched my fist hating this as this attitude always angered me. This wasn't how I had expected the meeting to go. Trying to calm myself down as much as possible as I didn't want to lose my shit right now, I asked again, pronouncing each word with a good heavy break, "Motherfucker. How. Do. You. Know. About. Her?"

He laughed out loud when I completely lost it. I turned my gun towards the roof and fired a total of two rounds, the noise resonating around the room when I heard men moving from behind when I pointed my gun at them and said, my voice ringing through the whole atmosphere as clear as day with my eyes all the while on Augustin, "One move, one aim and you'll end up in hell. Drop the guns."

They looked at Augustin who just nodded and they all lowered their weapons. Pointing the muzzle of my gun back towards him, pressing it against his forehead harshly, I asked in a deadpan tone, "How?"

The fucker furrowed his forehead as if in deep thought, displaying a pathetic play when he got up, came and stood in front of me and raised both of his hands as if in surrender, "Ashton, I don't intend to fight. I don't want to start a fight. Just give me what I want and we will part as great friends."

"You hell wouldn-"

"We just need the girl and in exchange you can have all these guns-"

Everything in me snapped when I pushed him backwards harshly, laid the gun against his head and grabbed his neck. I. Was. Seething. In. Anger. My nostrils were flaring in rage when I looked at him, "First of all, she isn't an object that you refer to her as an it. Second of all, she isn't someone whose body I'll sell to disgusting pigs like you to taint on, use on and fucking sin on it to get your shit load of a fucking shipment in return. Thirdly, how do you know about her, is what I'm asking for the last time you son of a bloody bitch."

"Are you sure you want to start a fight Ashton? You are outnumbered."

I retorted back immediately, maintaining eye level, "I was always sure when I stepped into this game Augustin. No need to ask me whether I'm hesitant or not."

But he was right about me being outnumbered *for the time being*. One of the rules in my mafia was to never show your enemy what you are really feeling. Especially fear. Or the sense that you yourself realize that you are weak. Never. I looked at him and had just opened my mouth to speak when he sighed and interrupted, "Ashton, I don't need her for myself."

"Then?"

He sighed, "Just.......for a friend of mine."

This angered me further when I moved and pressed my gun brutally under his jaw, "What do you even mean by all the

## Chapter 21

crap leaving your mouth? And. Tell. Me. Everything."

He relaxed against my hold, looked me in the eye and replied in a bored tone, "No".

I further pressed the gun against his neck, leaving marks that his veins were being visible now, "Spill."

"Shoot me."

I knew what game this fucker was playing. Obviously I couldn't kill him, he knew about Sophia and some other person too according to him. If I killed him, his party would get sure and my girl would be in more danger than she already is. And right now, I needed to coax information out of him.

"Go on. Shoot me Ashton. It would do you no good. Hell, you wouldn't know how I got to know about your angel." He laughed mockingly at me when I felt weak. For the first time I felt powerless. How did he know I called Sophia angel. What was happening? I had the same thought again that the traitor might be one of my own men but they had sworn on my dead mother's grave. How can they lie? I mentally shook my head. Somebody else was the traitor and I couldn't figure it out.

I came closer to him and gritting my teeth, I dangerously whispered, "I don't care. Tell me."

He started laughing when he softly pushed my gun to the side, leaned forward and whispered, "Step up the game buddy."

And the next thing I knew, there were hundreds of bullets flying across the room. Augustin's fucking dogs opened fire and started shooting us. I threw him aside and hid behind his table, occasionally peeking to fire back. My heart was racing abnormally when I heard the shatter of a window breaking and some shouting followed. People were screaming when only Sophia's angelic face came into my mind.

He targeted her.

They targeted her.

And to get her, the easiest target was Everleigh which meant that the little one was also in danger.

Full of anger, I again took a glance from behind the desk and fired a headshot, one of their men dropping on the floor. I aimed at three others and shot them in a split second as they lay dead on the ground. One of them secretly jumped from the side of the table to kill me, when I pointed my gun at his under jaw and fired a bullet, momentarily slowing his stance when I aimed at his heart and fired till he fell dead in front of me. What a fucking pussy? He wasn't even wearing a bullet proof vest. Not that I was complaining though.

The shooting proceeded as I changed the clips when I heard heavy footsteps and the door burst off of its hinges and there stood my men. We just kept on firing when I suddenly collapsed on the hard cold floor and a gut-wrenching pain

## Chapter 21

pierced through my leg.

A bullet went through my left leg and I would be kidding if I said it didn't hurt me. I held it and groaned when Massimo came by my side. Not letting him look after me even for a moment, I pulled Massimo by the collar of his dress shirt, "Don't fucking care about me at the moment. Capture everyone and take them back home. Tie them up in the basement but don't do anything to them. That party is mine to entertain. Secondly, talk to Viktor through your ear piece and make sure that Sophia and Everleigh are safe. Now hurry."

I was rasping for breath when I looked at my left and saw a pool of dark crimson red blood surrounding me. It was damn painful when after about five minutes, the firing stopped but I could still hear distant screaming coming from below.

Massimo and Andreas came and hefted me up on my feet. I wanted to walk on my own but the damn bullet did hurt a lot. Putting my arm across Massimo's shoulders we made our way downstairs. The ground floor was eerily quiet and the club felt strangely empty.

*

Reaching home, I made my way limping towards the hospital wing from the backstairs to avoid running into Sophia. I didn't want her to see me in this state. Once was more than enough. It might freak her out even more than she already is. She didn't even know yet that I was in the mafia. I feared how she would react once she knows.

My huge guess was that she would want to leave me but it would be too late. I will already have left her way before than that but obviously with high ass security. Augustin might think that I have Sophia but I will make it sure that her departure is hidden from many. I never wanted to leave her but her recent stunt left me with no option.

I limped in the hospital wing when Jenna, the old nurse came running to me. She had been working here since I had opened my eyes. She was the one who had helped mom in delivering me and had helped her go through the rough pregnancy as dad was never with her. Or was barely with her.

Her forehead creased in tension, "Oh dear. What happened to you, my son?"

Since the day mom passed away, she used to call me son and I didn't mind it in the least bit.

I grunted, "Nothing much. Just some firing took place and I got hit by a bullet in my leg."

Her eyes widened in horror when she came and stood in front of me, crossed her arms together and scowled, "Oh so it's nothing?"

"I mean, I mean, yeah it's nothing, just………It's just a bullet." I somewhat ended lamely.

## Chapter 21

She huffed when she went back to her mini office and told me to lie down when I went and sat on one of the beds.

She came back with her equipment, put her glasses on the end of her crooked nose, and looked at me, "It might hurt."

I nodded when she went to work and I had to admit that it did not hurt at all. Nopes. Not in the slightest.

It?

It fucking hurt me like a sonovabitch. I closed my hand in a fist and pressed my mouth shut as painfully strong as I could in agony, when she started her work. She took the bullet out and honestly it was agonizingly painful. She treated me, wrapped up my wound and told me to lay down for at least half an hour which I declined immediately and proceeded to get up but she pushed me back down.

"Ten minutes. Please son, just rest for ten minutes."

To make sure her hard work didn't go to waste, I agreed and laid down thinking about a gazillion things when the door of the hospital wing opened and in walked Massimo.

"How are you?"

"Better. How is Sophia? Is she safe?"

"Yeah, she and Everleigh are good. They are both watching a movie in their room. I checked up on them before coming to meet you."

I nodded, "Good."

Massimo was somehow warming up next to me which was a bit suspicious but I let it go.

He wouldn't deceive me.

"We were only able to capture seventeen men. Three escaped."

I kept looking up at the ceiling when I asked, "Augustin?"

"Escaped."

I felt a new gush of hot pure anger when I jumped out of bed. Damn the ten minutes, I wouldn't spare anyone. I made my way out of the hospital, trying not limp anymore, to go and meet my special guests. The only thing on my mind was Augustin. How did he know about Sophia? Who else knew? What was he hiding? What was he planning? Where the fuck was he? All of these questions had the same answer.

No idea.

That's when I tilted my head to the side and said the only thing to Massimo which came into my mind.

"Block the roads, advance the CCTV footage at least till a thousand kilometers from here for the time being. I need

## Chapter 21

activity of transportation around my house."

\*\*\*

I trudged down the steps towards the basement when I stopped dead in my tracks. I had completely forgotten it. I mentally facepalmed myself and went into my office instead and called Doctor Bills.

"Good evening, Boss. Is everything okay?"

"Yes yes, I just wanted to ask you about Ms. Sophia's progress after the incident. How is she doing now according to you?"

"Boss, she is doing much better now, she isn't experiencing any more pain, her diet is going well and she is in good health now."

I rubbed my hand across my forehead to ease out the tension a bit, "Do you think she can travel?"

"Yes boss, of course. The car won't hurt her. Just, drive safe."

"No, I meant, travel by plane. Can she do that? Will it be okay?" My voice came out a little lighter than my usual dark voice because I couldn't let my guard down in front of the doctor but it was hard, damn hard. I never wanted to talk about this right now.

"Yes yes Boss, no issues. She is doing great."

"Okay."

I disconnected the call and threw my phone on the table. I sat on the chair letting it support my weight and closed my eyes resting my head on the desk. I never wanted to do this. I hated doing this but there was no other way. There was no other option and I couldn't do anything about it. She tried to take her life away, what could be more alarming than that? And I didn't want to hurt her anymore. I brought her here in an attempt to get close to her, to love her like the queen she was. To give her everything that she deserved. I wanted to see her smile and laugh openly in my arms in order to be able to get down on one knee one day and propose to her. But I couldn't see that day coming at all.

Everything seemed to have finished the moment I got to know about Sophia's suicide attempt. I felt my cheeks getting wet when I realized that I was crying. And I never cried.

Ever.

But here I was. As weak as a dead man, with no one to calm me down and nothing to bring happiness in my life. Someone rightly said that sometimes, you have to step out of someone's lives in order for them to be happy. You just have to leave them to see a genuine smile on their face. Even if you love them to death. You have to leave them because you love them and you want them to be happy. Always. Oh, how right that was and I was about to do the exact same thing.

I loved her to pieces but I will still let her go.

*Chapter 21*

Wiping my eyes, I turned on my laptop and booked two flights to send Sophia and Everleigh back to America.

For good.

I was done.

Everything was finished. This chapter was closed once and for all as I wouldn't fall in love ever again.

# Chapter 22

## ASHTON

The underground was exceptionally cold this time. I rubbed my hands together and blew on them to make them a bit warm. I peeked from outside and saw each one of them in a separate room. I nodded to one of the guards and entered one of the cellars.

"Bring four more here and throw the rest of them right in the opposite one so they can witness the-" I paused for a dramatic effect, "welcome."

The guard nodded and did as I told.

All four of the men were sitting in front of me, tied to a chair

## Chapter 22

with silver chains digging in their skins. There wasn't a tinge of fear in their eyes. Oh boy! Just wait for a couple more minutes. Let the fun begin.

I wore my black gloves and started circling around the four of them before I looked up and addressed the ones sitting in the opposite cellar, "Today, you guys will only be witnessing what I'll do, if these" I pointed back towards the four men sitting behind me, "don't obey me and spill everything. Today, you will just witness and you then will decide for your own self to" I started ticking on my fingers, "One, tell me everything, or-" I didn't have to complete the sentence. They already knew. "So, choose wisely."

I turned back towards the four men. Sitting on the chair placed in front of them, I rested my arms on my knees and looked at them.

"So, do I need to introduce myself?"

They were all damn quiet, none of them uttering a single word. I could feel the surroundings getting more and more cold and I could practically see the fear crawling up their skins. They weren't best at hiding their emotions. Oops! A mistake, I guess. But also a reason, they didn't belong to one of the best mafias.

I clapped my hands together, "Since all of you know me and since I do not have ample time to waste, I'll get straight to the point. My rules are simple. Answer me whenever I ask you a question or bear the consequences. I wouldn't spare a glance to your history, whether you have a family to feed, whether you have your pregnant woman or women at home to look after to, whether you have to right now go home and hand over your daughters to the love of their lives or welcome a daughter home. I. Just. Simply. Wouldn't. Give. A. Fuck.

And believe me when I say I won't, I definitely won't. I'll cut off your dicks and feed it to you, I'll rip out your fucking organs and throw the leftovers in the rubbish bins after feeding them to you, cut off your heads and send it to your families as a gift. Believe me, I'll do that. So, you better answer me."

I became quiet when I suddenly remembered, "And yes, don't even think of lying. I'll personally drop you to hell and back."

I looked at the other men in the opposite cellar and smirked to see several pair of widened eyes.

"And the same goes for you all, the only difference? Today is not your day."

I smiled when I lowered my head a bit and rubbed my hands together. After about a minute, I looked up at them, "Have you all digested that or should I explain it further?"

They didn't give an answer which angered me more than I already was. I swiveled out of my seat and slapped the nearest guy right across his face, the voice echoing around the cold chamber. There were several harsh intakes of breath.

## Chapter 22

"I. Said. Answer. Me. When. I. Ask. You. Something."

The men were practically mildly shaking when they all answered in unison, "Yes-yes."

I pulled one of the men's ears and bent down, "Yes. Sir."

They took shaky breaths and whispered, "Yes-yes sir."

I got up slowly and made my way back to my seat.

I released a breath, "So…tell me. How the fuck did Augustin know about her?"

They all lowered their heads and didn't utter a word. Yes, I was expecting that and I was ready to make them go through hell and back in order to get the information.

I again got up and started circling them. I could see their backs shaking in fear but it was all their fault. They were doing this to themselves. I stood in front of the prison bars, hands behind my straightened back looking at the men who were not being interrogated at the moment and could see them gulp in fear when I started talking, addressing to the four men sitting behind me. All the time watching the thirteen men sitting oppositely.

"You are doing this to yourself. Tell me how did Augustin know about her and I wouldn't hurt you. You delay it," I turned back facing them, "I'll make your life a living. Rotting. Hell of a mess. So, you better answer me before I get to work because one thing's for sure, I wouldn't go easy on you."

They swallowed and again lowered their heads. Such dogs!

I went and stood in front of one of them, on the extreme left, "What's your name?"

The surrounding was silent. Such pin drop silence.

He kept his head low and didn't answer me when I bent a bit and put my elbows on my knees, intertwining my hands together, "What is your name?"

The fucker remained silent when I suddenly slapped him hard.

"Mic-mic-michael."

"See, that wasn't hard."

He gulped when I harshly pulled his ear, "And Michael…….I hate it when someone stutters. So, avoid that." He nodded his head when I continued, "So Michael, what family do you have at home?"

His voice came out small and silent, that I had to bend down further to hear him, "Just a wife sir."

I nodded.

"Michael, was it a love marriage?"

## Chapter 22

He nodded.

"Hmm, I don't think your wife would enjoy spreading your ashes around. So tell me, How. Did. Augustin. Find. Out. About. Her?"

He remained quiet. Why weren't they giving up? They knew they were helpless, powerless, under THE ASHTON ROMANNO. Then, why the fuck weren't they giving up already?

I exhaled a force breath, "Okay, as you wish."

I went to the table placed at the back of the room and got a knife. I tested the blade and boy was it sharp! I slowly made my way back to Michael and stood in front of him, "You sure you don't want to answer me, Michael?"

He didn't respond which boiled the already building up anger within me. I took his right hand and placed it on his thigh and with a firm slash, cut his thumb off. He screamed in pain, the voice resonating around the underground and his thumb fell on the floor, blood immediately pooling around my feet.

"I told you, you are bringing this upon yourself. Tell me. How did Augustin know about her?"

He kept on screaming when I slapped him again and shouted in anger, "STOP SCREAMING."

He immediately quietened down and started whimpering

when I asked for the umpteenth time, "Bloody answer me will you?"

I gave him a rough two more minutes to give up but the fucker didn't. I rolled my eyes and within a mere second, cut all of his fingers off of his right hand.

His screams resonated around the room when I moved to the second person sitting on his left, not before addressing Michael, "This is just the start buddy."

I turned my attention towards the next one, "What's your name?"

"Easton, sir."

"Easton, I wouldn't waste more of my time. Answer me."

He also kept silent which was seriously annoying the fuck out of me. Why wouldn't they just give up when they knew that one day, they will have to tell me. So why go through so much of agony? So much of pain?

I ripped his shirt open, the buttons falling on the floor and slashed as many cuts as I could on his abdomen. Picking up the bottle of vinegar, I opened it and poured it on his wounds, the blood sizzling and his screams echoing around the cellar. Their screams were music to my ears now. Pure music. And I was enjoying it but was also getting pretty annoyed by them.

I stepped in front of the third one when he started whimpering. "Sir, sir, believe me I'm new. I have no idea. Sir, seriously, I had no clue. I was the bartender sir."

He started crying and I scrutinized him.

"When did you join?"

"Sir-sir two days ago. Sir, I promise I have no clue about this. I swear to God, sir."

I narrowed my eyes and folded my arms looking at him when I moved to step in front of the fourth one. He looked me dead in the eye and said out aloud, "I don't care what you do to me Ashton Romanno, but I sure as hell wouldn't let *my* boss down." emphasizing the 'my'. I chewed the inside of my cheek, looking at him when I held out my hand towards my guard, eyes still glued on him when I asked, "Pliers."

Moments ago, he was shaking, where did the sudden boldness come from?

I heard some shuffling when a heavy metal object was placed in my hands. With my left hand, I harshly tugged his lower jaw down opening his mouth and with the pliers, I cut all of his upper row teeth. He pinched his eyes close and started screaming but I didn't care. I carried on doing my work when I grabbed the knife again and slashed across his left cheek letting the blood drop. Turning back towards the guard I asked for some pepper which I threw on his open wounds, his shouts entering my ear canals.

I looked him from under my lashes, "Last thought?"

He still didn't reply when I nodded and picked up a saw in my hands, "This was for being involved with the party who is there to hurt my girl and that sudden boldness you just showed which was hell annoying." and turning on the saw, I turned around to see thirteen pairs of widened eyes gazing back at me when smirking, I cut half of his right leg off, throwing it right at his face.

I took a step back and took off my gloves looking at all the men there.

"Believe me, this wasn't my worst. This was just the beginning. I'll torture you till you won't even remember your name. This was just the starting. I'm giving you another day to think this through. Believe me, I would go to any lengths to get what I want."

I gave them one last look before I threw my bloodied gloves on one of the men's faces and was about to leave when I turned back and looked at Massimo, pointing towards the third man sitting behind me, "I need information on this so-called bartender." He nodded when I glared at them and left the room.

Fucking pieces of dog shit.

\*\*\*

I trudged down the steps after taking a shower and made my

## Chapter 22

way towards the kitchen. I was starving when I remembered, I neither had had dinner properly yesterday, nor breakfast or lunch today. I was about to enter the kitchen when I felt a harsh tug on my pants and I looked down to see Everleigh looking up at me with large marble shaped, white glossy eyes.

I looked up to see Sophia running and reaching us just in time when damn, did she look gorgeous in jeans and a white crop top especially with her prominent, sexy collarbones on display. I had promised not to fall in love with anyone again but I couldn't help it. She was so goddamn beautiful, like an angel. I forgot Everleigh was standing next to me when I shook my head and bent down to her level. Putting my hand under her chin, I looked at her, "Yes princess?"

"I,i,i want to go out somewhere to eat dinner." Her voice was so small, so sweet and she was so excited when she whispered, "Pwweasee." that I couldn't help but feel love for the small princess.

I opened my mouth to say something when Sophia came forward and placed her hand on Everleigh's shoulder, "No munchkin no. We have enough food at home. He is busy at the moment."

She whined a sad why when I smiled a bit and shook my head. "No no, it's okay. I'll take out time for her."

Grabbing both of Everleigh's hands, I pulled her towards me, "Get ready then. We'll leave in twenty minutes. Is that okay?"

She screamed a joyous yes and threw her arms around my neck, hugging me and I couldn't help but hug her back. She was cute, Tara wasn't lying. And come to think of it, where was that stupid female of a donkey?

*

I wore a black dress shirt with blue pants. Running my hands through my hair to add a bit of volume and wearing my Rolex watch, I made my way downstairs and started to check my mail waiting for the two sisters to come down when I heard the clicking of shoes. I looked up from my phone and holy smokes, Sophia couldn't get any better.

I couldn't think straight anymore, I was so lost in her. She was wearing denim jeans and a much much much better crop top than before, her shoulder blades looking as prominently sharp as ever that for once I wanted to just lovingly place a kiss there till I could see her blush. She also wore a small white bracelet, black earrings and she had pulled her hair up in a high wavy ponytail.

Her makeup was balanced and not too over and she looked mesmerizing. Everleigh, on the other hand, was itching to somehow just fly off the stairs and make her way outside. She was wearing a knee length pink frock and had her hair pinned back together in a braid.

They both made their way down next to me when I saw Sophia gulp and she lowered her head a bit.

## Chapter 22

I put my fingers under her chin and raised her head up, softly rubbing her chin. She gazed into my eyes and I felt pure love dripping from my eyes into hers. God, how much I loved her would be something so difficult to measure and how damn hard would it be to let go of her would also be something so very extremely difficult to measure. I looked at Everleigh and spoke, needing her not to see what I did next, "Straighten up your frock, love." and as soon as her head moved down to examine her dress, I moved my hand back and took off Sophia's hairband letting her hair fall freely in waves.

She lowly gasped and brought her head up, looking at me, when I moved my hand through her maroon red hair, letting it add volume to the already beauty owning them as I said, "You look more beautiful with your hair down."

She slowly smiled a small smile and that was enough to make my heart beat wildly. I brought my mouth next to her ear and whispered, "You look beautiful, angel."

She swallowed and tucked a strand of hair behind her ear and muttered a small yet a beautiful thank you. I held out my hand for Sophia to hold when she did but then my gaze immediately went to Everleigh who was looking at our hands, and was jumping on her feet a bit, her face and her sad pout clearly telling that she wanted to hold my hand but remained quiet.

I bent down to pick her up in my arms and started tickling her when she fell into fits of laughter and kept nuzzling her head in the crook of my neck when after some time I finally stopped, taking in a deep exhaled breath to calm myself down. God, this was exhausting. I smiled at Everleigh and again held my hand out for Sophia to hold.

She smiled and put the small of her palm in my big, calloused ones and it felt so warm, so peaceful, so………...so fucking perfect.

We sat in the car and I randomly started driving around the streets when I asked them, "So where do you guys want to go?"

Everleigh shouted from the backseat, "MICKEY D'SSSSSSSS!"

I glanced confusedly at my left at Sophia, "Mickey Ds?"

She laughed, "Mcdonald's. She meant Mcdonald's."

Oh. "Oh."

I nodded and drove there, occasionally looking sideways to see how God actually took his time to make her. Sophia was perfect. Flawless. And above all, anything a man could ever ask for. I was ready to lay out my life for her but the sad part was she wasn't happy and would be leaving me in a rough two more days. I couldn't get attached to her now, it would kill me. I silently drove and let time decide the events.

*

We had an amazing time and Everleigh was ecstatically happy.

## Chapter 22

She played in the play place for about an hour, and ate to her full when on our way home, she slept during the ride. I carried her up the stairs to their room and tucked her in bed, Sophia following along. I made sure to cover Everleigh with the comforter so that she wouldn't feel too cold and turned the air conditioner on. Turning around, I saw Sophia standing with a silent smile on her face.

I just wanted to hug her, to kiss her, to let her know how she meant the world to me. To let her know that I was nothing without her, just a living drunk mess, helplessly hitting every dark corner in this world, barely managing to find his footing and so lost, so dark, so devil-like that I just wanted her to lighten up every cob-webbed dark space within me and nobody else. I wanted to embrace her and never let go.

But I didn't.

I walked past her, said a small goodbye, closed the door behind me and made my way out. I was not even half a meter away, when I felt a hand on my arm stopping me from moving. Turning around, I saw Sophia standing when I got close to her and tucked a strand of her hair behind her ear, conversing softly with her, "What happened? Is everything okay?"

She seemed unsure when she asked, "No, are YOU okay?"

I furrowed my head in confusion, "Yeah, why?"

She made her way closer to me, "You……seemed off today. Like…a bit upset. Is everything okay?"

Fuck, I loved this woman beyond my imagination. How could I let her leave me? How would I survive alone in this damn of a house if she wouldn't be here when her mere smile, her mere existence would be constantly running in my mind, telling me again and again, grinding in my brain that she is here somewhere, she is somebody and the only body who captured my senses and nobody else. I smiled sadly, unable to control my emotions when I held her hand and squeezed it, "I'm fine sweetheart. Just a bit tired. I suggest you go and sleep."

"You sure right? You can talk to me."

I smiled again when I moved forward and placed a gentle long kiss on her forehead, my eyes closing in on the softness, "Go to sleep, angel. No harm will come to you."

And with that promise that I made, she nodded her head and went back to her room, leaving me to stand in the corridor for God knows how long. Till today's morning she had three days left to go back to America.

Without me.

One down. Two more to go.

# Chapter 23

## SOPHIA

I was ecstatically happy. A guard came yesterday to inform me how we were leaving for America today and I couldn't believe it. I wanted to go back to the place I had spent my entire life in, was born there, was raised there, dad and mum fought there, I became like a mother to munchkin there. I made many friends there and enjoyed some parts of it, if not all.

I was willing to go back with him and show him each and every place that meant the most to me and Everleigh. Although I knew how rich he was, a little pathetic sightseeing by me wouldn't hurt much. Another thing which made me a bittt happy was that I would be able to continue my job, earn for myself and not totally depend on his money.

Packing up my bags and giving them the last final lookover, I got ready and looked at myself in the mirror. I was wearing jeans and a white shirt fitted inside my jeans with a smart belt around the two, adding beauty to the whole outfit. I wore silver hoop earrings, a bracelet and black Nike's to go along with it.

Mild makeup covered my face with silver glitter on my cheekbones as I have always loved that. I also had tucked square sunglasses inside the pocket of my jeans to wear during the ride. I tied my hair up in a messy bun leaving some strands hanging down plastered to the side of my face. Checking myself for one more time and seeming satisfied with the way I looked, I went out to wake munchkin up to get her ready.

The part I was most excited about was showing him the places which meant the most to me. The places where I always went to when things got tough for me or when I needed peace just for a few minutes. I couldn't wait to sit there with him as well, under a tree and let peace envelop us.

*

We made our way down the stairs and the guard opened the door for us. The car was empty and munchkin ran and jumped to sit in it when I stayed behind. Walking up to the familiar looking guard whose name was moose something, I asked him, "Wouldn't he come with us?" And I felt so stupid

## Chapter 23

that I still didn't know the handsome guy's name.

"He is getting ready, he is just about to come. Please go and sit."

I nodded, "Thank you." and went to sit in the car.

Barely five minutes might have passed when the door opened and he sat in and GODDDD! HOW HOT HE LOOKED! He was wearing black coloured suit pants, a black dress shirt hugging his muscular body perfectly well with his muscles bulging out and damn, did he have some muscles there. He had his suit coat hanging around his arm and an expensive looking watch adding to the beauty. His hair were looking a bit rough, adding volume to his personality and just how I liked it.

"Hi." Even his gruff voice turned me on.

Before I could reply, munchkin became giddy and said in between short giggles, "Hello!"

She looked cute doing that but I thought she was getting a bit too close to him which to be really honest, was disturbing me a lot. And I don't know why.

They talked all during the car ride, with munchkin occasionally watching YouTube on his phone, while I just stared out. It was so quiet. So peaceful. Funny how the world is full of different people. How we never know who may need who, who is struggling and who is on the verge of giving up.

Sometimes, people change places to find the only person whose mere existence will bring peace to their life, their soulmates. While some find and cannot catch them. Or if they do, something drift's them apart and no one makes an attempt to come closer, in fear of rejection or in fear of anything going wrong. 'What ifs' destroy so many relations which could be saved.

It's funny how the world keeps on moving and yet we don't know what is going on in another person's life. We never know when someone is about to lose their shit. We have no clue that for example, the car to our left, the person in there might just be going to end their life or might just be going to meet his newborn. It's so complicated, so convoluted.

The car stopped to a halt and we stepped out. I inhaled the beautiful clean air of the airport and couldn't help but squeal. Especially over the fact that I would love to show him the mini waterfall in the park where I always used to go for peace when life used to get too difficult for me to handle all alone, with a small baby by my side.

*

We followed him and came into an open field where a large airplane stood, waiting for us. Munchkin dramatically slapped both of her hands on her cheeks and started to run towards the plane. I couldn't help but laugh out loud and followed her. This is exactly what I wanted. To go back to America with the person I was growing feelings for. With the person with whom I knew I might have a future with.

## Chapter 23

I was walking when something kept feeling odd. I wrapped my arms across my chest and rubbed them. I had a feeling that something, somewhere was wrong but I decided to ignore it. I kept on moving when I couldn't take it anymore. I was taking in deep breaths and my heart was beating wildly. This had never happened before with him right behi-

I glanced back to see no one following me. What? Where was he?

I turned back to see him standing at the very far end, with his hands in his pockets looking at me.

Not looking, staring.

I was confused. Why wasn't he coming? Why was he standing so far away? The plane might leave. I glanced back at the airplane to see munchkin already in and made my way back to him. Out of my peripheral vision, I saw him walking towards me and immediately my speed increased. I always wanted to be next to him, for better, for worse. I never wanted to leave his side.

Ever.

He came close to me and tilted my chin up, "Did you forget something, Angel?"

I wanted to respond with, 'Yeah you.' but decided to not say it so bluntly and instead asked, "Why are you standing there? Why aren't you coming along?" My voice always came out small and soft in front of him.

A sad expression flashed across his eyes but he quickly masked it that someone could easily tell that it was an illusion. He smiled and further bent his head down to properly look at me, when he cupped the both of my cheeks, came closer and whispered, "I'm not coming angel. You and Everleigh go."

My world stopped.

In a heartbeat.

It came crashing down.

I forgot how to breathe, how to think, how to move. Everything in me completely stopped and I just looked at him. There was a hollow sensation in the pit of my stomach. My heart felt heavy and it was beating so wildly that I couldn't control it.

"Why?" My voice came out so small, so tiny, not even more than a mere whisper but I was surprised that he heard me.

He removed the lone tear which escaped my eye with the pad of his thumb when he pressed his forehead against mine, "It's your home, darling."

It was now or never. I had to decide. I had to say it. I knew it was the only right choice to start something between us even if I had to be the one to make the first move. And honestly, I

## Chapter 23

didn't care. I was ready to be the first one to do something. Anything for an us to be an us.

I looked him deep in the eye, when mustering up the courage I finally said my thoughts out loud, "What if I say you are my home?"

He sucked in a harsh breath and his eyes widened. I could practically feel my heartbeat going a million miles per second for how crazy it got. He opened his mouth several times but nothing came out. He and I both, were at a loss for words. It was like as if time had stopped, as if the second's needle had forgotten how to move. The air seemed to have stilled. We couldn't hear anyone, couldn't see anyone. It was just the two of us, looking at each other, waiting for what was about to happen next. And the next thing broke my heart, shattered it into a million pieces.

He withdrew his hands from my cheeks and took large strides back. Looking down, with his hands in his pockets, he muttered angrily, "GO!"

I didn't know when it happened but I started to cry. I couldn't control my tears and they just flowed down freely because for the first time in my life, I got someone who actually cared for me, who actually spoke softly with me, looked out for me and the first person who made my heart fangirl for him. His hugs were the only ones I started to crave for and his company was the only one I looked up to. And now this? Now he decided to leave me? Not once did he look up to see how he had broken my entire world in just less than a mere second.

Angrily wiping my tears away, I went up to him, grabbed him by the collar of his shirt and pulled him close, and spat out, "If you weren't ready to start anything, you shouldn't have even brought me here in the first place."

Anger, hurt, pain and betrayal were laced in my voice, dripping from my eyes. Another stream of tears flowed down my cheeks when I pushed him back and turned around, to leave.

To leave him for good. To leave the man I wanted to spend my entire life with. The man I wanted to grow a family with because he himself wasn't ready for this and willing to strive for it. I was so done. Ready to leave everything behind once and for all.

I angrily started to walk away when I felt him pull me back harshly by my arm. Our chests collided but somehow this made me more and less angry at him at the same time. More angry for him leaving me and less angry for again seeing those beautiful features stand in front of me. I was madly in love with him knowing it was too early for this but I couldn't control how the heart works. And I certainly couldn't control when my heart and mind decided to be on the same team. I held up my hands in front of my chest and moved away.

"I'm sorry." His voice flared up the already building up anger inside of me.

## Chapter 23

"What do you mean you're sorry? If you weren't ready, why did you even bring me here huh? Why did you show Everleigh all these riches and then all of a sudden just throw her out? You do understand the fact that she is a five year old and these things do attract her and you do bloody well know the fact that I don't earn much and I cannot provide these things to her, then-" I hit his chest, "why-" again hit his chest, "did-" hit, "you-" hit, "do this?" and sniffled back tears again as I let my arms fall by my side.

Everleigh would be ruined because she was so used to such stuff. You get used to riches in less than a day but it takes years for you to adjust to poverty.

Never had I ever thought that this day would come but I guess I was wrong. He remained silent. He didn't utter a single word when I was fed up. Shaking my head, I turned around to go away when his voice, his next words…..they stopped me dead in my tracks. Frozen. Rooted to the spot.

"I couldn't keep you happy."

I couldn't comprehend that on what basis was he saying that? How can he say that? How can he tell whether I was happy or not? I furrowed my brows in confusion and turned around, staring at him, waiting for him to continue.

He took in a deep breath and looked sideways, motioning his guards to leave us alone. Once the area was clear, he started to speak and every word he spoke chiseled my heart. I believed my heart to be a fragile one for all the shit I had gone through but whatever he said stopped my world. I felt heartbreak and only true heartbreak. The one that I had never felt before.

"I tried to keep you happy, believe me. I tried each and every way but it never worked. I'll be damn honest with you, I haven't ever been in a relationship before. I have never been with any girl, I haven't spent time with any girl, so I don't know how to keep one happy. I don't know how to show love and I'm sorry for that. Sorry for being an asshole but I can't help it." He spread his hands in exasperation at this when he pointed his finger at me, "Everleigh would still get all of the riches even if u guys are not with me, I'll make sure of that. I never left my mini angel all alone, so kindly never say that, but let's get back to the point here.

I tried and I kept on trying to keep you happy but I just failed. You tried to take your own life away, what could be more alarming than that? When do you try to take your life away? When you are so tired, so fucked up with your surroundings, so genuinely exhausted that you can't take it anymore. You don't want to end life but you want to end the pain. Your environment, your surrounding matters. And what happened? You couldn't control it. You couldn't bear living here that you tried to take your life away. I tried to make it better for you but if in the end *I* am the reason that someone loses *their will to even live*, then I-"

I ran towards him, collided with his chest and crashing my lips onto his, I finally kissed him.

## Chapter 23

I didn't care if he liked it or not, whether I was good at it or not but I just kissed him and took all of the breath away. He froze at first, his hands stopping midair. He remained like that for some time when I thought that either I was doing it wrong or I shouldn't have done that. I was about to loosen my grip and move away after a few, when he circled his arms around my waist, pulled me in closer and deepened the kiss.

I swear I could feel butterflies in my heart. There was a tingling feeling in the pit of my stomach and I couldn't control it. I couldn't think anything else, it was as if my mind was foggy, the signals not passing. My legs lost feeling, but his strong hold around my waist held me up.

I was smiling and could feel *his* smile against my lips. He pulled me in even more closer till our noses were touching and never let me go. I wrapped my hands around his neck and dove down deeper, snuggling into his embrace and he pulling me more closer than ever, never letting us break apart.

He broke the kiss to take a deep breath and placed his forehead against mine, breathing heavily. I smiled a wide smile and giggled, "I don't want to leave you."

He looked at me, as if in deep thought, "You sure?"

I smiled and nodded, unable to form words.

He brought his mouth close to my right ear and whispered, grazing his teeth against my ear lobe, making me shiver on the contact, "You come right now, I wouldn't let you leave me then kitten. It wouldn't be an easy game."

He moved back to look at me but I pulled him by his collar, "I would love to be a part of this game, sir."

He smirked and bent down, placing a soft kiss against my lips. It immediately reignited the hot flames within my body and I felt like jumping in the air when he straightened up, "So, you want to come back home now?"

I nodded when he called one of his guards to bring Everleigh back.

*

And oh yes, we were met with a grumpy Everleigh.

"I wanted to go on that planeeeeee." She whined.

But for the first time everything seemed perfect. He picked her up and started tickling her when he grabbed my hand and all three of us went back.

To start a new journey.

Both not knowing how it will end up.

But nevertheless, ready to try it.

# Chapter 24

## SOPHIA

I was midway unpacking all of my clothes and placing them in the closet when there was a pronounced knock on the door. Looking towards the door, I allowed whoever it was to enter, "Come in."

It opened to reveal my Mr. Hot when suddenly I felt butterflies in the pit of my stomach. He looked at me and suddenly furrowed his eyebrows in confusion, "Why are you doing the unpacking?"

I also replied with confusion swarming my mind, "What do you mean?"

He came inside and pulled me away from the suitcases, "No need. The maids will do that. I came here to ask you something by the way."

I pushed my hair out of my face, "Yes?"

He rubbed the back of his neck and seemed a bit nervous when he kept opening his mouth trying to say something but nothing coming out, when after a few seconds which felt like hours, he just sighed and shrugged his shoulders, "Do you want to go have dinner with me? Just the two of us?"

I couldn't believe he had asked me that. I was internally screaming when I just nodded as the words wouldn't make their way out of my mouth.

He smiled a bit when he said, "Great. Then we'll leave in-" he checked his watch, "an hour?"

I whispered, "Okay."

He nodded and left the room when believe it or not, I started dancing. I was jumping up and down due to the massive excitement. He hadn't called it a date exactly but at least it was something.

Three maids came in and helped me unpack and quickly ironed the dress I had initially selected and then rejected to wear. Munchkin was with Lily, watching a movie and annoying her and to be honest, I didn't care now. She should annoy somebody else as well other than me. After about an

## Chapter 24

hour, I took a peek at myself in the mirror and looked………presentable.

I thought initially that it might be a bit too much but Emma, another one of the females here was head over heels in love with the dress. It was black in colour, going all the way down to the floor, with a slit revealing my left leg completely. I felt a bit awkward in it but she wasn't listening. Pushing me into the washroom, she made me wear it. The dress was being held up by black straps. It left some of my neck bare and outlined my breasts. It was beautiful but I thought it was a bit too much for the first dinner but nevertheless, I decided to give it a shot. Giving my makeup one last glance, I exited the room and made my way downstairs.

## ASHTON

I was impatiently tapping my foot and kept glancing at my watch. I hated it when people were late. Absolutely. Hated. It. She was two minutes and thirty-five seconds late now but obviously I couldn't say anything to her. I was going through my phone when I got a text on my business mobile from an unknown number as only closest people had my personal number. I usually gave out my business number for several security reasons.

Unknown number: *Ashton, this is my new number, you may as well just save it, but I'm giving you a month, maximum. A month to hand over your angel to us or…….relive the consequences. Augustin.*

Relive. RELIVE.

What the fuck?

Suddenly, the flashback of my past resurfaced back into my mind, the sound of the knife slashing across the tiny particles of air and then through layers and layers of skin and life, a body hitting the floor harshly, the brutal sound of a fallen warrior instilling in my ears and mind, never leaving the memory to fade away, me being unable to scream and unable to help, feeling so helpless, so shook, so fucking stunned. Nothing. I could do nothing at that time. But this time? I returned back to reality and just shook my head.

No.

No.

Absolutely not.

I won't let that happen to Sophia.

Ever.

I was useless when my past angel needed me, fucking powerless. The woman who loved me till death and who I loved till death…………..I couldn't save her. I couldn't do anything at that time to stand up against her enemies, against the men who were so ruthless to kill women and babies and what not. I. Fucking. Failed at that time. But this time?

## Chapter 24

This time I was the Don of the Italian mafia, the one people feared and cowered at just the mere mention of name. And never took the risk to cross their paths with me. And whoever did, knew too well what I did with them. I wouldn't spare anyone who moves even an inch, to hurt the person I love. I was buried deep in my thoughts when I heard the clicking of heels and looked up to see my queen coming down.

She looked absolutely, ravishingly gorgeous. She truly looked like a queen, with the long black dress, the slit in her leg exposing it turning me on even more. The top of her neck was bare which instantly made me hard as I could see her tempting cleavage. What was this girl doing to me?

She came down the steps when I walked towards her to hold her hand as soon as she came down. Standing next to me, she tucked her hair behind her ear, a sign that she was nervous. She was always nervous around me.

I bent down and whispered in her ear, making sure she felt butterflies in her stomach, "You look stunning, gorgeous."

She looked up at me and gazed into my eyes, whispering after around two to three seconds a soft thank you, with a red tint appearing on her cheeks, making her look even more cute.

I held out my hand for her to take and together we went out into the night.

*

### The Mafia And His Lost Queen

"What do you want to eat?"

"Anything." Her beautiful voice was melodious to my ears, fucking beautiful and soft. Enough to calm a raging storm inside a dead forest and to lighten up a dead man who hasn't been breathing fresh air since decades.

"No, but still, any preferences?"

She was silent for a minute when she perked up and replied, "Steak with mashed potatoes." and then she giggled, "Haven't had that since longgggg."

I chuckled when I made a U-turn and drove to the nearest restaurant.

*

The atmosphere was all I could ever ask for. There were minute LED lights, young breeze was blowing, the air smelt of fresh flowers, there were candles surrounding us on the rooftop. It was neither too hot nor too cold. The dinner was fantastic and the person sitting right in front of me looked so fucking angelic.

Sophia's features were prominent in the moonlight, her sharp collarbones were visible, her beautiful, light, pink coloured cheeks, her red silky hair flowing down in waves, the way her beautiful slim hands held the utensils to cut the food. She was composed, smart and above all, beautiful.

## Chapter 24

She put both of her arms on the table and bent, looking sideways at the surrounding and below at the ground floor parking area when I could see a bit more of her cleavage and I averted my eyes there and then. I couldn't control myself and a boner would have looked so embarrassing, so I had to look away.

"Tell me about yourself."

I froze midway eating and looked at her. Hmm. Good question. Interesting.

Putting the fork back on the plate, I also placed my arms on the table and bent forward, looking her dead in the eye. And funnily enough my angel was doing the same. And gosh did I just want to pull her forward and kiss her lips again. But I decided to let that go for now and answer her question.

"I am the only child. I lost my mother when I was eight years old. My father hasn't been much around me all those times I grew up, so I have been doing everything by myself. How about you?"

I didn't tell her each and every detail of my past because firstly, I wasn't used to opening up and secondly, we weren't that close right now. So, let the time come and I myself will tell her everything.

She was looking at me when her soft voice broke the air, "I'm sorry to hear about your mother and I'm sure your dad must be working to earn for you, maybe that's why he didn't have time to spare you some."

I just looked at her and smiled. Oh kitten, how you didn't know the slightest of the truth but okay. Let it be like that for the moment.

She continued, "As you know, I have a younger sister, my mum was a drug addict and she used to be out most of the times, drinking, flirting, sleeping with God knows how many different men. Dad, like yours, was never home. I used to do a job, double shift, earn money to feed mum and munchkin. I was pursuing my career in medical and…. yeah. That's about it. Nothing special." she chuckled.

I gazed at her. She was just like me. A broken soul. One who grew up themselves, with no one to hold them during difficulties, no one to calm them down when hell broke loose. No one to hold them and tell them that everything will be okay. No one to bring happiness in their lives. Absolutely no one. She was just like me.

I promised myself there and then again, that I would try my level best to make sure she never cries here again. One thing that I knew now was that she did have some feelings for me, for the way she acted out at the airport. She chose me over her family, over her job, over her previous home. She chose me and I will make it sure to make this place her *home* now. Better than the first one. Forever.

"What do you work?"

## Chapter 24

I choked on my own damn spit. What did I work? How will I disclose this to her? She may run away from me. Then what? How will I control myself? How will I keep myself sane? Obviously, I couldn't lie. If I wanted her to be mine, I had to make sure I don't lie so that she knows everything. To make a bond strong we have to stop lying to each other. But I couldn't risk it right now. So I thought to think over this properly before disclosing it to her.

"I do business."

"What kind of business?"

"Can we talk about work sometime else? I came here to give you time. I don't want work to make its way in when I'm giving you time."

She nodded frequently, "Yeah, yeah you are right."

I sighed in relief. Thank God!

After a minute she asked, "Umm, I know it's late, but can I know what's your name?"

And I immediately replied with a playful smirk on my face, "Mr. Extremely rude."

She playfully rolled her eyes which snapped me. I grabbed her chin and brought her face closer to me as her eyes widened, "Tsk tsk kitten, I hate it when someone rolls their eyes at me. Don't do it again."

I could practically see her chest heaving up and down owing to how fast she was breathing in when I smirked internally and left her chin as she sat back. The effect I had on her.

"Tell me, what's your name?"

I held my fork midair and gazed at her as if in deep thought, "When you didn't know my name, what do you used to call me?"

Her eyes widened and I saw her gulp.

Hmm.

Interesting.

"Nothing."

I dropped my fork with a clang on the plate and bent forward looking at her, "Darling, I know when one is lying. So, tell me the truth."

She started rubbing her hands back and forth fastly, "Can you leave it?"

Oh, now I really wanted to know. She should know how stubborn of a man I am.

I chewed the inside of my cheek and looked mockingly at her, "Nopes."

## Chapter 24

She again rolled her eyes at me and bending her head low, she muttered, "mrhot. "

I screeched a bit loud, "MR.HOE?"

Her head immediately snapped up, "What? No no. Absolutely not. No."

Oh thank God! I swore I heard Mr. Hoe.

"Then?"

She hid her hands under the table and started rubbing them which was another wrong move to make me horny.

She was hesitating a lot when I had another strategy in mind then. Paying the bill, I got up, held Sophia's hand and made my way downstairs slowly, with her trailing behind me to make sure she didn't fall. We got to the car but before getting in, I in a flash of a second, pulled her harshly in front of me and swiveled her around, pushing her against the hood of the car and leaned in.

She sucked in a harsh breath obviously not expecting this, when the slit of her dress parted revealing her whole leg completely to me.

To get the answer quickly, I placed first my fingertips at the side of her thighs, and then slowly my whole hand, maintaining my gaze with her, looking strongly into her eyes as she looked back into mine. I slowly started inching my hand upwards the back of her thigh, feeling goosebumps arise over her entire leg, and simultaneously pressing my body into hers getting to a point where our noses were touching.

I could feel the rapid intake of her breath and honestly, same. I was having the same feelings but I was better at hiding it than my angel.

I looked dead into her eyes, signaling how I meant each and every syllable that left my mouth, "What do you used to call me, kitten?"

She opened her mouth and closed it shut and refused to speak when I further moved my hand up her exposed thigh getting closer to her private region. She made a strangled squeal when as soon as my fingertips reached her underwear, she rasped out with a shaky breath, "Mr. Hot Mr. Hot Mr. Hot."

I smirked and let my hand move to circle her back, when I pulled her into my chest and kissed her left ear. Nudging my nose against her cheek, I whispered, "I like that name baby."

Her hands resting on my shoulder turned into fists over the sudden hot emotions as she was out of words and needless I need to say, out of breath as well when I moved back and straightened my coat, "For the record, my name is Ashton."

She looked at me for a second, then two, then three and then her eyes widened after a painful minute and she stammered, "Can-can I know your full name?"

## Chapter 24

"Take a wild guess."

Taking in a deep breath, she whispered, "Ashton Romanno?"

I smiled into the dark moonlight, put my hands in the pocket of my suit pants and nodded, "The very same, angel."

# Twenty-Five

## Chapter 25

### SOPHIA

To say I was surprised would be an understatement.

I was shocked.

Hell shocked.

HE WAS ASHTON ROMANNO.

**THE ASHTON ROMANNO.**

I had heard since quite some time that he was the deadliest man ever to walk on the face of this planet. I had heard that he was in the mafia, kills people, is involved in many ugly

## Chapter 25

shipments, shoots people dead on the spot if they cross him and was someone who nobody ever wanted to cross paths with, and I couldn't believe that I had been living in *his* house, in the don's house, that I had fallen in love with him and that I had kissed him for crying out loud.

Of all the people, it had to be him.

He was dangerous. He was known to be ruthless, cruel, cold hearted. He was known to never have loved anyone before and he never had cared for anyone ever before.

But………….that was all wrong.

He had been nothing but been my angel all that time. He had made me smile when I never wanted to. He had shown me love when nobody had done that to me since childhood. He made me laugh when no one could. He made me feel butterflies in my heart when no one had the ability to do that. I should have ran away from him the moment I knew that he was in the mafia. I should have packed up my bags and left this place for safety. I should have created a havoc till I was far away from this man. Far away from his home. His mafia. From everything.

But I didn't do that.

I did nothing of the sort.

I knew that the mafia was never a good place, never a good business, but I was stuck. I was stuck here as I couldn't leave him. I had feelings for him and I wanted to have a life with him. I wanted to proudly call him my husband one day and have a mini him or her running around the house only in their diapers. How cute.

I wanted this. I wanted all of this. And that's the reason I never left him there and then. Not for his money, or his reputation, or his fame.

No.

For his love, for his caring ability. For him. I decided to live here, live with him and to give this new life a chance. We never know when it might be THE ONE for us.

Gulping and tucking my hair behind my ear, I just nodded because I literally had no idea how to react. He looked at me for a long time, scrutinizing me, thinking God knows what when after what felt like hours, he advanced towards me slowly.

I should have felt scared, terrified and petrified that a mafia leader, a drug dealer and a gun lord was coming towards me and I had nothing to protect myself at all. He could shoot me with his gun right now and end my life but instead of where one would be trembling and close to tears because of the fear? I felt none. I didn't feel as a point of target because I knew he wouldn't hurt me. I just knew that.

He came more closer to me and lifted my chin up, "Let's go somewhere and talk, okay?"

## Chapter 25

I just nodded, my throat all clogged up when I got into the car, him closing the door behind me.

*

The sun was glowing a bright orange colour and casting a soft romantic glow on the sand. The beach was desolate and we both were the only ones who were there. He held my hand and we made our way towards the water. It was a beautiful weather, with cold wind blowing across my face, a beautiful silence filling the air.

And just the two of us.

We were near the water when he bent down and started to unbuckle my shoes. I immediately bent down to do it myself but he wasn't having it. Taking both of my heels off and placing it next to his shoes and socks, he again held my hand and together we walked forward, finally stepping into the cold icy water, when believe it or not, I giggled.

It was awesome. Damn awesome. It was such a beautiful feeling and I wanted to somehow just capture these feelings in a bottle and keep it safe in my heart. I was itching to just run freely and for him to run after me and catch me, like normal boyfriends do with their girlfriends, but we weren't till that stage right now.

Walking a bit further, he pulled me to his right and we sat on a big ass rock placed in the middle of the land.

## The Mafia And His Lost Queen

The landscape was beautiful. The sun was setting with a beautiful glow, a moderate cold wind blowing across us and our feet dipped in water. Everything was silent, peaceful and perfect with the person I loved sitting right beside me.

We were quiet when he spoke, looking away from me, towards the opposite end of the horizon, "I have been in the mafia for quite some time now. This is my life. I do this daily and I cannot leave it. It is a dangerous world, I know," he looked at me, "but I promise to keep you safe. I can protect you with my life, I swear angel." He grabbed my left hand in the both of his and placed it on his heart when my heart soared at his actions.

He suddenly looked down and brought both of our hands back on his lap, "But I can understand if you would want to leave. Self-security is the foremost important thing and believe me, I get it. So, if you want to leave.....I wouldn't stop you, I-" I placed my hand on his mouth to stop him from talking.

He looked mildly surprised at my sudden action when he looked at me and it was my time to hold his chin up. I scooted closer to him to the point the only thing between us were the fabric of our clothes. I leaned in, looked into his eyes and whispered, "I want to try this ride."

He bent down and touched his forehead with mine, "You sure baby?"

I giggled and nodded yes when he ran his nose along my

## Chapter 25

jawline, bringing it slowly under my left ear when he placed his mouth right next to it and whispered, "Welcome to the game, darling."

I was ecstatically happy and was practically jumping my knees up and down when all of a sudden, he grew serious, "I wanted to talk to you about another thing."

I looped my arm with his and looked at him, "Hmm?"

He turned his body fully towards me, "Why did you do it?"

"Did what?"

"Why did you try to kill yourself?"

The atmosphere changed and the temperature suddenly dropped when I gulped. I knew this question was coming but this soon? I had no idea. I was making up my mind as of what to say when he interrupted, "If you want time, I can give you that, but I want to know one day, I need to know."

I bobbed my head up and down and nodded but I wanted to tell him now. Something within me wanted to just let go of some burden from my shoulder away, when taking in a deep breath I whispered, "I wasn't in my right senses."

"What do you mean?"

I swear I loved him even more now. He was paying full attention to everything that I was saying and this was the first time someone had done that for me. I never had anyone to tell my stories to, to convey how much of a pain I was in, but today I finally had someone to whom I could tell everything, someone I could confide everything in, totally let my heart out. I inhaled and opened up about my life, from the day I was born till today, letting some of it out. Some.

"My parents never got along together well. Ever. Mum and dad used to fight a lot. Dad used to hit her and she sometimes used to hit back when the beatings got severe. Other than that, she used to just silently take the beatings. It came to a point she couldn't take it anymore. She was so………done." I was whispering now. I looked into his eyes when he nodded, the gaze alone giving me strength. I opened my mouth to speak again when he put his arm across my shoulder squeezing it and dragged me impossibly closer to him when I relaxed more.

"My mum left us when I was barely eight. She used to go get drunk, sleep with other men, used to pleasure them, all just to get rid of the pain dad lashed upon her. Dad was usually never home. He used to be out gambling or sometimes working for someone to get money to feed himself.

I started working when I was eight. I left my school as I didn't have the fee to pay for myself and munchkin both, and I figured out that munchkin's education was more important than mine, so I sacrificed mine and instead sent her to school. I used to work day and night, giving two shifts, occasionally three, just to make more money to make sure no one slept with a hungry stomach. Especially Everleigh."

## Chapter 25

I took a breath, "The point being, I didn't have a great past and dad's beating was something I could never forget an-...." No. I couldn't tell him. I. Just. Couldn't. So I decided to keep that piece of information with me for now. A secret. "So, I used to get nightmares, which increased to becoming panic attacks and I was all alone in that. Always."

I gazed into his beautiful steel grey eyes with a few tears in my eyes and whispered impossibly low, "That day I was having a panic attack and I ran out looking for you but you weren't home. It was too bad, severely bad and I didn't know what to do. I didn't know what I was doing and I just...... did it. I just did it-," and my voice came out as squeaky as I cried harder remembering Everleigh, as I held my head in my hands, digging my nails in my scalp, "not caring that my little sister was right outside and could see me the next day in a bathtub full of blood with the stench of a dead body and how much it must have scared her and made her living childhood a living graveyard was something that didn't cross my mind once. I really don't know why."

I covered my face thinking the horrids Everleigh could have gone through if worse had happened, when he lifted me up from under my armpits and straddled me on his lap. I buried my face in the crook of his neck, locking my arms around him and cried my eyes out when he just ran his hand up and down my back, calming me down.

The best part was he didn't force me to stop crying, he didn't forcefully tell me to suck it up, to be strong, to conquer it. No. He just let me cry, letting me get rid of every type of emotion I was bottling up inside. For the past, God knows how many years.

And God, how good it felt. I felt free, less burdened and light. I felt much better than before. When my hiccups steadied and I calmed down, he pulled me a bit back by my waist and gazed into my eyes.

He wiped away my tears with the rough pad of his thumb and held up my face with the both of his hands, his voice coming out all dark, gruff, rough and strangely sexy, "I'm sorry angel that I wasn't there. I was in a meeting at that time but I'm so sorry hun. I promise to be there whenever you need me from this day forward. I promise."

I closed my eyes and laid my forehead against his and just nodded. My heartbeat slowed down and I felt at peace. How beautiful was this feeling, I never knew.

Still with our foreheads touching, he moved some hair away from my neck, his touch sending electric sparks down the septum of my heart, and whispered, "I promise nothing will ever hurt you again. I promise you. I will be there to protect you whenever you need me and I promise I'll try my level best to make sure you never shed a single tear. Ever. Let me be your guardian, Sophia. Let me be your soldier. Let me keep you safe, darling. "

I was so overwhelmed that I had no idea what to say or how to react. Grabbing his face in the both of my hands and with tears in my eyes I whispered, "Thank you."

## Chapter 25

He shook his head, "Never thank me for keeping you happy. That's your right, sweetheart."

I just took in some deep breaths when he asked me the next question I was avoiding badly, "Did your dad ever hit you?"

I hesitantly nodded a no when he gave me an expression as if to say I-caught-you-lying-again-so-better-play-a-better-act-than-this.

I refused to reply when he held my chin and brought my face up, "Darling I need to know, did he hit you?"

"Can we talk about this later?"

"This means a yes, doesn't it?"

I raised my shoulders high, "Could be, could be not."

"Where?"

I heaved a sigh and rested my head on his left shoulder, "Please. Let's talk about this later."

He breathed in deeply and kissed the back of my head, running his hands through my hair, "Okay, but I won't let it go."

I smiled knowing by now that he was a stubborn man, "I know."

He slapped his knee, "Shall we go now?"

I swallowed and nodded a yes getting up from his lap.

I was about to leave when he called me, "Sophia."

My name sounded so soft, so fragile coming out from his mouth, like some soft cotton and it actually felt nice to me.

I turned around, "Yeah?"

He beckoned me to come close.

I groggily walked up to him when he placed his hands on my waist, pulling me in close and made me stand right in front of him. He bent down, holding my face in his hands, touched his forehead against mine and whispered, "I would like to have you with me and I promise to keep you safe. No hurt, pain or trauma will ever come to you angel. Ever." and with that promise he leaned down and softly pressed his lips against mine, silencing the world around me. A kiss full of love, passion, promise and a determination for an us to be an us.

I closed my eyes upon the softness and held onto him, never letting him go.

# Twenty-Six

## Chapter 26

### SOPHIA

I was more than happy today. He had promised those things to me which none had ever. Not even my own biological parents.

I did my hair, wore a t-shirt and some denim pants and jogged down the stairs towards the kitchen. Everleigh was sleeping so I guess I could spend some time there. Emma was working when I cleared my throat dramatically. Emma and I had gotten very close and we were practically like gossiping best friends now.

Her eyes widened when she quickly ran towards me and gave me a bone cracking hug. I immediately sneezed as she was covered with flour and it entered my nose, tickling me. She didn't notice that I was sneezing because of the flour when she grabbed my arm and pulled me towards the nearest stool making me sit there, "How did it go how did it go how did it goooo?" She was squealing so loud and bouncing on her toes that I couldn't help but laugh.

"It was okay I guess."

She put one of her hands on her waist, picked up the wooden roller pin and waved it in front of my face, "No missy no no. I want all the details. All the juicy details. Come on come on come onnnn."

I rolled my eyes and started laughing. What was this girl?

Getting up, I poured myself some orange juice and started telling everything to her. She widened her eyes, made dramatic oh's, and giggled at all the right places. I was midway telling my story when she screamed, "HE KISSED YOU?"

I giggled, "Yes yes, now sshh."

I tried to quieten her down a bit but she just won't stop.

"HE KISSED YOU SOPHIA, HE KISSED YOU FOR CRYING OUT LOUD."

She swiveled around when she dramatically put her hands on her forehead and leaned against the counter, "I think I'm

## Chapter 26

going to have a heart attack."

I rolled my eyes and took the roller pin, hitting her lightly on the head, "Oh shut up and get back to work."

She held the both of my arms and shook me, looking at me with widened eyes, "He kissed you. Register that. He. Kissed. You."

I opened my mouth to say something when a deep, dark voice resonated around the room, immediately affecting the temperature, making butterflies awaken in the pit of my stomach and goosebumps to appear on my arms.

"Who kissed her?"

Mr.Ho- wait, Ashton. Yes, Ashton.

Ashton walked in wearing a black suit and a white dress shirt, with his hair combed perfectly. He was full of drooling sexiness when I just gulped. He glared at me in an amusing way when I didn't know what to do or say. I turned around to silently ask Emma for help when she exited the kitchen saying in a low voice, "Let me set the table."

And I? I was left standing there, speechless with my mouth open. Did she just exit the kitchen? DID SHE JUST LEAVE ME ALONE?

I slowly turned my head around and looked at him coming to terms with the fact that yes, we both were now alone in the huge kitchen. Gulping and rubbing my hands together, I just said a hi to him which by God, came out as a squeal and looked hell stupid.

He smirked and came up close to me and brought my chin up. I gazed into his dark raging eyes when I guess he just changed his mind. He picked me up, placing me on the kitchen counter and snaked his hand around my waist, pulling me in close when my breast was touching his chest. I subconsciously put my hands in front of me on his chest and could feel the hard muscles underneath.

Placing his lips on my ear, he whispered hoarsely, "Did you sleep well, kitten?"

I immediately closed my legs when he noticed it and parted them by standing in between. Mr. Sexily annoying.

I inhaled deeply and replied with a low yes when he kissed the side of my cheek, "Good. I better go to work now."

I nodded and smiled weakly at him when he bent forward, placed his hands on my thighs and kissed me when I immediately wrapped my arms around his neck and my legs around his waist, bringing him in more closer. He wrapped his arms around my waist, getting us together more firmly when I swear my heartbeat was going a million beats a second and I didn't do anything to slow it down, just because I didn't want to.

And as always, the kiss was enough to lighten up my world, to

## Chapter 26

make me feel loved and praised…..not useless or as a burden.

He pulled away and gave me a kiss on the nose when he backed away. He was about to exit the kitchen when he stopped, turned around and looked at me, "And don't tell everything we do to everyone. I'm sure this is not the end, it's just the mere start."

He winked and left the kitchen leaving me shocked.

He. Did not. Just. Say. That.

I was coming to terms with what he had just said when an energetic Emma came jumping in. I rolled my eyes and slapped my hand across my forehead.

What had I gotten myself into?

## ASHTON

I was typing away on my laptop when there was a knock on the office door.

"Come in."

The door opened and I looked up to find myself groaning again.

Nina.

Why the fuck was she here again?

She seductively walked up to me and without asking for permission, sat on the chair placed in front of my desk when I looked at her boringly, "Why are you here?"

She suddenly looked worried and started fidgeting with her hands which was so unlike Nina. I sat upright on my chair and grew alarmed. If Nina was fidgeting….. meant it was something not good at all.

"I-i don't know how to disclose it to you."

"Tell me."

"I don't know how you'll react."

"Just tell me what's fucking wrong?"

"It's not something easy to digest."

Okay, now this was annoying me when I gritted my teeth and let her see how angry I was getting, "Nina, you very well know much I hate this. Get straight to the fucking point."

She blurted out, "I'm pregnant."

"Ookkaayyy. Good. Congratulations." I genuinely had no idea what to say to her.

She looked at me as if she couldn't believe me, "What? That's

## Chapter 26

it?"

I raised and slumped my shoulders, "Yeah, what else? Congratulations, you are about to be a mother. But why would you tell me all of this? You want me to take care of all the expenses? Now, is that what you want? Ask the dad then. You want a break from the mafia? Isn't it too early to be asking for this?"

She looked at me as if I had grown two heads. We both were silent for a while when I was genuinely confused. What was going on? I raised both of my eyebrows and opened my mouth to say something when she interrupted me.

"It's yours."

Twenty-Seven

## Chapter 27

ASHTON

What?

What the fuck?

I asked her to repeat again what she had said, just in case I had misheard her.

"I am pregnant and the baby is yours."

"How far along are you?"

"Two months."

## Chapter 27

"And you decide to tell me this now?"

"Yes."

"Why didn't you tell me this when you found out?"

"I wanted to give you a surprise to show you how happy I am to finally start a family with yo-"

I slammed my hands on the desk, "Get out!"

"But-"

"I said, get out."

"Ashton-"

"I SAID, GET THE FUCK OUT!"

She scrambled on her feet and hurriedly left the office.

She was definitely lying and cooking something nasty up as this couldn't be true. How was this possible? This sure as hell couldn't be true. How could I let this happen? What about Sophia? Neither would I leave her, neither was I ever ever ever damn okay with the thought of killing my own child and I sure as hell didn't want to. Yes, the mother might not be the one who I wanted but after all he or she would be one of my own blood. How could I kill the innocent soul before they even came into this world? And that too, my own.

I ran my hand through my hair and exhaled in frustration. What the actual bloody fuck was this mess?

Shaking my head, I called three of my main men into the office.

*

Massimo, Andreas and Phoenix gathered around my desk.

"I wanted to talk to all three of you about the security. As you all know, Ms. Sophia and her younger sister are more in danger now than before, so I wanted extremely tight security around here. So, what's the progress?"

"It's quite strong as far as my supervision is concerned." I nodded. I always knew Massimo was good at his work.

I looked at Phoenix and Andreas.

"The newbies are creating a bit of a problem but nothing more." Phoenix answered.

"And the gates have been well guarded. As you know, there are guards constantly on rotations around her room so I would say it's going perfect on my side." Andreas informed me.

I sat back on my seat and crossed my legs looking at Phoenix, "What do you mean the newbies are creating a problem?"

## Chapter 27

"They can't get their hands on aiming and firing properly. They keep missing and it's getting frustrating now."

"And why is that happening?"

He shifted on his feet nervously, "I don't know why boss, but they just can't get a grip on it."

He seemed agitated when I clapped my hands together and got up, "Okay, if that is the case, I'll teach them today then." and without awaiting any response I left my office. Not that I needed any. I wanted to desperately take out my anger and my frustration after the news Nina told me.

I was passing by Sophia's room when I heard her soft giggles and I stopped.

Her voice, her aura, her smile and the peace that automatically came by being with her.... I fell for it. All of it. And I couldn't just shrug off the feeling, not that I wanted to anymore. She had me wrapped around her finger. She made me feel happy, calm and relaxed in ways no one had ever done. How I used to keep finding ways to get this level of comfort when I just gave up.........only to get that gift from her, suddenly, out of nowhere. I rubbed the back of my neck and made my way downstairs towards the training grounds.

*

It was exceptionally hot down here and I could see everyone sweating. Eyeing everyone menacingly as I was too mad,

### The Mafia And His Lost Queen

I was shocked to see Nina standing there, sharpening her knife and cleaning her gun, and reluctantly I made my way towards her, "What are you doing down here?"

Keeping her eyes on the blade, she replied arrogantly, "Why do you care? Not the first time I am here now, am I?"

I roughly grabbed her by the elbows and shook her, "Leave. I wouldn't repeat myself."

"What if I say no?"

What is the problem with females? Why do they suddenly change when they get pregnant? Surely the hormones don't kick in so quickly.

I rolled my eyes in annoyance, "If not for your own self, take care of the baby you are carrying."

She came more close to me when she whispered tauntingly, "Ours."

I felt revolted. How can a part of my heart wish that the child she was carrying had never been conceived? How can I wish that my own blood could have not made way into the woman I hated the most's womb?

Yes, I would love my child a lot and yes, I would give him or her the time and love they deserve but somehow, I was hating this. Not wanting to talk to her, I gave her the last warning to leave when she obliged. Right now was not the

## Chapter 27

moment to test my patience. Because I definitely won't have that at the moment.

Standing in front of the newbies, I wrapped my arms across my chest and glared at them.

"You know there is a reason my mafia is the strongest to ever exist and I would only be keeping those people who are capable of protecting this mafia and my family. So, whosoever of you can't do that even after this basic of a training-" I pointed my hand towards the door, "get the fuck out right now. Get the fuck out and the bullet of my gun will meet you before you leave the double doors because nobody is leaving this place alive."

Everyone gulped but didn't dare to make a move. As expected.

"You sure all of you want to stay?"

They nodded a yes when I gritted my teeth in anger and scolded them, "Then bloody step up the game! It's been a month since you guys have been training and still you don't know how to shoot properly. Are you serious? Since you can't learn it the easy way, I thought of doing it the hard way this time. Today, I will be teaching you how to shoot and I will make it damn sure that the one person I call………gets a fucking grip on it. And believe me when I say I will make it sure?" I eyed them, "I sure as hell make it sure."

I smirked to see horrified expressions on their faces but their fault, they brought this on themselves.

I scanned every person in the row when I called the one sitting afar, a bit from the right, who seemed scared out of his fucking mind but still came up, walking groggily.

I raised my gun and pointed towards his private area, "Go back and walk up to me confidently, or I'll shoot you in your nuts and believe me you won't have kids again."

He gulped and walked back to where he was sitting only to come back to me without any tinge of fear and with a completely normal expression. I could feel that he was about to faint as he was damn scared but he had to hide that feeling which he kind of did do it good. Just a bit more of a practice and he was good to go.

"What's your name?"

"James, boss."

"Hmm, James……..you see that target right in front of you?" I pointed towards the circular dartboard placed at the far end.

He silently nodded when I handed him a gun, "There are four bullets in this gun and I need each and every one of it to hit the exact center of the board. Fail to do so……..I'll show you the hard way. Go on."

He nervously swallowed when he aimed, took in a deep breath and fired. And fired. And fired. And fired the last

## Chapter 27

shot and God how pathetic he was. Not even a single one made its way towards the center.

I narrowed my eyes into slits and looked at him. "What the fuck was that? Is that how you are going to protect my family?"

He had no words when I got up, snatched the gun out of his hand, reloaded and aimed towards the dartboard and fired all four rounds. Lowering the gun, I saw all of the four bullet piercings right through the center of the dartboard when I looked back at him.

He smiled a hesitant smile when I just glared at him finding no reason to cheekily smile like a dickhead. He nervously coughed to cover it up when I loaded the gun with one bullet and handed it back to him again, "One last chance. Hit the bullseye."

He seemed pretty determined when he spread his legs apart and fired, the bullet piercing through the air and this time not even hitting the dartboard. I slapped my hand on my forehead. What type of idiots were they?

Annoyingly grabbing the gun from his hand, I pointed towards the board, "Go and stand there."

"But-but-"

"If you cannot, the door is open, get out. My bullet will make its way through your dead brain."

He shivered but nevertheless went to stand in front of the board. I ordered Phoenix to place a box of cigarettes vertically on his head. All of the newbies were silent, gazing horrifyingly as of to what I was about to do.

I spread my legs a bit apart, raised the gun in front me, aiming the box and maintained my ground when before shooting, I addressed to him, "You make one move James and there is a huge possibility of you losing one of your eyes, so it's my suggestion, don't move."

He shivered a bit but still managed to stand still. I took in a deep breath, strengthened my stance and looked back at Phoenix, "Train them the way I am doing. I don't want any more excuses." and with a bang I shot, the box completely toppling off of its head, leaving him unscathed. He exhaled a huge breath and slumped when I again shot, pointing my gun towards the air when he immediately straightened up.

"Don't you dare ever slump again, you get me?"

He gulped and nodded when I guess he finally remembered and whispered, "Yes boss."

I placed another dartboard a few centimeters away from me and gave him another gun. So the scenario was that he was standing in front of the dartboard and I was standing at an angle of thirty degree from his line of sight. "James, you will shoot again, in the center while I will have my gun pointing towards you. One failed shot and you never know when I miss the dartboard placed right behind you and *accidentally*

## Chapter 27

hit you.

So, put some space between your legs, balance and steady out your arms, look at the target and taking in a deep breath, fire. Don't exhale while firing, you move while exhaling and your aim gets misaligned. So don't be nervous when you are shooting, nervousness always makes a person unstable, whether physically or emotionally or mentally-" and here only Sophia came into my mind. How she used to act nervously when I was around her. Cute!

"So," I turned towards the rest of the newbies, my voice booming around the room, "never ever ever be nervous when in combat." I emphasized the 'ever', "You will surely lose. Never ever let your enemy know that you are nervous or scared or maybe that you have no clue as to how to save yourself. Never. The enemy's eyes, are like an eagle's eyes. Damn sharp. So, never let anyone know about your flaws. Be confident and be brave even if you feel nothing but. That's what it takes to be hell competent."

I turned back towards James, "So James, I wouldn't repeat myself. I will be having my gun pointing towards you and let me assure you it has bullets-", it never had bullets, I was bluffing to train him, "and no one can count on my anger, certainly not you, so I hell wouldn't be responsible if anything happens. Do as I said and fire. If you can't get to the bullseye right now, fire near it but do it. On your mark....NOW!"

I raised my gun towards him when he glanced nervously at me but did as I asked. Barely a minute might have passed when with his stance solid and him not being nervous anymore, there was a large booming voice in the room and he lowered the gun down. I looked at my right and smirked at the result.

Bullseye!

I never learnt how to appreciate people or congratulate them and that's exactly what I did. I didn't say a well done or a good work or a good job. I just nodded, placed my gun on the ground and went to stand right in front of the board. I moved a bit to my left and moved my right arm away from my body so that the center of the board was right under my armpit.

"Fire."

His eyes grew wide in horror, "But-but boss-"

"I SAID FIRE!"

He shakingly raised his weapon when I seethed, "Dare to miss it."

And oh yes, he heard it. He put some space in between his legs, calmed his breathing down, took in a deep breath, furrowed his brows in concentration and slowly curling his fingers around the trigger, he pulled it. The bullet did not hit me at all but when I looked down, I was proud of the result. He had hit it once again right in the center of the board.

## Chapter 27

I looked at him silently saying a good when I turned towards the newbies, "Get a hand on this art. If you can't, let me know. I would love to train you."

I turned around and made my way to leave the room when I stopped right next to Phoenix who was leaning against the wall, "Work hard or I'll make sure that you do."

And with that, I made my way out of the training ground to go get a cold shower.

I told you, when I said I will make it sure that the one I call gets a grip on it…..I sure as hell make it sure.

# Chapter 28

## SOPHIA

"Can we watch a movie, Sissy?"

Munchkin's voice brought my attention back to her. I closed my book, smiled and ran my fingers through her hair. At first, I thought to deny it as I didn't want to disturb him but I also wanted to meet him so bad. It had been around two days since we had last seen each other. Neither did he come for breakfasts, lunch or dinner which was pretty disturbing to me. Emma tried to calm me down by convincing that maybe he was busy with work. At the end, I now knew he was the head of the biggest mafia so obviously, he would be busy.

I looked at munchkin and saw her big dovey eyes when I

## Chapter 28

laughed and nodded. I felt like annoying him for some reason. Grabbing Everleigh's hand and fixing my hair, we stepped out of the room and started walking through the large corridors taking them wherever they did because I didn't know the route to his office till now. I was about to turn left when munchkin pulled me exactly towards the right.

"Munchkin, where are you going?"

"To his office."

What?

"How do you know where his office is?"

She kept on walking pulling me along, "I've been there."

Hold up now! I stopped in my tracks and pulled her back, "What do you mean you have been there? When? How? Where was I?"

She was silent when I got agitated, "Everleigh, answer me dammit."

"Which question?"

I rolled my eyes, "When?"

"When I saw you in blood sissy."

"Whe-" and that's when I remembered. My suicide attempt.

*The Mafia And His Lost Queen*

And I remembered Ashton telling me how she had found me. Swallowing the large lump in my throat, I just nodded and started walking again. I had seen his office before but I didn't know the way from our room. Awesome! The one falling in love didn't know and the rest of the whole world knew. Just great.

We reached outside his office when I suddenly became unsure. I whispered, "Let's leave it munchkin. He is very busy these days."

"Whyyyyyy?" Her squeal was so loud I hastily covered her mouth.

"Munchkin, try to understand sweetie, he is a very busy man-"

She cut me off mid-way removing my hand from her mouth, "But I want to watch. And with himmm."

I took in a deep breath to warn her again when the door opened and I looked back to see the man of my dreams standing there. He looked dashingly hot as always in his- DID HE ALWAYS WEAR SUITS? His hair were ruffled and his expression seemed worn out which made me think he was too tired. Even for his own liking.

I swallowed and stepped aside a bit when he asked, "What happened?"

"Noth-"

## Chapter 28

"I want to watch a movie and sissy says no. I don't like this now." Munchkin ranted this out so fast and I felt betrayed. God!

He smiled and bent down, pulling her towards him, "And why did sissy say no?"

"She said you are busy, that you are a busy man. Are you a busy man?"

He smiled, "No, not at all."

She left his hands, came and stood in front of me, "You lied to me."

What?

I glared at him, narrowing my eyes into slits, daring him to continue lying and not rectifying his mistake.

He chuckled and pulled Everleigh back, "I'm kidding, your sister isn't wrong, princess."

She hung her head low. HA! TOLD YA!

"But I can definitely take out time for you."

Okay, I take my words back.

Her head perked up and she squealed, "Really?"

He chuckled and nodded.

"I want to watch a movie pleaseeee."

He huffed a tired okay and got up closing his office door behind and picked her up in his arms. He held out his hand for me to hold which I graciously accepted and we went upstairs towards the cinema.

*

"Which movie do you want to watch?"

"Frozen."

Surprisingly, we both groaned at the same time, making me laugh internally but he still agreed. Even I was annoyed with that movie now. The first time I saw it, I was head over heels in love with it, but when munchkin started watching it daily, forcefully making me sit next to her, it did get annoying after some time.

He adjusted the projector when he looked back towards us, "You guys fancy some popcorn?"

We both eagerly nodded our heads when he smiled a bit. And that smile was enough to lighten up my mood, my world and everything in me.

He came and was about to sit next to me when munchkin whispered, "Please sit with me."

## Chapter 28

"But I want to sit with your sister, princess, I have to talk to her about something."

She pouted and nodded but had tears in her eyes when she suddenly hiccupped. The drama queen!

He sighed and rolled his eyes when he got up and made his way to sit next to her, on her left. She immediately grew happy when he asked, "I'm sitting with you now, are you happy?"

"Yeah." She giggled.

"Now, please let your sister sit next to me."

"Yeah okay." She shrugged it off so casually that I was shocked but it was okay. I was happy to get to sit right next to him.

I got up and sat to his left when he handed me the popcorn, our hands grazing each other's, sending sparks down my body.

\*

Halfway into the film and I was getting agitated now. He wasn't talking to me, the movie wasn't finishing, Olaf was getting a bit annoying when I just started moving back and forth on my seat repeatedly.

"You good?" Ashton asked me.

"Yeah why?" SEEEE? I EVEN SOUND LIKE OLAF WITH THE *YEAH WHY*.

"You keep moving. What's wrong?"

I huffed in annoyance pointing towards the screen of the projector, "This is sooo annoying, I swear to God."

He smirked and leaned in next to me, putting his hand under his chin and gazing dreamily into my eyes with that damn handsome of a smile, "And why is that, may I ask?"

"She's been watching this daily since quite some months now. Daily. And it's annoying you know."

He groaned and looked back towards the screen, "Oh believe me, I get it."

Hmm. Amusing.

Now, *I* placed my hand under my chin and leaned next to him, "So is that why you groaned when she said this."

He came more closer to me, our faces mere inches apart when he whispered, "Yesss."

I chuckled when he said, "Happened many years ago but my cousin's daughter loved this too and she used to watch it every other day with me. It was torture to be really honest so I don't know how you are still sane and beautiful after watching it for a gazillion times."

## Chapter 28

I chuckled and looked down. Whenever he talked to me, complimented me and said sweet things to me, it made me blush. It sent shivers down my spine, my heart could feel million jolts of electricity and I couldn't stop it.

I looked back up to see him still gazing at me lovingly with that stupid, beautiful smile on his face when I asked, heat rushing to my cheeks, "Whattt?"

His smile grew wide, "Nothing."

I leaned forward and ran my hand along his hair, straightening them, his eyes drooping close due to the softness.

"Can I ask you something?" We both were now conversing in just whispers.

His eyes half opened again, "Hmm?"

"Why haven't you been coming to breakfasts or lunch or dinner? Did I do something?"

His eyes widened, "No angel, no. You never did anything. And believe me if I was mad at you, before walking away, I'll inform you that I'm mad and how you are supposed to make it up to me. And I'll deliberately stay mad at you for some days. You know, just to show some ego."

He winked and smiled an innocent smile when I hit his arm playfully, "Tell me, why haven't you been coming?"

"I was busy sweetheart, I couldn't take out time to eat."

"Did you eat something in your room or office then?"

He nodded a no when my eyes grew wide, "So have you been staying hungry all those days?"

He again shook his head no, "No no, I have been having protein shakes."

"That's it?"

He said a yeah when everything in me exploded, "Do you know food is so important for you? If you wouldn't eat food, you wouldn't have the energy to do work, your muscle contraction will be weak, your neuron coordination will be low, the main synthesis of li-"

"Love, I don't understand medical terms, but I do get your point. Let's talk about something else."

I was flabbergasted but I left it. I did get my point across.

"So, tell me more about yourself." I was interested to know more about him and I could tell he was half asleep by now. When was the last time he slept?

"What do you want to know?"

"Anything."

## Chapter 28

"You ask me."

"Favourite colour?"

"Black." Damn, he was quick to respond.

"Favourite song?"

"I don't listen to songs."

I opened my mouth and my eyes grew wide, when inhaling a large breath, I was about to say something but he cut me off, "No. Just no. Next question."

Okay Mr. Impossible.

"Favourite subject."

"Accounting."

"Eww."

This time his eyes grew wide, he sat upright and looked at me, "Don't. You. Dare. Say. Ew. To. That. Subject. I. Love. It."

"I took a trial class of it back in my days and I couldn't understand anything."

I swear his voice came out so squeaky, "That's because you aren't made for that subject. Or that field. You were meant to be in the medical side of the numerous types of professions and you are, don't say ew to that subject. I'm deeply offended, you pigeon."

I again widened my eyes, "Who did you call pigeon may I ask?"

"You."

I folded my arms and looked back at the screen, my lips forming in a thin line, "Ant."

"Snake."

"Alligator."

"Hippo."

I sucked in a harsh breath when he laughed.

And. I. Was. Stunned. I had seen him smile but to actually hear him laugh? It was the first time and God how I loved it.

"Did you call me fat?"

"Did I say you were one?"

"You just called me a hippo."

"Which doesn't necessarily mean I'm pointing to you being fat. It can be any other feature."

## Chapter 28

"So basically, you are calling me ugly?"

He smacked his lips together, "Yups."

"Are you serious?"

"Nopes."

He smiled and I rolled my eyes in amusement when I could feel his hand under my chin pulling me close, "What did I say about rolling your eyes kitten?"

"That you love it."

"Even you know I never said that." and with that he leaned in to kiss me and suddenly I forgot everything. I forgot my surroundings, the voice of Elsa singing behind me. Everything stopped and it was just the two of us. Our lips were moving in sync and it was a perfect match. His hand left my chin and made way towards the left side of my face when he grabbed it and just brought me more close deepening the kiss while I held onto his arm for support.

I could do this forever and I wouldn't get tired. He pulled away and rested his forehead against mine breathing in heavily.

Gazing into my eyes, he whispered, "I'm tired, let's go. I want to sleep."

"But Everle-" and she was asleep.

I looked at him to see him already up and adjusting his belt when he said, "You think I'm going to kiss you while she is awake? That also at this age of hers?" He bent low to pick Everleigh up as he continued, "While you were busing being nervous around me with your head bent low, she was already asleep."

I tucked a loose strand of hair behind my ear and nodded silently. He turned off the projector and carried Everleigh towards our room.

I swooned in and anyone passing by could easily tell I was madly in love with the one and only Ashton Romanno, the don of the Italian mafia. The monster, the killer, the ruthless one but my angel, my guardian, my protector. And I couldn't wait to tell him that I wanted him to be mine and me to be his. I think I was definitely definitely definitely falling in love with the man behind his worn mask.

**Twenty-Nine**

# Chapter 29

## ASHTON

Sophia and my bond had been growing ever so strong since each passing day and I had never been more than grateful to have someone in my life. She calmed me down in ways no one could, except of course my mother but I didn't want my chain of thoughts to wander over there, it was too painful and deeply agonizing.

Everleigh was ever so cute and sometimes the main bridge between Sophia and I, connecting us. Sophia always brought peace into my fucked up world like no other person had ever managed to do so. Whenever shit went down, she was somehow always there for me, consoling me, calming me down even when I didn't show it and funnily enough, I always did. I could breathe easily when my queen was with me and it was like as if she completed me.

I lost a part of myself when I was eight years old and finally after fifteen years, about to be sixteen, I found the part that I had lost. Someone else had filled it in, something I had never even expected would happen, but it did. And I would rather want her to do it than anybody else.

My army was growing stronger than ever, the house and clubs were all guarded properly and Sophia and Everleigh were safe up till now. Massimo, Andreas and Phoenix were training my army hard and it was good to hear that the newbies were getting ahold of strategies. The only thing which was constantly disturbing me like fuck was Nina.

She was carrying my child and it added to my already building up difficulties. Why? Why did it have to be her? I couldn't imagine that I could be so careless. Rubbing my jaw and looking in the air, I kept on wondering as to how was it possible?

I remembered that I had taken every safety precaution that I could, but then how? The only thing which made sense to me was that maybe it was too harsh that the condom had broken but still, it wasn't possible.

Massaging my forehead in frustration and deep annoyance, I focused my attention on the fact that I had kidnapped Everleigh on her birthday and the cute child didn't even get a decent gift. So getting up and grabbing my wallet, I

## Chapter 29

snatched the car keys from my table and made my way to the garage. Sitting in my car and bringing the monstrous engine to life, I drove out into the streets to visit the nearest malls in hopes of finding anything for the both of them as Sophia might feel bad if I only gave Everleigh something.

\*

The mall was unusually quite busy which did not make sense to me at all but understandable since I barely came out shopping, and whenever I did for myself, I always had guards to clear out my paths five to ten minutes before I arrived at the place. So, it was usually only me in the shopping area buying my clothes.

After about half an hour of roaming around doing useless window shopping, I chuckled to myself at the next thought.

I hated shopping.

Even when I used to do it for my own, I never spent more than twenty minutes to get my wardrobe full but today, I was genuinely confused. I wanted to buy something for Sophia which she would actually love. Yes, I had spent more time with her since the past month but still, believe it or not, I didn't have a single clue as to what she liked or disliked in these matters. I sighed in annoyance when I entered a fabulous looking shop and started roaming around.

There were several abundant pearl necklaces and different wristbands along with packs of beautiful hair bands and all the girly stuff which I felt weird walking in through and could practically feel bile rising up my throat. I felt nauseous and close to throwing up when straightening up my coat, I fastened my pace to get the work done as quickly as possible.

After a few seconds, after I lost around ninety percent of my patience, I picked up some bracelets, hairpins and some hairbands for Everleigh. There were several beautifully decorated notepads with glitter pens and different sort of paints, when I picked one set of all of them wishing she would like it as anytime now, I could throw up.

Turning around the corner I saw a line of………………… ..wings? I arched an eyebrow and wondered why would children wear fake pink barbie wings WITH WANDS? Whattt?

Shaking my head and ignoring that, I went towards the other end where many perfumes were displayed and I checked the scent of each but it didn't match the scent power from the shop I used to buy my perfumes from. So deciding to get Everleigh's stuff from here, I would go to the shop I used to go and get Sophia a decent perfume.

I collected all the things and started to make my way towards the counter when my eye caught a hoodie. Abandoning my route, I made my way there and read what was written on it and to be really honest, I found it hell amusing, "**SARCASM AND ORGASM. TWO THINGS MOST PEOPLE DON'T GET. THE ONES WHO DO ARE SMILING RIGHT NOW.**" And I was genuinely smiling. I was itching to buy this for

## Chapter 29

Everleigh to have a look at Sophia's face but I changed my mind because I knew she was going to have me for it.

Going through more, I found the perfect match for her. It had a light grey shade, another one of my favourite colours with the letters, **DONOT READ THE NEXT SENTENCE** written in bold and an italic font on the top and a small sentence written beneath which I obviously and definitely read, of course as I couldn't buy one with swear words written on them.

So reading the next line it said, **YOU LITTLE REBEL. I LIKE YOU** in much small letters. I silently smiled to myself. Yeah, it was the ideal one for her. So guessing her size to be medium as she was a bit bulky, I asked for a fresh piece and made my way towards the counter, but not before grabbing a pair of those wings and wand for her as well as somehow it was itching me to not buy that. Why? I have no clue.

While paying the bill, I heard a shrill deep cry of a child which gave stimulus to a sharp headache within me. Looking to my left, I saw a young girl holding her, I assumed to be her mother's legs, and laid on the floor crying as her mother tried to console her, "Susan, sshh, don't create a scene love, I don't have money."

"BUT I WANT ITTTTT." Her hysteric cries could be heard around the whole store and it somehow disturbed me. A child should never need to shed a single tear in pain or agony ever in their life and being a person who had gone through that situation, I knew better as to how it felt, even if mine wasn't this shopping case.

Her mother hoisted her on her hips and while apologizing with one of the standing salesman, placed a white coloured, small teddy bear hastily back in the rack and made her way out of the shop.

Paying for the my stuff and the hoodie, I silently looked back to my right towards the mother who sat on a bench consoling her crying daughter. Without thinking further, I picked up two teddy bears and paid for them asking them to wrap one separately as quickly as possible. One of them was for Everleigh of course and the other one for her.

Walking outside, I wordlessly made my way towards them and nudged the girl on her right shoulder. With tear-stained cheeks, she moved her head and looked back at me and I would be lying if I said she didn't look cute. Her little nose was red from crying and her cheeks, white as snow. I motioned for her to step down from her mother's lap which quite surprisingly she did without hesitation. I was guessing she was mad at her mom. Way too mad.

I held the both of her hands and looked her in the eyes, her mother carefully eavesdropping to whatever I was about to say to her and alarmed at the same time because obviously, I was a stranger.

No one had really seen me. No one really knew how I, Ashton Romanno, really looked like and I did that on purpose to avoid attention. My name was more than enough to instill

## Chapter 29

fear in people where I had to.

"You know, I have a daughter too who is just of your age and equally as beautiful." and yes Everleigh really was beautiful.

She looked at me and didn't say anything. Not that I had expected to because obviously what could she say, so I continued, "So I couldn't see you crying, and……."

I opened the small of her palm and placed one of the wrapped-up gifts in her hand. She looked down at the gift and quickly tore the wrappers, eager to see what was inside when I controlled my smile looking at her impatient self. Her eyes widened when they landed on the teddy bear when she lifted her head to look up at me. I just passed a smile her way, ruffled her hair and whispered, "Stay happy." and got up to leave the mall.

I was about to exit the double gates when a pair of tiny arms wrapped themselves around my legs when I looked down to see her hugging me with her cheeks plastered against my legs.

I bent down and smiled at her when she grinned back and thanked me. I just nodded my head when she ran back to her mother and together, they went the opposite way when I couldn't help but imagine Sophia and I to be having a daughter. Or even a son. It would be so beautiful.

Heaving a sigh, I went out of the mall to go and get my queen her present.

## MASSIMO

Ashton was shopping for Everleigh's gifts and I decided that Ella too would get a gift for Everleigh's birthday, doesn't make sense, I know but it's not necessary that everything needs to make sense and hence? She too would get a present and it would be AN OREO SHAKE FULL OF LAXATIVES!

WITHOUT DIAPERS!!!

I honestly never forgot that incident making a mental note of how boss humiliated me for asking for diapers without any hesitation. The fuck was that bitch!

## ASHTON

Throwing my car keys on the bedside table harshly, I quickly went to my walk-in closet to change into my sweatpants. It was a damn long day in the office as well and I couldn't wait to just lie down and let my aching muscles relax for once. I'll talk to my men tomorrow regarding a few issues as well.

## THE NEXT DAY

I slumped heavily in my office chair and held my head. It was hurting me a bit when I got up and downed down two tablets of Advil. Coming back to my seat, I called Parker to my office.

## Chapter 29

He peeked his head through the door, "Yes boss?"

"Come in."

He slowly made his way and stood in front of my desk.

"The last time I gave you a task, you fucked it up." I took in a breath for a dramatic effect. "You fucked up the entire shipment. This time, I wouldn't spare you if anything goes wrong. I promise I'll give you a hard time to the point you yourself will beg me to kill you and believe me I won't. Got it?"

He gulped and nodded which angered me. Slamming my hands on the desk I shouted, "GOT IT?"

"Yes-yes boss."

"Stutter one more time."

"Sorry boss."

I scrutinized him before lowering my voice again, "I am sending some old guns with you. Take them to Charles, the one living in the North of Carolina. I have already talked to him, the guns just need a bit of modification, they will then be as brand as new. I need the whole lot of thirty-five guns, all set to be back by no less than two weeks. Am I clear?"

"Yes Boss."

I nodded, "Go to my warehouse, the one which is ten kilometers from here and collect them. You are dismissed."

He bowed his head before leaving my office, "Yes boss."

I heaved a heavy sigh when I called Massimo, Andreas and Phoenix to my office.

"Yes boss?" They all asked in unison. All my life, I daily heard a 'yes boss', an 'okay boss' and a 'it's done' boss to a point it was slightly annoying. A simple yes would suffice but it would weaken the strong hold I've kept on them and I didn't want that. They should respect me and fear me always.

I gestured for them to take a seat.

"I need more explosives. Upgraded, better ones. After the fight with the French and knowing the power I hold, I have taken those guns as well as payback for daring to mention Sophia in their shitty mess, which was also a bit easy since all of their men were captured by us. So free guns. Moreover, to ensure safety, all have been screened for any possible microphone or camera or anything harmful, which could possibly burn down my family and my whole empire but it all came out clean.

Now knowing as to what has happened, and knowing how many mafia families are against us, it would take them no time to form an alliance with the French and come for us and I sure as hell wouldn't be sitting in front of the gates with cheese pizza in my hands to welcome them, so I need

## Chapter 29

further measures to keep everyone safe here. Any ideas?" I always had the habit of getting straight to the point and not delaying it or messing around as I didn't have time for that type of shit.

But before they could say anything, the other question which had been keeping me awake almost all nights suddenly popped up in my brain, "And what about Augustin? Did you trace him? Any clues?"

Massimo sat up straight, "I tried a lot of research but the fucker was good with it, we found nothing by now. As you know, we have arranged a better IT tech than James, let's see what we can get."

I nodded, "Okay, fair enough. Just make sure the new tech isn't the snitch, I wouldn't think a second before I slash his throat and rip him to pieces. I wouldn't tolerate anyone targeting my family."

Massimo just gulped and nodded when I continued, "Yes, so what about the explosives?"

"I'll look around in the market, though it would be difficult to find." Phoenix replied.

"Why?"

"Boss you know the French had the best, no one can match their production."

"I know that and I fucking know that explosives from them is out of option now, so what next?" Nowadays, even the name of the French triggered me a lot and arose anger within me like no other.

"I can do some research and let you know." Massimo offered.

I nodded.

"And Andreas you? What about you?"

"I need to make some babies at the moment, so I'm kind of busy." he stretched his arms wide and admitted unashamedly.

My eyes widened and Massimo's cheeks turned a funny shade of pink when he chuckled, "Just kidding just kidding, don't go apeshit on me. I'll arrange something. I'll try my best."

I swallowed a large heavy lump in my throat when I nodded and said in barely more than a whisper, "You better."

These three were getting more and more closer to me day by day, especially when Sophia came and I just wished none of them was the snitch cause if one of them was......I wouldn't be responsible for any spilt blood or any funeral. I just simply wouldn't.

They got up and started to leave when Andreas stayed behind.

"Yes Andreas?"

## Chapter 29

"Promise me you won't go apeshit on me."

"I won't."

"Oh thankgo-"

"I won't promise that I won't go apeshit on you. I definitely might. Chances are I so rightly will."

He gave me a bored look when he turned around and started to walk away, "Then forget it."

"You move one more step and I'll shoot you in the balls."

He swiveled around with his hands on his hips, "Why grandpa?"

What the fuck?

He suddenly started laughing which confused me, "What?"

Between hysteric laughs, he said, "Nothing, just the face that you made."

I rolled my eyes in annoyance, "What did you want to tell me?"

He took in a deep breath when he held the palm of his right hand up high and said aloud with his eyes closed, "By God, I wish I get out of this office alive, and by God I'm telling the truth that it is nothing but pure humour and pure truth, but you Ashton Romanno, my love, look cute as hell when you are embarrassed."

And with that, he dashed out of my office leaving me stupefied.

I was coming to terms with what had just happened when I got a call from Jessica and I automatically smiled while picking it up.

"Darling it's done. When are you coming?"

I got up, readjusted my suit before walking out, "On my way."

Thirty

## Chapter 30

ASHTON

I parked my car outside her shop and stepped in.

"There you are love." Jessica was always cheery and smiling which left me wondering how broken was she from the inside but I never asked. I hated it when people used to ask me about my private life as I took that as overstepping the boundaries, so I thought maybe she may also not appreciate the question so I left it hanging at the back of my head.

I smiled and held the little silver coloured box she was holding with a little glittery silver bow on top. Without opening it, I asked, "How much for it?"

She waved her wrinkled weak hands in the air dismissing my question, "No no nothing, keep it as a gift from me. This is the first time you are here, buying something after so long, so I am assuming she is someone special right?"

I chuckled along with her when I nodded my head slightly, "You can say that, but Jessica, I won't be leaving until you charge me some amount of money."

She rolled her eyes, puffing her cheeks out, "Same as when I saw you come out of your mother's womb, stubborn as ever."

I laughed, "That is a habit I unfortunately can't leave."

She breathed in, "Okay, five dollars will do the deal."

I rolled my eyes when I made way towards the nearest expensive looking one, "This costs for five thousand dollars and as you made this especially on my demand, I'll pay you eight thousand."

I reached my hand into my wallet when I felt a harsh tug on my arm and suddenly, I was being dragged behind. She was literally dragging me when I looked at her confused, "Jessica?"

"Get the hell out, you donkey."

I suddenly understood, she was throwing me out of her shop when I stopped, mustering all of my strength and held her by both of her arms looking dead straight into her eyes,

## Chapter 30

"Jessica, you know me very well so you should know I won't go without paying you. This amount of money is nothing to me, as you know and I'm totally fine with paying you this. If you have ever felt love for me, ever, just accept this."

She opened her mouth and closed it shut several times, not being able to speak up. Guess, I have been doing this a lot lately to so many different people on so many different occasions.

She uttered a weak 'son' when I held up my hand midair stopping her again, "No. Just no. Take it. Enjoy your life and get something you really want."

She wiped away a lone tear which escaped her eye and accepted it while whispering, "Your mother would have been so proud of you".

I just looked down and swallowed, painful memories resurfacing back in my mind when I forcefully smiled, nodded my head and exited the shop when I got into my car and silently looked at her.

Jessica was an eighty year old woman, divorced twice and married a third time with the love of her life, only for her husband to pass away from a heart attack many years ago. She has three sons, and all of them left her once they got married which to be really honest was a very shit move to make despite knowing that their mother had cancer. But the assholes still left her and told her to deal with it, and since then, I've been paying for her chemotherapies and whatever treatment she needed.

Luckily, she won the battle of cancer a year ago and has been cancer free. I still did pay for her monthly checkup just to be sure that the tumor didn't reappear.

My mum used to come to her a lot for jewellery and stuff, tagging me along and when I took over as the mafia leader, I promised myself to handle all of her hospital expenses so that she could stop worrying. I silently looked at her cleaning the windows and crying when I exhaled a breath and looked down at my left to see the little box sitting beside me.

I slowly brought it into my lap and carefully opened it seeing the extra present I had gotten for my angel when I smiled silently.

Jessica truly did outdo herself.

*

## SOPHIA

I woke up stifling a yawn and looked outside. It was sunny, the birds were chirping and the sky was a beautiful golden crisp of a colour. Large pine trees could be seen, adding aesthetic to the nature's already present beauty. I sat up and stretched my arms, kicking all the tired muscles to wake up when I got up and got ready to go downstairs.

## Chapter 30

I entered the kitchen when Emma came running and gave me a bone cracking hug, "I woke up in a ridiculously good mood today for reasons I absolutely have no idea of."

I laughed when she looked back at me, "Why are you down here, why not with prince charming?" She wiggled her eyebrows in mock and started to hit me playfully.

I tried to form my lips in a thin smile but failed miserably, "Oh shutup. I thought of helping you make some cookies and cakes upon Everleigh's demand. I am good at baking."

"Yeah sure, only I won't eat them."

"Why?" Not going to lie, but as much as this was confusing, it did hurt me.

"Because prince charming will eat it all up, including you, so I wouldn't have the chance to eat," she stopped after looking at my widened eyes and heated red cheeks before adding, "your cookies."

I smacked her on the arm, "Oh stop it already, will you? I'll start."

"*Sure, angel.*" She mocked once again.

I rolled my eyes playfully when I got to work.

First thing I'll make, is a cake. Yes, a beautiful, big, mouthwatering, yummy cake.

\*

I forgot how to make the cake.

Totally.

Like deadass, deadass.

I dashed up the stairs to find the recipe from my phone when I smashed into a wall but suddenly someone grabbed me and started apologising, "I'm sorry miss, I'm so sorry."

I suddenly backed away maintaining a distance and saw that okay, it wasn't a wall but rather a muscular man. I mean, WHY IS EVERY MAN HERE SO MUSCULAR AND HARD AS ROCKSSSS.

I nodded and backed away, "It's okay it's okay. Who are you by the way?"

"Phoenix, boss's major left hand."

I nodded, "I see I see."

"I need to get going miss. It was lovely meeting you."

I smiled, "Same here."

Grabbing my phone and eyeing the sleepy head who was still sleeping, I dashed towards the kitchen and continued baking.

## Chapter 30

*

I guess I was so tired that I slept again because the next thing I could feel was as if someone was shaking me when I stifled a yawn and turned around, opening my eyes only to be met by a pair of raging, steel grey ones. Oh, how I wish this could happen daily.

I looked at my right to see the bed empty and frowned. Where was Everleigh?

I looked back at Ashton and got up, sitting on the bed when he removed a strand of hair behind my ear and said, his deep voice sending shivers down my spine and awakening the dead butterflies in my belly, "It's six now, darling. You were exhausted I guess when you slept, but everyone is waiting for you downstairs since the past five hours to celebrate Everleigh's birthday party which we missed. I didn't want to wake you up yet but if you slept any longer, your night sleep will be ruined."

I widened my eyes when I looked at him, "FIVE HOURS?"

He nodded.

"Why didn't you wake me up?"

"No one disturbs you until unnecessarily. So now, get up, get ready and come downstairs. We are waiting for you."

I lowered my eyes and nodded when he straightened up but

not before tucking another loose strand behind my ear and coming very close to plant a soft kiss on my cheek, letting his hot lips linger there for a few seconds which felt like minutesss. I shut my eyes close and clenched my hands into fists soaking up the sweat they were releasing as my body heated up like no other, my inner fan girls screaming like never when he with a last kiss, he got up and slowly left the room to let me get ready.

I squealed in excitement and fell back on the bed holding my head with my right hand and placing my other hand on my chest to control my heartbeat. God! What was this man doing to me?

*

The living room looked beautiful as hell. There were balloons everywhere, vases and vases of flowers with banners decorating the walls spelling out, "HAPPY BIRTHDAY MUNCHIES!" I stifled a laugh as this was so cute. There were many presents gathered up at one side, mini tables surrounding the entire room with different types of eatables ranging from cakes, chocolate cookies, molten lava and loads of chocolates to sandwiches, burgers, pizza's and what not.

There was fake confetti decorating parts of the floor with the room full of nothing but beautifulllll pink, white, purple and golden led mini lights. There was a beautiful homely scent wafting around the room, strangely calming enough and I just stood at the staircase drinking it all in as I could never give Everleigh this much before even if I wanted to.

## Chapter 30

I had celebrated five birthdays with her, technically four and I couldn't ever give her this lavish of a celebration as even the beautiful golden chandelier casting it's light below looked royally magnificent as ever.

Emma was chasing munchkin who was laughing openly and in return chasing the Moose named something guard who was deliberately running slow but was making sure that munchkin couldn't catch up.

Blinking back tears, looking at her happiness and what didn't I do exhausting myself just to see those pearl white teeth show when she laughed, was beyond my imagination. I just smiled taking it all in and praying once again to God to keep my little munchies happy. How beautiful was this feeling, I couldn't draw or map it up even.

I have always wanted to be this much happy, have always wondered having my own family, in some small of a house with the love of my life, a normal working man. But I had never ever imagined, that I would find my happiness in the home of a mafia don. Never. Knowing how dangerous was the work he did, but if this was the price of our love? Then so be it. I was still wishing to make my place in his heart forever and for him to hold me close till the end of times. I removed a lone tear when come to think of it, where was Mr. Impossible.

I roamed my eyes around the room in search for him when I already saw his in my direction and his x-ray gaze did wonders to my heart. It looked as if he wasn't just looking at me, but deep within my soul, the barriers opening to give him easy access to every scar that I carried hidden.

He looked hot as always but this time he was wearing more lively of a colour. He had a navy-blue dress shirt on with black coloured suit pants and a black coloured coat. His hair was slicked back and he was looking dashing as ever. He was looking at me when suddenly coming out of his, I guess transfixed state, he made his way towards the stairs.

I started making my way down when he held out his hand as I reached the bottom and I graciously took it when he leaned down and whispered in my ear, "You once again look gorgeous, angel."

I smiled a nervous smile and muttered a thankyou when I pulled him by his tie and ruffled his hair, adding volume into it as I whispered, "I love your hair more when they are ruffled and not gelled back. And you yourself look amazing pigeon." and with my fist against his chest, I pushed him a bit back, smirked and ran away from his hold because I really wasn't in the mood of arguing the names of different kinds of animals to exist on the face of this earth with him once again.

I glanced back to see an amused look on his face when he quickly raised both of his arms and bent them a bit waving them in the air, mimicking a bird when I changed course and charged back towards him, "Did you just call me a bird?"

He had the same stupid, annoying boyish grin on his face as

## Chapter 30

he placed his hands inside the pockets of his suit pants and shrugged his shoulders, "My lips were sealed."

"Okay. Did you just *act out* that I'm a bird."

"Hmm. Maybe."

"Well okay, I like it then, you hen."

"Thank you, my Elephant."

I sucked in a harsh breath when he laughed out loud for the second time in his life I guess and put his left arm across my shoulder and started dragging me along towards the living room, "Believe me angel, as much as I love this war, currently I'm not in the mood for it."

I huffed out annoyingly, "Yeah same."

He pinched my right cheek, "You look cute when you are annoyed."

"I look even more cute when I'm away from you."

He dramatically widened his eyes, "Is that so now?"

I grinned a cheeky grin when I muttered a small no and ran to stop Munchkin from running around madly.

*

## The Mafia And His Lost Queen

Emma quietened everyone down and started speaking, "Okay guys, after a verrrrrry long time we are celebrating a birthday and why the fuck is this bitch here?"

The door to the living room opened and a very beautiful young woman walked in. I instantly looped my hand through Ashton's arm and pulled him close, jealousy running in my veins like fire spreads in a jungle and narrowed my eyes at her when Moose got up, "She's my girl, got any problem?"

I slackened my grip on Ashton's arm when he chuckled and Emma retorted back equally in anger, "Yeah sure, I arranged all of this, who the fuck called her?"

"Well, suck it up cause she's mine and she will come wherever I go and I never told you to decorate all of this."

"Well, she could have helped-"

"You could have asked."

"She has eyes, could have seen-"

"You could just leave the room if it is giving you that much of a problem."

"Why sh-"

And Ashton spoke in his calm voice, "Stop."

I was surprised.

## Chapter 30

Hell surprised.

Yes I knew Ashton had power, but this much? Just a word uttered so softly and everyone actually stopped. Not going to lie again, but he did look hot with that much of power.

He had his hand up in the air when he looked at the both of them, "Whatever differences you both ladies have since the past I guess, seven years now, solve it. I won't have daily fights here. I definitely wouldn't tolerate that, so resolve whatever issues you have. Massimo, Ella-", Ella looked at Ashton when he said, "Go sit together. Emma," she put a scowl on her face and looked at him, "continue."

She rolled her eyes in annoyance when I felt Ashton tense up beside me. He hated it when people rolled their eyes. I instantly put my hand on his left arm and rubbed it, feeling the muscles relax underneath as he curled his arm around my waist and pulled me in close.

I guess Emma had lost her enthusiasm when she just muttered, "A very great happy birthday to you munchies, there are your presents baby." she pointed to where they were and with a sour mood, went and sat on the sofa.

Munchkin not caring for the mood of the atmosphere, not giving an ounce as to how tense the surrounding was, jumped up and ran to get her gifts when I whispered to Ashton, "What's wrong with the both of them?"

He shrugged, "I don't know. All I know is that they had a

fight seven years ago and since then, whenever they look at each other, they feel like putting a bullet through each other's skulls."

"But why? Why that long?"

He rolled his eyes and exhaled a heavy breath, "Women."

I playfully hit his arm and whispered a shutup when he smiled.

Everleigh placed all the presents in the middle of the room and started tearing up the packaging when I muttered, "Easy munchkin. Be gentle."

But she never listened to me. She kept on opening each one until she had a white teddy bear, some hair accessories, notepads with all kind of glittery pens, paint brushes, paints, a barbie doll with a large cooking play set, a set of colouring books with crayons and a grey hoodie.

"The barbie doll is from us potato, Ella and I." Moose said.

She squealed, "Thankyou uncle M and aunt Ella."

Uncle M? Wow, I didn't know they both were this close. Yes, they used to play together but I never knew they were so close.

"And the cooking set is from me, beautiful." Emma chirped happily.

## Chapter 30

I then added, "And the colouring book and crayons are from me munchkin."

"And the rest is from me." Ashton's deep voice resonated around the room. She widened her eyes and so did I. This was too much for her. She got up and ran around the room hugging each and everyone until she came to Ashton and hugged him.

She looked up to him, "I don't know your name."

Massimo spoke up, feeling giddily excited, "He's John Cena."

Laughter wafted around the room when Ashton glared at him before turning to munchkin, "My name's Ashton."

She whispered the name Ashton again and again, when she looked up at him and whispered, "Can I call you whatever I like?"

Ashton just chuckled, "Call me whatever you like."

She suddenly chirped up, "Ashie, Ashie."

His smile kept planted there but his whole face tightened till I could see his jawline muscles straining against their hold. I suddenly could see all the veins on his hands and arms announcing their presence when he just nodded, smiled and whispered, his voice tearfully hoarse, "Ashie it is then."

She grinned when she came up to me and gave me a bone

cracking hug.

*

The party went somewhat great after opening the presents because Ella left early since Emma was very rude with her, and to follow her along, Moose also left. The rest of the part went in eating a variety of dishes. Ashton did love the cookies and the cake that I made and I was genuinely happy for his appreciation. While Munchkin, Emma and Ashton were watching a movie, I excused myself and went upstairs to get something.

I knew we were arranging Everleigh's party and since Ashton had done a lot for us and even made me feel loved when no one had, I wanted to thank him and got something for him as well. Trotting down the stairs, I stood back and looked at the man who was capturing my heart in so many ways when I saw him sitting on the floor, with a single leg raise way of sitting.

His left leg was resting on the ground and the right foot was on the ground, making his whole right leg lift up in an arch. He had his right arm on top of his right knee, watching the movie when I went close, bent down and nudged him on the shoulder, calling him to move back a bit so that we had our privacy.

He skidded back and whispered, "Yes Angel?"

I rubbed my left hand on my thigh as I was nervous and kept

## Chapter 30

the right one behind my back hiding the gift when I spoke, "Can you come with me for a few minutes? I want to talk."

He nodded and got up, "Sure."

Holding my hand, we both went upstairs in my room when he closed the door behind and without turning on any lights, letting the moonlight peek in through the curtains, he moved me and made me stand near the bed and stood in front of me, looking me deep into the eyes.

I suddenly got hell nervous and looked down, immediately raising my head back up, swallowing the embarrassment, when I could feel his chest rise up and down from laughing silently as he bent down and whispered in my ear, "It takes guts to look down there and I'm still proud that you did."

Heat crept up my cheeks like no other when I stuttered, "N-no, I n-never meant to look that way, I just-" I cleared my throat and spoke, "wanted to thank you for everything that you have done for us up till now and I had no idea how to say a thank you, so I got you something. Might not be that expensive or you may not like it, but nothing else came into my mind."

He smiled and put his hands in his suit pockets, "You didn't have to get anything for me angel-" when I interrupted him, "so I got you this." I slowly brought my right hand in front showing him the wrapped up gift and just whispered, "Hope you like it."

I was nervous as hell when the corner of his lips tugged up in a small smile and he grabbed the box from my hand and started unboxing it. A perfume in a black coloured glass bottle emerged from the wrapping when he looked at me, "Where did you get this from?"

"A shop."

"When?"

"Do you like it?"

Obviously he'll go mad at me if I tell him when and specifically how did I get it but now was not the time.

He took off the lid, placed his index finger on the nozzle, and kept looking at it, kept looking, kept looking as if thinking something when as soon as I spoke, "Wha-" he moved forward towards me in a flash, so damn quickly before I could register what was happening.

Throwing the wrapping on the bed, he curled his left arm around my waist and pulled me flush into his chest when I immediately placed my hands in front of me, on *his* chest. He pulled me more closer, placing the side of his face with my side and with his finger still on the nozzle of the spray, with the bottle still in his right hand, he touched my stomach and slowly started to inch his hand up.

My breathing hitched, my heart beat racened, butterflies awoke like never and I felt myself pulsating everywhere when

## Chapter 30

reaching my neck, he kissed my cheek and sprayed a bit of perfume some distance away from my left ear. My eyes rolled up when he leaned in further and moved his head towards my neck. My legs gave away when he strengthened his hold around my waist and touching his nose to my neck till a point I could feel his heated breath, he inhaled.

He inhaled and I closed my eyes again upon the sensation, curling my toes in. My stomach was doing abnormal flips and I just closed my legs, praying he didn't see this.

He muttered a little hmm when he placed a light kiss on my neck, earning a shiver from me and backed away before bringing his mouth to my left ear, *"ljubavi koja je lepa, hvala."*

"What?"

He leaned further in when he was dangerously close to me and whispered, "It means, love that's beautiful, thank you."

I tucked a strand of hair behind my ear and whispered a welcome when I asked again, "What language was that?"

"Serbian."

"You know Serbian?" I was surprised.

"Yes Amore."

"That was Italian." I chirped up excited as a young child.

He laughed his sexy laugh, "Yes that is."

I smiled back when he suddenly grew serious.

"Hun, as much as I appreciate this and I like this, I'm sorry."

What?

"What do you mean?" I was genuinely confused.

"I didn't get you something."

I just shook my head as I wasn't expecting anything. I hadn't received anything since as long as I remember so it was totally okay, "It's okay, no pressure. I got you one, you gave me happiness, I'll take that as a gift."

Something flashed across his eyes but he just smiled.

I was suddenly tired when I yawned, "I think I'll go to bed. Today was a long day."

He nodded his head when I exited the room and half shouted to Emma, "Please get Everleigh to bed when you guys are done."

\*

I was again being woken up for the second time in a day, and again, by the handsome one himself, Ashton.

## Chapter 30

"Meet me outside whenever you are ready." and with that he left the room.

What?

I looked at my right to see Everleigh sleeping and then checked the clock to see it was two in the early morning. What happened so late that he abruptly called me so early? Was my mum okay? Was my dad good? I hope they were. Confusedly, I went to the washroom to brush my teeth and wash my face before leaving the room. He was standing with his back to the wall and was staring at the roof when going up to him, I asked, "What happened? Is everything okay?"

He didn't respond and just held out his hand for me to hold. We started walking up flights of steps when he opened a glass door and out we came onto the rooftop. I gasped at how beautiful it was with the gorgeous sight to see, the houses with lights turned on in some of them, many many trees and greenery adding beauty to the whole area.

The street lights fit so perfectly well with the whole landscape that one could stand here and stare for it forever. I wrapped my arms around myself slightly shivering for reasons I don't know.

I felt his presence before he placed his hand on my lower back and guided me towards the end of the rooftop. Reaching there, we looked at our surroundings and there was some sort of serene air enveloping us. It was peaceful, calm and silent with the sky as black as it could get, hundreds of lightings all around the houses and the person I was falling for standing right next to me.

He held the both of my hands and turned me sideways when he looked me in the eye, "I also got you something, I never forgot you in the first place."

My eyes lit up when I looked into his eyes, "Really?"

He chuckled and nodded when coming more close to me, he whispered, "Just like you, I had no idea what to get you. Yes, it isn't as much as Everleigh got but that is the only thing I could think of. I loved your gift angel, and I hope you love mine as well."

I inhaled a deep breath, waiting, when he put forward a small silver coloured box in my hand and waited for me to open it. I carefully held the box in my hands, undoing the ribbon and finally taking off the lid when I took a sharp intake of breath.

"Ash-ashton." My voice came out all small and squeaky as I couldn't explain the feeling. How beautiful was this gift I couldn't tell. It was a small golden coloured necklace with the words Angel written in some kind of slanted font I wasn't familiar with. It looked so magnificent and was so carefully made that I instantly fell in love with it. I was speechless when I looked up at him with tears in my eyes as he asked, "You like it?"

Words weren't forming when I just nodded sniffling back.

## Chapter 30

"You want me to put it on for you?"

I silently nodded when he grabbed the necklace and stood behind me, pushing my hair softly out of the way. His hands grazed the back of my neck, arising goosebumps all over me when subconsciously I moved back bringing us closer. He fastened the necklace behind my neck, its cold surface resting against my warm skin when he came back and stood in front, gazing at it.

He whispered, "You look beautiful in this."

I glanced down and it actually looked breathtakingly gorgeous when no proper words for a compliment formed once again and I couldn't help but just whisper back, "I love it. Thank you so much."

And with that I wrapped my hands around his neck and buried my face in the crook of his neck, him wrapping his arms around my waist snuggling me in close when we just stood there for God knows how long, both of us smiling a genuine goofy smile.

And oh yes, he was wearing my perfume, I could smell it.

# Chapter 31

## ASHTON

Angel loved the necklace I got her and I knew it the moment Jessica handed it over to me, that she would love it. I had made sure that the crafting was in the font that I had selected and that it was made of pure gold. Fixing my suit coat and stepping down the last stair, I was about to enter the kitchen when I heard excited chatters from inside.

"Yes yes yes." Sophia was squealing out loud and I couldn't help but lay my ear next to the door and eavesdrop. What was all the squealing about?

"You. Have. Got. To. be. Kidding. Me."

## Chapter 31

I rolled my eyes.

Emma.

"No, I'm not. He came up to me, at like two in the morning I guess and woke me up taking me to the rooftop and gave me this." Pure excitement was dripping from her voice when it dawned on me.

She was talking about the necklace and that's when I smiled to myself.

Glad she liked it.

"How did you react?"

I moved closer to the door to hear clearly. I also genuinely wanted to know this, knowing eavesdropping was bad but I had never done a good act in my life so may as well add this to the list.

"Emma…I..I honestly had no words. He left me speechless. Never in my life had anyone ever gotten me anything like this and believe me this is so close to my heart. I wish we both end up together but God forbid if something does happen and we cannot be one…." she was silent for a second when her voice got quieter and hoarser, "I cannot forget this. I don't care what awaits for the both of us but I sure as hell wouldn't lose this. I'd rather die than lose this." She chuckled at the end leaving me standing there in silence.

I was dead quiet.

She continued in a more hushed tone that I pressed myself further against the door wishing that either the door doesn't open to me falling inside or someone pushing me from outside till I fell inside. That would be too horrible and I'll kill whoever does that.

"I-i think this is a part of himself that he gave to me, Emma. Since the time that I have been here, believe me he has been a closed book. I cannot read him or get to know whether he is happy, sad, angry or disturbed. He always has the same expression which is so annoyinggggg as I cannot determine his mood," I chuckled to myself at this when she continued, bringing my attention back to her, "I have always seen him very reserved and keeping everything to himself. But last night..........last night was different.

I just felt as if he gave me a part of himself forever and believe me Emma, I'll guard it. I'll guard it like I've never guarded anything before. I don't care if he breaks my heart or leaves me or ignores me, but I definitely wouldn't break this piece of himself that he gave to me. Ever."

I heard a sniffle when Emma's voice croaked, "You guys are perfect, Sof."

Sophia chuckled when I just laid my head against the door of the kitchen and sighed. Her voice always brought calm to my raging world and I craved for more of it with each passing day.

## Chapter 31

"Can I ask you something Emma?"

"Yeah sure girl, go ahead."

"For how long have you been working for Ashton?"

"Sof, it's been about, I guess, quite some years now."

"Hmm, has he always been like this?"

"Like what? Amazingly sexy and lavishingly hot? So, yups."

I rolled my eyes in annoyance. She clearly knows what Sophia meant.

"Oh shutup," I could feel amusement laced in her voice, "you know what I meant. Hot tempered, angry and very reserved?"

"I mean……yeah Sof and believe it or not, I don't blame the guy."

"What do you mean?"

Yeah exactly. What did she mean?

Did she know?

Did Emma know?

"Look, my mum used to work here for Ashton's parents. I

was born when Ashton was around three years old. When I grew up, my mother became extremely sick. Sof, she had severely bad lung infection and there wasn't any transplant available, so the doctors were like, she has less time to live and that was when she asked me to go find a job and make a suitable living but Sof, I loved this place.

I grew up here and I wanted to do nothing but stay here. It's like my home now you know, where I grew up, where I spent time with my mum and where my mum breathed her last. I did everything here. Hell, I even got my period here," both of them laughed at this when she continued, "So, she told me everything that happened and what trauma Ashton had to go through." and I swear to God, my hands turned into goddamn fists and I was just itching to go to the gym and lash it all out brutally, at the realization that Emma knew each and everything.

She continued, "She told me all of this due to a reason, Sof. She kind of knew Ashton so she predicted he would act out this way. She warned me beforehand that Ashton might turn out like the way he is now and after hearing the whole story, I don't blame him man. The guy has been through some real deep shit."

"What real deep shit?"

I immediately stiffened, the blood in my mere veins running cold as ice.

"Sorry Sof, as deep as our friendship is, I don't think I can

## Chapter 31

tell you that. That is Ashton's place to tell you, something if he wills, he will tell you himself. I could tell you but that wouldn't be fair on him, even I don't know much of the details to his story, just a bit of an insight you can say. Give him some time, get close to him, I know he will tell you. I have never seen Ashton more alive than ever. Yesterday was the first time I actually heard him laugh and that was the moment I knew you are the one for him."

There was silence after this.

"Sof?"

"Hmm?"

Fuck. Even Sophia's hmm was beautiful.

"Don't break him, Sof. Don't break him. Believe me, he is becoming alive again after so effing long. Stay with him. Don't leave that man. He deserves happiness. He deserves to be happy, to live a joyous life and to have someone with him. Always. He is just broken. Heal him."

I heard a sniffle which I assumed was Sophia's when she whispered back, "Nahh, I would stick to him like an annoying jellyfish does." They both chuckled a small laugh earning a chuckle from me as well when I silently turned around only for my eyes to meet Massimo's who had a small smile on his face.

While passing by me, he squeezed my left shoulder and

whispered, "Glad to see you again brother."

Yeah, Massimo and I had grown together since we were in our diapers.

And yeah, eavesdropping isn't always bad.

The only problem it created? My ego just got greater and oh kitten……now you are definitely on one hell of a fucking ride.

## SOPHIA

"I just want to sleep, sissy."

I looked suspiciously at munchkin, "Baby, are you okay?"

"Yeah. Why?"

"You just woke up like two hours ago, hun."

She stretched her arms yawning, "I'm just tired, mama."

I froze for a minute as my mouth sealed itself shut. It seemed as if time had frozen too. I felt as if I was paralyzed, I couldn't move a muscle, nor even a limb. I was rooted, stupefied to the point that I found it hard to even breath. She just called me mama and I couldn't help to stop the tears from leaking out. Blinking back the hot tears, I opened my arms for her to cuddle in when she jumped and nuzzled next to me, "Okay,

## Chapter 31

go to sleep then, I'll wake you up when lunch is ready."

"Okay, bye."

"Bye, I love you baby."

"I love you too."

It barely took her five minutes to go to sleep and another five minutes to hear a pronounced knock on my door.

I whispered, "Come in."

The door slightly opened and in poked the head of the most hottest man I had ever known. Ashton gazed at me when I just beckoned for him to come in. Everleigh was sleeping in my lap and if I moved a bit, she would wake up and today I was not in the mood to disturb her. She had just made me the happiest sister to ever exist on this planet and so, I didn't want to ruin her sleep.

He softly closed the door behind and came and sat at the edge of the bed and looked at Munchkin, lost in some thoughts when he shook his head and looked back at me for a long time, his brows furrowing when he whispered, "How are you?"

I smiled a genuine smile when I whispered back, "Great. You?"

"Why are you crying?"

"I'm not."

"Sweetheart, by now you should know that I know when one is lying and when one is not, so come on, tell me what's wrong."

I hiccupped back a sob looking down at Everleigh when I looked back up at him and whispered with tears running down my face, "She called me mama today."

He was silent. Dead silent. His eyes widened a bit but he remained quiet. After a minute, he brought his forehead ahead and bumped mine to his, smiling, "You deserve that, don't you think?"

I nodded my head, "But I never expected that."

"I did."

"What?"

"I had expected that this would happen one day."

I just blinked and looked at him, nodding, "I'm listening."

He raised both of his shoulders and dropped them, "It was obvious. The way you care for her, the way you look after her and are always there for her. It's just like being a mom. I had the feeling that this was coming."

I smiled once again when I sniffled and looked back at him

## Chapter 31

again, "I asked you, how are you?"

He nodded his head, "Yeah, yeah good."

There was some silence when he spoke again, "Did you have breakfast?"

"Yeah. You?"

"Yeah, yeah."

Another silence.

"Everything good right?"

I smiled, "Yeah."

Another painful, awkward, long silence.

He scratched the back of his neck, "Did you have a good sleep last night?"

"Ashton, what did you come here for?" I smiled.

He pointed his forefinger towards me, "Good question. Indeed, a very good question."

I chuckled and looked at him wondering what he was going to say.

"I was wondering if you wanted to go out for dinner tomorrow?"

"Yeah, I have never gone with Emma before, I like the idea. It will be a good break."

He formed his lips in a thin line and gave me a bored look when he got up, muttering a yeah, and started to walk away when I laughed and grabbed his arm, pulling him back and making him sit back on the bed, "I was kidding. Yeah, I'll go out with you."

He nodded his head, "Good. You should."

I raised my eyebrows, "Oh really? Why?"

"You don't usually get a really hot man to take you out to dinner very often."

"Cocky much?" I smirked.

He came close to me whispering in my ear, "Oh you have no idea, kitten."

I laughed again, "Believe me, now I do."

"Really? Is that now?"

I nodded, smiling, when he asked, "And how is that may I ask."

I put my finger under my chin and pretended to think, "Hmm.

## Chapter 31

First of all, let's start with just saying that you are stubborn as hell."

"Absolutely."

"Second of all, you have no sense of humour."

"Nopes. Absolutely not. And just so you know, especially and obviously not with cute animals."

I was confused, "What do you mean?"

He showed a silent smile when he nodded his head, "Nothing."

I shrieked, "You can talk to animals?"

He confidently nodded his head.

"Howww? How do you know what they are saying?" I was amazed.

He shrugged his shoulders, "I just know. They speak and I can understand."

"Which animals can you fully understand?"

He got up and slowly picked up munchkin from my lap, placing her a bit far from us on the bed and covered her with the blanket when he came back and sat half cross legged on the bed. He took my hands in his and pulled me close till our noses were a few micro centimeters away from touching when he whispered, "Just say….the first animal…..let me make it very damn clear, it was a cute one-"

I interrupted him, "Explain his or her's appearance."

He furrowed his brows in concentration, "An extremely majestically beautiful one. I saw her and I couldn't take my eyes off of her. She seemed to put me in a trance. A trance I could never get out off."

I chuckled, "Weird feelings you have for an animal, I must say."

He bent his head low and nodded, "You can say that, but not for long I guess."

"What do you meannnn?"

He smiled again and shook his head back and forth, "Nothing, nothing."

I pulled his hands more close, "God you are so annoying, tell me, which was the first animal you fully understood."

He narrowed his eyes watching me closely when he whispered, "Let's just say, a beautiful female pigeon."

And that's when it fucking dawned on me.

What the hell?

## Chapter 31

I pulled my hands away from his grip when he erupted into laughter and I swung the pillow which was right next to me, hitting him square in the face, "That's what you get for insulting me."

He suddenly grew serious and looked at me with those beautiful narrowed grey eyes of his, "Did you actually just hit me?"

I replied a confident yes and swung the pillow again when he caught it midair and pulled it, dragging me along when I was practically in his lap. Putting his hands under my armpits, he picked me up placing me on his lap when I was straddling him. Wrapping his arms around my waist, he pulled me in very close till our chests were touching.

It sent electric pulses down my body and I felt as if I was on fire. I wanted to close my legs together but it was near to impossible. I started to breath in deeply when we both just gazed into each other's eyes. Grey to blue. Perfect. The most perfect match I could ever ask for.

He tugged me down when I was plastered against him when he whispered in such a way that goosebumps erupted all over my body, "Getting naughty are we now?"

I smiled a cocky smile when I placed both of my hands around his neck, "You allowed me."

"I regret that."

I raised my eyebrows, "Do you now?"

"Nahh."

I laughed when he closed in on the distance and kissed me. It was as always, a tender one when I could feel the same tingling sensation in the pit of my stomach. My brain wasn't functioning anymore and it was as if I was drunk on his kisses. He pulled me in close from my waist, never letting me go when I just deepened the kiss, holding his face with the both of my hands. After every one, I wanted more and more and more. We held onto each other tightly when we broke the kiss and took in some breaths.

Leaning his forehead against mine and nudging our noses together, he asked, "So you down for tomorrow night?"

I just whispered a drunken yes and smiled looking at him.

It was honestly the perfect life I could ever ask for.

So perfect.

When he just ruined it.

"Are you ticklish?"

I carefully started to get off of his lap, "Yes and don't you dare-" I never got to finish my sentence when he started tickling me, as I broke into fits of enormous laughter KNOWING FULL WELL THAT MUNCHKIN WAS ASLEEP.

## Chapter 31

I clawed my hands at him repeatedly to make him stop but Mr. Ego just wouldn't budge.

"Ashton stop. Stop pleaseeee."

He kept on tickling me when I fell off the bed but the Mr. never stopped. Picking me up from the ground, he quickly left the room with me, opened the door of the room right next to ours, quickly shut it close, locked it when he threw me on the bed and got on top of me, tickling every part of my abdomen that he could reach. I was sure my uncontrollable laughter could be heard all over the mansion but he didn't care.

He stopped for a second, taking in a deep breath and just looked at me. His eyes held some sort of tinkle that I had never seen. It looked beautiful, so beautiful on him. His storm raging, grey eyes shone and he looked as royal as ever. Barely five seconds might have passed when he advanced more closer to me.

I was under him and couldn't escape while he was on top of me caging me in when he gradually bent down and claimed my lips. I wrapped my hands around the back of his neck, pulling him further closer to me and was too absorbed in his kiss with my mind foggy and my body drunk, when he suddenly started tickling me again.

I shrieked and shouted trying to get away from him but he never decided to put a brake. Falling on the floor, he picked me up again and continued the punishment when he suddenly just pulled me harshly against his hold. I had my hair plastered all over my face when wrapping my hands around his neck and placing my forehead against his, I just gazed into his dreamy eyes.

My ears, nose and face were beetroot red of a colour and I was laughing way too much when he just pulled me impossibly more closer.

We both were breathing in heavily, our chests rising and falling rapidly with each passing minute, the air surrounding us was humid, and we could feel some sort of heaviness between the two of us, some sort of rope keeping the both of us connected when we were just clinging onto each other.

He kept staring into my eyes, to a point I felt my head heavy. Anyone gazing into his eyes could easily get hypnotized. A different sort of emotion flashed across them when he removed a strand of hair from my face and touched his nose to mine, waiting for his breathing to calm down when he finally whispered against me, in that damn sexy of a voice, earning a harsh breath from me.

Finally.

The thing that I had been waiting for.

For so, so, so damn long.

## Chapter 31

"I love you, angel."

————————END OF PART I————————

# END OF BOOK I

"The Mafia And His Lost Queen, Part I.' ends here. Hope you all loved the starting journey up till now. Do give me your reviews on my socials mentioned, as well as on Goodreads. I would love to hear from all of you. You can join the Facebook group, as well as the Discord group to let me know your thoughts as well.

Part II will be coming out this year, hopefully in a few months and trust me on this when I say……..you are going to love it a thousand times more. Promise.

Until then? Stay happy, stay blessed and thank you to all for always being there for me through thick and thin.

Peace!

Signing off,
   A.Z Chaudhry

## About the Author

I am a 19 year old, who started writing when I was barely 16. Writing has always been my passion and a way for me to let my emotions sink away from my body onto a paper via ink. I have always found it as a space for me to breathe when times get tough. I can portray my feelings through the eyes of characters and somehow, this makes the book more relatable because many people here are broken souls, fighting warriors and strong champions who know what depression feels like. They know what it feels like to suddenly lose touch with the world or suddenly lose all of your energy, hope and the shine in your eyes. I, myself was going through this phase, struggling the fighting battle and that is how TMAHLQ came into being.

"Failure is part of the process of success." -**Robert T. Kiyosaki**

"Sometimes things have to go very wrong before they can be right." -**Unknown**

**You can connect with me on:**
 https://www.facebook.com/profile.php?id=100009408883077
 https://instagram.com/anachaudhry123?utm_medium=copy_link

# Also by Ana Chaudhry

### The Mafia And His Lost Queen Part II

Sophia is a penurious, troubled girl fighting her inner demons and caging monsters, trying to run away from her past life as much as she can, however far that she can but finds every road ending with a blockage, finding every path with a stop sign and nothing but dead ends. Not giving up and still pushing all of her energy to make ends meet, she doesn't give up until her life takes a turn and that too when the well known, owner of the prestigious Italian Mafia's mob boss takes a glance at her, his heart never allowing his eyes to misalign once they have settled on her.

On the other hand, his life is fucked up, messed up, ruined to ashes but he is still living and is the king. He knows when to shut down his emotions, when to snap, when to hold things under control and when to wage highly successful wars. He doesn't believe in love or happiness and vows to die alone. But will he be able to complete this vow of his when he sees a set of pure electrifying blue eyes which make him completely stop on his way. And not stop him only, but his goddamn stubborn heart. What will be the fate of Ashton Romanno?

*Coming soon!*

Printed in Great Britain
by Amazon